CROSSING ALL BOUNDARIES

SUZANNE NEMEC

Lori,

Hope you enjoy this copy of the book that began it all. ♡

Thank you for being part of our Reader group.

May we all be so lucky as Jennifer to find someone who loves us so much, they risk everything to be together.

"Some love stories were never meant to end."

Love, Suzanne and my spirit guide, Josh

6/2/19

Crossing All Boundaries
book 1 of the Destined To Be Lovers saga

Cover designed by Dane Low of Creativindie

Interior layout by Standout Books

Editors: Ashley R. Carlson and Lauren Wise of Midnight Publishing

ISBN-978-0-9990417-0-3 (Paperback)

ISBN-978-0-9990417-1-0 (Kindle)

www.SuzanneNemec.net

CONTENTS

To my spirit guide—Josh. Thank you for sharing so much about the other side with me. I could have never written this book without you.

ACKNOWLEDGMENTS

Thank you to my computer guru husband, Michael, for all your love and support! Elizabeth Baker, for reading and listening to countless drafts and panicked phone calls. My sister Christine and my mom, for lending me your ears time after time. My Reiki/metaphysical teacher and friend, Dominique Lassauge, for everything you do. To my editors, Ashley R. Carlson and Lauren Wise, of Midnight Publishing, for your unwavering dedication. And to the many friends and readers who've shown their support, I thank you.

A very special thank you to Sandy Anastasi, creator and author of the *Sandy Anastasi System-Psychic Development* series, for all your many validations, teachings, and your friendship.

PROLOGUE

180AD

The crowd was becoming restless, and Astraea sensed their need for blood to be shed and death to be served to those whose only crime was to have been born into slavery or Christianity. No one was deserving of such cruelty. She turned her gaze away from the soon-to-be blood-soaked ground to look around the arena. The spectacle was a sea of color, with women adorned in their finest garbs as if attending the most festive of parties alongside their shameless escorts. She looked away from the sight of a man slipping his hand down a woman's dress to grab her fleshy breast. She'd seen the same scene many times amongst the spectators, and knew the man's other hand would soon be under the woman's skirt, giving pleasure—foreplay before the events to follow.

September had been unbearably warm, and today was no exception. Astraea wore a lightweight blue dress that maintained her modesty, with a floor-length hemline and a neckline that stopped just shy of the pinkish hue encircling her nipples. Modesty and coolness of the garment weren't the only reason she'd worn the dress; it was also Demetri's favorite. Memories of last night lying naked in Demetri's arms after hours of pleasuring pushed away the horror of the games that were soon to transpire. Using her peripheral vision, she searched for her lover in the senate box across the aisle, but saw only the usual spineless councilmen and Demetri's empty seat. *Where are you, my love?*

"Astraea, my darling, I hope you're not too bored?" her husband asked.

The sound of her husband's voice made the hair on her arms stand straight and her stomach tighten. When she failed to respond quickly enough he began caressing her arm with a clammy hand, causing bile to rise in her throat.

"I've planned a special event for you that's sure to pique your interest and put a smile on your beautiful face, my faithful wife."

There was something dark about the way her husband had spoken the words that increased the speed of Astraea's heart. "How kind of you for thinking of me."

Deep inside Astraea felt only hatred for the man she'd been forced to marry when she was fifteen years old. If not for the savages of Rome who'd invaded her village and killed her family and her people, she would've been free to marry someone she loved. She would've been free to marry Demetri.

"You can thank me later tonight when we're alone," her husband responded.

I'd rather plunge a dagger deep into your chest and cut out your heart! If not for the plans she and Demetri had made to run away together, Astraea would've been tempted to kill the evil man sitting next to her. Her husband's only interest in her was during the darkness of night, or after he'd had too much wine. Unlike her retched husband, Demetri actually cared about her wellbeing and respected her opinions. She'd suffered enough cruelty to last many lifetimes and had the scars to prove it, but no one would stand up to the emperor's favorite cousin.

The sound of horns announcing the emperor's arrival saved Astraea from having to reply. Her eyes once again searched the endless stream of faces for Demetri, but the crowd was now standing, waving flags to greet the emperor who stood behind the driver in a gold chariot pulled by six black Arabian horses. Behind the chariot, twenty or more Roman guards carrying whips and what looked to be five-foot lengths of iron chains followed. Astraea tried to turn her mind away from the possible disturbing uses for the chains, but couldn't shake them from her thoughts.

She'd watched men and even women whipped only for the spectators' pleasure. One or more were placed in the center of the arena, stripped down until barebacked or close to naked, and held in place between two guards with ropes while a headsman holding a five-tongued whip positioned himself. Once in place, the headsman angled his body for optimal aim as he waited for the crowd to fall silent. Only then did he swing his arm around and slash the strips of leather against the victim's skin, cutting deeply into their flesh.

Astraea closed her eyes in an effort to fight off the memories of the many victims' excruciating screams.

"What's the matter, Astraea?"

"The heat—it's making me ill," she responded to her husband, hoping that this time he'd take pity and order her back to her quarters.

"You two!" her husband called to her ladies-in-waiting. "Fetch Astraea a jug of water and the fan-bearers," he ordered before turning back to her. "The emperor would be greatly offended if you were to leave. I'm sure with some water and a breeze, you'll survive."

One event after another, each more horrific than the previous, brought the crowd to their feet while vendors passed out cooked legs of lamb, bread, and wine. The sight of the spectators gleefully tearing the pungent meat off the bone and washing it down with mugs of wine turned Astraea's stomach. By late afternoon the crowd had subdued but her nerves hadn't, as Demetri still wasn't in his seat. *Where are you, my love?* she wondered again and again.

"Oh good. It's time for my special treat, Astraea. I hope you like the participant," her husband sneered

Astraea's heart began beating faster than a wild bird and she could no longer breathe. Even though her husband didn't speak his name, she immediately knew why Demetri wasn't in his seat. She froze in place and could only stare straight ahead, praying she was wrong, but all went unanswered when she caught sight of Demetri in the arena. She was vaguely aware of the gasps that exploded around the amphitheater when the crowd noticed their favored state senator in shackles. At the same time, murmurs from the ladies of the court displayed their displeasure and a few mentioned Astraea's name as if she'd been the one to sentence her lover.

They're right! If I hadn't fallen in love and lured Demetri into my bed, he'd be safely sitting in the crowd, she realized.

The guards paraded Demetri in front of the emperor, who in turn signaled for the event to begin. Demetri's eyes met Astraea's for the first time and they softened, holding no hint of fear, only love and compassion for the woman to whom he'd given his heart.

Astraea fought away her impending tears as Demetri grappled with three gladiators at the same time, her fists clenching until her nails dug into her palms. Fighting the urge to hide her eyes, she didn't take them off him as she willed him to victory. Dressed in little more than a loincloth his exposed skin began to glisten under the bright sun, and the wavy brown hair she'd woven her fingers through the night before had darkened from exertion. Each time Demetri swung his sword, beads of sweat followed suit as he quickly toppled two of his opponents. The sounds of the crowd reverberated around the Colosseum, its high walls serving to amplify the noise. It took all of Astraea's restraint not to shout out with the others, but instead she used the precious moments to pray to the God Demetri spoke of so often.

The last opponent left standing was a tall hulk of a man who held a net in one hand and a dagger in the other. Demetri used his smaller size to his advantage and made quick work of defeating his opponent; as the other man fell to the ground, her breathing resumed.

Flowers rained down from the stands in celebration of Demetri's win, and Astraea's heart soared as high as the sun when her victorious lover stood alone, smiling and waving at the frenzied spectators.

Astraea and her husband were seated next to the emperor, Commodus, and Demetri took his place of honor in the arena in front of them. As was customary, he raised his sword in salute, but his eyes locked with Astraea's to pierce her soul with their intensity and love for her. She risked a slight smile and nodded her head in an appropriate gesture for a statesman's wife. Then suddenly Demetri's expression changed, and to her horror he crumpled to his knees, never once tearing his gaze from her. A large man stood behind Demetri and yanked a dagger from her lover's back, beginning to wave it around as if he were the victor instead of having just murdered Demetri in cold blood.

Astraea's heart shattered when Demetri fell forward onto the dirt. *Please God, if you're as Demetri says, the mightiest God, then you have the power to save him.* As if Demetri and his God heard her silent prayers, her lover raised his head and looked into her eyes—before all hope was lost. In horror, Astraea watched Demetri take his last breath.

Disapproving jeers rang out around the arena and mayhem followed. Her husband's guard grabbed and escorted her back to her quarters; once alone, Astraea's legs gave out and she collapsed to the floor, sobbing.

"My lady, what can I do to help you?" asked Luna, one of Astraea's ladies-in-waiting.

"Please, help me die," Astraea pleaded.

"No, my lady, you mustn't say such things!"

"Then there's nothing you can do. Leave me alone with my pain and my loss." Before Luna reached the door, Astraea called out to her. "Luna, wait—if you want to do something, help me see Demetri one last time. Please try to find out where they've taken him."

"I'll see what I can do. I know a caretaker who works in the catacombs below the Colosseum. I'll ask him."

"Please hurry, Luna. I must see Demetri one last time!"

An hour later Astraea and Luna followed the caretaker down a silent, bone-chilling corridor located under the floor of the arena. Though the living quarters of the gladiators and guards were situated on the opposite side, they met no one the entire way.

The room where Demetri had been placed was dark, but when the caretaker lit the three torches hanging on the wall they filled the cold chamber with a soft glow. It took a few seconds for Astraea's eyes to adjust and focus on Demetri where he lay on a stone platform.

Regardless of what we've done, Demetri is a leader in the senate and should be laid out in a manner deserving of his status. "Please leave me," Astraea commanded. When Luna and the caretaker hesitated, she ordered them to leave again. This time, they dutifully followed her wishes.

Her lover felt cold to the touch, and in an instinct to warm him, Astraea removed her cloak and draped it over him. "This is my fault, my love. Please forgive me."A strangled cry escaped, followed by retching sobs as her heart filled with unbearable sadness and the thought of living without him became inconceivable. Demetri's eyes were closed, making him appear so peaceful that she wondered if he'd found his God and, if so, whether he'd already arrived at that paradise called heaven.

Astraea caressed Demetri's cheek and lowered her lips to his, kissing him gently. Unlike the night before, he didn't reciprocate or take her into his arms. In her grief, she pressed her cheek against his chest in sorrow while her long, dark hair draped across him. Suddenly, a hard object next to his body caught her attention, and she began feeling around until she'd located the culprit and brought it out into the light.

Demetri had always spoken of destiny, reincarnation, and signs from above, and she took it as the sign she'd been looking for. *Please forgive me, Demetri, but I cannot live without you.*

Astraea raised the dagger covered in Demetri's blood above her head and spoke the final words straight from her broken heart: "Demetri, I'm completely yours and only yours. *Forever.*" With one fluid motion, Astraea plunged the dagger into her chest and fell onto Demetri**'s** body, driving the blade deep enough to stop her heart and the undetectable glimmer of hope she she'd been carrying.

Demetri gazed down at his lifeless body in confusion. He'd never felt more alive or buoyant, as if he'd been set free from all worldly ties—except for one he wouldn't dream of severing.

He was trying to figure out how to merge himself back into his physical form when he heard footsteps in the corridor. As a child, he'd lost his ability to hear in his right ear when he'd gotten sick, yet now his hearing was attuned enough to hear the far-away steps perfectly. *How can this be?*

"Demetri, I've been waiting for you," a musical, feminine voice called out softly.

Demetri looked around but saw no one. "Show yourself! If you don't come forward, I'll know you're nothing but an ungodly illusion whose intent is to deceive."

Before him, a beautiful woman appeared. *An angel?* She had long, wavy hair the color of sunlit gold, oversized ice-blue eyes and skin so pale it was as if she'd never seen the sun. Her lovely features and smile seemed kind and reassuring, and held no ill will or harshness. The sight of someone so angelic reminded him of the tales of mystical, false gods.

"Declare yourself before I drive a sword through you!" Demetri warned, reaching for his sword. When his hand came up empty, the angel's laughter mocked him.

"Do not fear me, Demetri. My name is Gisabella, and I mean you no harm. I know this must all seem like a dream or illusion, but it isn't. I've been watching you for many lifetimes, waiting until you were seasoned enough to take your soul home forever." She'd found him to be one of the strongest and bravest men she'd ever watched in battle. Impressed by his ability to remain level-headed even when all the odds were against him, Demetri was exactly the man Gisabella needed for her prized army.

"Shhh..." Demetri hushed her when he noticed the room was no longer empty. "Astraea," he whispered.

This is a first! Gisabella stared in disbelief at the man who dared to quiet her. *Who does he think he is to address the great-granddaughter of Zeus in such a fashion? Doesn't the fool know I can disintegrate his soul? I've done away with others for far less!* She watched in fascination as Astraea laid her cloak over Demetri's cold body and lightly kissed his lips. There was something so profound in the way the young woman—no more than seventeen, by the look of it—caressed the corpse's cheek that Gisabella's heart ached for the first time in centuries. When Astraea's wretched sobs shattered the stillness in the room, a few tears escaped from Gisabella's own eyes and fell to the ground.

Gisabella failed to notice the knife in Astraea's grip or the intention running through the girl's thoughts until it was too late. An excruciating, animalistic sound came from beside Gisabella, and she turned to see Demetri—a man who'd casted women's hearts aside for lifetimes —*sobbing*. She'd always believed him to be heartless, which was a trait she looked for in those selected to join her army of protectors. If not for his readable thoughts, she would've believed he'd taken Astraea as his lover only for the sake of revenging the girl's husband for swindling half of his land. This unexpected turn of events surprised Gisabella like never before.

"What are they doing?" Demetri demanded, his voice more terrified than harsh at the sight of his beloved Astraea being surrounded by three ghostly creatures.

"It's okay, Demetri, calm down. They're here to help Astraea transition to heaven." Before Gisabella could surround the situation in calming white light, things amplified.

"Demetri!" Astraea screamed out in desperation, her arms outstretched as she fought to get to him.

"Release her at once!" Demetri shouted, running towards her only to be frozen in place before he'd taken his third step.

"You can't save her now," Gisabella warned coldly. "She made her choice when she took her own life, and must now face the penalty."

"'Penalty?' What are you talking about? She's done nothing wrong but to escape from her murderous husband!"

"It's a penance I cannot change. When Astraea took her life, she inadvertently caused a ripple effect in many other lives, changing hundreds of people's destinies in a way that is irrevocable. Her penalty isn't so bad; she only needs to experience twenty-five-hundred additional lifetimes before she's able to reside in heaven."

"I demand you do something to save her!"

Gisabella held up her hand, halting the three guardians holding Astraea. "What are you prepared to offer me in exchange for my leniency, Demetri?"

"I'll do anything you ask if I can share a lifetime with Astraea as my wife," Demetri offered.

"Wise man," Gisabella smirked, getting exactly what she'd wanted. Unfortunately for Demetri, the lack of boundaries in his foolish offer left him completely at her mercy—yet one look into his desperate eyes cooled her frosty heart. "I will give you and Astraea a lifetime together after she's served some of her penalty, *if* you agree to spend your future serving me as one of my elite protectors. The life I'm offering you is prestigious, and unlike those protectors in my army, you'll work for me directly. If you don't accept, you'll never see her again."

"If you let us say goodbye, I give you my honor that I'll serve you well," Demetri promised, bowing to kiss the ring on Gisabella's extended hand.

"Let her go and stand back," Gisabella commanded the three spirits.

The moment Astraea was released, she ran forward, meeting Demetri halfway to fall into his strong arms. Two hearts aching to become one as their lips desperately sought each other melted into one, bound together forever by their undying love.

"I promise someday we'll be together forever," Demetri whispered, hoping no one other than Astraea had heard him.

"I love you. Please don't leave me," she pleaded.

"I'm afraid I must; it's the only way we can be together in the future. Never give up hope on me and my love for you. Know that my heart and soul are yours for all eternity, and I'll never forget you." Demetri held the woman he loved against him, engraving the memory of how she felt into his mind and vowing never to forget their last few moments together.

"Goodbye, my love," Demetri murmured, before kissing Astraea and his heart farewell.

"I promise to always hold you in my heart and to believe," Astraea choked out between ragged sobs. Soon the image of the man she loved faded from view, becoming a distant memory of a past lifetime.

Once Astraea was removed from the scene, Gisabella looked at her newly acquired protector, who was glaring back at her with contempt. *Great, seems I didn't make such a good deal after all,* Gisabella thought. Nevertheless, she'd waited many lifetimes for a strong leader who was extremely intelligent and wouldn't back down from a challenge. His soul was old and he'd fought many battles using both brains and brawn, which made Demetri one of her most sought-after prizes. Now that she knew his weakness lay deep in his heart, he'd be easy to control. *Like the man said: he'd do anything for Astraea.*

"As I was saying before you rudely *shushed* me, I'm the high priestess who's in charge of heaven and earth, and every dimension in between. This means that every soul, both living and in spirit, must answer to me. I rule along with twelve council elders to ensure that each dimension stays separated and every soul follows the doctrine given to us by God. You exist only in spirit form now, and as my protector, all your future lifetimes on earth have ended."

"Except for the one you agreed to give me with Astraea," Demetri reminded her.

"My mistake." Gisabella glowered at the man's audacity. "During the next five years you'll go through a rigorous training program, learning and developing every offensive and defensive skill ever known. You'll become an unstoppable force designed to protect the most gifted souls on earth. Most of your time will be spent working with one gifted visionary at a time, making sure they develop their gifts and keeping them alive until they've completed their destiny. Once they do, you'll be assigned another visionary charge."

"Five years of training seems like a waste of time. Why don't we agree on two?" Demetri held back a smirk when Gisabella's face pinched in the most unbecoming way. "Do you think we can continue this discussion later? I haven't eaten anything for hours."

"You've got to be kidding me! You're *dead*, Demetri! You don't have to eat."

"Maybe so, but I want to. Or is that not part of your deal? If so, I'm surprised anyone listens to you."

"Fine, I'll bring you to my house so you can stuff all the food you want into your oversized mouth! At least it'll keep you quiet for a bit." Gisabella's eyes turned frosty, daring Demetri to say one more word. Her prized protector was becoming nothing more than a pain in the ass, and she began debating if he was worth the effort.

"Okay—if you feed me, I promise I'll mind my manners."

"One more thing: your name is no longer Demetri. From this moment on you'll be known by your original birthright name of Joshua. Understood?"

"Whatever you say, Your Highness," he mocked.

"You will call me 'Your Excellency,' and you'll *not* speak to me unless I address you. Do you understand?"

"Whatever you say, Your Excellency," the newly designated Joshua responded in a dull voice. "Why 'Joshua?'"

Gisabella squelched her sharp retort when she noticed the insurmountable loss in Joshua's eyes. She'd only seen that depth of extreme despair once, and feared that without the aid of black magic, he may never become the great protector she'd envisioned. Upon realizing that

Joshua's irritating sarcasm and attitude was his way of covering up his pain, Gisabella softened her tone. If she wanted this man to pledge his allegiance to her, she needed to use a different tactic besides force.

"Joshua, take hold of my sleeve and don't let go. We'll be at our destination in less than a minute," Gisabella said, holding out her arm. Once he'd taken hold, she transported them to the home located in her own private dimension.

CHAPTER ONE

1,787 YEARS LATER

Josh opened the door to his disheveled apartment in a dimension located above the earth's atmosphere. His weary eyes gazed over the stacks of files, books, and assorted papers that blocked his path; they'd doubled in size over the past ten years he'd spent on assignment. After he balanced the chemist's folder on top of the lowest pile, he ran a hand through his dark hair while surveying his cluttered domain. *Screw it*—a book and a snack was a better way to start his vacation than cleaning up.

He headed towards the cleanest room of his apartment, where he was sure his closest, most trustworthy friends were waiting to welcome him home. He'd missed them a lot. They were the friends who'd listened to years of his often-jaded rhetoric over the council's handling of protection and security procedures, and they knew to keep their opinions to themselves as he unleashed his grievances all over the kitchen walls, floor, counters, and sometimes even the ceiling.

He hadn't always been so cynical, but the centuries had tainted Josh's view on things. Maybe it was him, or maybe he'd finally wised up to the fact that no matter how hard he tried, he was never going to stop the growing number of disgruntled fellow protectors. What was the use of dwelling on it? It wasn't his job to care so much, or take it upon himself to boost morale. If the council hadn't grown so useless, caring only about keeping their seats on the board, things would've been different. A few like himself were still clinging to the values of long ago in an effort to keep each dimension separate. If the interdimensional lines were to blur, all the souls on earth would be at risk of obliteration, and the ramifications to every other dimension would be devastating. The best he and the other protectors could do was to protect the universe's doctrine so that every soul could continue to live in harmony.

Josh slid open the door and walked into the kitchen, his eyes skirting around the room until he smiled for the first time in months. His friends were all there waiting; the companions who'd kept him company during the lonely years. They'd shared many meals and late-night snacks, helped him through countless sleepless nights, and had celebrated his many awards and achievements. In addition to his best friend, Gisabella, he owed them his gratitude for helping him sharpen his skills through the years. Thanks to them, he possessed the profoundness to transform the ordinary into refined palatable pleasures that often impressed even the most arrogant of gastronomes. Yep, they were all there—his trusty Vitamix, his confidant fourteen-cup Cuisinart food processor, and even his razor-sharp cutlery greeted him.

But he was *most* happy to see that his longtime companion—the one that had helped him through many lonely nights and empty mornings—was polished and waiting: his espresso machine, offering Josh the first taste of pleasure he'd had in years…*ahh*. The thought of greeting the sun sated in heady, caffeinated pleasure as he had years ago in Rome made him long for those hot, sexy days once more. The memory of mornings on a terrace overlooking the cobblestoned streets with an eye-opening, aromatic espresso in his hand and a long-legged, dark-haired woman in his bed was engraved in his psyche.

Too bad that was the *only* part he remembered. Even now he'd give anything to recall the nights with her, and how his loins had wrapped around her…*damn, why now?* Why must his mind torment him with sparse glimpses into a distant memory that had no beginning or end? Were they even real? Josh had no answer for this or the many other fragments of his memories that had gone missing, other than Gisabella's explanation of how he'd been hit in the head thousands of years ago by an asteroid; it made no sense then nor now, but it was the only response he'd ever been offered.

Before his libido grew to be hotter than a Diethylzinc and air explosion, Josh reached into his wine fridge and pulled out a bottle of 1969 Louis Jadot Beaujolais-Villages, chilled to a perfect fifty-four degrees. He uncorked the bottle and poured the dark red liquid into the largest goblet he could find. Breaking all protocol, he gulped half the glass down before the wine had caught its breath. He savored the rich, fruity bouquet; it had been months since a complex vintage had lingered on his palate. He cut Gruyère cheese into cubes and placed them on a small plate with a few Bremner wafers and some roasted pecans, then topped off his goblet before heading to his favorite leather chair with a book about ancient Roman battles. Silence was the only sound he wanted that night.

An hour later he was nearly a part of the book, immersed in the second Punic War while riding an elephant behind Hannibal across the Alps, when Gisabella summoned him. *Well, that was short-lived!* He slammed his book shut. *I can't let this go to waste,* he thought, popping the cheese into his mouth and draining his glass of wine.

Without warning, Josh found himself being transported through the galaxy to arrive almost instantaneously inside Gisabella's personal residence—a privilege she reserved only for him. They'd spent centuries working together, and had become great friends. She sat before him in her high priestess attire, and although they were close, he greeted her formally as "Your Excellency," then bowed and kissed her ring.

"Joshua," Gisabella greeted, indicating for him to sit. "It's a pleasure to see you, my friend. I commend the quality of the work you've recently finished. The council is pleased."

Now would be a good time for Gisabella to tell me that I've earned a month off.

As though reading Josh's thoughts, Gisabella added, "You deserve a vacation, and I wish more than anything I could grant you one. However, an emergency has come up and you're the only person I trust for this assignment." The look of disappointment in Josh's eyes was tangible, but Gisabella put aside her remorse and handed him the girl's profile and life-path. "I need you to leave right away to watch over this young girl. I'm also entrusting you with some of Jennifer's development and training. I hope I can count on your full support," she said, pairing the new assignment with an apologetic smile.

He took the folder and envelope, but refused to return the grin. Once again, no vacation. Not even one or two days off to recover. *Who is this "Jennifer?"* Was she so important no other protector could handle the assignment? Josh flexed his hands to keep from forming them into fists, and blocked his thoughts so the high priestess wouldn't know what he was thinking. He knew better than to give Gisabella ammunition to play one of her demented "getting your goat" games. He was in *no* mood.

Josh's silence was not a good sign, nor did Gisabella have to read his mind to know how irritated he was. "You're my closest and most loyal friend, and the only person I trust to keep the girl safe and teach her how to use her gifts when she's ready. Most of all, Jennifer must be kept alive at all costs."

Gisabella didn't elaborate on anything about Jennifer's destiny or the job she'd been born to do. Josh would find out soon enough, but for now it was best to keep him in the dark just as she was doing with the council. The last thing she wanted was for her second-in-command, Garth, to discover the girl. It was common knowledge that he'd been looking for a way to dethrone Gisabella and take over the council for centuries, but so far she'd managed to stay one step ahead of him. With no way of abolishing Garth's ancestry claim to her position, Gisabella had no choice but to play nice until Garth acted upon his threats. If knowledge of Jennifer were to get out, Garth would get his wish and the universe as they knew it would be decimated.

"You have my full support, of course, Your Excellency." Josh could only assume that Jennifer was highly gifted due to the fact Gisabella was handling the case. He wondered if there were rumors of Jennifer's destiny or whereabouts, or possibly a bounty being offered in exchange for her life. Why else would Jennifer's protection be an emergency?

"Thank you, my friend. These past few weeks there's been much turmoil, and a few visionaries' lives were inadvertently placed in danger. As a result, two protectors have been placed on leave for their insubordination. Frankly, I'm at my wit's end." Gisabella didn't wait for Josh's response before she changed the subject. "Now that that's settled, please stay and join me for a cup of tea. I baked blueberry scones with sweet honey butter."

"Blueberry scones?" Josh confirmed. "Baked from scratch, huh? If they're anything like your previous outstanding homemade goodies, I'm in for a treat." *More like a night hung over the toilet,* Josh added internally. As a spirit, sickness was never an issue—*except* when it came to Gisabella's cooking. On the bright side, it couldn't actually kill him. "I don't believe I've ever had the pleasure of sampling the honey butter you mentioned. It sounds quite good."

It took skill, but his speech sounded believable; he'd maintained his poker face the entire time. All lies! His friend hadn't successfully baked one item in her entire existence, and his stomach protested at the recollection of the burnt hacksaw-hard bricks she'd served him the year prior. Worst of all, Gisabella played her high priestess card to its fullest, so he had no choice but to consume each of her many cooking disasters. With any hope, the scones she offered were from a bakery on earth, or the one that had just opened in his dimension.

"You can relax, Josh. I didn't bake them," Gisabella assured him. Her position gave her the advantage of being able to mingle amongst people on earth without difficulty, which Josh envied; protectors were only capable of doing it on a limited basis, usually when they needed to save their visionaries from danger.

"No offense, Gisabella, but that's a big relief," Josh chuckled.

She didn't take offense. Josh's extreme perfectionism over food—the way it was prepared, smelled, tasted, and presented—drove her crazy. Through the centuries she'd known him, Josh had become the ultimate foodie-snob! To her, it all tasted the same.

It was decided that Josh would set out in the morning to look over Jennifer's situation and take over her protection and training, and he knew not to ask questions or express surprise when Gisabella told him she'd dismissed all the girl's spirit guides and angels.

"I hope you'll enjoy this assignment, Josh. She's a delightful young girl, and I have a feeling you'll like working with her." Gisabella blocked her thoughts and maintained her smile, making sure not to give away any clues about her true motives.

"Thank you, Gisabella. I'm honored you've selected me. You have my word that I will guard Jennifer with my life, as I guard yours," Josh said, glad he hadn't refused by the look of pure relief that immediately bloomed in Gisabella's eyes.

Before he departed, he bowed and kissed Gisabella's ring and raised his green eyes to her ice-blue ones. It was his turn to dish out a dig. "The blueberry scones were delicious. I'm sure if you'd baked them yourself, they would've come out just as good." His straight face faltered, and he snickered. "Then again…pigs would have a better chance of flying."

The corners of Gisabella's mouth upturned into a smile, as his sarcastic comment showed her Josh was okay with being assigned to someone else so quickly. She watched as he transported back home, sighing in relief. With Josh's acceptance, all she had to do now was sit back and watch.

CHAPTER TWO

Gisabella had a lot to do before sunrise on earth when Josh was due to arrive for his assignment. She waited until Jennifer's household was quiet and all were asleep before she made her move. Dressed in normal mid-1960s fashion, she headed down to earth and into Jennifer's bedroom.

Gisabella took a moment to study the sleeping girl before reaching into a purple velvet pouch and pulling out some magical sparkling dust. Careful not to awaken Jennifer, Gisabella lightly blew the dust that would cause Jennifer to believe she was dreaming towards her face, then surrounded the young girl with protective white light and took hold of her hand. Together they faded, becoming nothing but pure energy as Gisabella transported them across the galaxy and into another dimension, then soared higher to the heavens and past all known realms until they reached the high priestess's private domain. It'd only taken thirty seconds from when they'd left Jennifer's bedroom to stand, once again solid in shape, in Gisabella's house.

"Welcome to my home, Jennifer," Gisabella said with a warm, reassuring smile.

"Where am I?" Jennifer asked. She glanced around the expansive yet cozy room before landing her eyes once again on the beautiful woman before her.

"I've brought you to my home so we can speak in private. My name is Gisabella, and I'm known as the High Priestess. My job is to ensure that everyone on earth, all other planets, and in every dimension follows all the rules and lives happily together. You may've heard of those dimensions called 'heaven,' yes?"

"I'm in heaven? Does that mean I'm dead?" Jennifer said in alarm. *I don't feel dead—or at least I don't* think *I do. What does "dead" feel like?*

"Oh dear, please don't be frightened; you're not dead, and I'll have you back in your bed safe and sound when we're done talking. Why don't you think of me as your fairy godmother—you know, like the one in Cinderella?" Gisabella said, doing her best to explain things in a way that a child of seven could understand.

"I'm not frightened," Jennifer stated defiantly.

"Good," Gisabella answered, happy that the girl had spunk. "Let's have some tea and cakes and talk." She led Jennifer to the table where tea in delicate floral-patterned china cups, matching saucers, and a large silver tray filled with pastries awaited.

"These are delicious! You bake a lot better than anyone in my family," Jennifer exclaimed, helping herself to another blueberry crumb square.

"Thank you," Gisabella said, not bothering to inform the girl that she'd picked them up at her favorite bakery on earth. "Jennifer, I wanted to speak with you about your future. I know you've seen and spoken with many ghosts—or 'spirits,' as they prefer to be called—and have enjoyed their company," Gisabella went on, pausing to gauge the girl's reaction. She'd been keeping a close eye on Jennifer, and had been glad to discover that the girl had stopped speaking to her family and friends about the spirits who visited her from time to time by the age of seven.

"Yes, they were my friends," Jennifer said brightly. She didn't have many friends in school, and the translucent visitors who'd come to see her on their way to heaven were nicer than the kids in her class. Jennifer's expression suddenly became crestfallen, as if some thought was too painful for the young girl to handle. "But no one comes around anymore," Jennifer said somberly.

"I know." Gisabella chased away the stab of guilt that lanced through her; she'd been acting in the girl's best interest when she'd prevented all spirits from appearing or speaking to Jennifer two months prior. "Jennifer, starting tomorrow you'll have one spirit who'll be watching over you until you're an adult."

As Gisabella's words registered, Jennifer's face brightened, becoming almost radiant. Another pang of guilt plagued Gisabella's conscience regarding the stipulations she was about to give Jennifer.

"Really? Who? Do I know them? Is it someone I've spoken to before? Or maybe it's one of the young girls who used to play games with me," Jennifer said in an overzealous rush.

"It's someone you've never met." *At least not in this lifetime.* "I'm sending him to watch over you and keep you safe. The difference with this spirit is that he's extremely shy," Gisabella said, nearly choking on her outlandish lie. "He doesn't like people to notice him, and he's *most* afraid of anyone who tries to talk to him."

"Why?"

Oh dear Lord, now what have I done? I've forgotten how inquisitive children are—especially the little girl starting on her fourth pastry. Upon further scrutiny, Gisabella noticed how underweight Jennifer appeared. *Didn't the girl ever eat?* Her nurturing side wanted to feed her a five-course meal and send her home with a huge care package of food.

"Sometimes there isn't an answer to why someone is the way they are."

"So if I say 'hi' or even smile at him, he may become upset and leave?" Jennifer asked, her mouth covered in pastry crumbs.

Hallelujah! "Yes. It's up to you to keep your knowledge of him a secret between you and I. Do you think you can do that?" Gisabella asked.

"I *know* I can," Jennifer vowed.

"Good. As you grow older this man will play an important role in your life, and I need you to promise me you'll never speak to him." ~Until you're eighteen years old,~ Gisabella added silently, implanting the last request into Jennifer's subconscious. "The only exception is if you need his help and no one else is there but him."

"May I ask his name?"

"His name is Joshua." *You don't know it yet, but the two of you will fall in love. Best of all, Joshua is your soulmate and once you're older, I can guarantee he won't be able to resist you.*

"Joshua…I love him already."

Gisabella's breath caught; what trigger point had she touched in the girl's heart to make Jennifer say such a statement? It was something she hadn't counted on at all. *No harm done—the spell I'll place on Jennifer will cause her to forget our meeting and erase Josh's name and who he is until she's older.* Until then, Josh would be nothing more than a shy spirit who must be ignored. Best of all, once she'd cloaked the girl's mind, Josh wouldn't be able to read Jennifer's thoughts or have any clue that she could see him.

No one must ever find out how Gisabella had taken Jennifer's former soul, previously known as Astraea, under her wing, waiting until Astraea had served a tiny part of the penalty for taking her own life before rebirthing her soul as Jennifer. More importantly, she'd instilled in the girl many gifts and abilities that would someday make her as powerful as Gisabella herself. Thanks to her, Jennifer's soul had evolved into a worthy partner for her strongest elite protector.

The time had finally come for Gisabella to satisfy the deal she'd made in exchange for Josh's allegiance. Her plan was perfect; Josh had died once before to protect the girl, and there was no doubt he'd do so again if needed. As much as Gisabella wished she could've given the two former lovers a full lifetime together, Jennifer had become too valuable to risk. *If Josh were in my shoes he'd understand, and would use his time with Jennifer to help her develop into the strong woman she needs to become to fulfill her destiny of greatness.* Not that Gisabella thought Josh would remember the girl he'd been in love with centuries prior. Other than sharing a few traits and having dark hair and eyes, only a few similarities remained in the way Astraea and Jennifer looked and acted.

"One more thing—no matter what happens, you can trust Joshua. He will never harm you and will always be close by, keeping you safe. You never need to fear him," Gisabella reassured.

"Thank you for the gift of Joshua, and the tea and those delicious pastries," Jennifer said, raising her hand to her mouth to stifle a yawn.

"You're welcome, Jennifer. I think it's time to bring you back home.

Remember, no talking about Joshua to anyone, not even your cats or dog."

"Cross my heart," Jennifer vowed.

Soon Jennifer was back in her bed, tucked in, sound asleep, and with no memory of all that had happened.

The break of dawn and Josh arrived on earth simultaneously in the quiet town of Stratford, Connecticut. The streets were empty except for a few cars driven by nightshift workers heading home and newspaper boys on bicycles flinging newsworthy headlines onto front stoops, their one-armed throws reminiscent of how they thought a pitch in the big leagues might look. A couple of early risers walking dogs were the only other pedestrians in sight.

Josh stood in front of his new assignment's home, which was on an exceptionally quiet road in a cookie-cutter neighborhood. Slight variations of color made each home a little different—all except for his new charge's house, which was painted dollhouse pink with white shutters and a pale blue front door. He'd seen a similar color palette on a faded "Old Glory" flag many years ago. An oversized, under-trimmed weeping willow tree, lush lawn, and slate walkway gave the house a welcoming feel, and he could see a brook running along the edge of the side yard.

He had left Jennifer's life-path and profile in his apartment, as it was his standard policy to size up new cases on his own. Josh wasn't concerned with the ancient words written at the beginning of time by the original council elders and the high priestess—at least not in the beginning. This visionary was young, and there'd be plenty of time for him to read Jennifer's paperwork as time went on.

First things first: he went up high in the sky and scouted for any sign of danger or unwanted spirits lurking nearby. From there he was able to see everything that went on around the house and neighborhood. That was the dull part of his job—waiting for activity to happen. Of course, he had the option of going inside Jennifer's house and checking things out, but it was too soon to start infringing on her and the family's privacy. That would come soon enough.

It was Sunday and all was quiet until 9:05 a.m. when the front door opened and the entire family hurried to their car. Based on Gisabella's description, it wasn't hard to figure out which of the three children was Jennifer; she was the smallest, and had dark brown hair. He followed them to their destination, staying close on their heels as they all piled out of the car and ran to the building's double doors.

Josh hadn't been inside a church of any faith in hundreds of years. It wasn't that spirit protectors weren't allowed to enter; he'd just never had a visionary attend before. It didn't seem to bother the family that they'd caused a disturbance by coming in late to a house of worship—all except for Jennifer, who looked like she wanted to crawl under a pew. With half the mass already over by the time they'd arrived, his fidgeting charge didn't have to suffer much longer. Once dismissed, the family returned to their vehicle and headed home by way of a long, scenic route.

When Jennifer climbed out of the vehicle and walked to the front door, Josh noted the girl's greenish tinge. *Motion sickness?* That was his cue to follow her inside. While Jennifer wasn't his youngest charge, she looked to be the skinniest one; all legs and thin arms, she appeared frail and out of place in the Sunday best that was clearly two sizes too big for her. He stood outside Jennifer's bedroom until she came back out wearing a pair of shorts, a T-shirt, and battered sneakers.

Once outside, Jennifer took off running full-speed across the street and into the woods. Any thoughts he'd had about her frailness were dispelled after Jennifer's speedy, hour-long, faster-than-a-jackrabbit sprint. When Jennifer had finally stopped galloping, she collapsed in the grass next to the brook, sweaty and breathing hard.

Josh attempted to read his new assignment's mind several times, but found nothing of any use other than a few tangled thoughts of horses, cats, dance, swimming, and frogs. When he tried to dig deeper, he could still only discern a collection of random words as Jennifer gazed at the sky. *What is she doing?* He couldn't help but shake his head and roll his eyes over her oddity. Soon more thoughts of objects appeared in Jennifer's mind: eagle, horse, ship, castle, angel, and others that had nothing in common. Then it came to him—she was picking out cloud formations! More random words flooded in and out of her brain, but he found not a single sign of one visionary thought that he'd come to expect from his charges, nor any other indication of Jennifer's supposed gifts.

After a week of following around the young skin-and-bones waif who spent more time alone outside than with her family, Josh decided that the girl was an unusually *ungifted* charge. Had Gisabella thought this was a good use of his protector skills? The only thing Jennifer needed protection from was the stray animals she continuously dragged home.

One year, two years, then three years crept by, each duller then the last, making Josh so crazed for excitement that he once wished some rogue spirit would show up so he'd have some fighting action. He was growing softer by the week, and other than a few brief excursions to pick up things he needed, he spent his free time reading every book he could find from the British Museum. On a day when Jennifer was ten, he was enjoying Captain Cook's three volumes of pacific voyages when the notion that he'd been put out to pasture crossed his mind. *That's it!* Josh thought, glancing over at Jennifer with a frown. She'd shown no visionary talent whatsoever, and he'd been monitoring her for three straight years. He resumed reading, the frown deepening as he resigned himself to the fact he'd been officially forced into retirement.

CHAPTER THREE

DECEMBER 1, 1978

Eighteen candles on the cake and the embarrassing paper hat on Jennifer's head meant she'd long ago missed her chance to be kissed at sweet sixteen, as so many of her favorite singers told her she should expect. *How could this have happened? Wasn't a girl's first kiss all but guaranteed by eighteen?* She hadn't even come close to having her first date, let alone holding a boy's hand. Had her recent obsession with kissing a boy been driven by the femme fatales in her school? They were the girls people couldn't help but notice, strutting around school in their short skirts and see-through blouses, with their perfectly applied makeup and magazine-worthy faces. *Who knew blue eye shadow could look so good?* The way they flaunted their femininity to lure boys into their web was impossible to ignore. To make matters worse, her closest friends had received their first kisses years ago and displayed them like a badge of honor. If her friends pointed out one more eligible donor to her cause, Jennifer was going to go ballistic. The last thing she wanted was to kiss a boy for the sake of getting it out of the way. Her first kiss—and every kiss afterwards—needed to be special.

The out-of-tune rendition of "Happy Birthday" from Jennifer's family members along with her Aunt June, added to her misery. *Maybe no boy will ever wish to kiss me.* She filled her lungs to capacity and blew out the candles in one sweep, making a silent, pleading wish to the heavens above.

As she raised her head, Jennifer's breath immediately stalled as she locked eyes with the man across the room. *It's him!* His gaze, like always, was intense and unnerving enough to cause her heart to skip. Jennifer had seen him often over the years, and he was the first of his kind who'd stayed around longer than a day or two. She hadn't seen any other ghostly visitors like him since she'd turned seven. Unlike the others, he'd never once tried to communicate with her—and who was she to start a conversation with a strange man standing in the house?

Similar to the previous spirits, his form was translucent. Despite the lack of a solid appearance, she could still distinguish his clothing, actions, expressions, and some of his features—but sadly, he'd never come close enough for her to see the color of his eyes. *Oh, how I wish I could see the color of his eyes.* If she had to guess, he was in his mid-twenties and mostly wore jeans, a sweater or sweatshirt, sneakers, and other similar types of casual clothing. One thing was for sure; whoever he was, he didn't know much about fashion because he only wore plain, untrendy things and never once showed up in bell-bottoms or a *Saturday Night Fever*-inspired white suit. Jennifer stole another glimpse his way. *White suit or not, he puts John Travolta to shame in the looks department!*

His visits had grown more often and longer, sometimes even all day, and she enjoyed all the times he'd shown up. Something was different about seeing her spirit friend tonight, however. Maybe it was the way he held her eyes hostage, or how hard it was for her to breathe. She'd never been afraid of him; on the contrary, he intrigued her. But tonight, the way he looked at her, with an easy grin and roguish mischief in his eyes, was creating havoc on her insides. She diverted her eyes to a safer view: her cake. A loud warning sounded in her head to ignore him, but her eyes soon drifted his way again.

Jennifer, look away…you can't see me, right? Josh thought, the night immediately taking a surprising turn. His charge's birthday party had started out dull, with Jennifer cracking jokes, laughing with her family, and still giving no indication whatsoever that she possessed any of Gisabella's proclaimed visionary gifts. He'd been protecting Jennifer for years and he genuinely liked the girl, who he found to be a bit awkward around people she didn't know well. The hours he'd observed her quietly drawing and painting, or studying the clouds, was the side of Jennifer that made his job easy. Too bad she had *another* side to her personality that made her fearless and led her to take risks, providing him with more work than all her other attributes combined.

Josh shook his head in disbelief of how from the time he'd started protecting her, Jennifer had managed to select the largest and wildest horses at the local stable to turn into docile mounts. The worst part, though, was her outdoor runs—or as he liked to call them, her cross-country marathons. They grated on his nerves! He always had to follow her as she ran for hours on the trails through a so-called nature park. *Park my ass!* It was more like an overgrown, wild forest! He half-expected the Big Bad Wolf to jump out and grab her. *Just let the beast try! Jennifer would be the last young girl that wolf tried to eat.* On the plus side, he had plenty of time to read and had enjoyed peeking over her shoulder while she sketched or painted. He even enjoyed lying on the grass nearby, studying the sky and pretending to help her pick out cloud formations.

Protecting her had its pluses; it allowed him the freedom to constantly look at Jennifer and study every detail of her appearance. He found sanctuary in her eyes—they were dark and soothing, like espresso in southern Italy: deep, thick, and satisfying. *A man could become lost in those eyes.* He moved his eyes to safer territory now: her lips, pursed together as she leaned closer to the table. He took in her full, plump lips, so irresistibly kissable, especially when she pouted. *Do her lips taste as sweet as they look? Wait—where the hell had* that *come from?* He needed to turn his gaze to a safer area. What part of Jennifer was safer? Her long, silky dark brown hair? Maybe her tan, well-shaped legs? How about her youthful, curvaceous figure? *Damn!* Maybe her hands would be okay…expressive and sensuous…*No, no, no, and absolutely* not*!* His eyes were drifting, causing his mind to respond with a resounding *no way!*

He needed to look at something other than the girl; his eyes settled on her cake. Jennifer was looking at her cake, too. His mouth broke into a sly smirk over how hungrily she was looking at her cake. A disturbing thought entered his mind: *had Jennifer's needs become womanly? When had* that *happened?* This was the same girl who'd not too long ago been at the movie theater with her friends, throwing popcorn at boys and giggling. Yep, Jennifer wanted that cake in the worst way.

Jennifer's eyes won the battle over her common sense as they snuck a peek at *him* once more. What was he looking at? Her cake? The way he was looking at it, he must've wanted a piece—*badly.* Could a spirit eat cake? Not just cake, but food in general, or would it go right through them and land on the ground? *Food for thought. Yikes! He caught me looking at him again.*

If Josh didn't know any better he'd think Jennifer was flirting with him, the way she was looking into his eyes and flipping her long hair back with the hint of a smile on her sweet, untouched lips. *Trust me, Jennifer; I'm not the kind of man you should be flirting with.* As a protector, he couldn't allow himself to become attracted or involved with one of his cases, especially one so pure and inexperienced as Jennifer. His thoughts once again headed somewhere they shouldn't. *I need to get out of here, and fast!*

Jennifer felt the gaiety in the room dissipate, replaced by a sense of loss inside her heart. The attractive spirit often came and went, and it hadn't ever bothered her before. *What is my problem tonight?*

"Hope you made a wish," Jennifer's sister Sarah said. Sarah was five years her senior, and in Jennifer's opinion was the much prettier one with her blonde hair, blue eyes, and flawless, creamy complexion. Not to mention that she was outgoing, had tons of friends, and was on everyone's party invitation list. They were opposites in every way. Sarah had also just gotten engaged to her boyfriend of five years. Her wedding to Dave had originally been planned for the next summer, but—much to their mother's dismay—had just been pushed to the second week of January due to Dave's recent job offer out of state.

"I bet she wished for a horse," Jennifer's brother Alex teased.

Leave it to my brother to rub salt into an open wound. Jennifer had often dreamt of a massive black stallion that was fast enough to outrun the wind, and had thrown away far too many birthday wishes on the elusive black steed. This year she would change her failed pattern and use her wish towards her first kiss.

Alex was three years older and took great pride in frequently teasing Jennifer, and though he was a pain in the butt, she liked hanging out with him. Like Sarah, Alex was in college and last month he and his college buddies had rented a house together.

"Of course. What else would I wish for?" Jennifer fibbed. The worst thing that could happen would be if Alex were to find out her real wish; then his comments and jokes would be *relentless.*

"Jennifer, look at your dad while you cut the first slice so he can snap your picture," Mrs. Parker instructed.

"Okay Mom." Jennifer posed the knife on the cake's surface while looking up at the camera.

"Smile!" Mr. Parker instructed. "I believe we have ourselves a keeper," he announced after snapping the photo.

"Thanks Dad." *I could have done without a photo of me in a paper hat. If that picture gets around school, I'm doomed! Everyone already thinks I'm a geek!*

"Who wants cake?" Mrs. Parker asked while holding up two paper dishes with large slices of frosted chocolate cake.

"I'll take one of the larger slices, honey," Mr. Parker said, smacking his lips together in exaggerated anticipation.

Jennifer watched the exchange between her parents with a cringe. *Get a room!* But then again, she was used to her mom and dad fawning all over each other, unlike her friend's parents.

"Aunt June, did I mention that Theodore and I are traveling to Spain in the summer?"

Jennifer's ears pricked. *Mom and Dad are going to Spain? This* is *news. I don't suppose you'd like me to tag along?* Her parents had been traveling the earth for as long as she could remember, and the pile of trinkets in her bedroom proved it to be true. Each time the three siblings were left home to fend for themselves, Jennifer's sister was appointed the official guard on duty. Unlike her busy mom and dad, Sarah had eyes like a hawk and never missed a thing.

Later that night Jennifer escaped outdoors, bundled in her winter wear. It being the first of December, the grass was laden with a coat of frost and the quietness of the night was broken only by the crunch of her footsteps. The sound soothed her soul but did nothing to pacify her thoughts or calm her eyes, which darted to and fro in the hopes of one more peek at *him.* With reluctance, she turned her thoughts to tomorrow's trail ride and how she'd be seated on her favorite horse: a chestnut mare named Brandy that loved to run.

What Jennifer didn't know was that there was someone in another world watching her every move as she walked back inside and prepared for bed.

Sometime after midnight on earth, Gisabella gazed into her crystal orb from across many galaxies and dimensions at the teenager asleep in her bed. She was happy to see that Josh was protecting Jennifer from above the girl's home. From her observations during the previous three months, she could tell that the protector had only recently begun to notice that Jennifer had blossomed into a young woman.

Overall, things had been too eventless for Gisabella's taste, but all that was about to change. With a wave of her hand she uncloaked Jennifer's mind and unblocked all the girl's thoughts, placing her plan for the two of them in motion. Now that she had made it possible for Josh to read all of Jennifer's thoughts and for Jennifer to need Josh's help, things were about to get a little more *interesting*.

The sun shone brightly the next morning and all signs of winter were gone, making riding conditions perfect. Jennifer arrived at the stable and went to work grooming and saddling Brandy as Joe, the owner of the stable, headed her way. He was a kind, older man who walked with a cane and wore a permanent smile on his face as though tattooed there.

"Hi Joe," Jennifer said, returning his smile.

"I see you and Brandy are ready," Joe said. "The other riders canceled, so there's no need for me to lead the trail ride. Since you know Brandy and the trails well, why don't you take her out by yourself?"

Wishes do come true! Jubilation filled every cell in Jennifer's body. "Thank you Joe. I promise to be careful and keep her speed down to a canter." The sheer excitement of riding alone made his offer feel like a miracle.

"If you're all set to go, you know the way." Joe gave her a leg up and waved goodbye.

"Thank you, Joe. I'll have her back in two hours." Jennifer loosened

Brandy's reins, applied some light leg pressure, and they were on their way. The bridle path was wide, and offered tree-lined seclusion. Sitting astride the mare with no conversation to distract her made for a blissful state, and Jennifer kept Brandy down to a walk to warm the horse's muscles before cantering.

Josh didn't like this one bit. Jennifer riding by herself without a house in sight was doing *nothing* to ease his protector instincts. Though she was a good rider, anything could go wrong, and he needed to keep a vigilant eye out to ensure she stayed safe. He watched as Jennifer encouraged her horse into a brisk canter. The way Jennifer's hair flew in the wind as Brandy's thunderous hooves covered the ground shot his senses into high alert.

Josh told himself that he was being overly cautious, but when he caught sight of a moving object slithering across the trail in Jennifer's path, his honed instincts came to life. *What the hell is a snake doing out at this time of year?*

Without another thought Josh transformed himself into solid form, barely making it in time to watch Brandy's eyes roll back and her nostrils flare at the sight of the large snake. Before Josh had the chance to alter the situation, Jennifer's horse reared straight up on her back legs, frantically pawing the air with both front hooves. The sudden stop and the horse's unexpected upright position launched Jennifer off Brandy's back and into the air. Without a second to waste, Josh leapt forward and caught Jennifer in midair flight, doing his best to cushion the impact of their landing with his body. Seated on the ground with Jennifer in his lap, Josh gazed into the gorgeous brown eyes he'd only ever seen from a distance.

"It's you!" Jennifer said, looking up at the man who held her close.

"You've seen me before?" Josh asked suspiciously.

"Yes, I've seen you around—*a lot.* But you were always translucent," Jennifer said, staring in awe at the man who looked to be as alive as she was.

This was a first! In all his years of protecting the most gifted visionaries in the universe, only one or two out of thousands had ever been able to see him. *Maybe there's more to Jennifer after all.* "You needed my help, and I needed to become solid to catch you," Josh replied.

"Oh," Jennifer said, seeming to accept his answer without further explanation.

"Are you okay?" Josh did his best to ignore what Jennifer's close proximity was doing to his senses. Regardless of his inner struggle, he wasn't in any hurry to stand or remove her from his lap.

"I'm not sure where you came from or how you managed to catch me in time, but I'm thankful. You didn't have to bother, though—I'm sure I would've been fine," Jennifer said, brushing off her pants.

"You were sailing through the air without a net," Josh reminded her.

"True. But considering I'm seated on a strange man's lap, *now* seems like the appropriate time to require a 'safety net.'"

"This coming from a girl whose head would've been split wide open if not for my actions!"

"I think you're exaggerating," she rebutted. *Why am I antagonizing him?*

"Am I?" Josh's eyes sparkled. He hadn't gotten to banter with a woman besides Gisabella in ages.

"Fine—thank you for your help. My name's Jennifer," she conceded, finding his surprised look over her introduction to be quite endearing. "And this is where you tell me *your* name," she prompted, biting the inside of her mouth to keep from smirking at his discomfort.

What? Josh was caught off guard by the girl's reprimand, and found himself sheepishly grinning at his young charge. Apparently she had no problem putting him in his place, even though she'd seen him in a ghostly state. He was impressed. *That took guts!*

"I'm Joshua. But please, call me Josh. That's what my friends call me." *Hint, hint.* He extended his hand automatically, unsure of whether she'd find his handshake different than the others in her dimension. He was pleased when Jennifer reached out without any hesitation and grasped hold of his hand firmly. Her touch shot shivers throughout his entire body, and Josh shuddered. *Did Jennifer feel the same electricity when we touched?* The rational side of his brain told him to let her go, but he ignored the warning. Past all reasoning, he continued to hold her for as long as she'd permit him. It was when he looked directly into her eyes and found himself unable to tear his gaze away that he decided one of Jennifer's gifts was the ability to bewitch him with just a look.

"Nice to finally meet you, Josh." Jennifer wasn't sure what she'd expected from the handshake; she'd never before encountered a spirit who'd transformed to "solid," but she hadn't thought his hand would feel so warm. Jennifer found herself reveling in how real Josh was—so much so that if she hadn't seen him in his spirit presence first, she would've thought he was alive.

She felt safe enveloped in his energy, and it seemed as though his existence alone kept the frosty air at bay. Up close Josh's eyes were more intense than she could've imagined, holding a touch of humor she'd never noticed. Best of all, she finally knew their hue: green, but unlike any shade she'd ever seen before. They weren't vivid green or bluish; if she were to have to label their color, she would've described them as "a smoky gray-green." The longer she gazed into his eyes, the more she became lost in their ever-changing shade, one that currently vacillated between a rainy day in the forest and vibrant emeralds in the sun.

"Would you like me to assist you back on your horse?" Josh asked, spying Brandy a few feet away grazing on some sparse blades of green grass.

"Yes, thank you." Jennifer flashed him a shy smile.

"Unfortunately that requires letting you go," Josh said, beginning to unfold his legs.

"Of course." Jennifer attempted to scramble out of his lap, but Josh was already standing with her still in his arms as if she weighed no more than a feather.

"Are you okay to stand on your own?" Josh asked.

"Um, *yeah*," Jennifer quipped. *Why am I finding his concern so irritating? Maybe it's because I've taken care of myself almost all my life.* It was true; most of her life she'd been left on her own while her parents came and went and her older siblings focused on their own lives. She was used to being alone, and proud of how self-sufficient she was. Perhaps that's why she felt annoyed over how the same spirit she'd found comfort in most of her life was now treating her like some sort of fragile, breakable doll.

"Wait here." Josh hoped his no-nonsense voice would keep Jennifer in one place. After the fall she'd taken, he didn't trust her to walk, let alone *ride* back to the barn by herself. He walked slowly towards Brandy, murmuring calmly to the mare, and was glad the horse allowed him to approach and lead her back to Jennifer. As much as he was dying to tell Jennifer what a "good girl" she'd been for listening, he was sure his patronizing remark wouldn't go over well.

"Thank you," Jennifer said, holding out her hand to take Brandy's reins. "I got it from here."

"That's okay. I'm already here, so I might as well give you a leg up."

"Fine," Jennifer sulked. Brandy *was* sixteen hands high, which made it harder for her to get back in the saddle without the assistance of a leg up or a mounting block. Without hesitation, Jennifer bent her leg and waited for Josh's offered help.

Josh placed his hand on her shin, lifting her easily back onto Brandy.

"Thank you, Josh. Will I see you again?" Jennifer asked as she gathered the reins and smiled down at him. She'd seen him daily for years, so the odds were in her favor.

"Absolutely, Jennifer—I look forward to visiting with you again. May I ask how long you've been able to see me?" No matter what her answer was, it wouldn't be good. If Jennifer had begun to notice him recently, it meant she'd developed doing so on her own, which was never a good sign. Or worse, Jennifer had seen him for a long time without his knowledge or proper protection put in place. If he'd been a lower spirit who hungered for energy, he could've easily taken all of Jennifer's and left her for dead.

"When you first started watching me years ago," Jennifer said. "If you're asking me if I witnessed each time you smirked or broke out into a fit of laughter whenever I did something dumb, klutzy, or silly, the answer is yes. Not to mention all the times you shook your head in annoyance each time I decided to go running. You *could've* continued reading instead of following me, you know." She didn't dare tell Josh that sometimes she'd gone running only to watch his hyped-up reaction. *I wonder what he'd think if he knew how many times I hid my laughter at his frustration?*

"Why hadn't you said anything until now?" Josh cringed as he recalled the many times he'd rolled his eyes at her endless obsession with running. Another, more upsetting thought came to him: why hadn't any indication of Jennifer's abilities been readable in her mind? The only answer came in the form of one name—*Gisabella.*

"Because I never needed your help."

"Oh," Josh choked out, surprised by Jennifer's matter-of-fact reply. Even though she was technically years younger than his selected spirit age, she'd managed to get the upper hand in their conversation twice and given him a firsthand taste of her quick-witted sarcasm. He found himself even more attracted to her because of it.

"Now that I'm up here and you're down there, would you care to ride back with me?" she said, voice oozing with sugarcane sweetness.

Once again she'd surprised him with her forwardness, and this time his concerns were many. *Didn't she have a clue about unintentionally flirting?* Thank goodness it was him and not some corrupted pervert who might've considered taking advantage of her virginity. A new concern arose within him: If his reaction from simply holding her *hand* had been hard to control, how was he ever going to handle their bodies' closeness on the mare? He'd soon find out, because there was no way he was going to refuse her offer.

"I believe I'll take you up on that," he said, trying to sound nonchalant. "It'd give us more time to talk." Josh flashed his best "I won't bite" smile.

Jennifer removed her foot from the stirrup so Josh could join her. As he hoisted himself up, Josh's face came within inches of hers, and his breath was sweet and heady, like an aphrodisiac to her senses.

"I hope you don't mind if I hold on to you, Jennifer. No offense, but I've watched the way you ride. I get the feeling if I don't, I'll soon be lying on the ground." His voice was barely above a whisper in her ear.

"Yes, I noticed how you watched me from a distance whenever I rode Brandy." Her voice came out shaky and breathy, like a silly schoolgirl with a crush on a movie star. "Don't think I didn't notice you shaking your head in disapproval over the way I rode. Yet you've never seen me fall off, have you?" Before Josh could say anything, she pressed her heels into Brandy's sides and her horse leapt forward into a brisk canter. Josh's grip doubled in strength and she was glad he couldn't see the laughter in her eyes.

Well played, Jennifer! Josh thought. She'd officially told him off for everything he'd done over the years. Never one to hold back from a challenge, he took advantage of their fast pace to tighten his grip, while he tried to convince himself there was nothing wrong with spending some time getting to know her better. *This is for research purposes to better protect her,* Josh justified—even if he *was* focusing more on the curve of Jennifer's waist than anything else at the moment.

Jennifer slowed Brandy down to a walk, telling herself it was in her horse's best interest and not because she badly wanted to spend more time with Josh. Each time he leaned in closer to say something, his warm breath caused her heart to flutter.

"Thank you for slowing down," Josh said, though what he meant was *thank you for slowing down so we can sit like this a little longer.* Jennifer returned the favor by giggling. He couldn't see her face, but knew she was blushing, as she often did. Her guard was down and something had changed, almost like a veil had lifted; Jennifer's thoughts had become ridiculously easy to read. Right now she was happy he was seated on Brandy with her, and she thought he was handsome… He stopped reading once she started delving into more private territory, about how amazing his breath felt on her neck, and how she adored the feeling of his hands on her waist.

Josh ruminated on the fact he'd lost the first few conversation battles with his young charge. He wouldn't let that happen again. "I take it Brandy is your favorite horse," Josh started, attempting to lighten the conversation; he'd become a lot more comfortable than he ought to be seated so closely to her. He needed to leave soon and distance himself from temptation, because Jennifer was having the strangest effect on him. He wondered if *this* was why he'd been sent to protect her—Jennifer's life force energy and aura were euphoric, a combination that'd no doubt attract many men. In addition, every misguided soul from all dimensions would believe that their comfort rested in her light. With such pure energy, even *he* had to fight off the urge to siphon a little. *Gisabella must have cloaked Jennifer's energy and her thoughts until she turned eighteen! What other reason could there be for not picking up on Jennifer's abilities sooner?*

He bathed Jennifer in a cocoon of protective white light to help keep her from harm, then blocked his own energy field in case she inadvertently transferred any of her own energy to him. The simple action of Jennifer's extremely empathetic nature without proper protection could transfer some of her energy to him, leaving her depleted and at risk of illness. Jennifer fit the typical profile of an empathic person who hadn't received enough love as a child. The combination made her someone who'd not only feel what others were feeling, but who would empathize with them to the point of giving away her own energy to help them. He would need to instruct her on how to be sympathetic and caring, *without* sacrificing her energy. It'd be one of the first lessons he'd teach her, and Josh felt a stab of remorse for not having done much to help her awaken her gifts. In his defense, today was the first sign Jennifer had displayed any visionary abilities.

"Yes. I love Brandy," Jennifer said as she turned around to look at him. Her breath hitched when she found there was only a span of inches between them. Josh's lips looked inviting, and his eyes had darkened to a vivid emerald green.

Josh glanced away before he did something he'd regret. Jennifer was far too naïve for the likes of him, and way too innocent for his taste. "Thank you, Jennifer, for the pleasure of your company. I'm afraid I must bid you farewell now." He was shocked over how badly he wanted to stay with Jennifer; it was as if he never wanted to leave her side.

"Must you? We were just getting to know each other." Jennifer had no clue of the power her ensuing pout had over Josh's decision-making.

"I must." *Because I want to kiss your sweet, innocent lips hard enough to bruise them, and I can't promise I'd stop until it was too late.* Josh jumped off the horse and smacked Brandy's hindquarter hard enough to carry Jennifer away.

CHAPTER FOUR

Jennifer took extra care dressing for school on Monday morning, secretly hoping Josh would make an appearance. Their time together had been too brief, and there was so much more she wanted to know about him. She ran a brush through her hair absently while recalling Josh's grayish-green eyes and bright smile for the thousandth time since Saturday. With a final stroke of lip gloss, she grabbed her books and headed to the door dressed in her favorite bell-bottom jeans and soft, emerald-colored sweater.

"Goodbye, Mom," Jennifer called out.

"Don't forget I have a meeting after work and your dad is working late, so you're on your own for dinner," Mrs. Parker yelled from the kitchen.

Ever since Jennifer was ten she'd fended for herself, settling for sandwiches or a can of soup while her dad worked a second job and her mother attended so-called meetings with her friends, ones that were held over dinner at a fancy restaurant or during a girls' night out. Sure, there were the occasional business meetings for the bank job Mrs. Parker held, but they didn't happen more than twice a week. Jennifer had stopped minding a long time ago, and now reveled in having the house to herself so that she might work on her latest masterpiece without interruption.

Donning her winter coat, Jennifer headed out the front door, trotted down the steps, and stopped dead in her tracks—it was *him.* The sight of a translucent Josh standing in her front yard beside the massive willow tree sent her adrenaline racing. It'd been cold the night before, and the evidence of such was reflected on the ice-coated, weeping branches touching the ground and the frosty fog surrounding them. The combination was an ideal, fantastical backdrop for Josh's ghostly good looks and his heart-stopping smile.

~Good morning, Jennifer,~ Josh messaged in Jennifer's mind, playing the part of "Mr. Cool" even though his heart was drumming a salsa rhythm and he felt a bit nervous. It'd been a long time since he'd conversed with anyone on earth, and a while since he'd spoken to a woman he found attractive. More importantly, it wasn't his usual practice to show himself or speak directly with his visionaries, opting instead to give solutions to problems and other valuable instructions through their thoughts. The last thing he wanted was for any of his charges to become dependent on him, taking away their ability to stand on their own two feet. But Jennifer was different, and he was having a hard time putting his finger on why.

"Good morning, Josh. Nice to see you again." Like the many previous spirit visitors before Josh, Jennifer heard his voice loud and clear in her head as if he'd spoken them out loud.

~Would you mind if I walked you to school?~ Josh asked.

"I'd like that." *Hopefully this time you won't go running off before you answer some questions.*

Josh found that her unblocked thoughts were once again easy to read, and while he enjoyed this about her, his job was to teach Jennifer to block her thoughts and keep telepathic individuals at bay. It would only take one spirit craving a fresh energy boost to pick up on Jennifer's unblocked thoughts and energy, placing her in grave danger. The first step was to instruct Jennifer on how to send messages, making it easier for them to talk in public.

~Act as if I'm not here so no one will think you're speaking to yourself. Smile if you heard what I said,~ Josh messaged.

When she flashed him a large grin, Jennifer was rewarded with a wink.

~Good girl! Now, keep your expression blank, like when you play poker,~ Josh messaged.

If she knew how to reply back, Jennifer would've asked him how to play poker and the hundred other questions she had. Instead, she remained quiet and forced herself not to beam ear-to-ear as Josh walked alongside her.

~I know you must have questions, and I promise I'll try to answer them. Why don't we try an experiment,` Josh messaged, and when Jennifer's eyes darted sideways towards him, he took it as a sign to continue. ~I'd like you to concentrate on something you'd like to know about me. For beginners, it helps if you silently say your question to yourself over and over inside your head while I try to pick up on what you're thinking.~

What should I ask? I can't ask anything that he'll think is silly or dumb. What's the formula for an organic combustion? Agh—I can't ask him about something which I've no clue about. Are you seeing anyone? Agh! Too desperate-sounding!

~No Jennifer, I'm not seeing anyone,~ Josh answered with a playful smirk.

Jennifer's rambling thoughts were interrupted by the sound of Josh's voice answering her unintentional question. *If only the ground could swallow me now.* The color of embarrassment rose all the way from her toes to the roots of her hair. *Why am I having such a hard time concentrating around him? "Because you like him!" her subconscious interjected. But, he's going to think I'm such an idiot!*

~I'd never think such a thing,~ Josh replied, once again responding to her unspoken remark.

Why not, most of my family thinks I'm one. Well, maybe not my entire family. Mostly Alex—he's my brother. I bet you already know that, don't you? Not the idiot part. Now might be a good time to tell you that I have a straight B average. Oh no—it's happening again! Please don't tell me you heard all that. It's true—I'm an idiot. Jennifer risked a glance at Josh to find he was doing his best not to laugh.

~As much as I find your labyrinthine thoughts refreshing, I believe you still haven't asked me a question,~ he teased. ~Go ahead, don't be shy.~

Where do you live? This time Jennifer thought of an actual question in her mind.

~I have an apartment in a dimension that runs parallel to the earth's dimension. I don't spend much time there, but it's home.~

Do others in your dimension have homes?

~If they so choose. There are many options during their stays there, such as houses, apartments, castles, and other kinds of dwellings. The main difference is that when a person on earth transitions upward into my dimension, or "realm" as it's also called, they can choose where and how they wish to live and spend their time. There are even whole families who transitioned from earth together and duplicated the living style they had while on earth. Others opt to forgo a place to live in lieu of traveling around the universe, while some people spend all their time learning from the highest scholars. Since everyone is healthy and there's no requirement to eat, drink, or sleep, with a little imagination you can have anything you wish—the sky's the limit!~

My dad describes heaven like that.

~Many say it's exactly like they pictured heaven, and most have taken to calling it so.~ Josh watched Jennifer's expression for any sign of discomfort over this revelation, but none came. ~There are many horses, cats, dogs, deer, butterflies, and other wildlife, with endless fields and meadows for them to roam in.~

It sounds perfect, Jennifer thought wistfully.

~Yes, it does sound rather ideal.~ *I better save the bad stuff for another time.*

You said, "During their stay?" Does this mean time in your dimension, like here on earth, is temporary? If everyone is healthy, it doesn't sound like they die from sickness, Jennifer asked internally.

~Yes—or it is for the most part, at least. A person can remain for one, two, or hundreds of years until they must descend to earth to be born again.~

Born again?

~Each person has to experience thousands of lifetimes, all designed to advance their soul to a higher plane of knowledge.~

So how high on this plane of knowledge are you? Jennifer's eyes drifted once again in Josh's direction in time to see the corner of his mouth twitch.

~Pretty high.~ *She's got a lot of nerve asking me that!*

If, as you say, you're only "pretty high up" on the scale, that means that you haven't obtained the knowledge you need to stay in your world. How many more lifetimes do you have left before you reach the top?

~None!~ *What an insolent girl! I should give her an earful about showing me my due respect as her protector and teacher.* After a quick reminder that Jennifer had no idea he was there on assignment, he let her comment go.

Jennifer cringed at the tone of Josh's one-word spurn and apparent disapproval of her question. *It's* his *fault for telling me to ask him "anything." I'd like to know if he misses life on earth. Having parties, tasting different foods, dreaming of the future and so many other things life here brings. My guess is he does—like all the others who came to visit.*

~Lots of people opt to eat, drink, enjoy food, and have parties, while others choose to use their time to accomplish any unfinished dreams and goals they never got a chance to on earth. *I* happen to love food so much that I've studied with many top chefs in the other realm, and when I have the time, I enjoy eating meals.~

~You can cook? My father can't even make a can of beans! Although I think he's just saying that so I'll make them for him.~ *So that's why Josh was looking at my birthday cake like he wanted to devour the entire thing!*

~You did it, Jennifer! You managed to send me a message.~

~I did? It didn't feel any different.~

~It may not have felt different to you, but you elevated your level of concentration high enough to send your words into my mind. We'll practice more when I walk you home after school. If it's okay with you, that is…~

~I'd like that very much,~ Jennifer messaged.

~Excellent. I'll be here waiting for you then. Have fun and learn lots.~

"Thanks for—" Jennifer raised a hand to her throat in horror when her voice failed after she'd spoken the first few words aloud.

~Never speak to me out loud when we're in public. It's the first lesson you'll need to learn if we have any hope of becoming friends,~ Josh messaged curtly. When Jennifer's previous exuberant mood nosedived and her eyes clouded over, he wished there was some way to take back his thoughtless words. *I'm such an ass! Be nice to the girl—she's new at this,* he reminded himself. ~It's okay Jennifer, no one heard you.~ It was clear to him by the way she perked up that his attempt to smooth things over wasn't lost on her.

~My voice—what happened to my words?~

~I'm sorry; my first reaction was to silence your voice. I know this is all new to you.~

~How is that possible?~ A tremor ran through Jennifer's body at the thought of Josh being able to do such a thing. Even though her instincts told her to run as fast as she could from him, she kept her feet firmly planted and any trace of fear was kept at bay, as if she'd been programmed to trust Josh.

~We can talk about that later. For now you need to head to class because I'm afraid if you stand in one spot for much longer, you're going to attract attention.~

~Goodbye, Josh,~ Jennifer said, using her newfound messaging skill before walking into school without another glance his way.

Josh flew above the school, where he spent the morning floating around and patrolling the area for any sign of danger.

Once in class, Jennifer found it hard to concentrate on such mundane things as mathematics when she knew Josh would be walking home with her. When the lunch bell sounded, she was up and out of her chair in seconds.

"Hi, girls," Jennifer greeted her three closest friends as she placed her lunch tray on the table. She'd met Elizabeth in elementary school, and together they'd befriended Colleen and Mary in junior high. Each of them had suffered years of persecution from fellow classmates, being labeled "outcasts" and "weirdos." Going through such adversity together sealed their friendship and made them kindred soul sisters for life. One by one each of her friends had outgrown their nicknames, but Jennifer had been unable to shed the name she'd earned in kindergarten even into high school.

Now seniors and in good standing, the four of them enjoyed a panoramic view of the football field from a prime location table. It was no surprise to find Mary gazing longingly at one of the uniformed teens practicing his throws; she was officially boy-crazy, often imagining herself to be in love at least once a month with different guys.

"Finally, Jennifer! We've been dying to know how your party went." Mary turned her attention away from the window, flipping back her blonde hair to gaze over with her bright blue eyes.

"Well?" Elizabeth prompted. She was the tallest girl in school, and had expressive hazel eyes that were offset by her thick, chestnut-brown hair. Unlike Mary, Elizabeth rarely dated.

"It was okay—family, pizza, cake." *And a handsome male visitor,* Jennifer added silently. Memories of all the times she'd been ostracized for speaking about the spirits who'd come to visit her kept her mouth wired shut about Josh. "My parents gave me this pair of earrings." She pulled her hair back so they could see. "And the *best* present is that they're going to Spain!"

"Party time!" Colleen said as her face lit up. Colleen's curly red hair had a mind of its own, and she often wore it in a messy bun. She'd been the last one to join the group, with Mary and her becoming instant best friends. The two shared a common hobby—boys! The only difference between the two was that all the boys asked Mary out, while Colleen still struggled to step out from behind Mary's shadow.

"I'll start a list." Mary opened her notebook book and wrote "guest list" at the top of the page.

"I can invite the boy I like from math class. It's gonna be the party of the year," Elizabeth added.

"No way! My parents will have my head!" Jennifer cried, throwing her hand over Mary's notebook to try and stop the list of names from growing longer.

"Relax—they'll never find out," Colleen vowed.

"Absolutely not. We can have a sleepover, but that's all!" Jennifer compromised.

"Ooh, even better! Who should we invite?" Mary continued, jotting down names.

"The four of us. That's the limit," Jennifer stated. Knowing Mary, she'd invite every boy in their school and no other girls.

"Geez, Jennifer, sometimes you're such a wimp," Colleen quipped.

"Very funny, Colleen. Maybe I should remind you of the time you dumped us all out of the rowboat when you saw a spider and panicked."

"It was about to crawl on my leg!" Colleen visibly shivered. "None of you seemed to mind when those boys dived in and swam to our rescue."

"That's when I got my first kiss." Mary swooned from the memory of the first boy with whom she'd fallen in love. "His name was Tom, no, wait—it was John. Yes, that was his name, John. He was so adorable, and we dated for three weeks until he had to move because of his dad's job transfer."

"We all felt badly for you," Jennifer sympathized. Although she'd never dated or fallen in love yet, the pain rolling off Mary had been so tangible that Jennifer had felt as if her *own* heart were breaking.

"I have good news," Colleen interjected, quite adept by then at distracting Mary from her sad memories. "I've been accepted to Connecticut University with you guys!"

"Really?!" Mary exclaimed. "But I thought you wanted to pursue nursing?"

"I'll be studying nursing at their sister school while getting a biology minor from the main campus."

"All we need now is to convince Jennifer to come with us," Elizabeth added with a glimmer of hope.

With graduation only six months away, there was the matter of which college Jennifer wanted to attend. She'd gotten a couple of acceptances, but none offered an art program even remotely at the level she desired. She still hadn't gotten up the nerve to tell her parents she planned on being an artist; they'd think she'd lost her mind, then repeat the same woeful tale of how she'd die of starvation without a normal paycheck, followed by the "bring home the bacon" lecture. *There are more important things than eating bacon, Mom and Dad.*

"I'm considering Connecticut University but I haven't made my final decision—I'll know more after my interview in two weeks. The fact that you're all going there *does* make it more appealing, but it all depends on their art department and whether I can convince my parents."

"I'm sure there's a way to do a double-major with a heavy concentration in art," Colleen suggested.

"I guess I could add a degree in marketing and then my parents would have to approve," Jennifer said, nodding. *Why hadn't I thought of that?*

After they'd made plans to go to the movies Friday night, they each headed off to their next class, with Jennifer practicing what she'd say to her parents so that they might allow her to pursue her true dream.

CHAPTER FIVE

Jennifer stared at the clock, willing the hands to move faster and for the dismissal bell to ring. After what seemed like an unbearable wait she escaped out into the fresh air, where true to his word, Josh was waiting.

~Hi, Jennifer,~ Josh messaged with an easy grin that was immediately reciprocated, proving she'd heard his message.

~I wasn't sure if you'd show up or not,~ Jennifer shyly messaged. Now face to face with Josh after reliving their previous conversations while pretending to pay attention in class, she found his good looks and self-assured mannerisms beguiling. It didn't even matter that he was a spirit; Josh was still hotter than any guy she'd ever met.

~I'm a man of my word.~

~I guess I have no other choice than to accept your word until you break it.~

~I get the feeling you don't think very highly of promises or a person's word of honor.~

~Why would you say that?~ *I didn't think he'd take everything so literally! Geez...it's time to change the subject.*

~No reason. I believe we were discussing how I silenced your mistaken outburst before you were late for matriculation.~

Matriculation? Who speaks this way?

Josh forced himself to bite back his retort. *What's wrong with the way I speak? It's always served me well before now. Maybe I should speak 1970s slang and see if she approves. Why is this girl so frustrating?* ~Jennifer, the ability to silence your voice comes from my knowledge of energy manipulation, meaning I'm able to change and neutralize the energy of your voice so that no human could hear it.~

~I'd imagine you must win lots of arguments this way.~ Jennifer delivered her message while hiding her snicker behind her schoolbooks. Too bad she hadn't counted on translucent Josh's ability to reach over and force the books downward, exposing her guilty smirk.

~It'd serve you well to remember that I win every argument fair and square, including those with young ladies who hide behind sarcasm, satire, and schoolbooks.~

~I can tell there's no way to win an argument or a conversation with you,~ Jennifer appeased.

~I'm glad you agree.~ Josh ignored the childish, foot-stomping thoughts running around in Jennifer's head. ~As a reward, you can ask another question.~

Jennifer squashed the comeback perched on the tip of her tongue. If she had any hope of finding out more about him, she'd better start playing nice.

~Earlier you said that you're a trained chef and love to eat. How is that possible? Even though I can't see completely through you right now, you're not exactly solid. For instance, if I were to give you a bite of my apple, how would that work?~ Jennifer held the leftover apple from lunch in his direction.

~You and your tempting apple exist in the earth's dimension, but since the apple's an object it also exists in the gateway dimension I'm currently standing in. Think of the gateway dimension as a mirror image of all things in your world—with the exception of people—that also serves as a link between our two worlds. This is especially true when a person dies on earth; first they must pass through the gateway dimension before they continue on into the dimension that most spirits reside.~

What on earth is Josh talking about? All I wanted to know was if he can eat food.

~That being said,~ Josh reached out for the apple. ~I've taken the apple's duplicated energy and as you can see, we're still each holding the same apple. This is possible because objects can exist in both the earth and the gateway dimensions.~

Oh my god—can he eat the apple or not?!

~When I take a bite,~ Josh bit into the crunchy red flesh of the fruit, ~it only takes place in the gateway dimension that I'm in, while your apple remains in your hand, untouched.~ Josh chewed and swallowed the apple while looking into Jennifer's wide-eyed stare. Her increased breaths and flushed cheeks stirred something deep within him. *This girl is trouble! Damn it, Gisabella! If I find out that you've placed one of your enchantment spells on either Jennifer or myself, I'll have your head on a platter!*

The way Josh bit into the apple with his bright white teeth and full lips made it impossible for Jennifer to look away. All hope of doing so was lost when her eyes partook in the vision of the juices glistening on Josh's bottom lip. The scene that was playing out before her felt biblical in every sense of the word, and the apple had become more than just an innocent piece of fruit.

~That's amazing! I didn't see the apple going down. I mean, based on ghost stories and such, I wasn't sure if you could eat, um, I mean…hold food inside you, or if it'd go through you and fall on the ground.~ *Agh! Talk about unedited stupidity!*

~Jennifer, I'm a real person who's alive, complete with organs and blood. I just happen not to be as solid as you are when I'm here on earth. Of course there are certain benefits to those living in the spirit dimension; we don't have to eat, neither is there a need for the body to digest or eliminate.~

~I never thought of it like that; of course you're as real as I am. Wait a minute! Are you telling me that you don't need to use the bathroom?~

~Never!~ *Except when Gisabella forces me to try one of her god-awful creations!* ~Even better, none of us age, unless we choose to change the age we've selected.~

~You mean to tell me that everyone in heaven gets to choose the age they want to be and that they never grow old? Can a person change their mind?~

~It's frowned upon to change your selected age, because it's based on what age each person was their healthiest while alive on earth. Even though no one ages, each person's wisdom increases at a normal rate, so there's no need to grow older physically.~ Josh quickly changed the subject before Jennifer could ask how old he really was.

~As for the apple, all spirits can take or move objects about in the earth dimension; although we're not supposed to, it happens quite often. With a little magic I learned from Merlin many years ago, I'm able to use the same principals I used with the apple to move objects from my dimension and place them into yours,~ Josh messaged before taking another bite of the apple.

~Merlin?~ Jennifer's face transformed in recognition. ~You can't possibly expect me to believe that you know "Merlin," the wizard from Camelot. He's not even real.~

~Don't let Merlin hear you say that. I can attest that he's very real, and that he's given up his wizarding days in lieu of teaching.~ Josh stopped before he disclosed that Merlin was in charge of teaching each of Gisabella's protectors. He needed to be careful not to reveal too much information about his job, until he was sure that Jennifer was open to the idea of having a protector. He hoped that when the time came, she would understand that his assigned presence there had nothing to do with their growing friendship.

~So, let me get this straight—you learned how to move an object from your dimension into mine from Merlin?~

~That sums it up.~

~Is that how you changed yourself to solid? You moved yourself into my dimension?~

~Not quite.~ Josh cringed, not wanting to go there. ~Alas, I can only move innate objects and must adhere to a long list of legal limitations of what I can do with them.~

~Then how did you become so solid to the touch?~ Jennifer messaged, followed by a head-to-toe flush. ~What I mean is...~ *Oh no!* Memories of how Josh's arms and chest had felt beneath her fingertips were forever seared into her mind. *Of all the times to begin daydreaming about the best day of my life. What's* wrong *with me?*

~No Jennifer, changing over to solid only happens in rare cases—for instance, it was only possible because you were flying through the air in need of rescuing. I can't stay solid in your world for long, and once you were safe and had ridden away, I became as I am now,~ Josh explained. Somehow he managed not to break into an oversized smile from her thoughts, but there was no way to hide the twinkle in his eyes.

~Does being solid feel much different to you?~

~Yes—it's as close to being alive on earth as I can get to the real thing, but there are a few disadvantages.~ He'd have left it at that except for the questionable look Jennifer gave him. ~When I'm solid in form, it's harder for me to move from place to place as fast as when I'm invisible or translucent.~ *And the loss of energy required to stay solid makes it harder to protect you!*

~Wait..."invisible?" You mean to tell me that there were times you were lurking around when I couldn't see you?~ Jennifer cringed.

~Seeing as though I never knew you were able to see me, I'd say that's a moot point. However, if you're wondering why there are times I prefer being invisible even from those rare individuals like yourself who can see translucent spirits, it's because it conserves my energy.~ *Making it easier to protect you and to win battles when the enemy can't see who's pummeling their ass.*

Jennifer noticed they had reached her house. *What now? Should I invite Josh in for some cookies and milk? By the look of him, I don't think he's a milk drinker; more like coffee or something stronger. Will I see him again? I have more questions! Maybe he'd like some lemonade—get a grip, it's too cold for that.*

~Thank you for letting me walk you home. May I do so again tomorrow?~ *Bewitching spell or not, I want to talk to you again too.*

~I'd like that, but only if I can ask more questions.~

~Agreed,~ Josh messaged, taking another bite of the apple as he faded away, leaving Jennifer open-mouthed and alone.

Once she'd gathered herself, Jennifer went inside the empty house and ran upstairs to the sanctity of her bedroom, where she spent the next hour lying in bed staring blankly up at the ceiling.

"Jennifer, I'm home," Mrs. Parker called out several hours later. "Hopefully you already ate dinner." When no answer was heard, Mrs. Parker shrugged her shoulders and went upstairs to change.

I'm in my room, and I've been left alone long enough to know when I need to eat, Jennifer silently answered, glad her mother couldn't read her thoughts like Josh.

"Oh, here you are, Jennifer," Mrs. Parker said. "Are you studying?"

"I was." *Although I'd rather be talking to the new guy I met.* "Hey Mom, I noticed we're out of eggs and some other items; I can drive to the grocery store and pick them up for you."

The look on Mrs. Parker's face spoke volumes about Jennifer's suggestion. "You know how I feel about you driving the car by yourself. Maybe when Sarah comes home, so she can accompany you."

"I'm eighteen now, Mom! Both Sarah and Alex were driving on their own by seventeen. This is ludicrous! I've had my license for two years, yet you still insist that I'm not responsible. You've had no problem with me being alone in the house since I was ten years old, yet you refuse to let me drive!" Jennifer cried, incensed. *Geez, will Mom ever forget I drove into the garage door? I couldn't help the fact it was opening at a glacial pace. Other than a few other minor miscalculations, my driving hasn't been that bad.*

"I never said you weren't responsible. I've simply pointed out how sometimes your head is in the clouds. I'll never forget that time you couldn't find your way home from school."

"I was in kindergarten, and the school was almost a mile from our house! I know the way to and from the grocery store," Jennifer argued. *If Alex hadn't run off with his friends, I'd have been fine!* "Why don't you just say the real reason you won't let me drive your car?"

"I promised your father I wouldn't keep bringing up your accident, but seriously Jennifer, how'd you manage to do so much damage to the house and my car without ever leaving the garage?" Mrs. Parker pursed her lips.

"It was an accident, Mom. For the ten thousandth time, I'm sorry. If it's any consolation, I haven't had one since." *Other than running over a curb or two, some missed stop signs, oh yeah, and the time I narrowly missed the neighbor's cat—thank goodness he was fast! Don't ask me why I sometimes flake out when I'm driving. My mind just wanders to more important things.*

"I'd prefer if you took someone with you," Mrs. Parker said, but when Jennifer's stubborn look didn't budge, she switched tactics. "Please try to understand that you're my baby and I feel like you've grown up so fast." Mrs. Parker's voice held a hint of emotion, accompanied by watery eyes.

"I know, Mom." It was pointless to argue with her mother when she began speaking of all the time she'd missed with Jennifer. It was only recently that her mother had begun to notice her, and that was because her two favorite children would soon be out on their own. As long as Jennifer could remember, her mother had worked all day and spent almost every weekend away with her father, or attending parties.

"Don't worry—you'll be driving to and from college soon. Just not in *my* car. If you decide to keep living here, maybe we can find you a used one."

Jennifer watched tears gather in her mother's eyes. She'd never seen this emotional side before. *Why's she crying?*

"Have you looked into business degrees like you said you would?" Mrs. Parker asked suddenly, regarding Jennifer with a clear-eyed, renewed strength.

So much for the brief glimpse of my mother's nurturing side. "I'm looking into a degree in marketing." *To go with my art major.* It wasn't a good time to tell her mom about her plan for two degrees. Once her mom came home after dining out and a few glasses of wine, she would have a much better chance of things going her way.

"I'm so glad you've come to your senses. With a degree in business, you can find a job anywhere."

"I think I hear Sarah. Can we borrow your car?" A quick change of topic was in order, a maneuver that Jennifer had learned over the years to distract her mother away from irritating topics.

"All right, but be careful and remember to pick up some peanut butter."

"Thanks Mom." She kissed her mom on the cheek and ran downstairs to convince Sarah into being her copilot.

Jennifer climbed into the driver seat of her parents' Buick and after much cajoling, Sarah joined her in the passenger seat. What Sarah thought of Jennifer's driving became obvious when she sucked in a breath and pulled on the seatbelt until it was as tight as possible.

"Would you relax?! My driving isn't that bad!"

"Let's just say I hope you've improved since the last time I rode with you. Honestly, Jennifer, how could you forget so many driving rules the minute you turn the key?" Sarah shook her head in exasperation.

"May I remind you that I passed my driver's test with flying colors?" Jennifer didn't bother to add how green the test giver had been when they'd exited the car.

"How much did you pay him?"

Ignoring Sarah's dig, Jennifer turned the key and brought the car to life, then reached for the radio.

"Oh no you don't!" Sarah said, looking at her sister in dismay. "You need your full concentration."

"Chill out, Sarah. You're beginning to sound like Mom." If this were actually true, Sarah would've been putting on lipstick, fixing her hair in the rearview mirror, and ignoring Jennifer as if she didn't exist.

"Yeah right. Mom let's you get away with murder because you're the youngest."

Not this again! Every conversation always came back to how lucky Jennifer was for having been ignored. Jennifer put the car in reverse and pressed the gas pedal ever so softly, successfully clearing all the hedges while keeping all four tires on the paved surface. With a careful glance each way, she backed out like a pro.

"See, I told you I've improved," Jennifer boasted with a proud smile.

"Congratulations! You made it out of the driveway without getting us killed!"

"Have you picked out where you're going on your honeymoon?" Jennifer quickly changed the subject to something a little more palatable than her bad driving.

"We're going to Bermuda. Pink sand and fun in the sun. Soon I'll be married and out of the house with no parents around to tell me what to do—I can't *wait*."

"I'm going to miss you, sis. You've always been there for me and now…well, you know, things will be different." Jennifer tried her best to keep her voice from cracking. When she was a child, Sarah was the only one who'd taken the time to show her any attention.

"I know, but it's part of growing up. Just think—next year you'll be in college, and maybe you'll even find you *own* future husband," Sarah teased.

"'Husband?' Now you sound like Mom!" Jennifer squeaked, though her imaginings had immediately veered to a certain man she'd enjoyed speaking to very much.

"Jennifer! Wake up! You just ran through a stop sign!" Sarah shouted.

"I did?" Jennifer glanced in the rearview mirror to see the object she'd missed. *Oh no! If Sarah tells Mom, I'll never be allowed to drive the car again.* "You distracted me by telling me that I have to find a husband! Please don't tell Mom or she'll never let me leave the house again!" It never hurt to throw in some exaggeration to get her way.

"Fine, but pay attention to what you're doing. The last thing I want is to lose my baby sister—especially now that you're not a little brat and we have more in common," Sarah snickered. "Before you know it, you'll be getting married too, and the four of us can hang out together."

"Don't rush things. I have no desire to date let alone get *married* until after college when I'm an established artist."

"That could take forever! Besides, you'll be next on Mom's radar; thank your lucky stars that she's left you alone so far. Once I'm married, look out! You'll finally understand what I've had to go through."

Josh shook his head. *Jennifer blew right by that stop sign! I can't believe it's the second one she's missed in three months. The only reason she passed her driver's test was because of my parallel parking skills and ability to stop her car.* A thought occurred to Josh then, about how some of his prior visionaries had had similar issues when concentrating on mechanical tasks. It'd always been the very gifted ones, and Josh wondered how far his charge's capabilities reached. When Jennifer parked the car and the girls climbed out, Josh followed, making sure they didn't run into any trouble as they shopped.

"These are a necessity for studying." Sarah held up a bag of red licorice.

"Seriously? I prefer a huge bowl of buttered popcorn."

"Too messy. Plus everyone knows that popcorn is best when eaten at the movies with a boy's arm around your shoulders," Sarah teased.

Jennifer hid her impending blush while pretending to look at the selection of candy bars. *What I wouldn't give to have Josh's arm around me.*

Their quick trip to the grocery store turned into a full shopping cart filled to the top with a vast array of snacks, peanut butter, eggs, and several other necessities. Back at the car, they loaded the trunk and clambered in before Jennifer started the car and mentally prepared herself for the drive home. *I will not become distracted. I need to pay attention and stop for stop signs,* she said over and over as she backed out.

"Doesn't it feel odd with Alex living at school?" Sarah asked as she tore open a bag of chips.

"I like not being picked on."

"He came home for your birthday."

"That was a nice surprise." Jennifer reached over and grabbed a few chips for herself.

Josh shook his head. *Great, now Jennifer's trying to eat and drive at the same time. She can't even handle driving when she has no other distractions.* He prepared himself for the worst, and didn't have to wait long before Jennifer failed to notice that a stoplight had turned red. With no time to message her, Josh employed his telekinesis ability to stop the car.

What just happened? Jennifer glanced down to make sure the car was still running.

"Thank goodness you stopped!" Sarah exclaimed. "Don't scare me like that—I thought for sure you were going to drive right through that red light."

"Oh. Sorry." Jennifer looked around the car as if it held the answer to what had happened.

~If I were you, I'd pay attention to driving instead of eating chips,~ Josh messaged.

Oh no! Josh must've stopped the car. That means he's watching us. Josh isn't interested in Sarah, is he?

~No, Jennifer, I have no interest in watching Sarah. You may wish to look at the light now, because it's green. Pay attention! I don't want you to get into an accident.~

~Thank you for helping me out,~ Jennifer messaged. ~The last thing I want is for my driving privileges to be taken away forever.~

~Then stop messaging me and watch where you're going. You wouldn't want to get lost, would you?~

Jennifer glanced at Sarah to make sure she didn't hear Josh's loud reprimand. *He's got some nerve speaking to me like that!* When the car slowed down of its own accord to twenty-five miles per hour, Jennifer balked. *What* else *is Josh capable to doing?* Her unspoken question earned peals of laughter. ~Get out of my head! Can't you see I'm trying to concentrate?!~

"Are you okay, Jennifer?" Sarah questioned. "Why are you all red? Who are you thinking about?"

"No one." *That you can see.*

"Please tell me you haven't picked up talking to unseen friends again." Sarah laughed at what she thought was a hilarious joke. "I swear you were the oddest child. I'll never forget the time you brought your invisible friend to school for show and tell. Talk about ruining your entire elementary school reputation and any chance for normal friends. Weren't you in fourth grade?"

"I was in kindergarten and six years old!"

"Either way, it was hysterical. Remember the way kids used to put sheets over their heads and follow you home from school?" Sarah chortled. "Mom was so embarrassed when the principal made her and Dad come in to discuss your behavior. How you ever ended up with fairly normal friends now is beyond me."

"Thanks for reminding me." *I wonder what she'd say if she knew about Josh?* Jennifer pushed the thought away, knowing Sarah and everyone else would never understand her unconventional friendship with the handsome spirit.

Jennifer breathed a sigh of relief when she put the car in park and turned off the ignition without further incident. Before entering her house she strained to hear a message from Josh, but none came.

CHAPTER SIX

The next morning, Jennifer glanced at the alarm clock and screamed inwardly. She'd had a restless night and the dark circles under her eyes were a reflection of that. *It's my fault for dreaming about Josh all night.* What was it about that man? She'd bet a month's allowance that Josh had no trouble sleeping—*wait a minute, does Josh sleep?* This and many other questions were to blame for her nocturnal difficulties. *Who am I kidding, Josh may not even show up this morning—especially after seeing the way I drive.*

When Jennifer exited the house she found Josh waiting for her, wearing faded blue jeans, a dark blue sweater, and a cream-colored scarf that looked more fashionable than warming. And, if she wasn't mistaken, he was wearing cowboy boots. *Nothing beats a man in cowboy boots!* Somehow she managed not to swoon or slip and fall into the bushes while gingerly picking her way down the frost-glazed steps

~Good morning, Jennifer. You seem a little surprised to see me. What's wrong? Didn't you think I'd show up this morning?~ Josh messaged with an "I'm happy to see you" smile.

~To be honest, no.~

~May I ask why?~

Maybe it's because my family and everyone else besides my three best

friends thinks I'm too boring or nerdy to hang out with for more than a few minutes. I can't tell him that! ~I figured you had better things to do than spend your time walking to school with me.~

~There's where you're wrong.~ Josh almost added *what would give you the idea that everyone thinks you're boring?* until he remembered the few times he'd witnessed her being shuffled out of conversations. When she was talking one on one or with her friends, Jennifer was at ease, but in groups she often faded into the background. *How can I help this wallflower blossom?*

Jennifer pulled her coat tighter. ~It sure is cold out this morning, isn't it?~

~Yes, it's chilly.~ *I can't very well tell her that I don't feel the cold or heat like she does, nor will I ever admit that I dressed differently in the hopes of impressing her. This is getting us nowhere! What happened to the girl from yesterday who wasn't afraid to call me out or challenge me?*

Why can't I think of anything interesting to say? Ugh—he must think I'm an idiot for sure now.

~May I ask you a personal question?~ Josh messaged.

What does he want to know? No—I've never kissed a boy or found one I wanted to kiss as much as you. In case you're interested, I'm free Saturday night and every weekend afterwards. I think you're handsome. Oh no...please tell me Josh didn't hear my thoughts! I'm gonna have to stop talking to myself. Maybe a plow will drive by and bury me under ten feet of snow. No wonder I've never had a boyfriend! Why can't I stop talking to myself?

~I'm sorry, Jennifer, but I didn't hear your answer.~ There was no sense embarrassing the poor girl over how she'd messaged every word of her random thoughts to him. *I'd better refrain from telling her how nice I think it would be to kiss her too.*

~A personal question? Sure, fire away.~ *Phew, that was close.*

~Have you seen many other spirits other than myself?~

I didn't see that coming. ~Yes—well, when I was a kid I did. Some of them hung out for days or weeks, but none ever stayed as long as you have. Now it's my turn. Will you be sticking around now that we've become friends?~

Josh received Jennifer's question along with the residual pain she'd experienced when the other spirits had left. Feeling her sadness made him want to gather Jennifer into his arms and comfort her. *This would be a good time to tell her I've been assigned to watch over her. Then again, if I do, she might feel like she's nothing more than a job to me.*

~I'm afraid you're stuck with me, because I won't be going anywhere for a very long time.~ Josh was pleased when his answer brought forth a sparkle in Jennifer's eyes.

~Don't you have family in heaven waiting for you to join them?~ It'd been a long time since Jennifer had let a spirit friend into her life, and she hadn't forgotten the pain of their frequent disappearances without a trace or goodbye. She didn't want to go through it again, *especially* with Josh.

~I grew apart from anyone I shared a previous lifetime with long ago.~ *Not that I'd remember them if we were reunited, anyway.* The unwelcome truth reminded Josh of how many pieces of his memory the asteroid accident had taken away.

~Don't you have any family or other friends beside me?~

~I have one other good friend who I've known forever, but I don't see her much.~

Oh—a "her." The thought of another woman in Josh's life created an unwelcome ache in Jennifer's chest.

~She's just a good friend, Jennifer.~ *Why am I justifying my friendship with Gisabella to this girl? It's not like I can ask her out on a date, right?* ~Gisabella has been my closest friend for years.~ *Why didn't I tell her how many years? Probably because "thousands of years" makes me sound way too old. What the hell is wrong with me? Too old for what? Get it together—Jennifer is too good for the likes of me.*

Gisabella, Jennifer repeated the name in her mind. *What an unusual name.* ~Where does your friend live?~

~She lives in a different dimension than you or I, on her own planet which is protected…~ Josh stopped himself before he said too much.

~Protected from what? Who is she? What does she do?~

~Looks like those questions will have to wait until later,~ Josh messaged, relieved to see that they'd reached Jennifer's school.

~All right, but I want to hear more about your friend and all about you and your life. Bye for now, Josh.~

~See you later, Jennifer,~ he messaged, watching her walk away. *I need to stop this before Jennifer becomes too attached! The last thing I want to do is break the girl's heart when my assignment ends and I'm forced to leave.* As soon as Jennifer entered the school, he headed to his preferred vantage point up above.

The moment school was dismissed, Jennifer exited and immediately went to where Josh was waiting. ~I believe you were going to tell me about your friend, Gisabella,~ Jennifer messaged the moment she saw him. She'd driven herself nuts all day wondering about his friend, coming up with dozens of possible answers she didn't wish to hear. *Maybe he dated Gisabella for years and still has feelings of love for her, or maybe she was so wonderful that Josh would never date anyone else.*

~What can I say—we're old friends.~ *"Old" being the definitive word.*

~Were you in love with her?~ Jennifer held her breath until she received his answer.

~No, I was never *in* love with Gisabella. I love her more like a sister or an aunt.~

~What did you mean when you said, "The planet Gisabella lives on is protected?"~ Jennifer asked with a quizzical expression.

Great—when did Jennifer turn into such a "clue-sniffing bloodhound?" She'd have a great career as a detective or news journalist. I think it's my turn to distract her. Josh turned and looked Jennifer in the eyes for a few moments, before he gave her something other than Gisabella to ponder. ~Has anyone told you that your eyes are the color of dark cioccolato?~

~What does "cioccolato" mean?~ Jennifer quirked her eyebrows.

~It's the Italian word for chocolate—if I were to have used such a common word to describe your beautiful eyes, I'd be doing them a grave injustice. But alas, I fear that if I'm not careful, I might find myself lost in them—ahhh, but then I would be your prisoner.~ It was true, especially now that Jennifer was looking back at him, all yummy-eyed and beckoning. *This is a dangerous avenue I'm heading down, as Jennifer isn't mine for the taking!* Josh opted to ignore all the reasons he should stop his feelings from growing deeper. If he was being honest with himself, it was already too late to change how he felt about her.

~You have beautiful eyes too.~ *Is Josh going to kiss me? How will that work with him being translucent? Will I pass right through him, or will he take me into his dimension like he did the apple?*

~We'd better keep walking.~ *Maybe it'd be easier if I answered her orig-*

inal question. ~You were asking about the planet Gisabella lives on. It's in another realm no one else knows about, and she's the only one who can transport people to and from her domain.~

~How does she transport people?~

~It's very similar to how the transporter works on the TV show *Star Trek*. The person turns into pure energy, transports to a selected point, then becomes solid. It's the fastest and easiest way to travel. We were all surprised when the creators of *Star Trek* came up with a concept that was almost identical to how we move about. Biggest difference is that I can transport anywhere in the universe I want to go—with the exception of Gisabella's planet—without the use of a machine.~

~Wow! That's amazing.~ *I love the way Josh's eyes light up when he's sharing things about his world with me.*

~Looks like we're here. I'll see you bright and early tomorrow morning.~

~All right,~ Jennifer agreed, watching Josh fade away. *He must've transported himself somewhere, or did Gisabella request him for a visit?* The idea hurt more than she cared to admit. *Why didn't I invite him inside for cocoa or a glass of wine? Josh looks like he might like wine—or maybe he prefers beer. Now that I'm eighteen, I can join him for a drink or two.*

By the end of the week, even though Jennifer had grown frustrated with Josh only walking her to and from school, she'd learned a lot about him and the dimension he came from. The idea that there was a council of elders and a high priestess who were in charge of every dimension, heaven, earth, and the universe, including the people and spirits living in them, was a hard concept to grasp. The whole thing was a little too *Twilight Zone* for her.

Her inability to summon up the courage to ask Josh if he'd like to come inside and the way he kept rushing off the moment they reached her house added to her disappointment each day.

When Jennifer went to the movies with her friends on Friday night, she kept replaying their conversations in her head while picturing his many facial expressions. *Why can't I stop thinking about Josh? Earth to me, he's a spirit from another world! Sure, Josh is interesting, friendly, mysterious, and cute. Who am I kidding? He's freakin' hot! Not to mention intense and a little dangerous.* When the movie credits began to roll, Jennifer realized she'd zoned out during the entire movie.

"What should we do now?" Colleen asked with a toss of her untamed red curls.

"Don't look at me—this shirt took my entire allowance." Elizabeth pointed toward her blouse and shrugged.

"Jennifer?" Mary cocked her eyebrow.

"You're all welcome to come over to my house. My parents are at some benefit dance and won't be home until midnight," Jennifer offered. Now that her siblings were rarely around, her house had become the preferred place to hang out. Although it offered lots of privacy, there was never anything good to eat. "We should stop and pick up some snacks."

"I second that!" Mary laughed.

Once they'd made it back to Jennifer's house and were seated in the living room with bowls of popcorn, chips, and M&M's, they chatted for hours.

"All right, let me think of a good question," Colleen said. "Okay, I got one: Describe your ideal boyfriend."

"That's easy—all of them!" Mary answered with a snicker. "Seriously, I like jocks, but mainly Chris Spencer!" She swooned and collapsed to the floor.

"You mean Mr. Quarterback Extraordinaire? Tell us something we *don't* know. All you do is stare out the window watching him practice. If you want him to notice you, why not start eating lunch under the goal post?" Colleen suggested, sending Mary into a fit of giggles. "What about you, Jennifer? Who's your ideal boyfriend?"

"Um…he has to love art, and be a passionate, kind person. Nature, running…I'd like him to enjoy those things so we could do them together. You know, just someone I like spending time with." To her dismay, the others groaned.

"Must you make your ideal man sound so boring?! Fast forward to how hot he looks!" Mary said, rolling her eyes.

What could she say? *My ideal man is a spirit no one else can see. Yeah, right. "I need a one-way ticket to the psych ward over here please!"* After a deep breath, Jennifer found herself describing Josh. "For starters, he's a little older and of Italian heritage, with possibly a little Greek mixed in.

Taller than me, so that when we kiss he tilts my chin up until our eyes meet. His brown hair is slightly wavy, and his eyes are an ever-changing shade of green that peers into my soul; his lips are full and kissable, and his strong arms and muscular chest are hard under my touch. Finally, his smile causes my heart to melt." When Jennifer finished, her friends were staring at her with glazed eyes and mouths agape.

"I'll have what she's having." Colleen's voice came out husky.

"Jennifer, we didn't ask for a description of some mythical Greek god!" Mary chuckled. "Get real! If you're expecting a guy like that to show up at your door, you're going to miss out on your best dating years. What about you, Elizabeth?"

"My ideal boyfriend must be taller than me," Elizabeth said.

"That eliminates most of the senior class!" Colleen chuckled.

"I don't know about that." Elizabeth's coy response earned her quizzical looks.

"Are you dating someone?" Colleen pressed, scooting closer.

"We've been seeing each other for a month now. I didn't want to jinx it by saying too much, or until Brad and I…well, you know," Elizabeth blushed.

"Get out of here! You finally did it with someone?!" Mary exclaimed.

"What do you mean 'finally?' It's not like my virginity came with an expiration date!" Elizabeth rolled her eyes.

"How was it?" Jennifer asked with concern.

"It just happened; we were kissing and touching and the next thing I knew, he had a condom on."

"Please tell me that's what you wanted too?" Jennifer asked cautiously. Elizabeth had only mentioned going out with Brad a couple of times, but she'd had no idea it'd become so serious.

"Sure. I mean, why not? Everyone else in our class is having sex."

"Even if that were true, that's not a reason to sleep with someone," Colleen said.

"I could've said no, but I like him a lot. And it's not like I have a line of boys banging down my door." Elizabeth shrugged, appearing a bit dejected about the whole matter. "He called me today and we have another date tomorrow night."

"Just remember that no matter how many times you've slept with a boy, you have the right to say no anyway. Maybe you should wait until you feel more comfortable before you sleep with him again," Mary said, taking Elizabeth's hand in hers.

"Thank you. To be honest, it wasn't very good. We were both nervous and he finished in less than a few seconds," Elizabeth admitted.

"Did it hurt?" Jennifer asked.

"Not very much. It was over so fast, and he didn't seem to be *that* big, if you know what I mean," Elizabeth said with a nervous giggle.

"I'm sure Jennifer doesn't know what you mean," Mary quipped. "I bet she's never even seen a naked boy!"

"I have too!" Jennifer retorted.

"We don't mean in your art books! No wonder Jennifer loves art so much—all those paintings of naked men!" Colleen snickered.

"The statue of *David* doesn't count either!" Elizabeth chimed in.

"In that case, I haven't," Jennifer confirmed with flushed cheeks.

Not even one?" Colleen questioned in disbelief.

"When have *you* ever seen a naked boy, Colleen?" Mary asked.

"I live with five brothers." Colleen's reminder resulted in a unanimous round of loud "ew's." "I'm *kidding*! You remember Arthur, the college boy I dated over the summer? At the time I didn't feel comfortable saying anything; you know, it was between Arthur and I. Anyway, we'd barely reached the heavy petting stage when we broke up. He called me the other night, though, and said he wants to meet up when he's here for Christmas."

"That's wonderful!" everyone agreed.

"I'll hear Arthur out, but there's no way I'm going any further with him until I know he's serious about our future. I couldn't face another heartbreak. Without all the sleepovers I've had with you girls the past few months, I wouldn't have survived."

"Should we maybe talk about something else?" Jennifer said, trying to divert her guests away from the subject she knew would take up the rest of the evening.

"What was your first time like, Mary?" Elizabeth asked.

"It was all right, but I was young and he was only a year older and kind of clueless. After a few months, it got a lot better."

For the next two hours Jennifer listened to her friends discuss boys, dating, and sex in detail. Things got totally derailed when Mary ran into the kitchen and came back with four bananas, determined to teach them the finer points of properly performing "fellatio" on a boy. After roars of laughter and tons of blushing, it was agreed that they'd never again eat a banana in public. By the time everyone left, Jennifer had a splitting headache and knew a whole lot more about sex than she cared to.

CHAPTER SEVEN

When Saturday morning arrived, Jennifer's usual accompanying "no school" celebratory mood did not. There'd be no walking to school with Josh, and it was too cold for a run or riding Brandy. She'd begrudgingly started on her homework when her mother knocked on the door.

"Are you sure you're going to be all right by yourself?" Mrs. Parker asked. "I've written down the number where your dad and I'll be staying. If I'd known Sarah was going skiing this weekend, I'd have made other arrangements."

"Seriously, Mom—I'm used to being home alone." *I've been alone every day since you began working!*

"Here you go, Jennifer," Mr. Parker said from the doorway, holding up some keys.

Are those the car keys? Be still my beating heart! At last, freedom to explore farther than a two-mile radius from the house.

"Oh no, Theodore; you can't seriously think Jennifer is ready to drive on her own!"

"Claire—our daughter is eighteen years old and a responsible adult. She's had a few infractions during the learning phase, but I think Jennifer's learned her lesson and it's time to give her the freedom she deserves."

When her dad turned and winked at her, Jennifer couldn't contain her enthusiasm; she lunged forward to give him a big hug. "Thank you, Dad. I promise I'll be careful."

"I know you will, pumpkin. We'll be home late Sunday night."

"Jennifer, would you be a doll and set up the Christmas tree? Your dad took the boxes down from the attic. Don't forget to make sure the lights are working before you put them on; if they're not, there's money on the counter," Mrs. Parker added.

It was hard not to miss the concern on her mother's face as Jennifer walked her parents out, but all of that was forgotten when she had the house to herself. *I've got some privacy and the keys to the car! I'd say this calls for some music!* Jennifer ran into the living room where the pile of boxes awaited. After flipping through some records, she chose an album of well-known Christmas music and turned up the sound. By the time "Jingle Bell Rock" began playing she was in full-swing, dancing around the room while unpacking the family's plastic tree. Once she'd set the tree up, Jennifer found the lights and began testing them. With one strand half-lit and all the others dead, she fetched her coat, grabbed the car keys and cash from the counter, and headed out the door.

I can do this. All I have to do is watch for stop signs, red lights, pedestrians, other cars, and obey the traffic laws. Jennifer started the car and tuned the radio station to Christmas favorites, placing the car in reverse. She hadn't driven far when she got the feeling someone was watching her, but the car was empty. *It must be Josh!*

~Josh, can you hear me?~

Looks like I'm busted! Josh's first thought was to do the smart thing and ignore Jennifer's message, but the pull he felt towards her was too powerful to ignore. *I swear, Gisabella, my attraction to Jennifer better not have anything to do with you.* Before he allowed himself to go through the list of reasons why he shouldn't accept Jennifer's offer, he answered. ~How did you convince your parents to give you the car?~ His comment earned him a sweet pout. *Damn—she's alluring.*

~If you're trying to be funny, you haven't succeeded.~ *Here goes nothing.* ~I don't suppose you're free tonight? My parents gave me the job of putting up our Christmas tree and I'd love some company. It's not much fun to set it up by myself.~ *Please say yes.*

~I'm not sure how much help I'll be.~

~As long as you don't knock the tree over or set the house on fire, you'll be a great help. We can make popcorn and sing carols.~ *Oh great—nothing like boring the guy to death the minute he arrives.*

~Okay, but only if I can join you now as your copilot.~ Josh tried not to guffaw at the expression of horror his stipulation had caused.

With Josh sitting next to me, I mine as well drive my parents' car off a cliff for what he'll do to my concentration. ~Sure, but please wait until the next red light before you make an appearance.~ At the next light she brought the car to a halt and glanced at the passenger seat to find Josh in translucent form, buckling his seatbelt.

~The light's green,~ Josh messaged. If he thought riding Brandy together was electrifying, sitting in such close proximity to Jennifer was ten times more intense.

~Don't take this the wrong way, but given your present condition, isn't wearing a seatbelt rather pointless?~

~I've watched you drive! No offense Jennifer, but even in my present condition on earth, I prefer to belt up. In fact, your parents should think about installing some three-point harnesses.~

~Do you even know how to drive a car?~ Jennifer turned to glare at him, but when her eyes met with Josh's smoldering gaze, she averted her attention and tightened her grip on the wheel.

~Be careful, little girl.~

~We have to get new lights for the tree.~ Jennifer shifted uncomfortably in her seat. *Why does he affect me so much?* It was true; his warning, much to her surprise, sent shivers through her body. ~Hey, do you want to get a pizza?~ She risked another glance at her copilot for an answer, but needed to look away again before she did something stupid like run over a curb. *Why is it so hard for me to act normal around him? Or breathe, for that matter!*

~Sounds like a plan.~ *Why am I grinning? It's pizza—not a five-course gourmet dinner.* The realization of how pizza with Jennifer sounded better than any meal he'd ever eaten made her offer that much more precious.

Once they arrived at her house, Jennifer carefully inched the car into the garage, gathered the pizza and the bag of twinkle lights, and led the way into the house.

"We're here," Jennifer said aloud, fishing the keys from her purse. It took a moment to calm her nerves enough to get the key in the lock. "Make yourself at home while I get us something to drink. I'd give you a tour of the house, but I think you know your way around."

~Yes, I've been here once or twice,~ Josh smirked. ~As nice as it is to hear your voice, I feel the need to warn you—speaking out loud can really mess with your brain.~

"Mess with my brain? What're you talking about?"

~Talking out loud uses several more areas of your brain than messaging does, so if you're receiving messages but answering vocally, it can jumble your brainwaves.~

"So you're saying that I have to message you even when we're alone?" Jennifer frowned.

~Unlike when we're out in public, I'm not forbidding you from speaking aloud, but I'd prefer you to use the same method of communication for ease.~

"You're right—I wouldn't want to be accused of messing with *your* brainwaves," Jennifer said. "I don't see the big deal; as a kid, I remember talking out loud to the spirits who visited."

~How'd that work out for you?~ Josh noticed a flicker of doubt in her eyes, but rather than delving into all the other reasons Jennifer should practice messaging, he yielded. ~Fine; talk out loud or message—it's all the same to me.~

"Okay then, I will. Make yourself at home while I get us something to drink." Jennifer peered into the fridge, chuckling at his obvious exasperation.

~Go ahead and laugh, Jennifer, but don't blame me when you mess up in public and start talking out loud to someone nobody else sees,~ Josh warned.

Josh is right, I can't afford to mess up; I finally have a normal life with normal friends. The realization that the last few sentences Jennifer had spoken aloud had made it much harder to concentrate drove home Josh's warning about attempting to do both at once.

~We have soda, beer, wine, milk, eggnog, and a ton of diet sodas; I swear my mom collects them in the hopes of finding one that melts away fat—not that she's heavy or anything… I mean, she looks fine…~ *Great time to have a case of babbling! He's going to think I'm incapable of having a regular conversation.*

Josh walked over to where Jennifer was standing with a can of Tab in her hand. ~Relax, Jennifer. I've spent enough time with you to know that you're a bright and witty woman I'd like to get to know better.~ He fought the urge to pull her into his arms, taking a step back instead.

~I guess it's pretty obvious that I've never invited a boy over to my house or been out on a date. Now that you're here, I'm not sure how this should work.~

Is she kicking me out the door? How did I manage to screw this up in record time?

~I don't suppose this is one of those occasions when you can become solid? If you can't, it's okay,~ Jennifer quickly added.

~Is that all? Here I was thinking you'd changed your mind and wanted me to leave.~

~Why would I do a silly thing like that? I've wanted to spend time alone with you since my birthday.~

~Me too,~ Josh admitted.~ I'm afraid there's only a limited number of times I can chose to be solid anytime during the following days: from sunrise on the day of each full moon until the following dawn, when you're in danger, Christmas Eve at midnight until the next morning, Halloween night—no surprise there—and on rare special occasions provided I've received permission from Gisabella or the council. To tell you the truth, I haven't had much reason for choosing my solid form until I met you.~

~I can handle being friends with you either way, but I'm a little unsure of how to offer you a beverage,~ Jennifer said with a shrug. ~Do I pour you a glass of your own or...?~

~I'll have whatever you're having.~ Josh waited until Jennifer had finished filling her glass and placed it on the table before he reached out and took the object's duplicate, then followed her into the room where Christmas tree parts and boxes were scattered about. ~I've never seen a tree like this one.~ He held up a lifeless wired branch with crinkled green plastic sticking out of it, doing his best not to laugh.

~A fake one in pieces, or one this old?~

~Both!~

Jennifer opened the box of pizza and placed it on the coffee table in front of them. ~Help yourself,~ she said, pointing to the largest slice.

Josh devoured it in record time, wiping his mouth with Jennifer's offered napkin. ~This is great pizza. Thank you for inviting me tonight.~

An hour after they'd finished eating, the tree's limp plastic limbs and lights were in place.

~Looks real,~ Josh said, trying to keep a straight face.

~Are you making fun of our tree?~

~Nope! How could you think I'd do such a thing?~

~This is my favorite Christmas song,~ Jennifer blurted out. In a moment of spontaneity, she forgot her nervousness and began dancing and singing around the room to Brenda Lee's version of "Rockin' Around the Christmas Tree."

Josh couldn't hide his amusement over possibly the worst singing voice he'd ever heard. If Jennifer hit one note during the entire song, it was by accident. It took everything in him not to beg her to stop, but it was her dancing that had him desiring an encore. He'd put up with Jennifer's horrible singing forever just to watch the way she danced, uninhibited and free.

~What's your favorite Christmas song?~ Jennifer asked as she flounced on the couch to catch her breath.

~This one.~ Josh changed the music over to an orchestra version of "Ave Maria" and began to sing.

The moment Jennifer heard Josh's voice, her eyes grew large and her mouth dropped open in shock. She leaned forward, mesmerized by the sound of his perfect tenor. His voice sounded so real inside her head that it was as if she was seated in a concert hall enjoying his standing ovation-worthy performance. *Now I know why they say angels can sing!* Halfway through the song she noted the words alternating between English and…Italian, maybe? Josh's eyes were closed and he stood stock-straight with his hands clasped in front of him, which allowed Jennifer the chance to take in every detail of him freely for the first time. When Josh finished, she leapt up from the chair with wild applause.

~Bravo!~ Jennifer sniffled and wiped away a tear that'd escaped. ~Where did you learn to sing like that?~

~I'm glad you approve. Like you and many others, I've had the opportunity to develop a few abilities during each of my past lifetimes that have carried forward.~ *Even ones I don't remember learning…* ~You, too, have learned abilities that are engraved into your soul; if you have any doubts, just look at your paintings and sketches—both are reflective of someone who's studied art for many years.~

A ton of empty boxes later, they stood back to admire the tree. ~Wait a minute,~ Jennifer messaged, running over to flick off the living room lights before returning to Josh's side.

~It's beautiful.~ Josh fought to keep his voice level. It'd been many centuries since he'd shared in a Christmas memory. He felt Jennifer's hand brush against and then through his hand, mingling their energies. Jennifer's unexpected touch was welcomed, and he found himself savoring the intimacy.

"Oh!" Jennifer blurted aloud when she looked down at their hands. ~Does that hurt?~ she messaged, eyes full of concern.

~On the contrary, it's quite the opposite. Raise your hand and I'll show you what I mean.~ When Jennifer held her hand up, he slowly moved his through hers, studying her expression for any sign of discomfort or fear.

~I see what you mean. It feels…pleasurable. Yes, that's the word I'd use to describe when your hand passes through mine.~ *In addition to soul-stirring and all-consuming.* ~Does this mean that unless you're solid in form, we can't hold hands without passing through each other?~

~Kind of, but there's a way I can make my energy denser. Hold up your hand again.~ Concentrating on the task, Josh touched his hand to Jennifer's, applying just enough pressure for her to feel his touch.

~That's so cool,~ Jennifer said in awe while pressing her hand against his translucent one as hard as she could. ~Does it take a lot of energy for you to stay like this?~

~Not too much.~ *Because I'm a protector.*

~Are you limited to only one hand or body part at a time?~

~Where do you want me to hang this ornament?~ Josh said, avoiding her question.

~That one should go closer to the top.~

After putting up all the ornaments they could find and searching an exorbitant amount of time for the tree topper with no luck, Jennifer and Josh agreed to rest on the couch for a bit.

Three hours later, Josh opened his eyes to find Jennifer asleep in his energized arms. *Holy fuck, what have I done?* After a brief scan of their clothed bodies and Jennifer's innocent expression, he released his breath. *Can my attraction for Jennifer be so great I don't have to concentrate on solidifying my energy to hold her?* Careful not to wake her, Josh stood and repositioned the blanket so that she was covered.

"Thank you for giving me the best evening of all my lifetimes," Josh whispered into her ear, kissing the top of her head. One last look at the tree inspired him, and with a wave of his hand, he used a little of the magic he'd learned from Merlin to leave Jennifer a special present.

"Goodbye, my sweet," Josh said softly. *I'll be back to personally watch over you shortly.* After putting his own type of security system in place, Josh transported to his apartment in the other realm to find Jennifer's paperwork.

CHAPTER EIGHT

Jennifer stirred and opened her eyes. *What am I doing down here?* When she recalled that Josh had helped decorate the tree, she glanced around the room but found no sign of him. *How could I have fallen asleep? Agh! Talk about being a bad hostess!* She sat up and faced the only light source in the room; all 300 of them. *Wait a minute. Where did that come from?* Jennifer distinctly remembered they hadn't been able to locate the treetop decoration, so chose to relax on the couch instead. Color rose to her face at the memory of sharing a blanket with Josh, and how warm and electrifying his energy had felt.

Upon closer examination, she could only surmise that the horse adorning the top of the tree with a young couple seated astride it and wearing Santa hats must've been a present from Josh. At that moment, the horse began pawing the ground while the miniscule look-a-likes turned their heads towards her and winked, causing her mouth to fall open in surprise.

A glance at the clock on the fireplace mantle indicated it was three in the morning, and thus not a proper time to send Josh a "thank you" message. According to her friends, calling any boy after midnight would come off as a booty call, and she wasn't ready for that kind of relationship. Jennifer's brow creased as she frowned. *Come to think of it, Josh didn't try to kiss me. For all I know, he might've only helped me decorate the tree because he felt sorry I was stuck doing it alone.* With that disheartening thought, Jennifer curled up on the sofa and fell into a dreamless sleep.

Josh arrived at his apartment to find it the way he'd left it when he began protecting Jennifer: cluttered and disorganized. *Where did I put Jennifer's papers?* He rifled through stacks of visionary folders and life-path envelopes on the coffee table, desk, and bookcase until locating Jennifer's paperwork in the top drawer of his nightstand. *A good place to find Jennifer—next to my bed!* Her paperwork was thicker than he remembered, then again, he'd barely glanced at it a decade prior. Once he'd started watching over Jennifer it hadn't seemed warranted, since she was always so ordinary—until that night, anyway, when he'd found himself feeling things he'd never felt before with any other woman. *How can this be happening?* He'd always done his best to avoid emotional attachments. *Maybe what I'm feeling isn't entirely of my doing.*

~So help me, Gisabella, if this is your sick idea of a joke—~ he began messaging, before a recording interrupted him followed by a loud busy signal:

~I'm sorry, but your message cannot be delivered at this time. Please try again tomorrow!~

~Not funny, Gisabella! I demand to be transported for a meeting with the high priestess to go over my current case.~ Josh sent off the message hoping to provoke a response, and it didn't take long before he found himself face to face with a very agitated Gisabella.

"You rang?" she snapped, leaning against her kitchen counter.

You don't scare me, I've seen you madder than this! he wanted so badly to say, but that would've been counterproductive. "Your Excellency, how kind of you to make time to see me," Josh said, each word dripping with enough over-the-top sweetness to cause a toothache. He bent down and kissed Gisabella's ring before meeting her icy stare. Clearly she wasn't pleased with his underhanded way of demanding an audience. "You're looking well, Gisabella," Josh said in an attempt to break her chilly welcome. *Great, nothing like a one-sided meeting.* "I don't suppose you baked anything, or would consider offering me a cup of tea *or something a lot stronger*?" A slight crack in her ice sculpture facade gave him hope. "Cut the crap, Gisabella—I could really use a friend about now."

"What do you want, Josh?" Gisabella asked, her voice betraying only the slightest hint of softness.

"Tea, cake, and a good friend."

"All right, but only if you're willing to try my new creation: pineapple, raisin, and whiskey meringue pie," Gisabella bargained.

"Bring it on!" *It's been a while since I've thrown up!*

Gisabella removed her formal high priestess garb to uncover the jeans and lilac tunic she was wearing underneath and began to plate some slices.

"You've outdone yourself," Josh said, looking down at the pile of mush Gisabella had the nerve to call "pie." Bracing himself, he tentatively picked up a forkful and forced himself to bring it to his mouth. As much as he wanted to pinch his nose and close his eyes, he knew better than to upset his hostess.

"Well?" Gisabella asked.

"It's interesting—surprisingly, it isn't horrible."

"I knew someday you'd like something I baked," Gisabella beamed.

"I suppose you know why I want to talk to you," Josh said as he forced down another bite. It *did* have one redeeming quality—whiskey.

"I see you have Jennifer's information with you. I take it you've noticed signs of the girl's gifts? It's always nice when you finally get around to reading your charge's information, unlike my other protectors who read it before they begin."

"I've noticed a couple of Jennifer's gifts starting to break through, but that's not why I'm here," Josh said, ignoring her dig.

Gisabella took a deep breath as she waited for Josh to approach the subject he was surely there to discuss.

"I've never been in this sort of position before, where I've felt the need to talk to you as both my friend and my boss. I'm not going to mince words. Please tell me you haven't been playing around with one of your spells. I need to know if you're the one responsible for the…*feelings* I seem to be developing for Jennifer."

"Well, well, it's about time a girl's caught your eye." Gisabella let out a soft chuckle. "I've waited a long time for you to fall hard for a woman, and I must say that seeing you now, all messed up and unsure of your next move, was *worth* the wait."

"I'm glad I could provide you with amusement," Josh said, inhaling deeply before playing his hand. "But you have it all wrong. I'm here to request a transfer."

"*What?!*" Gisabella croaked. "There's no way in hell I'll ever transfer you off Jennifer's case. Get this through your thick skull right now—you're stuck with the girl!"

"I thought as much. So how did you do it? With one of your love potions or some illegal spell you conjured up? Perhaps you used some new wizardry learned from Merlin? Which one did you use to make Jennifer like me?"

"Is that what you think? That Jennifer likes you because of some *spell*? For such a smart man, you're pretty dumb sometimes. You're quite the catch, you know."

"A 'catch?' What could I possibly have to offer Jennifer but a temporary love affair with a ghost?!"

"You have more to offer her than you think. When did you become so introspective? Centuries ago you would've lured a girl like Jennifer to your bed without giving a second thought to what it would do to her when you disappeared!"

"Let's just say that got old fast. Hearing girls crying out for me for weeks at a time wasn't worth one lusty night under the full moon. Jennifer's a good friend, and she deserves better than a romp in the hay. The last thing I want to do is break her heart." *Or my own.*

"You could claim Jennifer as your mistress until her life-path pulls her away. It's worked well for other spirits who've become attached to someone who's living."

"You make it sound so easy—'Claim Jennifer as your mistress until she meets the man she's destined to marry on earth'—all the while expecting her to be happy with a once-a-month-in-the-flesh fuck under the full moon. You're delusional if you think that will satisfy either of us."

"Let's cut to the chase; what would it take to make you and Jennifer happy?"

Josh pretended to think of the response that was already in his heart.

It was clear Gisabella's stake in getting the two of them together was pretty high. He'd heard of instances when an especially powerful visionary needed to lose their virginity before their nineteenth birthday to awaken and preserve their gifts. *Could that be the reason? If so, why the secrecy or the rush?*

Josh squared his shoulders before stating his demands: "First, Jennifer's feelings must be allowed to develop on their own without any interference from you. That means none of your spells or any other trickery. Secondly, she and I are allowed to marry before I take her as mine." *Poker face, don't fail me now!* He did his best to maintain an even gaze despite Gisabella's horrified expression.

"You want to *marry* the girl?!" Gisabella stammered. "Are you out of your bloody mind? You'll get us all banished by the council, or worse! What you're suggesting is considered an act of treason; no such union between two dimensions has ever been done before. Tread lightly, my friend, because if you don't bed the girl, I'll find someone else who will!" Gisabella had stretched the truth a little, but she held her ground. *Let's see just how serious you are.*

"You're bluffing! Take it or leave it, Gisabella," Josh said, preparing for the fallout after his ultimatum. Instead, Gisabella remained silent. "I believe we're done here, so if you'll excuse me, I have to get back to my future wife. Great talk! I suggest you keep working on your mush pie—eventually you may bake something edible."

"Oh no you don't! You're not going anywhere, mister," Gisabella shouted, stopping Josh in his tracks.

"Does this mean you accept my offer?" Josh crossed his fingers behind his back. He didn't know if his desire for Jennifer was spell-induced or real, but what he *did* know was that there was not another soul in all the universes that he wanted to be with other than her.

Gisabella hid her delight behind annoyance. She had Josh *right* where she wanted him, and if all went well Jennifer would soon be married and deflowered—an event that would open the door and bring forth all her gifts, allowing her old soul persona to flourish under Josh's care. If she hoped to keep Josh in the dark about Jennifer's lineage, then she must concentrate on his silly demands. *Where did Josh learn to negotiate? He's horribly inept at it. Doesn't he know you're supposed to start with a huge list of unreasonable demands, thus giving yourself room to negotiate?* Her conscience would never rest if she didn't sweeten the deal in his favor; it was the least she could do for her closest friend and the valiant protector who'd served her well.

Gisabella laid out her demands. "You may wed Jennifer under the following conditions: First, you must marry Jennifer by February fourteenth. If the two of you aren't married by that date, then all bets are off and you'll be removed as her protector. Second, Jennifer's destiny and life-path state she must marry another man in eight years' time. That cannot be changed no matter what stunt you may try and pull. Jennifer's heart has been preprogrammed to fall in love with her predestined husband. And finally, your marriage must be kept a secret. I'll perform the ceremony myself here in my garden." Gisabella herself hadn't been given this small courtesy, and had suffered an agonizing broken heart when she'd been forced to leave the man she loved to marry her life-path husband.

Josh nodded to all of her demands, still in shock that she was even considering such a request.

"I'll even throw in a honeymoon and use of my house and stables so you can take your new wife horseback riding. The way I figure it, you can bring Jennifer up at midnight, spend four days together here, and only four hours will have passed down on earth when you bring her back. I'll even grant you with a few extra opportunities to become solid on earth," Gisabella offered. "For all this you agree not only to marry Jennifer, but to consummate your union within twelve hours of saying 'I do.' Well? Do we have a deal or not?"

"I don't suppose you're willing to tell me why you want Jennifer and I together so badly? I assume you have more interest in our legal and physical union than my 'wedded bliss.'"

"Why would you think I'm getting anything?"

Josh held his tongue; Gisabella wasn't one to tell him something she didn't want to, and he'd already gotten what he'd ultimately wanted. "Remember, Jennifer must fall in love on her *own*; no tricks, or the deal's off."

"I give you my word." Gisabella's eyes sparkled as she reached into the pocket of her jeans and extracted a small box. "I believe you'll be needing this."

Josh reached for the blue velvet box, looked inside, and whistled. "By the looks of this ring, I'd say you knew I was a sure bet." Upon examination, the engagement ring's intricate, platinum band was the ideal setting for the exceptional marquise diamond it held. If he had to guess, he'd say it was "five-carat ginormous."

"One more thing—Jennifer must remain as pure as freshly fallen snow until your wedding night." Gisabella could barely squelch her amusement at Josh's foul expression. "I'll be happy to give you some tips on how to woo a woman," she teased.

"I may be a little rusty, but I think I remember how it's done." Josh tried his best to sound confident. He hadn't a clue how he was going to convince Jennifer to agree to such an outlandish idea. *I must be out of my freakin' mind to think I have any chance of making her my wife.*

"You won't be needing these." Gisabella snatched Jennifer's profile and life-path from Josh's hands. "Reading them now would be cheating." Gisabella smirked at his outraged expression; clearly Josh had planned on using the romantic preferences listed in her past lifetimes to work his way into the girl's heart.

"Your underhanded games will make my marriage to Jennifer all the sweeter." After a brief moment, Josh's grin faded. "I have a favor to ask of you."

"Ask away." Gisabella held her breath. *What could he possibly want now?*

"When Jennifer and I marry, there's something I'd like to give her." Now that he was speaking, he wondered if Gisabella would find his request silly. "I'd like to give Jennifer my last name."

"Is that all? Have you explained to Jennifer that no other dimension uses last names besides earth?"

"I haven't—but all the same, she'll think it odd that I don't have one." He ran his hand through his hair in frustration. "The thing is, I can't tell Jennifer my last name because I don't remember any of them." His voice cracked in defeat. "It doesn't have to be one of my 'real' ones; if you don't know what they were, then give me any last name. I don't care if it's something common like 'Smith' or 'Jones'; I just want to give Jennifer my last name before her life-path husband gives my wife his." His heart ached at the thought of losing Jennifer to another man.

"Smith it is, then!" Gisabella tried to smile, but the look in her friend's eyes was painful to see. If there were any way to change the future she'd do it for him, but it was too late to alter Jennifer's destiny.

"Mr. Joshua Smith. It has a nice ring to it, doesn't it?"

"Yes, Mr. Smith, it does sound nice. I believe the future Mrs. Smith will think so too."

"I hope she likes it. Suppose she doesn't?"

"Seriously?" Gisabella rolled her eyes. "Jennifer will love any name you give her because it's yours." Gisabella shook off the guilt that threatened to take hold. "Happy courting, Josh! Don't forget, hands off everything below Jennifer's waist until after you're married!" After getting the last word in, Gisabella transported Josh back to his apartment.

Once back at home, Josh let loose a barrage of profanity that wasn't fit for a drunken sailor's ears. *I can't believe she took away Jennifer's paperwork and changed the rules midstream.* After a quick look into his crystal ball to ensure Jennifer was safe, he went into the kitchen and made a cup of hot, rich espresso to help him strategize.

Five hours later, Josh was traveling back to Jennifer's house to begin phase one of his well-thought-out plan.

CHAPTER NINE

Mmm, blueberry pancakes. Jennifer inhaled deeply, filling her senses with the hunger-inducing aroma. She was seated across from Josh on a terrace overlooking an ancient cobblestoned road eating breakfast. Josh reached out and caressed her face, saying the most beautiful words of love while looking into her eyes.

"Josh, you weren't kidding when you told me you could cook," Jennifer mumbled in her sleep. "I never knew breakfast could be so divine, my love." Another deep, aroma-infused breath later, and her eyes popped open. *Why did I have to wake up before Josh kissed me?* The distinct scent from her dream lingered in the air, and when she figured out the enticing smell was actually coming from the kitchen, she bolted upright and raced in that direction.

~Good morning, Jennifer. Did you sleep well?~ Josh greeted her, doing his best to keep from taking her into his arms.

~Yes, thank you.~ *I must still be dreaming.* Jennifer took in the sight of her translucent man-friend flipping pancakes, squeezing oranges, and stirring a pot of some unknown contents. Josh was sporting a five o'clock shadow, answering her unspoken question about hair growth in heaven, and his hair was mussed in a sexy way. Other than that, he looked his normal put-together self, dressed in jeans and a blue denim shirt. As they'd gotten to know each other the veil that existed between their dimensions had thinned, making it easier for her to see that Josh's ever-changing eyes were bluer in pigment that day. *I must try and duplicate that color; what a wonderful, sultry sky it would make.*

"You weren't kidding when you said you could cook," Jennifer blurted out, instantly experiencing déjà vu from her earlier dream. ~Ugh! I keep forgetting to use messaging!~

~Don't worry, you'll get used to it,~ Josh reassured. ~Now you understand why I insist you communicate this way. If you'd like, I can teach you how to make these and other recipes.~

~I'd like that very much.~ *Alone in the kitchen with Josh for hours? Sign me up!* When a pleased expression filled Josh's face, she knew he'd read her thoughts.

~What should we do today?~ Josh asked, hoping she'd take the hint that he wanted to spend the day together.

We? Maybe he's just being nice because I'm home alone. The unwelcome thought entered her mind before she could derail it.

~Jennifer, I want to spend time with you. In truth, I like you a lot and I enjoy your company. Not because I don't have any friends to hang out with, or anywhere to go, but because I love talking to you and would like to get to know you better.~

"I love talking to you, too," Jennifer said so softly it was like a whisper of wind. It was impossible not to feel unnerved by Josh's ability to read her mind, especially the self-deprecating kinds of thoughts that frequently filled her head. *What other random thoughts has he read? It's official—I can no longer think about anything stupid or embarrassing, though that doesn't leave much else.*

~Since you have the car keys and me as your copilot to keep you out of trouble, we can go to the movies or visit the library.~

~Movies! No offense, but I've seen your nose in a book more than you've watched me jog,~ Jennifer teased. *Movies, popcorn, and holding hands sounds perfect.*

~I think it does too,~ Josh said, answering her unsaid statement before standing to clear the table. A glance at the color in Jennifer's cheeks made him cringe. *I'm officially the universes' biggest jerk! Now the poor girl's afraid none of her thoughts are sacred. I need to fix this before I lose her trust.* ~I think it's time I teach you how to block your more private thoughts, so I can't read them so easily. I used to hate it when Gisabella would do that.~

~How long did it take you to become good enough to safeguard them?~ Jennifer asked a little too eagerly.

Less than a minute. ~Judging by how fast you learned how to message, I'd say by the time we're seated at the movies, I won't have a clue what you're thinking unless you've unblocked your thoughts on purpose. Let's practice on the drive over.~

~Who knew something as elementary as imagining a brick wall could stop you from reading my mind?~ Jennifer messaged a half hour later as she parked the car at the movie theater.

~You don't have to sound so pleased.~ Josh followed Jennifer up to the ticket counter and looked on as she purchased one pass. *Damn! I forgot to give Jennifer the money for her ticket—some escort I am.* It wasn't like he had a lot of earth money, but he did have a few bucks saved and could ask Gisabella for a loan if needed.

Once inside the theater he guided Jennifer to one of the emptier rows and selected two spots next to the aisle. Once seated, he envisioned a protective, white light around them to ensure no one would be tempted to sit next to her.

~You don't mind if I share your popcorn, do you?~ Josh messaged.

~Not at all.~ Seated next to Josh in the darkened theater filled Jennifer with excitement. *Is this a real date? If so, it's my first!* When their hands brushed together as they reached into the popcorn bag, she felt a surge of adrenaline. Twenty minutes into the movie and the popcorn was all gone, though Jennifer couldn't recite the plot to save her life.

Josh waited until the empty container was lowered to the floor before reaching over to hold Jennifer's hand, feeling the connection all the way down to his toes. A glance at her face told him that she, too, was enjoying their shared touch. He brushed his thumb lightly over her hand, and the result was so intoxicating it was as if he'd had three gin and tonics in rapid succession. The sound of Jennifer's sharp intake of breath verified she felt their magnetic attraction too.

~I'm confused, Josh. Who's that guy speaking to the blonde?~

~At this point I could ace a quiz on every facet of your hand—the softness of your skin, the way you squeeze it when someone yells from the screen—but what the movie's about? I have absolutely no idea,~ Josh messaged with a lopsided grin.

Jennifer diverted her gaze to his full, kissable lips, no longer capable of looking away. A squeeze of her hand made her aware that she was mooning at Josh in an "I'm crazy for you, kiss me now" kind of way. Embarrassed, she turned her attention back to the movie and kept her eyes frozen to the screen as Josh gently raised her hand to his lips to plant a kiss there. A soft moan escaped her mouth, and she'd never been more thankful for darkened theaters and loud movie pyrotechnics.

~I don't think I've ever enjoyed watching a movie more,~ Josh messaged on the way back to the car.

~I agree—best movie ever!~ *He's still holding my hand!* The feel of Josh's energy made his touch *more* real, in a sense, than if he'd been a living guy on earth. Although not solid, it was possible to feel how his long fingers and thumb were wrapped around her smaller hands. Josh's touch felt warm and comforting, but now she was experiencing so much more from a simple graze of a finger…*could it be love? Get a grip! There's no way a guy like Josh could fall in love with me. No one could be that lucky.*

When they arrived back at her house, Josh walked her to the front door and she gazed up into his eyes. ~Would you like to come in for some ice cream or cake?~

~Thank you for the offer, but I think it's best if I leave and you get some rest—tomorrow's a school day. I'll be back in the morning, waiting out front to walk you there.~

~You're probably right.~ *Why doesn't Josh kiss me? Maybe he's shy?*

When the door closed, Josh's grin widened. *Oh baby, I might be a lot of things, but shy isn't one of them.* He wanted Jennifer's first kiss to be special, and one that they would both remember forever.

That night Jennifer dreamed of Christmas trees, green eyes, bitten red apples, and lips she longed to kiss. She awoke early and hopped out of bed, eager to walk to school with Josh.

"Good morning, Jennifer," Mrs. Parker said, greeting her in the hallway.

"Did you and Dad have a good time?"

"Yes, it was nice to get away."

Seeing as though you're always "getting away," I can't imagine it feeling any different. Jennifer bit back the words that'd formed on her tongue. In truth, she liked having the house to herself, and had grown used to her parent's busy travel schedule—but it still stung to be reminded of how little they seemed to miss her when they were away.

"The Christmas tree looks wonderful; did you have any trouble?" Mrs. Parker asked, studying her daughter's face.

"It was no bother." *Especially with Josh stopping by to keep me company.* "None of the lights worked so I had to run out and buy new ones. I left your receipt and change on the counter." Jennifer rolled her eyes over the shift in her mother's expression when she mentioned driving the car, as if the end of the world were upon them.

"Please tell me you didn't run into anything—I mean, run into any trouble?" Mrs. Parker said, quickly correcting herself.

"Not unless you count the five cars I sideswiped or the front bumper sitting in the middle of Main Street." Jennifer hid her smirk when her mother's eyebrows creased with concern. "I'm kidding—nothing happened."

"Don't worry me like that!" Mrs. Parker admonished.

"Sorry, Mom. I'll see you later." Jennifer made a mad dash out the front door and down the steps to where Josh was waiting.

~Good morning, baby,~ Josh greeted.

Josh called me baby! Be still my racing heart. Jennifer made sure to guard her thoughts like he'd taught her.

Josh reached for Jennifer's hand. ~Look—we're the perfect height for each other.~ When she looked at him in confusion, he clarified. ~Despite our five-inch difference, our arms still match up—so to onlookers, you look no different than when you're walking on your own.~

Why am I feeling so shy? It's a fact, I'm socially unable of holding a conversation with a guy I want to kiss. I need to say something before he thinks I've lost my ability to speak. ~My Mom thought the tree came out nice,~ Jennifer blurted.

~I enjoyed decorating the tree with you.~ *I wonder what Jennifer would do if I told her there's a full moon on Thursday? Or how she'll react when she sees me solid for the second time… If she agrees to marry me, it'll be a monthly event.*

~I read in the paper that there's a full moon Thursday,~ Jennifer messaged, with her heart somewhere in her throat. *Nothing like blabbering on about how badly I want him to be solid.*

Did Jennifer read my mind? Josh concealed his concern. ~Curious, are you? Or do you have another reason for wanting me to be solid?~ *Let's see how she handles this question.*

~I know what you're doing, and I'm not falling for your roundabout way of getting me to list all the benefits I get from you being solid,~ Jennifer said coquettishly.

~In that case, maybe we should agree to do something fun together Thursday after you get out of school.~

~What about ice skating? The pond is frozen and we'd have the quiet end to ourselves.~

~I don't know how to skate, but I can watch.~

~Finally, something you don't know how to do! I can teach you, and I think my brother's skates will fit you. My parents are going to an awards dinner and won't be home until after midnight, and Sarah's staying overnight with her friends—so when we're done skating we can have hot cocoa and watch television at my house.~ *And make out.*

~All right, but be forewarned: I'm bad…at skating.~

Jennifer looked into Josh's eyes, trying to gauge if he'd been referring to something other than the outdoor activity. *Is solid Josh different than translucent Josh?* She squinted, studying his face, but saw nothing in his expression that'd lead her to believe anything was amiss. On the contrary, Josh looked like the same gentleman she'd gotten to know so well.

Once in front of the school, Josh let go of Jennifer's hand and watched her head into the red brick building. With only two months to convince Jennifer to marry him, he had his work cut out for him. Failure wasn't an option, since the last thing he wanted was to say goodbye to the girl who'd all but captured his heart. If he'd read her profile when he'd had the chance, he might know what Jennifer possessed that made him hunger for her. *Maybe we shared a forgotten past lifetime, or Jennifer was some sort of siren who earned the right to be reborn as a human yet retained her abilities to entrance a man's soul…* Since Gisabella had taken Jennifer's life-path and profile he'd never unlock those answers, but on the bright side now he didn't have to read about the man she was obligated to marry in eight years' time.

There was a part of him that wanted to do the honorable thing and break off all contact before Jennifer fell in love, so she could find happiness with someone on earth. Their being from two different dimensions meant a doomed relationship from the start, and if he broke her heart, it would destroy him. Jennifer deserved so much better, but he was too selfish to let her go. *Jennifer's the only thing in this god-forsaken universe that matters; she's my one and only chance for happiness.*

It was then that Gisabella's words came back to haunt him: "If Jennifer doesn't agree to marry you by February fourteenth, you'll be removed as her protector." Recalling the warning was enough to cause a sharp, stabbing pain in his heart, giving him a tiny sample of what it'd feel like to lose her. *Who am I trying to fool? How am I going to get Jennifer to marry me by then?*

CHAPTER TEN

Thursday turned out to be a picture-perfect day for ice skating: sunny, not too cold, with no wind or snow in the forecast. Jennifer exited the house with both pairs of skates. She slung her freshly polished skates over her shoulder, each one adorned with fluffy pink pom-poms and bells that jingled every time she took a step. Filled with anticipation, Jennifer tried her best not to run as fast as she could to Josh. *Try to show some restraint,* she chided herself.

When she arrived at the pond, the other skaters were at the busy end filling the air with joyful laughter and huddling around the bonfire for warmth. She was glad Josh had decided to meet her at the quiet end of the pond, where it was peaceful and romantic. Jennifer sat down on the wooden bench and began to put her skates on, crisscrossing the laces so they were as tight as she liked. She was so wrapped up in her lacing that she didn't even hear Josh arrive.

"Oh! I didn't see you…" Jennifer's voice trailed off at the sight of Josh in the flesh and gloriously solid. She'd always thought translucent Josh was extremely handsome, but seeing him solid for the first time since they'd ridden Brandy stole her breath away. He looked like he belonged on the silver screen or in *GQ* magazine, yet there Josh stood, smiling down at her. *What could Josh possibly see in me?*

"Hello Jennifer." *Doesn't she know that* I'm *the one who isn't worthy of her?* When the time was right, he'd declare his love and wipe away any self-doubts she had. "How do I put these things on?" Josh held up the skates she'd brought him.

"Umm," Jennifer's attempt to form even the simplest of words faltered, and it took several long moments to regain her equilibrium. "You should grab a seat first." Before she had a chance to move over he sat down, pressing his leg against hers. Between his deep voice and physical touch, she became hopelessly lost in the moment. *Dear God, please give me the ability to combine words into coherent sentences!*

"Are you sure it's possible to balance on this thing?" Josh said, running his index finger along the thin steel blade. "Maybe we should go for a walk in the woods instead." He didn't bother to hide his desire as he made eye contact with Jennifer.

"Sorry, but I'm already wearing my skates," she stammered before turning a shade of red that was too dark to hide. *Why am I so nervous? He's the same man who helped decorate the tree and heard me sing. Oh no—Josh heard me sing! That alone would chase any sane person away.*

Josh tried his best not to crack up at her unblocked thoughts, but when the hint of a snicker turned into a roaring guffaw, there was no way to hide how many of them she'd inadvertently shared.

"Hey! What are you laughing at?" Jennifer asked, even when she knew the answer. "If you don't stop laughing, I'm going to push you so hard out there you'll land on your butt!"

"Don't worry—the way I skate, I plan on being on my butt out there most of the time already," Josh howled, unable to catch his breath.

"You really are a hunk," Jennifer blurted out. "And now that you're here in the flesh, I'm a little overwhelmed by you."

Josh's laughter ceased. "You have that all wrong, baby—I'm the one who's overwhelmed by you. I can't believe you have no clue what a smart, beautiful, and sexy woman you are."

"'Sexy?' Now I *know* you're not being honest."

"Oh, I'm being honest all right, and while you may not believe it now, I promise that someday I'll convince you about how sexy you are."

"Not as sexy as you," Jennifer whispered.

"You only think so because this is the second time you've seen me solid," Josh said patiently. "Go ahead and take a good, long look; stare, if you must—but get it out of the way, because I'm the same man you've spent time with in translucent form." Josh closed his eyes to give Jennifer the freedom to explore his features uninhibited.

Jennifer took a deep breath and stared for a moment, then lifted her hand to Josh's face and caressed his cheek before tracing his lips with a finger. It was as though Josh were the earth and she were the moon, and she leaned closer, unable to resist his gravitational pull. Before their lips could touch, however, Josh's eyes opened and he moved back to put some space between them, a flicker of doubt flashing in his green irises.

Damn. Why won't he just do *it already?* "Being able to touch you in solid form feels different—in a good way." Jennifer moved her hand down Josh's arm until she was holding his hand. "The other way is good too, but now I don't have to worry I might accidently go through you."

"Good point," Josh smirked. He lightly kissed Jennifer's hand before releasing it, then bent down to put on his skates while Jennifer glided onto the ice, her skates' bells jingling the whole time. Josh soon shuffled over, nearly falling twice and cursing repeatedly as he fought to join her.

"Maybe I should just stand here and watch you skate," Josh said, frozen in place as Jennifer went in circles around him. To make matters worse she began performing a series of spins and jumps, adding to his humiliation.

"Oh no you don't! Take my hands," Jennifer offered with both of them extended.

"Okay, but if you fall you'd better not take me with you."

"I'll try to remember that," Jennifer said sardonically. She held Josh's hands tightly and began to guide him. "Move your right foot first. Good! Now your left one. Don't worry, I won't let you fall. Excellent! Again, right foot, left foot, right, left…you're skating!" Jennifer cheered, skating backwards with Josh's hands firmly grasped in hers as he followed her lead. Soon she was able to let go, and watched him skate a few yards before he lost his footing and fell.

"Are you all right?" Jennifer asked, skating to his side.

"I think so." Josh shook his head in disbelief over how easy she made it look. "Don't you ever fall?"

"Not since I was six." She skated backwards a few feet and spun around.

"Show off!" Josh called out.

"Take my hands and I'll help you up," Jennifer instructed. Josh grabbed hold, tugging on her so that she lost her balance and fell on top of him with an ungraceful thud.

"Looks like your twelve-year-old record of not falling is officially ruined!" Josh gloated, wrapping his arms tightly around her.

"You cheated!" Jennifer's rebuttal sounded half-hearted at best. She rested her head on Josh's chest and intertwined her legs with his while focusing her gaze on his mouth. *I want to feel his lips on mine.*

"I think we're melting the ice because my clothes feel wet. Maybe we could head back to your house?" Josh fought back the urge to kiss Jennifer right there on the ice; it would've been too risky out in the open where everyone could see them. When his lips met hers there'd be no way he could keep his wits about him, and he still needed to guard Jennifer in public. It was not a risk he was willing to take. Plus, he wanted their first kiss to be much more than a brief moment that would eventually be replaced by Jennifer's other memories.

"That's it? You've only skated four minutes, and three of those were spent on your butt," Jennifer mocked. To her surprise, Josh bench-pressed her until his arms were straight and she was outstretched over him, looking down into his eyes.

"I'm going to stand you up now," Josh warned.

Once Jennifer was upright, she began skating around Josh, performing more jumps and spins while laughing at his attempts to stand. The last thing she noticed before she toe-picked deep into the ice and lifted off into a double rotation jump was Josh unlacing his skates. The fact she'd found possibly the only kink in Josh's perfection made her giggle, which was unhelpful while traveling through the air attempting to touch down on two thin, stainless steel blades. Her ankle gave way, bringing the rest of her body down so hard that she never heard the sound of the ice cracking. The only warning she received was the look on Josh's face mere seconds before she plummeted into the icy water.

As hard as she tried to move her arms and legs, she wasn't strong enough to fight the pull downward from the weight of her skates and clothing. Even with the air trapped inside her clothes, Jennifer sank quickly. The icy water had knocked precious air from her lungs as she struggled to hold on to the last breath she'd taken, and her body's attempt to warm her heart robbed her limbs of all heat, leaving her extremities useless. All she could do was helplessly gaze upward at the sky through the hole in the ice and pray for one last look at Josh's face.

"*No!*" Josh immediately yanked off his other skate, rushed to the hole in the ice, and dove into the dark water. He kicked furiously until he caught sight of Jennifer and was able to grab her around the waist. As soon as he had her in his arms, Josh transported them both to her bedroom. Jennifer's eyes were shut, her coloring was a sickening bluish tint, her breathing was shallow, but her heartbeat—while worryingly slow—was steady.

"Jennifer, can you hear me? Damn it, answer me!" Josh shouted, tightening his hands around her arms and trying to shake her awake. With all the signs of hypothermia and her semiconscious state, he couldn't waste another moment. According to his calculation, the water's temperature was around forty degrees Fahrenheit and Jennifer had been submerged for twelve seconds, leaving only fifteen minutes to warm her before she slipped into a coma or worse. With a wave of his hand, he filled the room with brilliant, healing light.

"Come on, baby—don't you dare give up!" Josh forced out, ignoring the tightening sensations deep inside his chest. "You can't quit on me—if you do, I'll lose you forever. Fight for us, it's our only chance to be together! Dying is *not* an option!" he shouted as tears welled up in his eyes.

Go away... So tired...want to sleep. Jennifer slipped deeper into the darkness surrounding her, until the man's voice was barely a whisper. *Peaceful, so peaceful. Let me sleep...*

"*No!* This isn't your destiny, Jennifer! So help me, if you don't open your eyes I'll pry them open!" Josh warned through gritted teeth.

Jennifer's eyes fluttered open to stare blankly ahead as if she wasn't able to see.

"Thank God!" Relief flowed hot through Josh's body. "I have to get you out of these clothes," he said shakily. He couldn't waste another precious moment—time was slipping away and if he didn't work fast enough, no amount of shouting or begging would bring Jennifer back to life.

Stop, let me go back to sleep. Was so peaceful. Jumbled thoughts came and went in Jennifer's mind, but her desire not to be disturbed went unheeded.

With one hand wrapped around Jennifer's waist to hold her upright, Josh roughly yanked one side of her waterlogged coat off her shoulder and then the other.

"Stay with me, baby! Whatever you do, keep those brown eyes of yours open," Josh coaxed. Resting her body against his for support, he clenched the bottom of her sweater and pulled hard, lifting it up and over her head and tossing it on the floor next to her coat.

Jennifer's eyes shut and her head sagged downward as she slumped into unconsciousness again. Josh listened in fear, expecting to hear Gisabella's command to transport Jennifer to heaven. ~Please don't call this one home,~ he begged. "Please Jennifer, you must stay with me; I refuse to be the one to transport you to heaven, never to see you again. Damn it, don't you know how much I love you?!" Josh shouted. "Wake up! Didn't you hear me?! I love you! Say it! Damn it, Jennifer—say it back to me! Baby, please say it back—tell me you love me too," Josh begged through tears that ran down his face as he pulled her listless body against him.

Sleep. If you love me, let me sleep.

When Josh received no response, he laid Jennifer on the bed in preparation to do chest compressions if she didn't start breathing on her own. A quick check of her carotid artery proved Jennifer's pulse was fading. The only hope he had of saving her life was to raise her body temperature so that her heart would keep beating. He briskly rubbed Jennifer's arms and legs, moving faster and faster to increase the warming friction.

Cold. So cold. Stop—it hurts. Love? The feel of Josh's intense energy slowly brought Jennifer back to consciousness, but her vitality was non-existent. She slowly opened her eyes, observing Josh as he removed her skates, socks, and jeans. In her soaked bra and panties, she was far too cold to care about modesty or being close to naked. Her frosted lips formed a tiny smile at Josh's attempts to divert his eyes from her scantily clad figure. Somehow, he'd managed to undress her in a manner befitting a gentleman.

"I'm sorry, Jennifer, but I have to take off your drenched undergarments—it's the only way to get you warm," Josh said quietly, hiding her nakedness with a blanket.

"Okay," Jennifer forced out. With only a thin layer of fabric separating her from Josh, her heart thawed, and with each heartbeat her blood reached places that'd been deprived of oxygen, creating a pins-and-needles sensation everywhere.

"Talking's a good sign." Josh's tone reflected the first sign of hope since transporting his frozen date home. He reached under the blanket and without one peek, went to work undoing and removing Jennifer's bra, then hooked his fingers into the waistband of her panties to slide them off. When done, he tucked the blanket around her and continued rubbing her extremities.

"Jennifer, I can only think of one way to warm you fast enough, and it involves body heat," Josh mumbled under his breath. "If you have any problem with you and I under the covers without clothing, let me know now."

"Please—I'm so cold," Jennifer chattered.

Before he changed his mind, Josh pulled off all his clothing except for his briefs and slid under the covers.

Jennifer welcomed Josh's muscular arms as he pulled her tightly against him, a move that helped her shivers to recede and her awareness to return. Best of all, when she opened her eyes she was lying on his bare chest. With a sigh, she savored the feeling of Josh wrapped around her nakedness and the way his heat fed life back into her, once again awakening her soul. A deep inhalation of Josh's memorable scent of vanilla, cinnamon, and pine reminded her of Christmas morning.

"Jennifer, how do you feel? Are you warm enough?" Josh asked when he felt Jennifer stir.

The way Josh's eyes looked into hers made time stand still. They were hypnotic, and had changed to a gorgeous cobalt shade. She didn't dare look away for fear he'd disappear. *I love him,* Jennifer realized, closing her eyes and tilting her lips upward.

"Please don't look at me like that." Josh looked down at Jennifer's slightly parted lips, ones that begged to be kissed. As much as he wanted to give in, he feared that after almost losing her, he might not be able to stop until he'd claimed her. Her energy told him that she was more than willing to follow his lead, and his hard erection was eager to accommodate their lust. As much as he hated to, he needed to get away from her; Jennifer was a virgin, and if he planned on keeping her one until they were married, he had to leave.

"Please, Josh," Jennifer murmured in anticipation. Her need for him was so fierce that she pressed her nakedness firmly against his hardened physique in an attempt to squelch the fire burning from deep within. A soft moan of desire left her parted lips, ones that ached to be kissed for the first time.

"Please don't, Jennifer, not like this. You have no idea what you ask of me," Josh warned.

"Why do you sound angry with me?" Jennifer asked.

"I'm not angry with you—I'm mad at myself for not protecting you from harm." Josh sat up, moving to the edge of the bed and running his hand through his hair.

"Why are you blaming yourself? It wasn't your fault; it was an accident, and thanks to your quick actions I'm safe." Jennifer sprang up and hugged him from behind, resting her face against his taut, muscular back.

"You don't get it. I'm your *protector*," he divulged.

"'Protector?' What are you talking about?"

"Jennifer, it's my job to keep you safe, but today I failed miserably."

"Safe? I don't understand."

"I was assigned to watch over you and keep you from harm. If I hadn't gone on a date with you, none of this would've happened. I crossed a line that I vowed I'd never cross." Once he said the words it was too late to take them back; all he could do now was watch Jennifer's expression change.

"Your job is to watch *over* me?! All this time I thought that you liked me…that you just chose to be near me. So you've been lying to me this entire time?!" Jennifer's voice cracked and she pulled the sheet tighter around herself. *What a fool I've been to believe a guy like Josh could ever be interested in me.*

"No!" Josh backtracked. "That's not it at all. Protecting you started out as a job, but once I got to know you, everything changed. Jennifer, I've fallen in love with you—so much so that I wish to marry you."

"*What?!* You just told me you should've never asked me on a date, and now you want to marry me?! I bet in three hours you'll figure out that you 'vowed' you'd never cross that line either."

"Jennifer, please listen. I'm being truthful when I say that I love you," Josh said, reaching out to her.

Jennifer flinched away and glared at him. "You had so many chances to tell me why you were here, but you lied to me, saying you were here as my 'friend.' How could I have been so stupid? I can't believe you made me fall for you, knowing that I had no idea your job was to watch over me. Well, congratulations, Josh! You actually made me believe that you were my boyfriend. I knew it! Deep down I knew a man like you would never find me interesting."

"I *didn't* lie about being your friend or being in love with you," Josh mumbled, hands dropping to his lap.

"But how can I believe anything you say now, Josh? I…I can't do this. Please leave."

"You don't understand—the only reason I waited to tell you was because I was afraid you'd think you were nothing but a job to me. Nothing could be further from the truth, and I hoped my marriage proposal would prove that."

Jennifer scooted further away from him, shaking her head. "I'd have to be absolutely crazy to agree to marry someone who's been lying to me for months—*years*, if you want to get technical! Get out of my room and stay away from me. I never want to see you again." Jennifer covered her face, not wanting to see the sheer despair in Josh's eyes.

"Have it your way," Josh acquiesced. "Don't worry—you won't have to put up with me much longer."

What? Jennifer opened her eyes just in time to see Josh fading away.

Once Josh had put some distance between himself and Jennifer, he thought his hunger for her would abate. It didn't! The fact he'd hurt her grabbed ahold of his soul and squeezed it until the pain was so severe he cried out from sheer agony. He placed his head in his hands, trying to block out the memory of how her naked body had felt against his, but it was useless—she'd stolen his heart.

He only had one option to keep her in his life: earn her trust again. If he failed another protector would be assigned to her, and the thought of never seeing Jennifer again was more painful than anything he'd ever experienced.

CHAPTER ELEVEN

Jennifer awoke the next morning with a heartache and a pounding head. She'd spent most of the night crying and resolving herself to the fact Josh had tricked her on purpose, leaving her no choice other than to never see him again.

"Jennifer, why aren't you awake? You'll be late for school," Mrs. Parker said as she bustled into the room.

"I don't feel well," Jennifer moaned.

"Do you have a fever?" Mrs. Parker laid her hand on Jennifer's forehead. "You do feel hot and your eyes are watery and red. Maybe you're getting a cold, or worse—the flu! Oh dear, I hope it's not the flu, it will go through the house like wildfire. I can't afford to catch that; your dad and I have that party on Sunday," Mrs. Parker fretted. "Maybe you should stay home from school, and if you get hungry there's a can of soup in the pantry. I'll be home after eight o'clock tonight. See you later!"

Jennifer watched her mother rush out of the room. *What a germaphobe.* She'd been left on her own when she was ill often, even the time she'd had the measles and had become delirious from lack of water. *I'm perfectly capable of taking care of myself!*

A glimmer of doubt crept into her mind then...maybe she hadn't been as alone or self-reliant as she'd once thought. If her memory served her correctly, she'd felt like someone was in the room watching over her, swabbing her face with a cool cloth and holding her head up so she could drink water. All this time she'd reasoned it was delirium that had caused the vision, but now she wondered if Josh had been the one caring for her. *How stupid I've been!* She chided herself for not following her gut instincts that someone like Josh could fall for her, and rolled over, hoping sleep would help block out the hurt.

It was afternoon when Jennifer awakened in a pool of sweat. The realization that she must've gotten sick from falling through the ice made her think of the fallout the day prior. In the middle of her commiseration a knock at the bedroom door startled her, and she turned her wide eyes towards it.

"I thought you might be awake," Josh said, peeking around the door like nothing had happened between them.

"You nearly frightened me to death! What are you doing here?" Jennifer shouted.

"Fine choice of words for someone who's here to take care of you." Josh noticed Jennifer's puffy eyes and knew they weren't caused by sickness.

"I told you that I never wanted to see you again," Jennifer mumbled, her attempt at an angry tone faltering.

"Don't worry, you'll be rid of me soon."

"Good!" Saying the word didn't result in the level of satisfaction she'd hoped for.

Josh carried a tray over to her bedside. "Sit up so you can eat some lunch."

Jennifer met his eyes with a steely gaze of her own.

"And don't give me any grief, because you won't like my response," Josh warned, causing Jennifer to rearrange her expression to something more subdued.

When she was seated upright he placed the tray on her lap and laid his hand on her forehead. "It feels like your fever broke."

Josh's actions caused a lump to form in Jennifer's throat, making it harder to swallow. Once she'd tasted the soup's homemade goodness, however, she ate hungrily.

"Would you like some more?"

"No, I'm good," she lied. In truth, she was anything but good. *How could you have made me fall in love with you when it was all a lie?* Jennifer kept a solid wall in place so her thoughts couldn't be read.

"I'm going to clean up the kitchen. Please put these on in the meantime." Josh placed a clean pair of pajamas on the bed and picked up the tray. Before he left the room, he turned around. "I suggest you follow my instructions because I'll be back in ten minutes—and I *won't* be knocking that time."

"Why are you here? Wasn't fooling me into believing you were my boyfriend and breaking my heart good enough for you?" Jennifer spat, bursting into tears the moment he walked out of the room.

Josh braced himself; now that he'd fouled things up so badly, he didn't stand much of a chance of making Jennifer his wife until he regained her trust. When he'd contacted Gisabella the night before and explained how Jennifer had kicked him out of her life, the high priestess wasn't at all sympathetic and blamed him for messing everything up. Of course Gisabella was right—he'd screwed up royally. Too bad he still had the job of teaching Jennifer how to use her visionary gifts. Somehow he had to find a way to work closely with the woman he loved and who presently despised him. *No problem, said no man ever!*

When Josh reentered Jennifer's bedroom, he prepared for a barrage of possible flying missiles, but what he found was more shocking than if she'd flung a brick at his head; Jennifer was standing in the middle of the room, topless. "What the fuck?!" He slammed his eyelids shut but it was too late; he'd seen enough of her perfect breasts to have them branded in his memory forever. "Jennifer, please cover yourself." His command came out more like a plea.

"Don't you like the way I look?" Jennifer's anger was doing the talking now.

"I think you know the answer to that," Josh said dryly, with one hand over his eyes to avoid any temptation to peek.

"What's wrong? Yesterday you claimed to be in love with me. Then again, that was after you informed me that I was nothing more to you than a job!" Jennifer pulled on the pajama top, feeling embarrassed at her brazenness but more upset by the way Josh had covered his eyes in horror. *A sure sign he isn't interested.*

"I took the liberty of writing down a few rules that as your protector, I expect you to follow," Josh continued without removing his hand from his eyes. "We'll begin your visionary lessons tomorrow after school, starting with how to surround yourself with protective white light." He spoke in the calmest voice he could muster as he followed protector protocol for dealing with a highly agitated attacker.

"Rules!" *Seriously?* "What makes you think I'm going to follow your rules after you *pretended...*" Jennifer couldn't finish the sentence. If Josh had come back that day and professed that his love for her was real, she'd have said the words that were in her heart. But yesterday's accident along with Josh's revelation and no-nonsense attitude were just too much to take. Soon a couple of tears turned into a deluge, and she sank to the ground.

"Jennifer, please don't cry," Josh rushed over and gathered her into his arms. "Please tell me what I can do to fix things with you. I'll do anything not to lose your friendship."

"Why did you have to come back today and make me soup instead of just leaving me alone?"

"Because I hurt you and I want to make things right between us."

"What do you want from me?"

"I want to be your friend again, and in time I hope to regain your trust."

"How can I trust you when you're required to be here as a rule-toting protector of some arbitrary, white-lighting school from heaven?"

"I swear on my soul, Jennifer, that things for me changed the day of your eighteen birthday. It was as if I noticed you'd become a woman, and from that point forward I've been unable to take my eyes off you. When we began talking, my heart opened for the first time in centuries. And when we decorated the Christmas tree together, it was the best night I've had in all my lifetimes."

"Why should I give you another chance?"

"Because, that's what friends do. They forgive each other's mistakes and overlook their flaws." He cupped Jennifer's chin and tilted her face upward until her red, puffy eyes met his. "I'm truly sorry." He waited for her to say something, but she remained silent. "Baby, please, I don't want to lose you. I know I made a huge mistake in not telling you sooner, but

I was afraid you would misunderstand and think that I was only spending time with you because I was required to do so. Jennifer, I've broken so many rules because of how I feel about you—it's real. It's all *real.* Please don't throw our friendship away."

"If you hurt me again…" She left her threat unfinished when he pulled her close and kissed the top of her head. "Hey, wait a minute, how come you're still solid? The full moon was last night."

"Gisabella was kind enough to grant an exception seeing as I mucked things up so badly with you. She thought it'd be easier for us to patch things up if I was solid," Josh said apologetically. "I told her how it was all my fault you almost died."

"I didn't 'almost die.' And when will you get it through your thick skull that it wasn't your fault? Are all bodyguards as thickheaded as you?"

"I'll have you know it's a prerequisite that all protectors must have a hard head." Josh flashed his smile and added darkly, "By the way, the next time you pull a topless stunt, don't expect me to be such a gentleman."

A surge of heat coursed through Jennifer's body, making all of her untouched places come to life and ache with need. *No, no, no! I refuse to desire him! Friends, that's all we are, and all we'll ever be. Josh was only grasping at straws when he said he loved me.*

"I promise that you won't have to worry about seeing me topless again, unless you peek in on me unexpectedly. Which reminds me—we need to set some rules." If the situation wasn't so dire, she'd have burst out laughing at the change in his expression. Clearly Josh wasn't happy that their friendship wouldn't include topless benefits.

"What do you have in mind?" Josh asked warily.

"You're not allowed in my bedroom or the bathroom unless you ask *permission* first! And you agree to respect my privacy."

"First of all, I've always respected your privacy and have never peeked in on you. Secondly, I'll agree to your demands, unless it's an emergency or you're in danger—then all bets are off."

"Agreed, but it better be a life-or-death situation and not something stupid like a hangnail," Jennifer warned.

"Fine—anything else?"

"You won't pretend to be in love with me," Jennifer said with a heavy heart. *It's better not to hear Josh's lies than to fool myself into thinking his feelings are real.*

"I give you my solemn word that I will never *pretend* that I love you." The words left a bitter taste in his mouth. *Because I love you for real.* Professing his true love for Jennifer in his thoughts was all he could do for now, until the time when she'd actually believe him. He hoped he'd still be able to convince her to marry him before it was too late. "Is that it?"

"For now, but I reserve the right to add more rules as I see fit," Jennifer warned.

"All right, here's my list. You can read it later." Josh hid his grin behind a stone-faced expression and handed her the three neatly written pages of rules he expected her to follow.

Jennifer flipped through the pages quickly, snorting with laughter as the terms "respect," "obey," and "no questioning my authority" jumped out at her. There were more than twenty-five altogether, regarding dress code, limited makeup, dating boys, no drinking, no parties, no dancing in public, and other nonsensical demands. She was halfway through the second page when she checked Josh's face for signs that it was his idea of a joke.

"Like you, I also reserve the right to add more rules as I see fit," Josh clarified before Jennifer had a chance to speak.

"I don't think there's a rule in the entire universe that's not on this list! I'll be sure to read them tonight with a red marker and return the revised version tomorrow."

Josh bit back a warning that she'd better not change one word if she knew what was good for her. Instead, he forced a smile at the woman whose usually welcoming brown eyes glared at him in a no-nonsense "I dare you to mess with me" way.

"I assure you, there are plenty more rules left in the universe that I'd be more than happy to add," Josh said.

"I'm sure you would. Just remember that I have plenty of red ink and I'll cross them all out. Better yet—a matchstick might prove more effective." Jennifer hit the page with her hand to express her disapproval. "Do you force all the women you protect to stop wearing makeup and attending parties?"

"No." Josh paused a moment to give Jennifer a false sense of victory. "I never had to give them a list of rules because all my previous visionaries, *that I can remember,* have been men."

"That tells me a lot! No wonder you're so bad at protecting me." Jennifer watched as Josh's demeanor immediately changed at her hurtful words. Before she could take them back, she found herself sitting on the floor alone. "Wait, I didn't mean what I said—it came out all wrong. I'm sorry." She reasoned Josh hadn't heard her and sent him an apologetic mental message, but he didn't come back. As much as she hated to admit, it felt good to hurt Josh after he'd shattered her heart into a zillion shards of hopelessness.

She climbed back into bed with a red marker and Josh's list of rules and proceeded to draw red lines through the ones she'd never be able to obey: "no long-distance running," "no bad driving," and "no sarcastic comments." She opted to keep the "no dating," "no parties," and "no dancing" on the list along with some others that her broken heart couldn't care less about doing with anyone other than him. *I wonder if I can give Josh a "no dating" rule? Why not!* After she wrote in a few rules of her own for him, she signed on the dotted line.

It was well past dinnertime when Jennifer climbed out of bed and went down to the kitchen in search of something to eat. To her surprise, she found a steaming plate of food waiting with a note:

I hope you like eggplant parmesan; it's one of my personal favorites. There's warm rolls in the oven and some dessert in the fridge. Sleep well and pleasant dreams.

Your friend, Josh

Josh's kindness made her feel worse. After all the harsh things she'd said, he'd made her a hot meal. Armed with the knowledge that maybe Josh was being truthful when he said he wanted to be her friend, she dug a fork into the hot eggplant parmesan and sampled his favorite dish.

CHAPTER TWELVE

Jennifer was thankful when Monday morning finally arrived. Two whole days and nights had passed without a word or sign from Josh, making it the worst weekend since the breakup of the Beatles!

A final look in the mirror gave her the confidence she'd need to face Josh—*if he shows up*. Pushing the bleak thought out of her head, Jennifer tugged at the bottom of her knitted miniskirt and pulled on her wool coat, fairly certain that the way her skirt stuck out less than an inch from the bottom of her coat wouldn't go unnoticed. Teamed with a snug lavender sweater, black tights and tall, leather riding boots, her ensemble was complete, and in direct violation of at least three of Josh's "protector rules."

Opening the front door, Jennifer braced herself for the chilly climate and frosty reception from her protector. A wave of relief washed over her when she found Josh waiting to walk her to school. *No, no, no—eggplant parmesan or not, I'm still mad at him.*

~Good morning, Jennifer. I take it you're feeling better today,~ Josh messaged, doing his best to feign happiness and not to escort Jennifer back into the house. *What the hell is she wearing?* His eyes traveled up and down his charge, twice. *Damn—she looks hot!* Josh wiped the grin from his face, reminding himself that Jennifer was heading to a school full of "girl-crazed" boys! *Doesn't she know that she's in violation of several rules?* ~Did you get a chance to read through the rules?~ *Ouch, wrong thing to ask!*

~I have them here.~ Jennifer pulled out the list and placed it on top of her schoolbooks, watching Josh help himself to the object's duplicate. Six facial cringes, five angry stares, four taunting smirks, three shakes of his head, two outright scowls, and an expression of his displeasure—left Jennifer's stomach in knots

~I see I'll need to buy you a new red marker,~ Josh said wryly.

~That won't be necessary; I have plenty more.~ Her sarcasm was reflected back at her in the form of Josh's darkening irises, causing her breathing to diminish and her legs to grow heavy.

~I'm glad to see you haven't lost your wit.~

~Nope, but you have.~ *Oh no!* Just when she thought Josh couldn't look more irritated, he proved her wrong. *I must play nice,* Jennifer told herself over and over until she caught the glimmer in Josh's eyes. *Great! He must've read my thoughts! Surely a breach of the rules I gave him. Unless? Oh no! How could I have forgotten about my "no dating" rule for him? I'm such an idiot!*

~I don't know about that—I think your thoughts have done much to improve my mood this morning. I'll make sure you receive a signed copy accepting the rules that I must follow.~

~I thought we agreed that you wouldn't read my thoughts,~ Jennifer messaged with a tone of indignation.

~I never agreed to that and I don't see it written here, so you're out of luck. Besides, you need to practice *blocking* your thoughts, so consider my telepathic attacks part of your training.~ Josh did little to hide his grin at Jennifer's exasperation.

~You. Are. So. Frustrating!~ Jennifer sent each word separately, further accenting her displeasure by speeding up, hoping to out-walk him. Josh's long legs made her attempt futile and though she contemplated running the rest of the way, she reasoned it'd be a pointless maneuver against his ability to transport or float above her.

~So. Are. You,~ Josh messaged back. ~After school I'll teach you some basic protection practices, which you'll need to add to your morning ritual.~

Jennifer stopped dead in her tracks and confronted him. ~What do you mean "I'll need protection?" From what?~ *Other than my heart from you?*

~We're almost at our destination. I'll explain everything later.~

With much effort, Jennifer refrained from demanding to know *that minute* and flounced away without another word.

Goodbye to you too! Josh watched Jennifer disappear inside the school. *This is going to be a long day.*

By lunchtime Jennifer's mood hadn't improved. First there was Mrs. Stellard's surprise quiz, and in English she'd missed a homework assignment given out the day she'd been sick. If that wasn't bad enough, the science proposal that'd taken her weeks of research had been rejected, and if she didn't come up with a new one by Friday she'd fail the class.

Great, how am I going to catch up and deal with Josh? I wonder whether he'll back off if I tell him about my horrible day so far. Somehow, I don't think protector Josh will care about my preferences. Jennifer was still talking to herself when she walked into the cafeteria. *I still don't get why I need protection? What on earth did Josh mean when he spoke of protecting visionaries? Yikes! I must be a visionary—nah—that doesn't make sense. There must be another reason why he's been assigned to me. Maybe Josh was sent to make sure I don't get in a car accident with some* other *much-needed visionary.* She stifled a giggle. *This is ridiculous; who'd care enough about me to warrant Josh's protection?*

"Jennifer, over here," Elizabeth called out, waving her arm in Jennifer's direction.

Jennifer greeted her with the biggest smile she could muster, but it came up short and looked more like she was having painful cramps than expressing happiness.

"Cool outfit, Jennifer! I didn't think you owned anything other than jeans," Elizabeth chuckled. "Seriously, you look fantastic. I bet once the 'in' crowd notices you, you'll be popular in no time."

"I think it'd take a lot more than a miniskirt to alter my reputation," Jennifer said. They'd often joked about not fitting in with the popular kids, and had started going out of their way *not* to several years before.

"To tell you the truth, they won't care about how odd or quiet you are when your legs look *that* good! Are you feeling okay? It's not like you to miss school," Elizabeth asked, giving Jennifer a strange look.

"The bug I had kept me in bed the entire weekend."

"You don't look so well now either. Is everything all right?"

"Nothing a bowl of ice cream and a night of TV won't cure."

"That bad? Maybe this'll help—I overheard Tommy Bicker telling one of his friends that he's asking you to the Christmas dance!"

"What?! E-Excuse me." *I think I'm going to be sick.* Jennifer put her hand over her mouth and ran out of the cafeteria towards the ladies room, barely making it in time to empty her breakfast in one of the stalls. She'd just flushed the toilet when she heard Josh's voice inside her head.

~Are you all right? Do you have a fever, any pain? Stand still for a minute and I'll do a body scan on you from here. Don't worry, it's only a precaution to make sure you don't have any blockages.~

~Don't you dare do a "body scan" or whatever else you've dreamt up on me! I'm fine—no fever or blockages! The only thing bothering me is my overprotective bodyguard who's freaking out and sounds as if he's ready to rush me to the hospital!~

~Then what's wrong? What did you eat for breakfast? I've seen the way your mom cooks—don't tell me she tried her hand at oatmeal again. If that's the case, no wonder you vomited.~

~I suspect my sudden run to the toilet was from finding out that Tommy wants to ask me to the dance. It must've been too much after the terrible weekend I've had.~

~Do you *want* to go to the dance with this Tommy guy?~ Josh fought back the unwelcome worry and doubt that threatened to ruin his chances with Jennifer.

~No, I don't want to go to the dance with Tommy or any other boy. I'm surprised you care! And according to your list of rules, I'm not allow to date anyone.~

~If you read the rule more carefully, it states that you "can't date any *other* boys."~

Other boys? Does Josh mean other than him? For the first time since Thursday's blowout, her spirits rose. ~I hate to tell you this, but if you signed the rules *I* gave you, you're not allowed to date at all,~ Jennifer clarified.

~I suggest you look at the paper I signed and placed inside your book bag,~ Josh messaged, trying to hide the merriment in his voice.

Jennifer dove into her bag and dragged out her copy, flipping to the rules she'd given Josh:

3. I agree not to date anyone else but you, Jennifer!

Jennifer stared openmouthed at the words Josh had added to the rule she'd given him. *Anyone else "but me?"* ~You do? I mean—how can I date you?~ Jennifer stammered. ~Friends don't date each other.~

~Have it your way for now, but know that if and when you change your mind, I'll be here waiting for you with open arms.~

~I have to go. Elizabeth must be wondering what happened to me.~ This was not the place she wanted to have a discussion as important as dating.

~Jennifer, please drink some ginger ale to settle your stomach.~

~I'll think about having some soup. Thanks for checking on me.~ The thought that Josh cared about her wellbeing, even if it was his job, comforted her.

When she reentered the cafeteria several Nerf balls flew by on their way to various targets, while a few other students played cards—hearts or solitaire, depending on the number of players. Jennifer walked back to her friends' table with soup, a pile of saltines, and a ginger ale in the hopes of quelling her queasiness.

"What happened to you? One minute I was telling you how Tommy wanted to ask you out, and the next you were gone," Elizabeth asked with concern.

"Sorry, I forgot something in my locker," Jennifer fibbed, not wanting to bring attention to her dash to the toilet. "I've decided to turn Tommy down if he asks me to the dance."

"Why would you do that? He seems really nice, and I thought you wanted to have your first kiss…unless you're hiding someone? That's *it*, isn't it? You have a secret boyfriend!" Elizabeth's eyes brightened.

"No, no. I've decided not to date until after college when my career's in full swing." Jennifer did her best to keep her face placid.

"You pick your *senior* year to decide that you don't want to date?" Elizabeth stared at Jennifer in disbelief. "Sorry—I didn't mean anything by it, I'm just surprised by your change of heart."

"As far as I can tell, boys cause nothing but heartaches!" Jennifer said, thinking of a certain someone. *They cause wonderful feelings too.* "Besides, I intend to graduate with straight A's."

"The way my grades are looking, I have a better chance of graduating with a boyfriend on my arm," Elizabeth frowned. "Hurry up and eat, we're going to be late for math."

"How are things going with Brad?"

"He's pushing me to go steady, but I'm not sure whether he's doing it so I'll agree to sleep with him again," Elizabeth sighed. "Maybe you have the right idea. I've been so worried about losing Brad that I failed my science test! How does Mary juggle them all?"

"Speaking of which—where *are* Mary and Colleen?" Jennifer asked. Her eyes followed Elizabeth's pointed finger out the window to where their friends were seated near the football field, watching several players practicing.

"Don't look now, but you'd better get your rejection ready," Elizabeth said in a hushed voice.

A sense of dread filled Jennifer. A month ago she would've accepted Tommy's invitation, but now there was only one man she wanted to be with—and she had little doubt that he was close by watching.

"Hi Elizabeth," Tommy said before turning his attention to Jennifer. "Hey Jennifer. I was wondering if you had a moment?"

Sorry, I won't have one of those until I'm in my thirties—and only if Josh hasn't kissed me by then! Putting her snarky thoughts aside, she scrambled to think of a nice way to turn him down. "Sure, Tommy," Jennifer said in her best disinterested voice; too bad Tommy didn't take the hint and proceeded to sit next to her. *Ick—too close.* Jennifer shifted a few inches away with the pretense of giving him more room.

"I know it's a little early, but I was wondering if you'd like to go to the Valentine's Day dance with me."

Jennifer heard Elizabeth choke. *Valentine's Day dance? How odd, why would I make plans to attend a sweetheart dance with Tommy that's two months away? I don't even know him that well.* Suddenly, as if a light bulb flickered to life inside her brain, she realized Tommy's motive. *He wants to begin dating me! Oh no! This can't be happening; I finally get asked out by a solid, in-the-flesh guy, but I have real feelings for Josh. I just don't know if we'll ever be able to overcome our differences.* The thought created a resounding ache in her heart, and she knew what she had to do.

"I'm sorry Tommy, but I can't," Jennifer said, trying to sound as apologetic as possible. Then in a bold move, she added, "I'm seeing someone else. He doesn't go to our school—he's in college." *What am I doing? Someone please close my mouth before I say another word.* The sound of Elizabeth's second round of choking and Josh's booming laughter filled her ears.

"Oh. I'm sorry, I didn't know you were seeing someone. If you'll excuse me, I have to get to class," Tommy said, taking off much faster than he'd arrived.

"You're seeing someone? Really?" Elizabeth said. "What happened to 'I want to wait until after college?' Okay Jennifer, spill the beans—beginning with the *who*."

~I'm all ears too, Jennifer. I agree with Elizabeth; why don't you start with the who?~ Josh chuckled.

"I said that so Tommy wouldn't feel bad. Now I have an excuse that I can use with any other boy who asks me out."

"I don't get it, Jennifer. For the past two years you've said you wanted a boyfriend, or at the very *least* a date to the senior prom. Why the change of heart?" Elizabeth voiced with concern.

"I *was* being serious when I said I wasn't interested in dating until after college—unless some gorgeous hunk who sings like a famous tenor from Italy and can't skate more than two steps without falling on his butt comes along and sweeps me off my feet."

So Jennifer wants to be swept off her feet, hmm? I can certainly try, and hopefully get her to agree to marry me in under seven weeks' time. I have to be nuts to think I can pull this off! Josh sighed.

CHAPTER THIRTEEN

The following day, Josh insisted on teaching Jennifer the first of many protection skills she'd need as a visionary. They'd been at it for an hour, and Jennifer's frustration was rising.

"Please tell me again why you're solid right now," Jennifer scowled. "Oh right, I remember—to irritate me!"

"That would be the second reason. The first is so I can help you hone your skills."

"I think you have them reversed!" Jennifer averted her eyes so Josh's striking features would stop ruining her concentration, but it didn't help.

"Try it again," Josh commanded.

"We've been at this for an hour," Jennifer whined. "Why can't I use a different color other than white? It's so boring. Pink would be so much easier to imagine, or better yet, turquoise, so I can pretend I'm on a cruise ship looking down into the Caribbean while sipping a piña colada."

"I bet you've never even had a piña colada."

"No, but they look good."

"I'll make you a deal," Josh bribed. "When you're able to surround yourself with protective white light for five minutes, we'll celebrate with piña coladas."

"In a coconut shell with fresh pineapple and cherry skewers and tiny pink umbrellas?" Jennifer said hopefully.

"I wouldn't dream of serving it any other way."

Jennifer closed her eyes, making it easier to visualize the words she was saying. "I'm picturing a white light coming down from above and surrounding me completely in a wide circle. The white light is pure and healing and it protects me from harmful energies, negative spirits... Agh! I keep forgetting what comes next!"

"You almost had it. Do it again," Josh instructed.

"It's your fault I can't keep a straight face whenever I get to the 'negative spirit' part," Jennifer scoffed.

"That's what makes this lesson fun for me." Josh didn't bother to disguise his shit-eating grin.

"You'd better go hunt up some coconut shells, because this time when I say 'spirits are negative' I'll be thinking of how irritating *you* are!"

"Whatever you need to tell yourself to get the job done. Again!" Josh repeated.

"I'm picturing a white light coming down from above and surrounding me completely in a wide circle. The white light is pure and healing and it protects me from harmful energies, negative spirits, energy vampires, and all other people and entities that mean me possible harm. The light soothes my soul and heals my body, giving me the protection and energy I need to sustain good health, while at the same time grounding my energy to Mother Earth so that I won't fall for trickery or false prophets." Jennifer continued to meditate on keeping the white light in place even when Josh began making faces and sending messages, trying to purposely distract her. His obnoxious behavior aimed at strengthening her concentration made her *that* much more determined to succeed.

"I knew you could do it, baby!" Josh cheered when she'd successfully conjured the white light for nearly six minutes. He ran over and almost scooped Jennifer into his arms, but stopped short at the last moment. "I believe I owe you a piña colada."

"Yes!" Without thinking, Jennifer threw her arms around Josh, closed her eyes, raised up onto her tippy-toes, and pulled his mouth down to hers. Her bold move failed miserably when her lips unexpectedly touched down on Josh's five-o'clock shadow. *He turned away! Ugh, how could I be so stupid?*

"Jennifer, I, um..."

"On second thought, I have a lot of homework—I'll see you tomorrow. Thank you for the lesson." *And the rejection.* Her mindless rambling filled the awkward silence, but there was no avoiding the look of pity in Josh's eyes. *Please just leave,* she willed.

"Do you want help with your homework? There's nowhere I have to be and I don't have much to do, other than watch over you. I'd love to stay and help."

"Thank you for your kind gesture—maybe another time," she responded, doing her best to save face. *Nothing like telling me he has nothing better to do than hang around with boring old me. Never mind doing everything in his power* not *to kiss me.*

"Are you upset?" Ignoring Jennifer's protests, he tilted her chin until her eyes met his. "Your eyes are watering—why?"

"Why shouldn't I be upset? The other day you made it perfectly clear that you're here only because it's your job to watch over me. Then you made me sign a rule saying that I couldn't date anyone else but you, leading me to believe you're interested in me, only to find out you have no better offers."

"Is that what you think? That I have no other offers? Trust me, Jennifer, I can get offers if I so choose, but I only wish to be with you. I know I hurt you and I need to earn your trust again, but don't think for one moment that I've stopped loving you. I give you my word as an elite protector that my love for you will never change."

"Then why did you turn your head when I tried to kiss you?"

"Because you're not ready! I don't want to rush things between us only to have my heart broken when you pull away."

Josh's words left her speechless. What could she say? *I promise not to break your heart or pull away?* She'd always been told by her parents and others that there were no promises when it came to love. Love given wasn't always reciprocated, and was subject to change; every magazine she'd ever read was full of stories about unrequited love, messy breakups, divorces, and cheating spouses.

"I feel like I'm ready to be kissed," Jennifer said shyly. "And in case you have any doubts, I don't want a broken heart either."

"What are you doing for Christmas?" Josh asked, switching gears.

"On Christmas Eve we go to my aunt's, but we're always home by eleven. Then on Christmas morning we go to church, open presents, and have a family brunch—not necessarily in that order. What do you usually do for Christmas? I assume you celebrate the holiday."

"It's been many years since I celebrated Christmas, but I'd love to see you and to give you your present. I have the option of becoming solid anytime after midnight on Christmas Eve until Christmas morning. Maybe you can sneak away for a couple of hours so we can spend some time together?"

"I'd like that. Hopefully you don't plan on using that time to teach me more protection lessons, because I've really missed your friendship."

"I promise, no lessons—I'll even do my best to act like a normal boyfriend."

"Is that your new title? 'Boyfriend?'" The term sent a shot of adrenaline straight to Jennifer's heart.

"I'd like it to be." A shift in Josh's weight was the only indication of how nervous he was *not* to receive the title he wanted so badly.

"So will your new title replace your protector one? It should, because I certainly don't need one of those. Besides, all this white light protection stuff is a little over-the-top, don't you think?"

"This coming from a woman I caught flying off a rearing horse and dove into ice water to save! It will absolutely *not* replace my purpose as your protector!" Josh said, counting to ten to calm himself before daring to speak again. "Jennifer, I wish to fill both of those roles in your life. As far as protecting yourself with white light, you must promise to do so every morning without exception."

"Only on one condition: that you tell me what makes me so special as to warrant your protection."

"I can tell you that you're intuitive and learn quickly. Other than that, you're right, I'm not at liberty to discuss your life-path or your destiny, nor do I know either of those things." *Because I was too stupid to read them when I had the chance.* "I can also tell you that as a visionary, you were born with a purpose that has to do with the greater good of mankind. It could be something as simple as giving a message or directions to someone, introducing two people, or—in rare cases—instigating a change that affects thousands of lives." Josh caressed Jennifer's cheek. "I've missed your friendship, too."

"I hope someday you'll tell me more," Jennifer said dreamily, more into Josh's touch than anything else.

"I honestly want to stay and help you."

"Are you any good at history? The rise and fall of Rome?"

"I have some knowledge in that area." *As in firsthand experience.*

"Good. Then you can stay and help." Jennifer walked over to the table with her history book and sat down, motioning for Josh to do the same. After two hours, there wasn't anything about the subject she didn't know. "Thank you for your help. How did you learn so much? Wait, let me guess—you've 'read every book ever written about Rome,'" Jennifer mocked.

"Yep, lot's of books." Josh hesitated, wondering how much sense it made to tell Jennifer about his days in Rome and his role in its decline. "On that note, I'd better get going before your mom and dad come home. I'll see you tomorrow morning," Josh vowed. Then he kissed the top of her head and disappeared.

It was Friday and the last day of school before their ten-day holiday break. The morning began with Jennifer's parents giving her the keys to the car and agreeing to let her drive herself to school and the mall afterwards. Elizabeth said she'd tag along, while Colleen and Mary had already made plans to see a movie with the two football players they'd met during their outdoor lunch.

As expected, everyone was distracted by the approaching holiday; some teachers even opted to host impromptu parties and games. When school was dismissed, Jennifer and Elizabeth hurried off to the mall.

"Who's left on your list?" Elizabeth asked.

"I need a present for Alex and one more for Sarah. I'm thinking of buying Sarah and Dave something for their new apartment. She's hardly home now that they're setting up their house together—hard to believe their wedding's three weeks away! How many are left on your list?"

"My parents and little sister. Anyone else for you?" Elizabeth asked.

My bodyguard-slash-boyfriend who claims to be in love with me—but I'm not sure if I should believe him. You don't know him, nor can you see him. Why not, you ask? Because Josh is a ghost. You should know, however, that they much prefer the term "spirit," as "ghost" is apparently a slang word they find degrading. "I thought I'd get something for one of Alex's friends who helped me with my driving test," Jennifer fibbed. When Elizabeth became absorbed in the song playing on the radio, she sighed, relieved for the lull in conversation.

Once in the mall, the crowds were so thick and the lines so long that they separated, agreeing to meet again in three hours. Jennifer selected a scarf for Alex and a pink lava lamp for Sarah and Dave to replace the one they'd broken. To that day it was unclear how the lamp had fallen off the nightstand, but whenever the subject was broached, the two acted strangely about it.

Even though Josh had said he'd be in meetings, Jennifer didn't take any chances. With her thoughts blocked, Jennifer pretended she was purchasing her final gift for someone other than Josh. The men's department at Macy's had tie-dyed, psychedelic T-shirts and some nice sweaters; they were stylish, but not the kind of personalized gift she had in mind. When she found an ornament shop, she purchased one of a couple skating; a risky choice since each time she mentioned anything to do with the activity, Josh scowled. The memory of lying naked in his arms that day heated her blood and colored her cheeks, and she blushed deeply when she gave both of their names to the engraver. Once done, she went in search of another gift. Ten minutes later she stumbled upon a picture frame shop, and went inside to check out the heart-shaped frame featured in the window display.

It'd been over a week since she'd fallen through the ice. Josh had hinted several times that he was still in love with her, and in her heart, she knew she'd fallen in love with him. There wasn't a precise moment that she could pinpoint when it'd happened; it could've been as early as when she'd blown out her birthday candles and looked up into Josh's eyes. She'd forgiven him for keeping the full truth from her, and they were working on rebuilding trust with one another, so the biggest question that remained was...did Josh still wish to marry her?

Jennifer paid for the crystal frame and wrote down the personal sentiment she wanted engraved. When done, she purchased some elegant foil and two matching bows for Josh's gifts, then headed back to meet Elizabeth at the food court, where they talked over hot fudge banana splits.

"How are things going between you and Brad?" Jennifer asked.

"You should have seen the look on his face when I refused to sleep with him after our last date," Elizabeth snickered. "When I explained how I wanted to save sex for when I was in an exclusive relationship, Brad agreed with me! Since then, things have been great and he's stopping by on Christmas!"

"That's wonderful! Looks like Brad's a nice guy after all."

"What about you? Have you changed your mind about going out with Tommy? I've seen the way he looks at you."

"I have no interest in Tommy or anyone else in our school."

"I didn't think so." Elizabeth checked her watch. "Oh no! My mother will kill me if I'm late."

Jennifer quickly paid the bill and they rushed to the car. Once she dropped Elizabeth off, she hurried home to wrap the purchased gifts. She finished wrapping the lava lamp and scarf and set them under the tree, then placed a photo of herself in the frame for Josh and wrapped both of his gifts as well. She finished them off with a card taped to the top of the biggest one.

With Josh tied up in meetings with Gisabella and the other protectors until late that night and her parents at a party, Jennifer was home alone. Before leaving, he'd explained how he'd placed some sort of "energized alarm system" around the house. When he'd started describing how it worked in detail she'd zoned out, finding that staring at Josh's kissable lips was far more interesting. When his mouth had stopped moving and transformed into a crooked grin, she'd darted her gaze away and forced herself to listen. Josh had explained how her privacy wouldn't be compromised and that she could go about her normal routine without worry. Before he left, Josh had given her a codeword to message if she needed him for any reason.

She now curled up with a bowl of popcorn in front of the TV. Her parents were at a party, Sarah was staying at her new apartment, and Alex wouldn't be home until Christmas. Having the house all to herself meant that Jennifer's thoughts wandered once again to Josh. *I wonder if he's done with his meetings. I wish he'd stop by for a quick visit and maybe even a goodnight kiss. Possibly the first of many. What is he* waiting *for? Maybe until Christmas—that would be so romantic.* She was still thinking of their first kiss when she dozed off.

CHAPTER FOURTEEN

Gisabella and Josh walked side by side into the elite protector meeting, one being attended by only the best guardians she'd acquired over the millennia. It was an event she held twice a year in an informal setting to honor their hard work. She'd shed her formal high priestess robes in lieu of a cranberry-colored gown and an elaborate diamond and ruby necklace with matching drop earrings for the occasion; the jewels had been a token of King Arthur's appreciation for her help in defeating the emperor Lucius.

"I want a word with you after this," Gisabella murmured to Josh as they approached the stage, greeting several of the 734 strongest protectors in the universe along the way. These men and women possessed the highest fighting abilities and intuition levels around, and had developed into some of the top psychics in existence. Each protector in her elite army had been through a rigorous training program with Merlin, who taught them every metaphysical property he knew. Merlin added lessons in magic and wizardry for those who were advanced, making them more powerful than all the others.

When Gisabella took her position at the podium, her four top elite protectors positioned themselves on either side of the stage as the audience went silent. She glanced to her left at Josh, bowing her head in respect of his rank above all others. Standing to her right was the second-highest protector, Sarnia, and beside Sarnia was Cornelius. Next to Cornelius was Lancelot, who'd spent so many extra years under Merlin's tutelage that Gisabella sometimes wondered whether the wizard still held a grudge against the younger protector's scandalous behavior on earth.

"Welcome, my most valued protectors in the entire universe and all dimensions; it gives me great pleasure to see all of you on this glorious night. With your hard work and extra efforts, we currently have nine hundred visionaries completely trained and ready to carry out their life-path destinies. Please join me in a round of applause for the hard work you and your fellow constituents have done."

Gisabella waited for the applause to die down before going through some of the details and mentioning names of protectors that deserved special recognition. She made sure to include plenty of pomp and circumstance, while she downplayed visionary attacks and those protectors who she'd fired due to issues in protocol. Tonight was all about celebration, and she kept the tempo of the meeting moving in that direction at all times.

When done, Gisabella turned to Josh to see if he had anything to add, but his grim expression told her what he really thought of the way she'd brushed the bad stuff under the table. She raised her eyebrows at Josh and winked, causing his scowl to deepen. Only a couple of protectors in attendance knew that she and Josh were friends, but none were aware of how their past had bound them together forever. Even though Josh couldn't remember, she owed such gratitude to him, and in time she'd help him to fill in the missing pieces of his memory. His amnesia was *her* doing, after all—so she was going to give him what he wanted more than anything, even if he couldn't remember her promise to him all those centuries before.

"Go in peace my friends, and remember to be on high alert as your charges celebrate their respective holidays," Gisabella said, ending the meeting. Loud chatter took over the event as everyone began visiting with the colleagues and friends they hadn't seen in months.

"Nice to see you again, Josh," Sarnia said in a low voice.

He didn't have to turn around to know who'd rested their hand on his shoulder, nor who owned that heavenly, seductive voice. "You too, Sarnia," Josh lied, keeping his greeting short.

"You're looking good—and very fit, for a man of your age," Sarnia purred.

Josh spun and faced the green-eyed vamp. Sarnia's bright red, wild mane of curls and angelic, heart-shaped face had a reputation for being used to fool her prey into thinking she *possessed* a heart. He had to give her credit for her persistence; as far back as he could remember, she'd been coming on to him. "Sarnia, I'm not sure what game you think you're playing, but I'm not interested," Josh said with no sign of nicety. "Why don't you go in search of another scratching post to climb while the room is still full of horny candidates?"

"Ouch! Don't you *get* it, Josh? I love the bad boy side of you. You remember, don't you?" Sarnia's red lips widened into a mischievous "cat that'd eaten the canary" smile.

A knot formed in Josh's stomach. *Is Sarnia part of my lost memories?* Another glance at her red hair and pale complexion gave him some relief that she was definitely *not* the woman from the memories that had haunted him for centuries. It suddenly occurred to him that the visions of his mystery woman had subsided ever since he'd caught Jennifer flying off Brandy. *Why is my lack of remembrance still bothering me even though it has nothing to do with my future wife?*

"You don't remember, do you? Why don't you come home with me and I'll help you relive a few of our rougher escapades," Sarnia coaxed.

"Not a chance in hell. Now, if you'll excuse me, I have a meeting with Gisabella. Claws off the shirt, kitty." Josh turned and hurried to catch up to the high priestess's side before she'd descended from the stage.

"Where have you been?" Gisabella turned to stare at Josh. "It's not like you to abandon your post."

"Sorry, Your Excellency. I was detained by a red-haired alley cat."

"Sarnia? Don't tell me she's still trying to lure you into her bed? When will that tramp give up?"

"I think tonight may've done the trick," Josh said wryly.

Gisabella raised an eyebrow in his direction. "I can see why Sarnia hasn't given up; you're one *fine* specimen of a man," she teased, knowing how much Josh despised any reference to his masculine good looks.

"Back off, Gisabella. Remember—I'm about to be married." Josh kept his voice low so no one else heard his declaration.

"You sound so sure of yourself. Pretty funny since you haven't even kissed the girl."

"So help me, if you go against your word or interfere in any way, I'll spend the rest of my years making your life miserable."

"You've got it bad, don't you?" Gisabella sympathized.

"Yes, and until I make Jennifer my wife and take her to bed, my soul won't be at peace."

"If it's any consolation, peace is overrated," Gisabella cajoled.

"You're an evil woman, my friend," Josh whispered.

"If there's anything I can do to help, let me know," Gisabella replied with genuine affection. "I'll be right back—something of importance is in need of my attention."

When Gisabella walked away, an old friend of Josh's started up a conversation and held his attention.

Gisabella found Sarnia perched on a stool. "Hello, Sarnia. Please don't bother to stand or try to say anything—just listen. If you ever approach Joshua or one of your colleagues again, I'll see to it that you're removed from my elite force and sent back to earth as a cat. I believe it's a fitting penance for all the men you've sunk your claws into, then shredded to pieces once you were done playing. For the record, Joshua is out of your league, little hussy. So back off, because I'm one person you *don't* want to anger." Sarnia recoiled as if she'd been physically struck as Gisabella continued. "Good—I can see you've gotten my message." Gisabella spun and walked away with a huge grin of satisfaction.

"Come, Joshua, I'm ready to go home now," Gisabella said loudly to give the impression that he was on duty and had no choice but to leave with her. This had always been the way they'd hidden their friendship and avoided any accusations of favoritism.

"Yes, Your Excellency," Josh said formally before they transported to Gisabella's personal residence.

Once there, Gisabella removed her shoes and went into the kitchen. "I'm in need of some tea and my slippers. Would you like a cup?"

"Sure. And I'm wondering if you can tell me something—Sarnia mentioned we had some sort of 'fling' once. Any idea whether that's true?"

"Sounds to me like you're concerned your new bride will refuse to marry you if she finds out."

"That's part of the reason. Jennifer's young, sweet, and very innocent, and I doubt she'll understand about my past or the long history I've had. How can I tell her I've lived through centuries but have no recollection of many of those years?" Josh ran his hand through his hair and moaned. "Please tell me I never hooked up with that sleaze! Sarnia looked like she wanted to devour me on the stage, then try and kill me for the hell of it," Josh guffawed. "That woman's some piece of work. If I ever hooked up with Sarnia, I don't deserve a woman like Jennifer."

"Don't let Sarnia get to you. I'm sure she lied to get a rise out of you, but no worries. I get the feeling that after my parting conversation with her, Sarnia won't be giving you or your future wife any trouble."

"Why the hell did you do that? I can fight my own battles," Josh shot back.

"I know you can, but it was one time I could do something to help you out. Which reminds me; if Sarnia ever comes on to you or any other protector, you need to let me know."

"Please tell me you're not keeping score. If so, you'd better get busy finding another million things to do to repay me. Speaking of which—I have a favor to ask you." *Here goes nothing!* "I'd like to meet Jennifer's family." When Gisabella's face paled, he could tell it was going be an uphill climb to get her to agree to such a thing. "Think about it; what new bride wouldn't want their fiancé to meet her family?"

"'Fiancé?' This is news! I didn't know you'd proposed and that Jennifer had accepted. Well then, if that's the case, I agree. If not, then you can hightail it back to earth and tell your girlfriend—who you've yet to even *kiss*—that if you show yourself to anyone but her, you'll lose your ability to be solid for the next ten years."

"I don't suppose there's any way you'd reconsider?"

"Absolutely not! Josh, you know better than to put me in such a precarious position."

"Of course I do. It's just that Jennifer was so excited that I had try."

"I'll tell you what I can do. Why don't you bring her here on

Christmas Eve at one minute past midnight earth time for a candlelit dinner? I'll see to it that the house is decorated and dinner's prepared."

"I don't suppose we can forgo the dinner part? I don't want you to kill my girlfriend."

"Fine—you can cook the dinner beforehand. With the difference in time between our dimensions, you'll have longer to spend together before you have to bring her back. It'd be a great chance for you to pop the question and finally give Jennifer the ring. Just remember to explain to her that no one but the three of us can see it—otherwise when she tries to show the ring off to her friends, they'll think she's delusional!" Gisabella laughed at her own joke.

"Where exactly will *you* be while all of this is going on?" Josh asked warily.

"Don't worry, I won't be spying or joining you for dinner. I have another home a mile away that I conjured up recently; it has a much better view of the lake and a gourmet kitchen."

Josh reached in his pocket and pulled out a small onyx sphere, studying the surface for a few seconds before replacing it.

"Everything okay?" Gisabella asked with concern.

"Jennifer's parents are out and she's home alone, so I'm keeping an eye on her."

"Maybe you should stop by in person. Women like that sort of thing, you know—a boyfriend who cares about them. The poor girl might need some reminding after the whole 'protector' fiasco." Gisabella cackled loudly when Josh cringed.

"You *have* been spying! Damn it Gisabella—why can't you ever mind your own business?!"

"Where's the fun in that? Watching you and Jennifer has been the most entertainment I've had in centuries. I swear, the two of you are perfect for each other, yet you keep doing everything possible to screw things up. I can't wait to see what happens when you try to give Jennifer the diamond ring; I bet she'll throw it back in your face. If I were you, I'd prepare to duck in case she has good aim."

"*Why* am I friends with you?" Josh quipped.

"Because we're a lot alike and no one else can put up with us. I can't wait until Jennifer marries you and the three of us get together for holidays; you'll bring the girl over so I can celebrate Christmas with the two of you, right? I haven't celebrated a real Christmas in years." Gisabella's eyes sparkled at the thought.

"Sure, why not. What do I have to lose but my dignity and my wife?"

After a second cup of tea Josh was transported by Gisabella back to earth, where he found himself standing in Jennifer's living room—in *solid* form. *This must be Gisabella's idea of a joke. Talk about scaring the poor girl to death.* Before he could leave, Jennifer stirred and opened her eyes.

"I was hoping you'd drop by to say goodnight. How was your meeting?" Jennifer sat up to make room for Josh on the couch. "I must've fallen asleep looking at the tree."

"The meeting went well, even if nothing important was discussed. Do you mind if I join you for a while?"

"Please, sit down. I'd love some company." Jennifer's voice held a touch of loneliness.

"Good, because the whole time I was supposed to be paying attention to Gisabella's speech, I couldn't stop thinking of you." He lifted Jennifer's hand to his lips and kissed it gently.

"Josh, I'm sorry for the terrible things I said to you last week. I don't want you to quit your job. I want you to stay."

"I'm not going anywhere, baby, not without you. Tonight only confirmed to me how much I want you in my life. Jennifer, I wasn't joking when I told you I wanted to marry you. I know we have a long way to go before you'd be willing to accept such an offer; there's a lot for you to consider, but I want you to know how serious I am about you."

"How would that work? Will my family be able to see you? I mean, I know you can't be solid all the time. But tonight you are, and it's not a full moon…"

"I'm afraid your family will never be able to see or meet me. Tonight I asked Gisabella's permission to meet your family, but she refused to give her approval. If I go against her wishes, I won't be solid for ten years. I knew it was a long shot, but I wanted to please you."

"That's horrible! She sounds incredibly mean."

"I know from your point of view it seems that way, but her job is to protect all the dimensions and to keep them separate. She's already given us permission to wed—that is, if you accept my hand. We'd be the first interdimensional marriage ever to take place. By doing so, Gisabella has not only put her job on the line, but her life." Josh noticed the nervous "deer in the headlights" look on Jennifer's face and knew he'd gone too far. *What am I doing? I'm rattling off all sorts of stuff like I'm proposing a business deal. I suck at romance!*

They had two hours alone together before Jennifer's parents came home, so Josh walked over to the stereo and selected Elvis Presley's "I Can't Help Falling in Love" before holding his hand out to her. *It's time to show Jennifer my softer side.*

"I've never danced with anyone before—I mean, well, *slow*-danced with anyone other than my dad. And I stood on his feet, so I don't think that counts," Jennifer babbled nervously.

"Don't worry, I got this." Josh took Jennifer's hand and led her into the middle of the room. "Put this hand in mine and your other hand anywhere on my shoulder or upper back, while I place my free hand on your waist so I have the pleasure of holding you close." Josh noticed Jennifer's heartbeat quicken as some extra color flooded her cheeks. "Now relax and follow my lead." Josh began to move slowly in place at first until Jennifer got the hang of it, before he began leading her around the room. "You're a natural at this—ouch! No harm done," Josh consoled after Jennifer stepped on his foot.

"Sorry about that," she giggled, leaning back in his arms to enjoy the feeling of being spun around and around. Soon her giggle morphed into unstoppable laughter.

Josh took the opportunity to try his hand at singing like Elvis. When the song stopped, so did his feet. He cupped Jennifer's chin and tilted her lips upward, beginning to lower his mouth to capture her sweet, innocent lips with his own—when the front door opened.

"Jennifer! We're home!" Mrs. Parker called out as she entered the house.

"Holy shit! I have to get out of here before your parents see me. I'll message you later," Josh blurted before transporting from the room.

Jennifer stifled another giggle, this time over Josh's petrified expression. *Surely not normal behavior for my strong protector.* Floating on air, she greeted her mom, who was too excited about the party they'd attended to notice anything different about the look on Jennifer's face. *Josh was going to kiss me!*

Later that night Jennifer was in bed replaying their conversation when she heard Josh's voice inside her head.

~Are you asleep?~

~No.~

~Good. I didn't get the chance to invite you to dinner tomorrow night because of your parents' unexpected arrival. Gisabella has promised us the use of her home, and if I pick you up at midnight, I'll have you back before morning.~

~Gisabella's? You're bringing me to heaven?~

~Don't worry, I promise to return you in one piece—even if I'd *like* to keep you there with me forever. Protector obligations and all that.~

~I wasn't worried about you returning me; I was worried about meeting your friend.~

~She's promised to mind her own business, so we shouldn't have any interruptions. Once we're alone, I can finally kiss you.~

~I sure hope so.~

~It's a Christmas Eve date! Now get some rest, baby, and dream of me.~

~Where will you be?~ Jennifer wondered.

~I'll be watching over you from up above.~

~That's nice,~ she said sleepily, unable to keep her eyes opened any longer. ~I love you, Josh.~

~I love you too, Jennifer,~ Josh responded, breaking into a huge, sky-illuminating grin.

CHAPTER FIFTEEN

Jennifer glanced nervously at the clock, then took another look in the mirror and smiled at how sophisticated she looked in her new cobalt dress compared to her usual jeans-and-sweater attire. A hint of blush, mascara, and lip gloss enhanced her features without overpowering them. Out of the corner of her eye, she caught sight of Josh's reflection.

"How long have you been standing behind me?" She tried to hide her excitement about his presence, but her oversized smile gave it away.

"Not long," Josh said quietly. Jennifer's parents were sound asleep and he intended to keep them that way. "Are you ready to go?" He didn't miss Jennifer's worried nod. "Don't be nervous, baby. I assure you, I've done this before and transporting is the safest way to travel between dimensions."

"I trust you." *Now if I could only stop shaking,* Jennifer thought as she looked at the handsome man who claimed to love her. Josh was dressed in charcoal slacks and a black sweater that accented his emerald eyes. For the first time she noticed he was wearing a watch; it had a large face with all sorts of dials and visible inner workings, but before she could ask which time zone it was set for, earth or the other realm, Josh interrupted her musings.

"Do you have everything?"

She reached down for the bag containing his presents and took the hand he offered. "I'm all set," Jennifer said, unsure of what to do next. Josh held her in his arms and looked into her eyes; the combination mesmerized her so much that she never noticed they'd moved out of her dimension and into another realm.

"We're here; that wasn't so bad, was it?" Josh asked.

"I didn't feel a thing." Jennifer looked speechlessly around at her surroundings; she was standing in the foyer of what appeared to be a very large home. To the right was a formal dining room, and in front of her was a curved staircase to the second story, where she surmised the bedrooms were located. Directly in front of her was a family room with an enormous fireplace and a massive mantle decorated with fir branches, pinecones, and candles in varying heights. An enormous tree with glass icicles and faux-feathered birds was tucked in the corner with a plethora of wrapped presents underneath. The whole scene made Jennifer wonder whether Gisabella celebrated the holiday season, or if the decorations were for her own benefit considering it was Christmas on earth.

Jennifer's favorite part of the house was the view out the wall of windows to the majestic mountains and mature pine trees beyond. A leather couch the color of melted caramel called out invitingly, but Jennifer had her eyes on the fur rug in front of the fireplace, hoping it was where they'd exchange their gifts and cuddle after dinner.

"Gisabella's house is lovely," Jennifer commented as she followed Josh into the enormous kitchen.

"I agree, the woman's got great taste. Would you like a glass of wine while I put the finishing touches on our dinner?"

"Please. Where's Gisabella? I know I said I was nervous to meet her, but it'd be nice to see your friend and thank her for making tonight possible."

"She built another house not too far from here."

"'Built?' I remember you mentioning something about people here having houses or castles," Jennifer vaguely recalled.

"Sorry—we call it 'building a house,' when in fact we find or draw the home we want and within a day or two it appears. There are several places people can go if they want to look through house magazines from earth. If you think about it, the whole idea of people here picking out homes designed with bathrooms, garages, and other rooms they'll never use is kind of funny."

"Do they just magically appear?"

"Yep. Each person is allowed one house, but they can opt to change it at anytime. I once heard a story of a man who changed his home once a month." Josh lifted a spoonful of amaretto cherry gravy to his mouth to taste for seasoning. "Try this and see what you think."

"Mmm, that's delicious!"

"Gisabella has a table set up for us outside so we can enjoy the sunset and rising stars. You should be warm enough with the outdoor fireplace." Josh led the way outside and held Jennifer's chair out. When she was seated, he pushed her chair in and kissed the top of her head, then leaned in close and spoke in her ear. "You look so beautiful tonight, and I'm so happy you're here."

"I'm glad to be here too." She was incapable of hiding the breathiness in her voice. Sitting outside under the stars with the man she loved was incredibly romantic, and the closest thing to being in a fairytale she could've ever imagined. Josh soon returned with two plates of delectable-smelling food before sitting opposite Jennifer.

She raised her wine glass for a toast once he'd settled in. "Here's to what an amazing chef you are, and to how lucky I am to be enjoying your culinary talents." It took effort, but somehow she managed to calm her nerves enough to keep from spilling her wine.

"Is everything to your liking?" Josh asked with a glint in his eye after a few minutes of silent eating.

"Everything is delicious." Jennifer's answer earned her an enigmatic smile, as if his question had been referring to something other than the food. There was no way she could ignore the rising sexual tension that crackled between them, or the growing ache blossoming deep within her nether regions. *Breathe, Jennifer,* she remind herself.

Don't forget to save room for dessert. It's a surprise."

"Josh, would you mind if I asked you some rather serious questions about us?" Jennifer mentally ran through the list she'd made earlier in the day.

"You can ask me anything," Josh reassured.

"You've mentioned marriage a couple of times, but I'm not sure how all that will work between us. I obviously have very strong feelings of love for you and would like to see where this leads, but I need to know more."

"What would you like to know?" Josh asked cautiously, leaning back in his chair. To the common observer Josh looked the epitome of confidence—it was a strategy he'd always used to camouflage his uncertainty.

Jennifer took two large gulps of wine and let the dark, fruity liquid warm her throat before she began. "If you're not able to meet my parents or my friends, then I assume no one will know we're married. Where will we live? Will you be my protector *and* my husband, or will someone else be assigned to watch over me?" She stopped speaking when she saw how pale Josh had become. *That's not a good sign.*

"Jennifer, what I'm asking of you won't be an easy decision. For our safety and Gisabella's, our marriage must be kept a secret, meaning only three of us will ever know about our union. I'd remain your protector and teacher, and, if you agree, I'd be honored to be your husband. In the beginning we would need to live at your parents' until we're able to afford a place." Josh's stomach clenched over how bad it all sounded. "My access to earthly money is very limited, as I'm not paid in earthly dollars to be a protector—it's the kind of job that comes with other benefits. In my dimension, I'm established and would be able to provide you with anything your heart desires. Not that I don't have *some* earthly money, but not enough to sustain us for long." *I sound like a horrible catch!*

Though it wasn't the answer she'd hoped for, Jennifer loved Josh too much to let such things stand in her way. After another sip of wine, she forced herself to ask the question she most feared. "Do you want children? I don't mean right away—I'd like to finish college first. Then I can get a job and we can find an apartment near where I work. I always thought two was a nice number…what about you?"

Josh paused long enough to finish his wine before addressing the hardest question Jennifer could've asked. "Since we're from two different dimensions, it's impossible for us to reproduce; this has been the case since the beginning of time. No spirit can impregnate or be impregnated by someone alive on earth." He tried his best to answer Jennifer's question honestly, without any influx of emotion, so as not to sway her from the cold, hard facts.

Jennifer's eyes filled with moisture. Josh had answered all her questions, but the answers didn't sound as appealing as she'd expected. *No one would know about us. We'd have no privacy living at my parents' house. We can never have a baby.*

Josh lowered his eyes. What had once seemed like a way to be with the woman he loved now appeared cruel and heartless. *I can't do this to Jennifer—trap her in an eight-year marriage with nothing to show for it but two broken hearts when she's forced to marry someone else. I have to let her go; it's the right thing to do.* "I'm sorry Jennifer, this is too much to ask of you. I don't have the right to make you give up so many things while I have everything to gain. It's not fair to tie you down to such an impossible life with me."

"Are you withdrawing your marriage proposal? Not that you've *officially* asked me… Come to think of it, I kicked you out the first time you blurted out that you fell in love."

"I want to marry you more than anything, but look at us; you're so young, and have your entire life ahead of you. All I have to offer is my love and commitment. What kind of life could I possibly give you? Hell, I can't even bring you to my apartment, because as a protector I'm in danger at all times. Not to mention how being married to me would put you at an even *higher* risk considering you're a visionary."

"So you're giving up? Let me get this straight—you made me fall in love and now you're pushing me away because you think you don't have enough to offer? Well isn't this *fucking* wonderful! I don't know what's more messed up; you, or the fact you don't think I'm strong enough to work things out."

"Watch your language, missy."

"Just *what* do you intend to do about it? Threaten me with some 'arbitrary protector' kind of punishment and then change your mind?" Jennifer spat out the words and then froze in place from the expression on Josh's face. The only sound was her angry gasps for air, and the tension between them could've been cut by a dull knife.

"Would you like some dessert?" Josh asked coolly, pushing back his chair.

"This isn't fair to either of us!" Jennifer shouted. The realization of possibly losing the man she loved sunk in, and she began to battle harder.

"What's the rush? Can't we try being engaged for six months and see how things go?"

"Jennifer, you don't understand." Josh stood and ran his hand through his hair.

"What aren't you telling me? I know you're keeping something from me," Jennifer accused.

"When I approached Gisabella and told her how I'd fallen in love and wanted to marry you, she told me I was crazy. After a lot of convincing on my part, she made me a deal: that if we married by February fourteenth, she'd perform the ceremony and approve our union. In doing so, she'd be going against the endocrine laws and the council and putting herself in grave danger."

"I take it you agreed to her offer?" Even as she asked, Jennifer already knew the answer. Keeping her voice low and subdued, she continued. "What *else* did you get out of this trade besides me?"

"Nothing—honest. I asked that you be allowed to fall in love without any trickery or spells."

"So you didn't give Gisabella anything else in return for her cooperation?" *The fourteenth?! That's in a month! I feel sick....*

"Besides the date we must marry, Gisabella's stipulations weren't too bad. Our marriage must be consummated for it to be legal, and I won't be allowed to interfere in your life-path."

"What does the last part mean—'life-path?'" Jennifer asked suspiciously. Even without meeting Gisabella, there was something about Josh's friend that she didn't trust.

"It means I can't alter or change the things in your life that are mandatory lessons. While you're alive I can change many things in your life, but I cannot interfere with your overall destiny."

"What does my destiny hold?"

"I don't know. Gisabella has your paperwork."

"So *that's* what you meant when you said you'd be gone soon! You promised you would never leave me! Apparently that's only true if I marry you by February fourteenth?! Josh, what have you done?" Jennifer choked out.

"I'm to be replaced on the fifteenth of February," Josh said somberly, his voice thick with remorse.

"So that's it? If I don't marry you by then, I'll never see you again?"

"I'm sorry, Jennifer; that was the deal."

"And now you've withdrawn your proposal, meaning you've resigned yourself to leaving," Jennifer said, fighting back the tears that threatened to overflow.

"I'd do anything to turn back the clock and change the terms so we'd have more time, but it wouldn't change who we are or the fact I have so little to offer you."

"Don't you get it? The reasons you listed don't matter as much as being married to you. As for Gisabella's timeline, I don't like how rushed it is, but if that's what you agreed to, then I guess we have to follow it. Do you still want to marry me?"

"Yes, more than anything—but it's not the right thing to do."

"So you made your decision." Jennifer shoved her chair back and stood. "Then we have nothing left to talk about."

"I'll take you home." Josh forced himself to appear indifferent so Jennifer wouldn't know how much pain she was causing at the thought of losing her. *How could I have imagined I deserved Jennifer's love?*

Once alone in her bedroom, Jennifer collapsed on her bed and gave in to the agony of their separation.

Back in the other realm, Gisabella gazed into her crystal ball only to find that Josh and Jennifer *weren't* together in each other's arms like she'd hoped. Now *what have you done, Josh? This will never do—I guess if I want my plan to work, I'll have to handle everything myself. Josh will thank me later, after he finds out how much Jennifer means to me.*

CHAPTER SIXTEEN

"Merry Christmas!" Sarah yelled excitedly, bounding into Jennifer's room. "It's after ten in the morning—don't think you're getting out of helping me cook brunch."

"Please go away," Jennifer begged, pulling the covers over her head.

"What's wrong?"

"Nothing." *I wish I could tell Sarah everything. But even if I could, she'd never believe me.* "My head's killing me."

"Do you want some aspirin?"

"Can you tell Mom I have a migraine and won't be down for breakfast or church?"

"I'll be right back."

"Thank you." Jennifer grabbed a handful of tissues and pulled the blanket over her head. She stayed that way the entire day, hoping no one would notice her red, puffy eyes or the growing pile of tissues that'd overflowed onto the floor. She'd received several unwelcome messages from Josh, finally discovering that the same wall used to block him from reading her thoughts could also block his incoming messages. With enough concentration, she was able to make the wall so huge that even her elite protector couldn't penetrate it.

There was nothing left to say now that Josh had made it clear he'd never marry her. If he'd found someone else or no longer loved her she could've accepted his rejection, but his reasons only left her with more questions, especially since he'd be forced to leave in less than two months' time. With no hope of a different outcome, Jennifer buried her face into her pillow and surrendered to the dark abyss of her exhausted, broken heart.

Two hours later, Jennifer was awakened by a persistent knock at the door. *Go away,* she thought, trying to ignore the repetitive thumping until the door opened.

"How do you feel?" Sarah asked.

"Not good."

"Maybe this will cheer you up." Sarah walked over to the bed with a present wrapped in gold foil and a red bow. "I found this on the front porch; it's addressed to you. Looks like you have a secret admirer."

"Please put it on the desk. I'll open it later."

"I told Mom and Dad to leave you alone and let you rest."

"I owe you. Mom never did understand PMS," Jennifer said, attempting to hide the real reason for her tears.

"Judging by the pile of tissues on the floor and not running to open your presents, I'd say it's more than PMS. You can't fool me; it's not like you to lock yourself in your room, and you rarely cry. Move over," Sarah commanded, shooing Jennifer to the other end of the bed.

"This reminds me of when I was five and you used to pretend you were my mommy," Jennifer sniffed, allowing Sarah to cradle her.

"You were such a little thing back then—what happened?!" Sarah teased. "I think it's time to get you a normal-sized bed; don't your feet hang off the end?" Sarah brushed the hair out of Jennifer's face and used a tissue to wipe her sister's tears. "Do you want to talk about it? Whatever it is, I guarantee it'll be easier to handle once you do. If it has anything to do with boyfriend troubles, I can help you. Lord knows I've had my share of heartaches."

"Thank you, Sarah—that means a lot. I'll be okay; I just need a day or two to get my head together."

"All right. But I'm here if you need me, and anything you say *will* remain between us. I won't even send you a bill," Sarah joked.

"Glad to know your services are so cheap." Jennifer's sardonic comment was followed up with a fit of much-needed giggles. Once they'd subsided, she drifted off to sleep in Sarah's arms.

"Jennifer, get up! You're gonna miss the ball drop!" Mrs. Parker called from downstairs.

It was Sunday, December thirty-first, and the last ten minutes of 1978 were ticking goodbye. Jennifer climbed out of bed and looked at the present that'd been sitting on her desk for the last seven days. She didn't need to read the attached card to know who it was from, nor had she bothered to shake or unwrap it. *I wonder if Josh opened his gifts from me.* The thought was unwelcome; if he had, then he'd have known that she'd given him all of her love and her heart. She pushed the notion away and pulled on her robe, heading downstairs in search of more ice cream and to join the others to watch the ball drop. It was an annual tradition which, according to her parents, hadn't been the same since Guy Lombardo had died.

Tuesday, January second, 1979 arrived, bringing an end to the holiday break. Despite all of Jennifer's prayers for a gigantic snowstorm to cancel school, the sun shone brightly, and all hope of avoiding Josh was lost. *I wonder what he'll do if I try to block his messaging in person?* Her stomach knotted; she hadn't seen or spoken to him in nine days, and wasn't sure what to expect. She had little doubt Josh would be waiting to walk her to school. As much as she longed to see him, the thought was unbearable. She eyed the unopened present from him and considered returning it, but decided she didn't feel like starting the morning off with an argument.

Her heart was aching when she opened the door and walked down the steps to where Josh stood waiting.

~Jennifer, I…~

~Please don't!~ Jennifer held up her hand before Josh could continue. ~If you tell me you're sorry again or how much better off I'll be without you, I'm going to start crying. And I don't have any more strength left for tears.~ She'd heard plenty of both from him before blocking his messages completely several days prior, so with her head held high, she did her best to avoid Josh's eyes as she walked past.

~I understand,~ Josh messaged, falling silently in step next to her.

He spent the rest of that day and six more doing his best to respect Jennifer's wishes. On the seventh day, when they reached Jennifer's house, he could no longer keep quiet.

~May I come in? I need to speak to you in private.~ Josh hoped his firm tone would convince Jennifer to invite him inside.

~There's not much left to say; you no longer wish to marry me and you'll be gone February fifteenth.~ Jennifer had never been more thankful for messaging, as it spared her from saying the painful words out loud.

~Jennifer, can we please continue our conversation inside instead of here in plain view?~ Josh pleaded.

~Fine.~ Jennifer stomped over to the couch and plopped down, tight-lipped and glaring.

~I met with Gisabella last night and told her how being here as your protector is upsetting you.~

~You did *what*? How could you do such a thing? Now you'll be leaving sooner?!~

~I thought it was better than making you suffer for another five weeks with me.~

~You *would* think so,~ Jennifer messaged while gazing into eyes that were a mirror image of the pain she was feeling.

~Gisabella gave me a list of things I need to teach you before I'm replaced.~ Josh shifted his eyes away from her brimming ones. He hated himself for each one of the teardrops he'd caused. *I'm officially the universes' biggest ass!*

~Why don't you tell her to go jump off a bridge!~ *This is all her fault!*

~If you don't mind, I think it's better if I refrain from saying that to my boss—I'm in enough trouble already. Promise me you'll at least try to work with me here, because you should know this stuff.~

~Don't expect me to be happy about it.~

~Why don't we start with something easy, like a game of energy hide and seek?~ Josh suggested hopefully.

"You want to *play a game?!*" Jennifer shouted, forgoing all messaging protocol in favor of berating Josh; it was far more satisfying to shout at him out loud. "First of all, I'm not exactly in a playful mood, secondly, I have a ton of homework, and thirdly, my head is pounding, so if it's all the same to *you* I think I'll go lie down. Maybe I'll be in the mood for one of your 'games' at the end of the month. Why don't you catch up with me then?"

~Jennifer, wait, it's…~ Josh called after the retreating figure running up the stairs. ~Okay then, I'll try again tomorrow.~

Ten days later, they'd reached the end of another week and things between them had only gotten worse. Each time Josh tried to bring up teaching Jennifer more lessons, she had a new excuse—and it wasn't the only issue frustrating him. The new year had brought several unpleasant changes with it, and perhaps the most irritating to Josh was the plethora of attention Jennifer was suddenly receiving from other men.

Josh was walking silently next to Jennifer when he noticed the green Mustang driving by for the third time. As it circled for the fourth time and slowed, his eyes narrowed and his temper flared. When the college-bound male beeped and waved, he saw matador-red. He'd watched the same driver checking Jennifer out three out of the last five days, and today Jennifer waved back!

~What the hell do you call that?!~ Josh could no longer hold back his anger or stop himself from wishing he could lock Jennifer away in her room. Since the night he'd withdrawn his proposal his protectiveness had grown tenfold, and nowadays it didn't take much to fray his nerves. Most of his nerve-splintering resulted in any hint of testosterone getting within twenty feet of Jennifer, which had begun to happen several times a day. It was as if she'd begun wearing a neon sign saying "*available girl!*" Lately he'd witnessed male classmates trying to catch Jennifer's eye, guys in cars offering her rides, and even many of her brother's friends talking to her. It was only a matter of time before one of them asked Jennifer out, and he shuddered when he thought about how he'd react to someone trying to move in on the woman he still loved.

~I was being neighborly,~ Jennifer answered.

~That guy doesn't live anywhere near your neighborhood,~ Josh growled.

~Did you just growl at me?~ If she wasn't so upset with him, she'd have found his growling *hot.*

~What do you expect when you're waving at strange men and acting as if I'm invisible?~

~I wouldn't be waving if you hadn't broken up with me,~ Jennifer retorted as she headed into school, leaving Josh to stand alone.

What am I going to do? I only have thirty-three more days before my time with Jennifer ends. How am I going to leave her?

Chapter Seventeen

"I can't believe I'm getting married tomorrow!" Sarah shouted excitedly in Jennifer's direction. "Is *that* your lunch—ice cream? I haven't seen you eat anything but ice cream for weeks." Sarah eyed Jennifer up and down critically. "When was the last time you ate a real meal?"

"I eat other things beside this stuff," Jennifer said, holding up a spoonful of pistachio.

"Look at you; I swear you're two sizes smaller! *Now* what am I gonna do? I warned you not to change your size; your bridesmaid dress is never gonna look right!"

"What are you talking about? I haven't lost weight." *Have I?* Jennifer hadn't had much of an appetite the past few weeks.

"If you didn't have hip bones, those pants would be around your ankles. So help me, Jennifer, if you don't tell me what's going this minute, I'm gonna tell Mom!"

"Please don't."

"Then start talking." Sarah crossed her arms expectantly.

"It's nothing, really," Jennifer stalled. *I can't tell her the truth.*

"Not good enough. I need more than that to keep my mouth shut."

"I like this boy and I thought he liked me, but then I found out he was only being nice because he felt sorry for me." Jennifer left out the details and how Josh would be gone after Valentine's Day.

"Are you sure he's not interested in you? Boys don't pretend to like a girl to spare their feelings, or give them a Christmas present." Sarah pointed towards the still-unopened package.

"He told me in no uncertain terms that he's not interested in a relationship."

"Look—I know at the moment it feels like it's the end of the world, but I promise that someday you'll find a boy who's crazy about you."

"I hope you're right." *I can't imagine falling in love with anyone other than Josh.*

"In the meantime, let's get some real food in you so you don't pass out during my wedding. Honestly—I've never seen you so broken up before."

"You're right! If he doesn't want me, there are plenty of other fish in the sea!" Jennifer vowed.

"You must be worse than I thought; you're quoting Mom! I think I'd better order us some pizza. We can spend my last night as a single woman hanging out."

"That sounds like fun." Jennifer brightened and hugged her sister. "I'm so happy for you and Dave. You're going to make a beautiful bride, and someday a wonderful mother," Jennifer said, managing to keep her emotions in check.

Gisabella summoned Josh to her home before dawn. She'd had enough of Josh and Jennifer mucking things up, and had devised a plan to put a stop to it all. Now she just hoped that Josh loved Jennifer enough to fight for her.

"Your Excellency, how nice to see you," Josh said, playing his losing hand like a card-shark with a gun to his head. There was no mistaking the anger in Gisabella's eyes or the frown lines gathered next to her downturned lips. "To what do I owe the pleasure?" Even *he* had to look away from her penetrating glare.

Two can play this game! Gisabella avoided the temptation to lash out at her friend in favor of a different kind of punishment. "I was straightening up when I noticed two unopened gifts sitting under the Christmas tree."

"Leave them," Josh snarled.

"You have to open your gifts from Jennifer; you can't ignore them forever." Gisabella pointed her finger in their direction.

"I'll take them with me," Josh said, doing his best to brush her off.

Unfortunately, her response was a "classic Gisabella" one. "You're *not* leaving here until you open them!" she roared.

With no other option available, Josh unwrapped the first box that contained an engraved ornament of a couple skating. With a lump in his throat he unwrapped the second present, pulling out a heart-shaped frame with Jennifer's photo inside. It was the inscription etched on the frame that gave him the answer he'd once hoped to hear:

Josh, I love you and my answer is yes!

With all my love,
Jennifer

He read the words twice before looking to Gisabella for guidance.

"Are you just going to let her go?"

"What other choice do I have? I can't give Jennifer the life she deserves."

"You mean a life with a man who loves her so much that he's willing to sacrifice his happiness because he thinks it will help her? Have you given any thought to what *Jennifer* wants? From my perspective, all you're concerned about is what you can't give Jennifer and not how much you *can* give her."

"It would be selfish of me to lock her into a temporary commitment until her life-path husband comes along. I can't imagine how hard it will be for us to say goodbye then."

"So you think breaking Jennifer's heart now instead of enjoying years of happiness together is the right thing to do? Why don't you go and ask the girl who cries herself to sleep every night which option she'd prefer? You might be surprised by her answer."

"But Jennifer wants children, and that's not an option with me," Josh said bitterly.

"Is *that* what's stopping you? Jennifer will have plenty of time for children with her life-path husband." The look on Josh's face redirected her argument. "So, this *isn't* about Jennifer…it's about you. I had no idea you wanted to be a father."

"I don't—I mean, I *didn't* until I saw the look in Jennifer's eyes. She loves me more than I deserve, and when she asked about having a baby with me, I couldn't continue. Gisabella, I've never loved anyone the way I love Jennifer; so much so that for the first time, I can envision myself as a husband and a father with her by my side."

Gisabella reached over and clasped his hand. "Please don't give up years of happiness with Jennifer because you wish for something that can never be; if you do, I know you'll regret it for all eternity. Jennifer's a wonderful girl who loves you with all her heart, and needs your protector skills and guidance. I'd hoped you'd be the one to train her; she responds well to your methods. As you can tell, she can be a bit of a challenge—"

"To teach?" Josh interrupted. "You got that right!" For the first time since arriving in Gisabella's home, Josh's lips quirked into a smile. "If I choose to follow your advice, do you think Jennifer will agree to marry me?"

"Why don't you ask her yourself? But you'd better do it before I hire your replacement. I interviewed two protectors who are capable of doing a good job with Jennifer, but I'm leaning towards Lawrence. I think she'll respond to him better than Gabriel, although I'm not too sure about Lawrence's reputation with the ladies."

"That Apollo look-a-like fucker? Are you *nuts*?! He'll spend the entire time trying to get into Jennifer's panties! How could you do that to her? She wouldn't stand a chance against that playboy!"

"What other choice do I have? I need a quick replacement, and even though Lawrence is in a lower squad, he's the strongest protector available."

"If he's so great, why isn't he part of your elite group?"

"He's had a few minor infractions that have held him back. But once he's proven how well he can handle your former charge, I'll see to it he stands on stage with you."

"'With me?' What the hell do you mean by that?"

"I'd rather hoped you would complete your assignment, but it seems that you let your personal feelings get in the way of doing your job. You need to step aside."

"Wait a minute—you gave me until February fourteenth to marry Jennifer."

"That was before you messed things up and broke her heart. If you're not going to marry the girl then it's time to let her go; doing anything less than setting Jennifer free would be cruel. You have until tomorrow night to make your decision—otherwise Lawrence will be assigned as her new protector."

"Tomorrow night?! That's too soon. You can't just renege on our deal."

"I know you think I'm being heartless, but I assure you it's for the best."

Before Josh was able to say another word, he found himself standing in his apartment. ~I wasn't done talking to you!~ When Gisabella didn't respond, his anger boiled over.

Fuck, fuck, fuck! I can't believe Gisabella pulled this shit! Lawrence? Of all the fucking dirt-bags—I can't believe she thinks he's good enough to be anywhere near my woman. So help me if that pecker hurts Jennifer, I'll cut off his balls and hang him up by his dick. It'd be far better than he deserves!

Josh kicked his way past stacks of files, sending them crashing to the floor as he went to the kitchen. It was the only place that'd help to calm his temper enough to think. Once there, he began opening and slamming cabinet doors and the fridge, sending a wine glass or two shattering to the floor in lieu of a large goblet. Next he headed over to the liquor cabinet and pulled out a bottle of twenty-year-old brandy. *Holy hell—this fucking bottle is older than Jennifer! What the hell am I thinking? What could she possibly see in me, a soon-to-be washed-up protector with nothing to offer her but my heart?* He poured out the golden-colored contents until the glass was full to the brim, then chugged half of it in a few gulps. The liquid blazed a trail from his lips to his stomach, where it sloshed around in his gut like hot lava.

An eighteen-year-old girl. How in the world did an innocent eighteen-year-old ensnare me in her web? An hour later, Josh reached for the bottle and poured the remaining few drops into his glass. *Jennifer, Jennifer, lovely sweet Jennifer—will you be my wife? "No," you say, "you have nothing to offer." Well you're damn right—I don't! The only thing I have to offer is my heart. Either way, yes or no, it's yours. I love you, Jennifer. Please be mine…* The bottle slid out of his hand just as his eyes rolled back, giving him the first few moments of peace since Jennifer had been thrown off her horse.

The next morning was Saturday, January thirteenth, 1979, and it arrived with blustering snow flurries and whiptail winds. The unexpected winter storm made it hard for Jennifer to keep her peach-colored hat in place as she followed Sarah and Dave from the limo into the reception hall.

Jennifer had been dreading that day, and it was as horrible as she'd imagined. The worst part was when Sarah and Dave exchanged their wedding vows; each speech was overflowing with love, and was in many ways what Jennifer herself wished she could say to Josh. She'd waited for him to approach the topic or give her a sign that he still wanted to marry her, but none had come.

Their separation had also taken a toll on Josh, who hadn't laughed in weeks. His eyes had lost their sparkle, darkening to a permanent shade of dull, dark charcoal.

"I miss you," Jennifer whispered once inside the building, but her pitiful cry went unanswered. She was thankful for the hideous-looking hat with netting that her sister had picked, as it hid her face well. The night before she and Sarah had stayed up until midnight, talking and laughing over all the silly things they'd done as kids. After today Sarah wouldn't be around much except for holidays and an occasional visit, adding to Jennifer's misery about Josh's departure in less than five weeks. The thought of losing both of them caused a few tears to escape, and Jennifer dashed to the ladies' room to fix her makeup and blot her eyes. With the sinks taken she was forced to use the full-length mirror on the wall, and Jennifer was stunned when she glimpsed the skinny, ashen girl before her.

It had been three weeks since their Christmas Eve dinner, and since then a constant lump in her throat had become the norm and she couldn't bring herself to eat anything but ice cream. *Sarah's right—I need to get over Josh; if he still wanted to marry me, he'd have asked by now.*

"There you are, Jennifer," Mrs. Parker exclaimed upon entering the ladies' room. "Hurry up, the photographer is trying to take photos of the wedding party. For goodness' sake, can't you at least put a smile on your face? I don't know what's gotten into you lately."

"I'll be right there." Jennifer pulled the netting down and left to join the others.

Josh watched the woman he loved fake a smile in the wedding photos, and it was one of the saddest things he'd ever seen. The last three weeks he'd been forced to watch Jennifer fade away to a vague, empty shell of the girl he'd once known. He hated to admit it, but Gisabella had a point; dragging out his departure until Valentine's Day was cruel. Too bad Gisabella'd made it clear that Lawrence was to be his replacement. Good old love-'em-and-leave-'em Lawrence—minus the love part.

Unaware of being watched, Jennifer picked at the frosting on her slice of cake while couples danced and held each other tightly under paper wedding bells. A detached, ironic smirk occupied her lips when she noticed that she was the only one seated at the head table, while all of the others were on the dance floor. *Will this day ever end?*

"May I have this dance?"

Not again, Jennifer cringed. She'd already turned away three other "sympathy offers" and had no desire to dance with anyone—*except Josh.* Her heart clenched at the thought, and she had every intention of turning down the man whose shoes looked so shiny they must've been purchased that day. Even when her eyes drifted up the man's perfectly pressed trousers, she wrote off the feeling that she knew him. It wasn't until she saw his gorgeous, tan hands and the watch he was wearing that her heartbeat sped up.

"I'm..." Jennifer's words caught in her throat when she looked up and saw the man she loved gazing down at her with a huge smile.

"It's a full moon, baby," Josh said by way of explanation, taking her hand to lead her to the middle of the dance floor.

"But what about Gisabella's warning? If you get caught, you can't become solid for another ten years!"

"What good is being solid without the woman I love?"

"I guess it's the same as being alive without the man I love."

"Sounds like we need to talk—but first, I'd like to meet your parents."

"You would? How should I introduce you?"

"As Joshua Smith. By the way, I hope you like the last name Gisabella gave me—because if your Christmas present means you still love me, then I want to marry you more than ever. Darling, I was a fool to push you away. If you'll forgive me, I promise to spend every moment of our time together making it up to you."

A couple of happy tears trickled down Jennifer's cheeks only to be kissed away by Josh.

"Jennifer, you're killing me here. Please tell me you'll consider being my wife, even with all the pitfalls I bring to our marriage."

"With such a romantic proposal, how can I refuse?"

"I'll let you in on a secret—I have a more romantic proposal in mind for later tonight once we're alone," Josh whispered. "Now take me to your parents, woman."

"Right this way, Mr. Smith." Jennifer led Josh to the table where her parents were, never once letting his hand go. When they'd reached her parents' table, her excitement over Josh's in-the-flesh surprise bubbled over. "Hi Mom and Dad! I have someone I'd like you to meet." Jennifer turned to Josh with love in her eyes. "This is my friend, Joshua Smith. Josh, these are my parents, Claire and Theodore Parker.

"It's a pleasure to meet you, Mr. and Mrs. Parker. Congratulations on the marriage of your daughter," Josh said, releasing Jennifer's hand to shake Mr. Parker's. He hadn't missed Jennifer's fidgeting at the mentioning of their eldest daughter's marriage. *It's not like I said "both" daughters.*

"Joshua, is it? I don't recall Jennifer ever mentioning your name," Mrs. Parker said, eyeing Josh up and down appraisingly.

Please don't give him a hard time, Mom, not when we're so happy.

"That's understandable, Mrs. Parker. I've been away at school, and during the Christmas break I was doing an internship abroad in a small province that had no phones."

Mrs. Parker turned to Jennifer with a smile. "It's a shame Joshua couldn't have joined us for Christmas dinner."

"I assure you it was my loss," Josh volleyed, reclaiming Jennifer's hand. "Maybe next time."

"What are you studying, Josh?" Mr. Parker chimed in.

"I was pursuing a bachelor's in molecular genetics, but when I found that I could have a better future as an engineer, I decided to study abroad in Italy where there's a growing need for specialized historical building engineers. I expect to finish my master's degree by the end of next year and have received several job offers." Josh did his best to sound like a student with a solid future.

"Really? That sounds like an interesting field. Must be awesome to study ancient buildings in Rome," Mr. Parker said, smiling at the idea.

"Yes sir, it is, and being in Italy gives me a chance to take in the culture and all the fascinating art."

"*Now* you sound like our daughter," Mrs. Parker said, not bothering to hide her disdain for the arts. "Jennifer and her art—honestly, it all seems like a waste of time to me."

"With Jennifer's passion and talent, I bet she could get a scholarship to a top school in the U.S. or even abroad. There's a need for talented artists to work with the government restoring famous works of art," Josh explained. "They only hire the finest people, and they'd snap Jennifer up in a heartbeat."

"You think Jennifer would be able to support herself with such a career?" Mrs. Parker asked.

"Definitely. She might not be rich, but she could support herself. Anyway, what's wealth when you're forced to do something you don't like?" Josh kept a blank expression when Mrs. Parker gaped at his none-too-subtle comment.

"That's what I've been trying to tell Claire," Mr. Parker chimed in once more. "Art has its own rewards, doesn't it, pumpkin?"

"Yes Daddy," Jennifer beamed, feeling for once like she had someone on *her* side. When her mother's expression soured, she changed the subject. "Josh is being too modest about his accomplishments. In truth, he has the most amazing voice and has studied with several opera coaches," Jennifer said, playing along even though she wasn't sure whether *that* part was fact or fiction. "Haven't you honey?" *Great! Now I have two sour lemon faces staring at me—Mom's* and *Josh's!*

"Please do us the honor of singing something!" Mrs. Parker gushed.

"If you're sure no one will mind, I'd be honored to dedicate a song to the lovely bride and her groom," Josh said, turning his attention to Jennifer with a heated gaze. ~What do you suggest I sing, my love?~

Yikes, who knew such a bland message could hold such irritation? ~You could always sing "Ave Maria" or another one of your favorites.~ Jennifer sent her message with the sweetest inflection she could muster, hoping he'd oblige her with a softer look than the one currently occupying his face.

~As you wish.~ "I would be honored to sing a special love song for the new bride," Josh offered, squeezing Jennifer's hand meaningfully.

"How wonderful of you," Mrs. Parker beamed. "I'll go make an announcement!" She hurried off to the microphone and commanded everyone's attention. "I'm excited to announce that Jennifer's date, Joshua, is a trained opera singer from Italy and has offered to sing for us." A round of applause erupted.

"Be thankful I love you," Josh whispered in Jennifer's ear before making his way to the stage and consulting with the piano player.

Jennifer smiled nervously at Josh. *Now what have I done? Oh right, I brought everyone's attention to my future husband, one who's not supposed to interact with the living!*

Sarah and Dave were called to the dance floor, joined by a slightly nervous Jennifer, Mr. and Mrs. Parker, and the remaining bridal party.

"I'd like to dedicate this song to the happy couple," Josh said with a nod to Sarah and Dave. ~And to the woman I love,~ Josh messaged with a wink.

The room was full of chatter as people mingled, but all went silent as Josh began singing "If Ever I Would Leave You." It was a song Lancelot had drilled into his head during one of their "full moon" outings centuries before.

Jennifer bit her lip to keep it from quivering. *Talk about that man being the center of my universe.* Like before, she took the opportunity to study Josh in solid form as he sang. *If he doesn't kiss me tonight, I'll scream.* When he was done, she joined the others in a jubilant round of applause.

"Thank you for singing at our wedding," Dave said, holding his hand out to shake Josh's.

"Congratulations to you both. Sarah, may I say what a pleasure it is to finally meet you. Your sister speaks highly of you," Josh added.

"Thank you, Josh. It's nice to see my baby sister so happy," Sarah said. "If you could excuse us for a moment—we'll be right back." Sarah pulled Jennifer away to talk privately.

"Sarah, please, stop pulling so hard!" Jennifer said as her sister's long, manicured nails dug into her forearm.

"I just want to make sure everything's all right between you and Mr. Drop Dead Dreamboat! He's the one who left you the Christmas present, isn't he? " Sarah asked and Jennifer nodded. "I can see why you've been so upset!"

"It's not like that. Sure, Josh is good-looking, but he's so much more; he's smart, funny, kindhearted, and he can sing!" Jennifer gushed.

"You don't have to explain; I can see it all over your face. In case you didn't know, that man's in love with you *big time!*"

"You think so?" Jennifer played dumb.

"I'd bet my life on it. The best part is seeing you smile." Sarah scooped Jennifer into a hug and gave her a kiss on the cheek. "I love you, sis! When Dave and I get back, you and your man should come and visit. I wish I could've seen the look on Mom's face when you brought Josh over to her," Sarah giggled. "She must've been shocked…you landed such a keeper! What in the world will she do for entertainment now that she doesn't have anyone left to play matchmaker with?"

Jennifer rolled her eyes. *Too bad after today no one will be able to see Josh or know that we're married. Sarah's right; how in the world am I going to stave off Mom and her matchmaking attempts?*

They stayed for a few more dances and watched Sarah toss the bridal bouquet, one that was fought over by Jennifer's many cousins. Jennifer giggled as the women dove for the bouquet like it was a football during the Super Bowl's final remaining quarter.

"There's a sound I've missed," Josh said, holding her tightly against him. "When can you leave?"

"Now, I guess—we had cake!" Jennifer tried to act like she wasn't affected by Josh's nearness, but her body was having a difference of opinion.

"Yes, I noticed how quickly you ate your piece and how you were eyeing mine," Josh joked. "Seriously baby, it's nice to see you eat something."

"What can I say? My appetite returned the moment I saw you."

"My appetite for you has never faltered," Josh said quietly, his eyes fixed on hers. "Now let's say goodbye to your family so we can go somewhere private and talk."

"Mom, Josh and I are leaving now," Jennifer yelled over the loud music.

"Okay. It was nice meeting you, Josh." After a brief pause Mrs. Parker added, "I'm not sure how far you have to drive, but you're welcome to spend the night on our couch."

"Thank you for your generosity. I may take you up on your offer."

"Are you two leaving?" Mr. Parker asked, joining the group.

"Yes, Daddy."

"My wife's right—feel free to spend the night at our house."

"Thank you, Mr. Parker. I'll see you both later then. Jennifer, do you have a coat?"

"I'm all set." With one hand in Josh's, she waved goodbye with her free hand as they left the noisy banquet hall.

CHAPTER EIGHTEEN

Josh led Jennifer outside to a secluded area, where he then transported them both to her house.

"I'm not sure how much time we have before Gisabella summons me," Josh said, doing his best to sound calm.

"Please don't tell me she'll make things worse for you than she's already threatened. I can live without you being solid, Josh, but I can't live without you."

"She's usually fair—but in this case, I'm not sure what she'll do. Don't worry, it's not like she'll send me away forever or anything." *I hope.* When Jennifer's face fell, it occurred to him that she'd seen through his attempt to sound positive. "Please don't let her ruin our moment, darling." Josh reached into the inside pocket of his suit and pulled out the small blue box that he'd been holding onto, before bending down on one knee.

"Jennifer, my love, I..." Josh began, then stopped.

She waited for Josh to finish his sentence, but nothing happened. *What now?* Her worried thoughts expanded when Josh's expression changed and he rose to his feet. "What's wrong?" Jennifer asked, unable to mask her worry.

"I received a message from Gisabella—she wants to see me right away. I'm sorry, Jennifer. I wanted this night to be perfect for you and I, but if I refuse she said I'll be demoted and removed from your side immediately. In case I don't return for a while, I want you to hold on to this." Josh handed her the blue box. "We are the only ones besides Gisabella who can see what's inside this box. Above all you must keep it and our love a secret; if the council were to ever find out about us, our lives would be in danger."

"Couldn't Gisabella give us a couple more hours?"

"Don't worry, I promise to be back as soon as I can. And when I return, I'll place what's in that box on your finger and speak the words that are in my heart." Josh cupped Jennifer's face with his hands and kissed her lightly on the cheek.

"Please don't leave me." Jennifer threw her arms around Josh's neck and buried her face in his chest.

"I should've kissed you weeks ago when I had the chance. Maybe if I had, we'd be married by now and none of this would've happened," Josh said in retrospect.

"Then kiss me now, so if you don't return I'll have the memory of your lips on mine." She forced herself not to cry as she looked up at the man to whom she'd given her heart.

He, too, needed the memory of her lips on his, so Josh cupped Jennifer's chin with his hand and lowered his mouth to hers. Her lips tasted as sweet as he'd imagined, and holding Jennifer in his arms became everything and more. The sparks they created were finally allowed to flame, and neither of them held back. There was no time for pretenses, and for the first time in centuries, his heart and soul were satisfied.

Josh's lips on hers awakened all of Jennifer's senses, and in her mind, it was the first and last kiss that would ever matter. His kiss started out soft and tender but, once heated, deepened into one she'd never forget. She willingly gave into his unrestrained, fiery passion, her frenzied response matching his ardent need.

She was lost in Josh's powerful arms when his solidness transformed to pure energy, and he faded away, leaving her holding nothing but empty air. Jennifer dropped to her knees, unsure of whether the high priestess Josh had spoken of could hear her words—but she had to try. She confessed how she'd been the one responsible for Josh going against

Gisabella's wishes and expressed her shame and remorse. "I'll do anything you ask of me if you help us be together. Please, Gisabella, have mercy on Josh and me. We love each other." Jennifer didn't know if the high priestess would care about her feelings, or whether Gisabella would even hear her voice amongst so many souls in the universe.

As expected, Josh found himself transported to Gisabella, who looked at him as if she'd like to commit murder—*his!*

"I don't suppose I need to tell you why I transported you here?" Gisabella heard Jennifer's attestation of love in that moment, and decided to use the girl's feelings to her benefit.

"I'm fully aware of the rules I've broken and the consequences you warned me about." Josh made eye contact with Gisabella's frozen stare. He didn't care about her threat of not being solid again for ten years, not when he'd seen how happy it'd made Jennifer.

"You deliberately went against my wishes, after I warned you of the consequences. Too bad your actions involved not only yourself but also the young woman who's been crying out for my mercy. You should really tell Jennifer she shouldn't make promises she may not be prepared to keep." Gisabella didn't have to wait long for Josh's reaction.

"Don't you dare touch her! This is between you and I—no one else, do you understand?" Josh shouted, taking an aggressive stance.

"Now that I have your undivided attention, I'll tell you what I want in return for my leniency."

"Go ahead." He bit his tongue.

"The most important thing to me is Jennifer's happiness, of course," Gisabella toyed. After making Josh stew a little longer, she alleviated his worry. "Relax, old man; all I want is for you and Jennifer to be married tomorrow night—here in my garden." She did her best not to burst into a fit of laughter at the expression of shock on his face.

"Thanks to your interruption, I didn't get a chance to propose, let alone talk about a wedding date."

"I know." Gisabella's eyes sparkled deviously. "That's what makes my idea so delightful. What better way to show my displeasure? Be thankful that's all I'm doing to you both. On the plus side, in light of Jennifer being so pure and your restraint in keeping her that way until your wedding night, I've retracted my original punishment of not being allowed to become solid for ten years. I think I've come up with something that will benefit each of us—after all, a man of your vigor must be dying to take the girl to bed. The way I see it, I'm doing you a favor." Gisabella leveled her gaze with his, daring Josh to say one wrong word.

"Thank you for your extreme kindness, Your Excellency. If you'll excuse me, I'd better return to Jennifer and let her know we're to be married tomorrow night."

"Wonderful news! I look forward to seeing you both then. Make sure you and Jennifer are waiting for transport in her bedroom at two minutes after midnight. Jennifer will be returned home four hours later earth time, giving the two of you four days alone up here for a honeymoon. Remember—she can't tell anyone. If the council were to find out about the laws we've broken, all of us would be hunted and disintegrated."

"I understand."

"Don't look so duped, Josh; it's not like you thought you could get away with going behind my back."

"Actually, all things considered, I'm pleased with the way things worked out. Now I get to marry the girl I love tomorrow night, and I have *you* to thank."

"For your sake, I hope Jennifer feels the same about our arrangement and doesn't tell you to get lost again. I'll even help you out by making you solid from now until the end of the honeymoon."

"We'll see you Sunday night. Do you think you can manage to keep your nose out of our business until then? I'd like to be alone with Jennifer without wondering if you're spying or messing around with one of your magic spells."

"I'll see what I can do to keep myself busy until then." Gisabella feigned boredom.

"If you're *that* bored, maybe you could arrange for some flowers and a dress for my bride-to-be. I'd hate for Jennifer's potentially unforgettable wedding day to be ruined by your limiting timeframe."

"I'm sure I can find some weeds growing in the garden that will suffice as a bridal bouquet. I'll tell Jennifer they're from you, of course; I wouldn't want to take all the credit." Gisabella flashed Josh a tongue-in-cheek look as she watched him disappear. *My sincerest wishes on your proposal, my friend, because you deserve some happiness. All I ask is that you make it special for the girl.*

When Josh arrived back in Jennifer's bedroom it was one minute after midnight, meaning their wedding would take place in twenty-four hours. *How am I going to tell her we're getting married tonight!* Jennifer was in bed with her eyes closed, appearing peaceful. Even in her sleep she taunted him, wearing a suggestive smile on her lips and barely anything underneath her blankets. He reached out and moved strands of untamed hair off her face, enjoying the erotic sensation of it sliding through his fingertips. His eyes fixated on her mouth and the sweet lips that would soon be his; he'd teach her to explore all the possibilities of pleasuring they could bring to each other. The thought of her as his wife pleased him, causing waves of arousal to circulate through his entire body. That night he would claim Jennifer as his wife, and give himself completely to her.

It'd been far too long since he'd been with a woman in the physical sense, but never had he given his love. His work had kept him too busy for any outside interests and didn't allow for time off, making relationships impossible. Jennifer was the only woman who'd made him crave *more* from a relationship. A crooked grin creased the corner of his mouth. She was different than any woman he'd ever met, and if he'd stumbled upon her standing on an island shore, he would've thought she was a siren who'd used her body in place of a song to beckon him forth. *Even if she were a dangerous siren, I'd still have pursued her.*

Josh smiled at the sight of the ring box clutched in her hand, but frowned when he noticed Jennifer had been crying based on the amount of tissues piled on the nightstand; a sign of his unexpected departure, surely. He traced the outline of her mouth, then brushed his lips against hers lightly until she stirred.

"Mmm, Josh," Jennifer murmured with closed eyes.

"I'm here, baby. I need you to wake up so we can talk and I can finally propose." To his surprise, Jennifer opened her eyes, bolted upright, and sprang into his arms.

"I've been worried sick; don't you dare leave me like that again!" Jennifer warned. "From now on I go where you go—got that?"

"I don't suppose that means you'll be accompanying me tonight to Gisabella's house?"

"I dare you to try and stop me. Does this mean I finally get to meet your boss-slash-friend?"

"I think it's safe to say you'll meet Gisabella, since she's to be the one performing our marriage ceremony." He waited for the fallout.

"Okay—that's more like it! I've been waiting for you to officially propose to me for weeks, so I can't tell you how happy I am that you've managed to book our wedding faster than it's taken you to put an engagement ring on my finger." Jennifer held up her left hand, doing her best not to laugh at his awkward smirk.

"If you'll allow me to remove this from your hand..." Josh took the blue box and knelt on one knee next to the bed. "Jennifer, the love I feel in my heart for you is so deep that without you, I'd cease to exist. I'm not sure if we shared one or many previous lifetimes together, but I must've loved you in each of them. There could be no other explanation for the depth of the love I have for you other than loving you many, many times over. If you agree to become my wife tonight, I promise I will love and cherish you forever. My darling Jennifer, will you do me the honor of becoming my wife?"

"Yes! Yes, I'll marry you! Josh, I love you and I can't wait to be all yours." Jennifer watched Josh open the box and take out a beautiful diamond ring, then held out her shaking hand and watched as he slid it in place. She stared down at the huge diamond with her mouth agape. "It's stunning," was all she could muster.

Josh stood and pulled Jennifer to her feet to wrap his arms around her, then pressed her firmly against his body. With one hand, he tilted her head and planted a hard kiss on her soft lips, letting Jennifer know she was all his, now and forever. Without any warning, Jennifer seized control of the kiss and threw down the gauntlet, staking ownership over him the same way he'd done to her. The amplitude of his physical response to Jennifer's well-played move was heady.

"Too bad my protector failed to tell me what a great kisser he is; then again, if I'd known that, all my lessons would've flown out the window in lieu of making out," Jennifer said between kisses.

Josh seized control once again and was soon invited inside Jennifer's mouth; Jennifer's response was so eager that he was encouraged to go further. Josh moved his hand downward undoing the buttons of

Jennifer's nightshirt, and cupped her breast, slowly rubbing his thumb around and across her nipple until it hardened beneath his touch. She pressed her breast deeper into his hand, willing him to continue with an arch of her back. He answered her need, lowering his mouth to her budding nipple to tease and flick it with his tongue. With each of her sweet moans he sped up his rhythm, caressing her other breast with his hand until it, too, was ready and eager to be treated to the same. He took pleasure in holding each of her delicate rosebuds between his teeth, increasing the pressure until she cried out, her body bowing in exquisite pleasure as she begged him for more.

"Please don't stop," she cried out with abandon. "Please..." Josh's pleasuring rendered her incapable of speaking; she wanted more—much more. Most of all, she wanted him with all of her heart, body, and soul.

"Mmm," Josh hummed as he lifted his head. His eyes locked with her espresso-rich ones, limpid and full of desire. He wanted to continue, but he'd made a deal with Gisabella and more importantly, he wanted Jennifer's first time with a man to be special and unhurried. "Jennifer, my darling," he whispered softly.

"I love you Josh!" Her voice was but a whisper as she rested her face against his chest, inhaling his familiar scent.

"Please tell me you want to be with me as badly as I want to be with you," Josh said, each word laced with urgency and need.

"Yes." Her answer was tentative, as she was unsure of what he meant. The "poison scene" from *Romeo and Juliet* played in her head. *Does Josh expect me to become a spirit?*

"As much as it would simplify our situation, if you were to become a spirit like me—if you killed yourself like Juliet did—you'd be penalized for thousands of years."

"I'm so glad I have a fiancé who can read my thoughts. Maybe someday you'll use them for more sensible things like when I want you to cook me dinner, need a backrub, or want to kiss you." Jennifer lifted her head and puckered her lips.

"We're going to have such a wonderful honeymoon in the same dimension with no one else around. Gisabella's offered us her home, and we'll have horses to ride with miles of fields and trails. Best of all, baby, because of the difference in the speed of time between our dimensions, we'll have four days together before you're back here at four a.m. on Monday morning. No one will be the wiser."

"Four days together—sounds like heaven." Jennifer cracked a smile.

"Would you mind if I spent the night? I don't mean here in your bedroom. I was thinking we could curl up on the couch in front of the Christmas tree—that is, if you don't think your parents will mind. To be clear, what happened a few moments ago will *not* happen again until our honeymoon. Only kissing from now until you're completely mine."

"I'm sure they won't mind as long as I change out of my nightgown." Jennifer failed to sound unaffected by Josh's honeymoon intentions, and clasped her clammy hands together to keep them from shaking. "Sarah and Dave used to fall asleep on the couch watching TV all the time, and my parents never said anything. They're cool that way."

Josh noticed the gold foil box on her desk. "I wondered why you never said anything about this," he commented as he picked up the gift.

"You're not leaving, are you? Please tell me you haven't changed your mind again," Jennifer panicked.

Josh's heart wrenched. "No, baby, I'm never going to change my mind about us—I'm all yours! I think I'll bring this downstairs so you can open it in front of me. Do you mind if I borrow your notebook?" When she shook her head, he picked it up and headed towards the door. "I'll wait downstairs to give you some privacy while you change—until after we're married, anyway." Josh flashed her a salacious grin and turned to exit.

Jennifer waited for the door to close before she reacted. *You'll be mine, too.* The thought brought a surge of heat flooding into her cheeks and an ache deep within. *We're getting married!* After donning some leggings and a sweater, Jennifer ran downstairs to where she found her fiancé waiting. Josh had removed his suit jacket, tie, and shoes, and had unbuttoned the top two buttons of his shirt. She saw that he'd taken off his watch and emptied his pockets onto the coffee table: a wallet, three small rocks of different colors, a set of keys to who knew where—*maybe his apartment?*—and what looked to be a small crystal orb.

He walked over and took Jennifer's hand in his. "Let's sit in front of the fire where you can open your overdue present." Once seated, he handed Jennifer the gold box. "Go on, baby, unwrap it. I know you want to," he said, flashing his pearly whites.

Josh's words instantly turned her into a shameless woman who was in serious need of more kissing. Once unwrapped, she lifted the lid and discovered an elegant platinum pen with a private engraved message meant only for her. "It's lovely. Thank you, Josh."

"Go ahead and give it a try." He handed her the notebook.

Jennifer began writing her name when suddenly the pen took control of her hand and began writing on its own:

Jennifer, please forgive me for how badly I've hurt you. I meant it when I said how much I love you, and I still do. I'll never forgive myself for what I've done to you. All I want is your happiness. I love you.
Jennifer, I long to hold you and kiss away your tears. My heart is forever yours.

Jennifer gazed down as the pen continued to move her hand, filling up the page with various sentiments. Even after she put the pen down, the words continued to magically appear. "How did you do that?" The awe in her voice was palpable, her expression wondrous.

"Your pen is magical and will only work for you. It's a sort of 'automatic handwriting' tool, where a person's spirit guide—or in your case, your protector—is able to channel thoughts through your subconscious. If you're intuitive, you'll automatically write them. This method is used by those who aren't developed enough to speak directly with their guides; thankfully, *we* don't have that issue." Josh pulled a matching pen out of his shirt pocket. "The best thing about our pens is that we can send and receive messages no one else can see. Our correspondence works differently—our messages will appear instantly on any nearby piece of paper regardless of whether the pen is being held. This method comes in handy if you're blocking my messages," Josh said dryly.

"Thank you for my gift. I love it, and I love you," Jennifer said shyly. As if remembering her manners, she then offered to make him a snack.

"No thanks. I'm not hungry, at least not for food."

"Come to think of it, I'm not either." Overcome by Josh's intensity, Jennifer twisted to stare at the flames in the hearth. *How did he get the fire started so fast?* The question vanished from her thoughts when she noticed the feverish look in Josh's eyes, and how they'd changed to the color of emeralds in the sun.

Josh's caress brought fire to Jennifer's eyes and soon he was lost in their soulful depth, awakened to how much there was to this young woman. He wanted to know more—what he *needed* to do was read her profile as soon as Gisabella agreed to give it back. *What a fool I've been!* Jennifer's closed eyes gave him time to study her face up close; while mesmerized by her sensual, erotic look, there was something so profoundly mythical about her, drawing him deeper into her bewitching spell. He lightly touched her lips with his and when her heartbeat quickened, he deepened the kiss, taking time to savor her sweetness while he gave into Jennifer's enchanting web of innocence.

"Mmm, I never knew a kiss could be so sublime," Jennifer sighed. The warmth of the fire mingled with the headiness of Josh's sweet and spicy scent was like an aphrodisiac to her senses. Being held in place by Josh's masterful hands while he leisurely kissed her ignited dormant embers buried deep within, while his artful technique caused her body to react in the most delicious way. She wondered if he heard her thoughts, because his kisses became urgent while his tongue sought permission to enter her mouth; she welcomed him in, meeting his tongue with her own. Her body was enveloped by Josh's solidness as he expertly explored her mouth, leaving her breathless and wanton.

He tried to stop himself before he went too far, but his body was coasting along on autopilot, taking over all of his rational thoughts. She'd met him halfway when she'd welcomed him into her mouth, pressing her breasts against his chest while trying desperately to deepen their kiss. He delved into her mouth with his tongue and, at times, passionately intermingled it with hers; his need responded to each of her panting, raspy, breaths—a show of how much more Jennifer desired. *A very good sign from my future wife.* A voice from within warned him to slow down and take his time, while other parts of his body were having a difference of opinion. His erection had grown in anticipation while his mind pictured how she'd look...*what the hell am I thinking?* Josh pulled away; he wanted Jennifer's first time with a man to be special, and certainly not in a place where someone could walk in and find them.

"Baby, I think you should get some sleep," Josh recommended.

"'Sleep?' I've waited all this time for you to kiss me, and you want to go to *sleep*?"

"That's correct. You need your rest, because I want my wife to be wide awake the first time I make love to her."

"Oh," Jennifer gulped. "Since you put it that way...goodnight Mr. Smith." Jennifer nestled closer, enjoying the feeling of being wrapped in Josh's embrace.

"Goodnight, my love." Josh pulled the blanket over the two of them and watched as Jennifer soon drifted off.

The crack of dawn arrived, and Josh opened his eyes to find Jennifer asleep in his arms. He'd heard her parents come home in the wee hours and head upstairs to bed without a glance their way. Now that it was morning and he was still solid, a thought went through his mind. *What would happen if Jennifer's parents saw me again?*

~Good morning, Gisabella. I was wondering—since Jennifer's parents have already seen and spoken to me, would it be more rule-breaking for me to make them all breakfast? Happy to say I didn't have to duck out of the way of a flying ring, either; it's on Jennifer's finger,~ Josh messaged.

~Glad to hear you didn't muck things up again, and everything is on track for tonight. As discussed, I have everything ready, bouquet of weeds and all. In response to your question, sure, what's one more infraction when you've committed so many others? My sincerest congratulations on your engagement, my friend.~

~Thank you, Gisabella. Looks like you have a nice side to you after all,~ Josh joked. Now that he had permission to stay, he stretched out his arm to retrieve his watch from the table, then wiggled his way out of Jennifer's arms and covered her with the blanket. He was in the kitchen when Jennifer strolled in and hugged him from behind.

"Good morning, baby," Josh said, snaking one arm around Jennifer's waist while he flipped pancakes with his other hand.

"It smells wonderful. Can I help?" Jennifer asked, doing her best not to swoon from the impassioned look in his eyes.

"I'm almost done here, so how about you set the table? I wasn't sure if your parents liked espresso or regular coffee?"

"I've never seen them drink espresso." Jennifer was setting the table when she whipped back around—*he's still solid!* "Josh, my parents are going to be down here any minute! They won't care that you stayed the night on our couch, but you need to leave before Gisabella freaks out again!"

"'Freaks out?' She'll have a good laugh about that one."

"Why must you go out of your way to get yourself in hot water with Gisabella? So help me, if you push her buttons and ruin our honeymoon, you're gonna have one irritated wife on your hands!"

"Whoa." Josh held his hands up. "I have Gisabella's approval to be here this morning. Let's just say she was in an *extra* good mood." Josh sauntered over and planted a kiss on Jennifer's lips. "Don't worry, baby, I have every intention of being solid for our honeymoon," he whispered in her ear.

"That's good," Jennifer sputtered. *If I'm this bad from a few suggestive words, what am I going to be like when we're alone together in the honeymoon suite?* "I have a few questions to ask you about—um—tonight." *Why is this so hard to spit out?* "I mean, our honeymoon."

"When we finish breakfast, we can go for a walk and talk then. It might help if I told you that I'm not going to do anything with you until you're ready. We'll take things slowly, and as you feel more comfortable, we'll move forward."

Before Jennifer could say anything more, her sleepy-eyed parents shuffled into the kitchen. "Morning, Mom and Dad! Why don't you both have a seat and I'll get you some coffee? Josh made us blueberry pancakes with blueberry compote. Wait until you try them; they're even better than the ones we get at the diner!"

"What a godsend you are, Josh. I don't think I could've kept my eyes open long enough to pour a bowl of cereal, never mind to cook," Mrs. Parker said, rubbing her eyes.

"I'll have a cup of extra strong coffee over here, please," Mr. Parker asked with a wave.

"If you prefer, sir, I made some espresso—but I'd better warn you that I like my espresso strong enough to wake up the dead." Josh winked at Jennifer, who looked as though she'd swallowed a fly.

"My wife's right, Josh; you're a blessing from heaven. I'll try a cup of your espresso—if it's as strong as you say, maybe my eyes will open the rest of the way."

"Yes, sir, coming right up." Josh handed Jennifer the espresso to deliver while he plated and served the food, then joined them at the table.

"What are you two kids doing after breakfast?" Mrs. Parker asked with a big smile.

"I thought Jennifer and I would take a walk and perhaps go out to lunch before I leave."

"Oh no, you're leaving already? We're just beginning to get to know you—and Jennifer seems to enjoy your company."

Oh Mom!

"I'm afraid I have some important matters that are in need of my attention." Josh looked at Jennifer and added, "I enjoy your daughter's company, too."

"Maybe when you're back in town we can all go out to dinner," Mr. Parker offered.

"I'd like that very much," Josh said, fighting back an odd sensation that expanded in his chest. He could get used to being part of Jennifer's family; going out to dinner, celebrating holidays, summer picnics, playing board games, and whatever else families did. Thoughts like those were dangerous, and no matter how hard they were to resist, he couldn't give in to their pull. Being married to someone alive in the earth's dimension would be challenging enough without forming further connections. If he did, it'd only be a matter of time before the council became aware of his marriage, which would bring disaster on them all.

~What's wrong?~ Jennifer messaged when she noticed Josh hadn't said a word in a few minutes.

~I need to get out of here.~

~Why?~ Jennifer asked with concern. ~You're not regretting proposing to me, are you?~

~Never! Would your parents be offended if we go for that walk now? ~

"If you don't mind, Josh and I are going to leave for a while," Jennifer said in her best "I'm not up to anything" voice.

"You two run along; we'll clean up. Thank you for making us breakfast, Josh. We hope to see you again," Mrs. Parker gushed.

"My pleasure, Mr. and Mrs. Parker. Thank you for letting me crash on your couch last night."

"Anytime, Josh—as long as you promise to make us breakfast," Mr. Parker said.

A little while later, Jennifer gazed out at the sparse winter landscape across the pond. She was seated next to Josh on the bench that held bittersweet memories of when she'd fallen through the ice and ended up naked in Josh's arms, only to have him leave.

"Jennifer—I want you to know that you can ask me anything," Josh began.

"As you're aware, my experience with men has been limited." *More like nonexistent.* "It's no secret that you're my first boyfriend and my first kiss." She knotted her fingers together.

"I'm well aware of how innocent you are, and promise that we'll take things slowly," Josh said, reiterating his previous pledge.

"That's not the answer I had in mind—or my question. I was going to ask how experienced *you* are. I assume that since you've lived many lifetimes, you've had multiple lovers?"

"I…can't answer that question," Josh gulped.

"*That* many?" Jennifer visibly cringed.

"That's not it—at least, I don't think so. I honestly can't remember all the details of the time I've spent as a protector, or my past lifetimes, so I'm unable to give you an honest answer. I'd be lying if I told you I haven't been with other women, some of who I vaguely recall, but I've never been in love with anyone other than you. The kind of love I have for you could only have come from loving you before; maybe even several lifetimes' worth. Jennifer, please don't let my past get in the way of our future."

"As long as you pledge your whole heart to me tonight, I promise I'll never bring up your past again."

"Baby, I believe you've held my heart in your hands since the day you were born. It's just taken me a while to find you."

"Me too." Jennifer's response earned her another passionate, knee-buckling kiss.

After spending most of the day together, Josh went home to his apartment so Jennifer could rest before their big night.

CHAPTER NINETEEN

Josh arrived at the door outside his apartment in time to see one of his neighbors walking—scratch that, *stumbling*—his way towards him.

"Hey man, it's been, like, *months*! Haven't seen you in months, man," Richard slurred.

"Yeah, I've been pretty busy on assignment. What are you doing here? I thought you were working?" Josh shook his head at his fellow protector's bloodshot eyes. Richard was a few centuries younger than himself, and a newer addition to their elite group. The jury was still out on how Josh felt about the guy, and showing up drunk at his doorstep wasn't helping Richard's case.

"Got the night off, yeah…you're missing a killer party upstairs, it's at some guy's place, I forgot his name…what was his name? Dave? Dan? Eh, whatever, doesn't matter…what *matters* is that I saw a total knockout standing outside your door earlier…total babe, hot damn…"

I sure hope I never sounded like this douche bag! "Are you sure she had the right address?" Josh said sardonically, not bothering to disguise the laughter in his eyes at the massive hangover Richard would have tomorrow.

"I tried to convince her otherwise, man, but she wouldn't listen,"

Richard frowned. "Said she wanted to see you, refused to leave, no matter how many times I asked…sorta insulting, man, I mean, no offense, but how does an old dude like you get all these chicks, it's bullshit—no offense." Richard held his hands up in surrender, teetering unsteadily.

The stench of whiskey filled the air, becoming more potent each time Josh's neighbor opened his mouth. *Whew! If I stand here any longer, I'll have a hangover too!* "For your information, I take my work seriously and don't have much time to bed a whole slew of women," Josh snapped, his patience fading fast. "Where's this so-called 'knockout?'"

"Shhh! Don't tell anyone, but I used my skeleton key. See—here it is." Richard fumbled with the long, thin key on his chain, one designed to fit every lock every made.

"What?! How'd you get past my alarm?" Josh scowled when Richard doubled over, clutching his belly as he laughed.

"Child's play, man. Get with the times, buddy, you gotta get with the times," Richard said, slumping against the nearest wall.

"I don't suppose you got her name?" Josh didn't bother to hide his growing irritation. He was all for having a good time, but Richard had crossed the line when he'd broken into Josh's apartment to let the girl in. The question *now* was, who the hell had Richard given access to? *This better not be Gisabella's idea of a bachelor party!*

"Red hair, she had this gorgeous red hair…you know what they say about red-haired chicks, they're dangerous…"

"Thanks, that's all I need," Josh said, doing his best to hide his grimace as he watched Richard stagger away. Josh entered his apartment, not knowing what to expect from his green-eyed tramp visitor. Within seconds he'd located Sarnia's energy—in his *bedroom. Shit. What's she doing in there?* Bracing himself for what he'd find, he entered the room.

"About time you showed up," Sarnia purred. "I almost started without you." Sarnia pulled back the sheet, revealing her nakedness while she began caressing one of her breasts.

"What the hell are you doing here?" Josh glowered.

"I'm here to see you."

"Sarnia, you must be delusional if you think I want *anything* to do with you. I thought by now you'd have gotten the hint, but apparently I haven't been clear enough. I don't want you, and I never will. Now please get out of my apartment before I notify Gisabella—"

Josh's words caught in his throat when in a flash, Sarnia had crossed the room to press her naked body against his.

"Feel better now?" Sarnia rested her hand on his chest and tilted her head to meet his gaze. "Don't fight it; you know how perfect we are for each other. Give me tonight to remind you of how great sex can be, *especially* now that I'm all grown up." Sarnia's hand traveled down the length of Josh's chest, swiftly moving towards his crotch.

Josh stopped listening when his eyes met Sarnia's piercing, wildcat-green ones. *No, no, no!* he said over and over in his mind, willing his body not to respond. It only took one thought of the woman he loved to regain control over the situation. "Sarnia, if you don't get the fuck out of here, I'll see to it that you're permanently removed as a protector."

"That's right, I forgot—you're Gisabella's pet," Sarnia hissed.

"The guy who let you into my apartment wants to screw you; why don't you go rub against him instead?" *He's drunk enough to think you have a heart.* Josh's eyes held no humor as he grabbed Sarnia by the arm and dragged her to the door. He was thankful she didn't try to zap him or use any other offensive energy moves, saving him the trouble of explaining to Gisabella why Sarnia no longer existed. Not that his friend would mind—she'd never liked the girl.

"Fuck you, Josh! Mark my words, you'll burn in hell for this!" Sarnia clenched her fists to stop herself from taking aim. She was no match for Josh—not like this, head to head. Instead, Sarnia would bide her time until an opportunity presented itself to revenge the man who'd cast her aside many lifetimes ago.

Josh watched Sarnia fade away, transporting to somewhere other than his apartment. The saying "hell hath no fury like a woman scorned" came to mind, but for all he knew Sarnia had listened to him and was in Richard's bed now. He'd had previous altercations with her but had brushed them all aside just like he planned to do with this one; Sarnia was the second-highest of the elite protectors, and he had no wish to destroy her career. *But if she steps over the line again, I'll personally send her packing.*

Josh poured himself a glass of "nerve potion"—also known as port wine. In a few hours Jennifer would become his wife, and if Gisabella had written him into Jennifer's life-path and destiny as he suspected, then she'd done so for a bigger reason than simply serving as her protector. There was no way of preventing Jennifer's predestined marriage to another man, leaving him two choices: he could fight his love for her and walk away now, breaking both of their hearts, or give Jennifer all his love for the limited time they'd be married before she was taken away.

What if there was a way to alter the plan? He gazed into his glass of ruby-colored liquid as if it held the answer. *There's got to be a way I can beat Gisabella at her own game.* He thought of how Gisabella had brought Lawrence into the picture. *To do what? Trick me? Force me into action?* The revelation of what Gisabella had done infused his blood with anger. *She's gone too far this time—high priestess or not, it's about time Gisabella received a taste of her own medicine.* His lips curled. *It'll be risky, but if Jennifer follows my lead and my plan is successful, there won't be anything Gisabella can do to change the outcome.* That night he'd give his whole heart to the woman he loved, with the hope that when Jennifer left him to marry another man in eight years' time, she'd come back to him when she'd finished her lifetime.

What can I do to make tonight special for my bride? A wedding gift, perhaps? It had to be unique; something Jennifer would always have, possibly even treasure her entire life. Time was ticking by and soon he'd have to leave to pick her up; hopefully she hadn't changed her mind. He shook his head free of all the "what if" scenarios, and concentrated on her gift.

I got it! What better way to show his full commitment to his bride than gifting a part of himself? Using a trick Merlin had once shown him, Josh envisioned a small, gold locket, so tiny no one would suspect it opened; instantly, a tiny locket hanging on a dainty chain magically appeared in Josh's palm. Once he'd placed his photo inside, he held the locket to his chest and willed some of his soul and heart's essence into the gift before sealing them permanently inside. Then he waved his hand over the locket and cast a spell so that only Jennifer could feel his heart beating and see his photo within. When he clasped the locket around his bride's neck, he'd be placing his heart in her hands forever; it was the least he could do for trapping her in an interdimensional marriage. Time was drawing closer, and he needed to hurry! Once the locket was secured in a red velvet box, Josh grabbed his razor and headed into the bathroom.

Back on earth, Jennifer's eyes darted to the clock for the millionth time. In less than five minutes, Josh would be picking her up to get married. *I can't wait to marry the man I love.* A noise caused her to jump and she turned to see Josh dressed in a black, tailored tuxedo, paired with a bow tie, gold cufflinks, and newly polished shoes—reminding her of James Bond. The sparkle in his eyes and his award-winning smile lit up the room, and though she'd always thought he was extremely good-looking, that evening Josh exuded pure testosterone and sex appeal. *What does he see in me? I'm certainly not sophisticated, nor do I look like one of the models on the covers of the latest fashion magazines.* Per Josh's last-minute instructions that Gisabella had a wedding gown waiting for her, Jennifer had dressed casually.

Josh offered her a single red rose, and Jennifer nearly slapped herself so that she'd stop staring long enough to accept his gesture. "Thank you," she croaked. Her thoughts, on the other hand, were a little more verbose —*take me, I'm yours, my Prince Charming.* It seemed a little too melodramatic to say out loud, especially for someone who wasn't wearing glass slippers.

Josh couldn't help but smile at Jennifer where she stood nervously in the middle of the room dressed in jeans, a pink sweater, and sneakers, with her riding boots held in one hand. She was clearly looking forward to riding one of the horses, but he wasn't sure if she felt the same about her soon-to-be husband. A blotch of fuchsia appeared on each of her cheeks, making him wonder if she knew what he was thinking. *I better block my more personal thoughts.*

He pulled Jennifer in closer and lowered his lips to her sweet, eager ones to taste their heavenly nectar. When he felt Gisabella transporting them he deepened the kiss, pleased when Jennifer kissed him back feverishly. Her body clung to his, trembling with need and begging for relief from the flaming desire that haunted her. His impending desire, once deeply buried, rose to the surface, answering her need and ready to be unleashed. When they arrived in Gisabella's garden, he was forced to release Jennifer's lips.

"Soon, baby," he whispered in Jennifer's ear, then took hold of her hand and led the way down the path to where Gisabella was waiting. The way Gisabella engulfed Jennifer in a warm and loving embrace surprised Josh—the high priestess had never looked more joyous.

"It's a pleasure to finally meet you, Gisabella," Jennifer said demurely. "Josh has told me so much about you, and I understand that we have you to thank for our marriage approval." Jennifer hadn't expected Gisabella to seem so kindhearted, and was equally surprised by the older woman's friendliness.

"You look beautiful, Jennifer," Gisabella said, beaming with pride. "Josh, make yourself comfortable while I bring Jennifer up to the house to freshen up. Come with me dear." She whisked Jennifer away, leaving Josh standing alone.

"Welcome," Gisabella said as she opened the front door. "My home is your home—please make yourself comfortable, and don't be afraid to ask Josh or myself if there's anything you need to make your stay here perfect." Gisabella took the opportunity to study Jennifer's face; the girl had grown up since she'd last seen her in person. She'd always kept a close eye on Jennifer's progress, and now that her training and safety would be Josh's responsibility as her husband and protector, she couldn't be happier.

Jennifer took the opportunity to study the house where she and Josh had once shared a romantic Christmas Eve dinner—one that had ended with their separation. *We're getting married, not breaking up!* They hadn't relaxed on the couch together because she'd demanded to leave, but now as Josh's future wife, it looked like a romantic place to curl up together after dinner while enjoying a warm fire. With the Christmas tree removed, the room seemed even bigger, but before she could daydream or look further, her hostess was on the move up the curved staircase.

Once upstairs, Jennifer followed Gisabella past a set of double doors on the left to a door further down the hall. When Jennifer was motioned inside, she caught sight of the gown hanging on the mannequin.

"Would you like to try it on?" Gisabella asked, softening her voice as she turned to face the nervous bride. "I had the gown designed for you to wear on your wedding day; it's crafted from the finest materials from other realms in the universe."

"It's the most beautiful thing I've ever seen." Jennifer's eyes were transfixed on the magnificent gown.

"Let's get you changed and see how you look." Gisabella observed Jennifer's hesitation. "It's okay, dear." *The poor girl doesn't remember who I am.* "Why don't you get undressed behind the privacy screen, while I tend to your gown?" When Jennifer was ready, Gisabella lowered the wedding gown over her head. "You look lovely, Jennifer—like a princess should!" The gown had instantly transformed Jennifer into an angelic vision, and she struggled to keep her emotions in check.

"I can't begin to express how thankful I am, Gisabella," Jennifer said, inspecting her reflection. "I hope Josh loves the way I look." She slowly rotated in the three-way mirror.

"You have nothing to worry about, my dear." Gisabella was relieved; Jennifer's exuberance validated that she was, without a doubt, in love with Josh. "Joshua is a lucky man to have you as his wife." She'd witnessed the way they both regarded each other for the first time, and was convinced of the depth of their love.

Gisabella walked over to a vanity to pick up the sparkling diamond tiara she'd worn for her own wedding day many millenniums before, during her last earth lifetime. "This tiara will be your 'something borrowed,' and your gown is your 'something new.' Now we need 'something old' and 'something blue.'" Gisabella pretended to look around the room for those two items, if only for the sake of appearance.

"I know!" she went on, holding up a bracelet box. "This is an ancient piece, so it can be your 'something old.'" She opened the box to show Jennifer a string of knotted gemstones. "This will also be my wedding gift to you. The anklet is made from the finest gemstones in the universe, and each of the stones serves a purpose that will help you find your way in life. It's imperative that you never remove it from your ankle."

"Thank you for your generous gift. I give you my word that I'll never take it off." Even though it seemed like an odd request, Jennifer was sure the high priestess had a valid reason.

Once Gisabella had fastened the unusual string of gemstones around Jennifer's ankle, she stood and appraised the handiwork. Josh, who was well-versed in gemology, would recognize the stones Gisabella had chosen to promote Jennifer's psychic growth and protection—along with a few others for his benefit.

"Last but not least: 'something blue,'" Gisabella said while picking up a large, flat, brushed-velvet jewelry case.

Jennifer watched as Gisabella lifted the lid and revealed a spectacular ten-carat, ice-blue diamond on a blue silk cord; when lifted into the sunlight, the room became filled with hundreds of sparkling spots. After being secured in place, the diamond rested in the hollow at the base of Jennifer's neck, cool and soothing against her skin.

Gisabella pooh-poohed away the tears that threatened to form in her eyes over how beautiful Jennifer looked, especially now that the girl's aura was glowing brightly in shades of lavender, silver, and white; a reminder of why she'd cloaked Jennifer as a child. Now that Jennifer was a woman, her energy could no longer be hidden, not even with Gisabella's most powerful spell. While Gisabella's gift of Jennifer to Josh was the best thing to ever happen to him, she didn't envy Josh's position. Once Jennifer was no longer a virgin, her gifts and abilities would develop on their own, making her all but impossible to hide. *Josh is going to have to stay on his toes to keep Jennifer safe.* Gisabella placed all her faith in her best protector, knowing that no other could hold a candle to him.

"We'd better get going—Josh must be wondering what's keeping us," Gisabella said, leading the way downstairs and outside to the path before turning to face Jennifer. "Wait here for a moment, my dear, while I make sure everything's perfect." She left the anxious bride standing in the safety of her garden to go in search of the groom, who she found waiting nervously in the same place she'd left him. *He looks like he hasn't moved an inch!* She tried not to laugh when she caught sight of how pale he looked. To think that she'd been concerned with *Jennifer's* nerves all that time! She led Josh a little farther down the path to where the ceremony would take place.

Josh had no choice but to follow Gisabella; when she stopped and pointed to the location Jennifer and he were to wed, his jaw dropped and his eyes opened wide. "Jennifer's going to love this," he said quietly. He smiled appreciatively before heading down the path outlined in pure white roses to wait at the altar.

When Jennifer suddenly appeared out of nowhere, her beauty took his breath away and left him spellbound. The young girl he'd thought to be a tomboy as a child and who'd become a beautiful young woman was now transformed into a princess! Jennifer's gown, youthful enough not to overpower her delicacy, showed him what an exquisite woman his bride was. Her wedding gown highlighted her exposed shoulders and the flawless skin he'd soon have the pleasure of caressing. The top of the gown's beaded bustier squeezed Jennifer's sweet breasts into submission and left him begging for more, while the sparkling layers of tulle at the bottom of the gown gave the illusion of wispy clouds and hid her sweet body from view.

I love him so much, Jennifer thought when she caught sight of her soon-to-be husband waiting patiently for her. She held a bouquet of white orchids, lilies, and roses tied together with an ivory-colored ribbon in one hand, while the other rested on Gisabella's arm. Josh's awestruck expression transformed into one of undying love, and he held out his hand to her.

~Join me, baby. I'm getting a little lonely standing here by myself,~ Josh sent off with an exaggerated wink. *Come on baby, show me a sign you're as excited as I am.*

~If you're that lonely, you could always run down here and get me, Mr. Smith.~ As hard as Jennifer tried not to laugh, she lost the battle and snickered, bringing a flush to her cheeks.

~There's the woman I love! I changed my mind—walk slowly, so I can enjoy every moment of how you look tonight.~ He was grateful for the long aisle so that he had plenty of time to study her as she approached. ~Don't look now, but I think Gisabella is on to us.~ Josh's smile grew larger when Gisabella's expression indicated she knew they'd been messaging privately. As Josh examined Gisabella, he noticed there was something different about her…but Jennifer's appearance had him so dazed he couldn't put his finger on what it was.

"Joshua, I give this woman to you," Gisabella said as she placed Jennifer's hand in his, holding their conjoined hands together in hers. The fire between them burned hot, giving the high priestess no doubt that the second part of the deal—Josh taking his new wife to bed—was as good as fulfilled.

"I accept this woman and promise always to love and protect her."

Josh said the words that were in his heart in a deep voice that radiated around the garden.

Gisabella took her position in front of the bride and groom. She wanted to make this quick, but nice. "Do you, Joshua, take Jennifer for your wife, vowing to protect and care for her, to be true to her, and to love her?" She waited, expecting him to answer, but none came. *~No!* Josh, we had a deal and you must agree!~ Gisabella's fury rose when Josh returned her message back to her, unopened.

Josh looked into Jennifer's eyes; she was so loving and sweet, and everything he could've ever hoped for in a wife and partner. "We've written our own vows." Josh ignored Gisabella's sharp inhale and locked eyes with Jennifer, stating his vows in a way that would tell the universe how he felt about the young woman before him.

"Jennifer, you are my one true love. I promise always to love you with both my heart and my soul. I will look after you, guide you, teach you, and hold you above all others for all of eternity." He hurried before Gisabella could stop him. "I give you my heart and my soul. I am yours and only yours, forever, until the end of time."

Gisabella's mouth dropped open. *What has he done?!* Before she could react, Jennifer began her vows to Josh.

"Joshua, you are my one true love. I promise I will always love you with both my heart and my soul. I will do everything I can to please you, treasure you, laugh with you daily, and hold you above all others for all of eternity." With her cheeks flushed and a shy smile, Jennifer repeated the exact words Josh had said to her. "I give you my heart and my soul. I am yours and only yours, forever, until the end of time."

After mouthing "good girl" to his angelic bride, Josh turned and looked at Gisabella. ~Checkmate!~ His message caused an immediate response from Gisabella, who glared at him with pure rage. He held his ground and waited to see what the high priestess would do next.

~Well played, Josh. Well played, indeed,~ Gisabella messaged back. The look of anger on her face transformed into a sly smile for his benefit. The two of them stared at each other for a full minute, before they broke into a fit of laughter and surprised poor Jennifer, who had no idea what had just taken place.

There was nothing Gisabella could do now: the words spoken there in that higher realm had linked them for good, except for Jennifer's destined life-path husband in eight years' time—that was a nonnegotiable obligation.

I did it! Josh thought. He'd come up with a way of tricking Gisabella, and Jennifer had followed his lead in repeating the same vows to him. Once Jennifer finished her life-path, she'd be his forever and there was nothing Gisabella or anyone else could do about it! Unlike earth marriages, their union could never end. Sadly, their strong commitment wouldn't change the destiny of her current lifetime, but once done, she would be all his. Best of all, once in heaven with him, Jennifer could never be sent back down to earth. Gisabella's response was what Josh had expected: shocked and mad at what he'd done. Someday she'd forgive him for his trickery, and when the time came, she'd hopefully accept Jennifer and him into heaven.

Having recomposed herself, Gisabella picked up the two platinum wedding bands she'd had specially created for the occasion and handed them out. "Please repeat after me: with this ring, I thee wed." Gisabella hesitated before continuing with the standard version of "to death do you part." Jennifer's eyes were full of love and hope, and Josh's were full of love and the unwavering strength the two of them would need for the future. She couldn't change the outcome of the vows they'd made to each other, and maybe Josh had done the right thing for all of them by taking Jennifer as his wife forever. Jennifer would now be Josh's responsibility, and Gisabella's days of worrying about the girl's training and future life-paths would be finished.

Josh held his breath. *Please, Gisabella, do this for us. I've never asked you for anything in my entire existence until now.* He left his thoughts unblocked in the hopes that when Gisabella read them, she'd have mercy on him and Jennifer.

Gisabella smiled at Josh and continued with the couple's vows. "Let no man or woman, anything or anyone, come between us or dare to tamper with the love we have for each other. From this day forward until the end of time, I pledge myself to you forever." She listened to Josh and Jennifer repeat their pledge to one another before she added her approval. "With my power as High Priestess, and with the light of God, I seal your vows and your marriage. I add my blessing in making your union so strong that no one can ever come between you." Gisabella's words resonated around them and sealed their vows forever. Looking at the just-married couple, she could tell how in love they were, and couldn't stay mad at Josh for what he'd done. In doing so, he'd placed Jennifer above all others and proved he'd stand by her side until the end of time. Yes, indeed! In bringing this couple together, she'd chosen well for both of them. Before Gisabella could add, "You may kiss the bride," Josh had Jennifer in his arms and was passionately kissing his bride.

Josh's all-consuming kiss left Jennifer breathless, enlightening her to the fact he may have more of an appetite for her than she'd expected. He held her tightly as they walked back down the aisle.

"Please enjoy your honeymoon. My home is your home. Dinner is set up for you a little way down the path in the garden." Gisabella hugged them and offered her congratulations.

"Gisabella—Jennifer and I would like to thank you for our beautiful and meaningful wedding," Josh said, speaking on behalf of both of them.

"You'll find the master bedroom has been transformed into your honeymoon suite." Gisabella's voice was thick with meaning, and Josh was sure to pick up on her witticism. She smiled at Josh to signal a truce. Now that he was Jennifer's husband, Josh had unknowingly raised his level from protector to a *much* higher status.

"Remember, my dear—never take off the anklet," Gisabella said to Jennifer, who nodded and thanked her for making their wedding perfect. Then Gisabella turned to the groom and gave her friend a tight hug.

"Josh, please take good care of Jennifer—she's all I have left," Gisabella whispered, stepping back to enjoy Josh's wide-eyed look as the implication of her words sunk in.

Before Josh could ask her about the comment, Gisabella had taken leave to the second home on her personal planet.

CHAPTER TWENTY

"We did it baby!" Josh flashed Jennifer a huge smile. "We've married each other forever and have Gisabella's approval!" Consumed by excitement, he picked up his bride and carried her down the flower-lined pathway to their wedding feast. Together they enjoyed a champagne toast and a selection of cold meats, cheeses, and fruit with crusty bread. *Thankfully Gisabella didn't attempt to poison us with her "gourmet cooking skills."*

"According to this note, dessert is waiting for us at the house," Josh said wolfishly, doing his best to keep from rushing up there with his bride.

"Why do I get the impression *I'm* dessert?"

"Am I that obvious?"

Yikes! Jennifer drank in the hint of a smile playing on Josh's lips and the way his head was cocked to one side—looking too irresistible for words. *What have I gotten myself into?* She loved Josh with all her heart and her body ached for him, but she was a little unsure of how to please a man, let alone her experienced husband. She'd only seen him solid a total of six times, and that alone caused some elevated panic and self-doubt. *What would a man who looked like a cavalier swashbuckler want with a naïve earth-dweller like me?*

"Jennifer, I'm not sure you realize how much I love you, or how *I'm* the one who's unworthy of you," Josh said, answering her unspoken thoughts. His sweet wife seemed unaware of her power over him, so he rose and took her hand in his, kissing her softly. When her response turned visceral and she deepened the kiss, he took it as a sign her anxiety had vanished. "Come, Jennifer—I want to make you my wife," he said, hoping his voice would coax away her fears. On the way up to the house he stopped several times to kiss her, and each time their lips met it fueled the fire between them.

Once in the house he led the way upstairs, where they found a trail of white rose petals leading the way to their honeymoon suite. Before opening the doors to their suite, Josh kissed Jennifer tenderly to ease her apprehension, lingering long enough to leave her breathless and ready for more.

The beauty of the room stopped Jennifer in her tracks. Its size could hold a party for 150 people and their closest friends! Across the room a romantic fire burned in a marble fireplace, and the flames seemed to dance as hot as her desire burned. *Is it possible for the flames to read my deepest thoughts?* What other explanation could there be in the dancing, erotic shadows cast around the room?

The bedroom was decorated in soothing shades of off-white and cream, and had a white loveseat for two facing the fireplace. A large off-white fur rug with two brocaded chairs and a small table between them completed the seating group. Vases filled with white roses were strategically positioned throughout the room, and two huge chandeliers hung from the castle-high ceiling above. The larger one was in the center of the room, with a slightly smaller chandelier over the king-sized bed. As Josh led Jennifer to the loveseat, her shoes clicked on the dark maple floors to break into her thoughts.

"I'm not sure about that bed." Jennifer's nerves took over her communication skills and, much to her dismay, Josh looked at her with a perplexed expression. "What I *mean* is it's so huge I'm not sure we'll be able to find each other!" Once the words were out of her mouth, she began to giggle. Soon it mutated into a gut-splitting, explosive howl, and she was thankful when Josh joined in, laughing just as hard.

"In case you aren't aware, I'm known far and wide for my tracking skills and my keen ability to locate a needle in a haystack," Josh boasted. "Since you're larger than a needle, I don't think I'll have too much trouble finding you."

They'd been friends for a while, but this was unchartered territory for them and Jennifer's first time with a man, so he wasn't about to rush her. Up until now his kisses had been affecting his wife considerably, but when he took her fully, she'd need to beg him to do so.

When his wife's laughter attack subsided, Josh reached out and brought her towards him until her body rested against his; she gazed up at him with her dovelike, virginal brown eyes. Jennifer's growing desire shone brightly and her heartbeat quickened as her girlish awkwardness disintegrated before his eyes. Left behind in his arms was a beautiful woman who was ready to be awakened for the first time. His lips touched her parted ones and he kissed her soft, succulent lips while her hands tangled in his hair, desperately trying to deepen their kiss. He held back, ignoring her attempts and forcing her desire to rise higher.

~Please kiss me harder!~ Jennifer resorted to messaging her demands for more. The cure for her deep ache rested in Josh's hands, causing her growing frustration to take over her senses. She pulled Josh against her, hoping to gain some relief, yet her gown was too full and the harder she tried to feel him against her body, the more frustrated and scattered her thoughts became. If he'd gotten her message or sensed how badly she wanted more from him, he chose to ignore her demands. *This is not at all what I expected from my lion-hearted, manly protector!* Worse yet, she could feel him grinning as he slowly teased her mouth, increasing her frustration and torturing her to the brink of sanity.

Without warning she was scooped into Josh's arms and carried over to the loveseat, then placed on her feet once more facing Josh. Her desire and need for him were too intense to take things at a slow pace, especially now that he'd chosen to ignore her advances; it was time to show her husband what she wanted! Reaching behind, she lowered her gown's zipper as Josh watched intently; his desire grew before her eyes and her power over him and his manliness was intoxicating. Grasping his arms, she guided him to switch places so that he was the one standing in front of the loveseat.

"Sit down," Jennifer commanded, feeling powerful as she made Josh bend to her authority. Her brazen move was rewarded by the glimmer she saw in his eyes.

"Excuse me? Did you just tell me to sit down?" *I like this side of Jennifer.*

"You heard me correctly—*sit down!*" Jennifer repeated with a renewed sense of boldness. Maybe it was the rush of adrenaline from exchanging their wedding vows or being in a different dimension, but she felt suddenly and completely uninhibited. The thought brought forth a renewed self-assurance; since Josh refused to heed her earlier requests for intimacy, she'd see to it that *this* time, he'd be the one hungering for her! His emerald eyes feigned relaxation, but the way his lips parted to suck in a sharp breath as he obeyed and took a seat proved to Jennifer that he was anything but.

"Quid pro quo," Jennifer said with confidence. Josh's telltale smirk confirmed that she'd been right—he *had* received her earlier message, electing to make her suffer on purpose.

Looks like my wife's on to me. Jennifer had backed up and was now standing three feet before him, lowering the top of her gown. Soon Jennifer's voluptuous, sweet orbs were in full view and begging to be taken prisoner. He forced his eyes briefly closed in the hope of regaining his equilibrium, only to reopen them to the same delightful vision: her luscious perfection. Either way, Jennifer had his undivided attention and he leaned back to avoid the temptation to reach out to her, opting instead to relax and enjoy her seductive show.

Jennifer gazed in awe at Josh's ever-changing eyes, a spectacle akin to the aurora borealis's hues and beauty. Gathering more nerve, she lowered her gown a little further as her sex dampened and her blood raced.

Now that she'd started, it was plain to see Josh wasn't going to help her out, made clearer by the way his mesmerizing eyes dared her to continue. *This is one dare I'm more than happy to oblige.* Taking her time, she gradually slid her gown over her hips to expose her favorite panties; they'd be next. Did she have the nerve? The answer was a resounding yes!

Crazed with desire, Josh used all his willpower to abstain from pulling her down onto the couch and taking her hard. It would've satisfied both of them, but he'd be left feeling horrible for taking her virginity in such a boorish manner. He took the hand Jennifer held out and watched with fascination as she stepped out of her gown and pushed it aside with her foot. He prayed he wasn't going to come right on the couch. *I'll concentrate on her shoes.* That's what he'd do, concentrate on her shoes until his throbbing subsided. He hadn't counted on this at all!

"So, you want to look at my shoes, do you?" Jennifer taunted, gracefully raising her left leg over his lap and resting her foot on the armrest. Josh paled as she bent at the waist while keeping her leg straight, stretching her body over his to unclasp the buckle on her shoe. Her childhood ballet classes were being put to good use!

"Oh, sweet Jesus," Josh blurted in a husky voice that sounded unnatural to his ears. *How much longer must I suffer?* He held his breath as Jennifer continued removing her shoe. Long hair dangling…brushing against his lap…breasts dancing…he hated to admit it but he had to glance away. By the look in his new wife's eyes, Jennifer knew she was in full control and looked to be enjoying his efforts to maintain his composure.

"Don't *come*—save that for when you're inside me," Jennifer whispered, pressing her breasts against him as she blushed scarlet over the scandalous words that'd tumbled out of their own accord.

Josh's mouth fell open in shock. *Had she really just said that?* "You *should* be blushing, baby," Josh said as he willed his erection to calm. His new wife now stood before him wearing only her lacy panties. With his direct eye contact, he challenged her to continue seducing him. After what Jennifer had said to him, he wasn't about to make this any easier. "Go ahead—I'm waiting." His voice was expectant and tormenting. *Let's see what you're made of, little girl.*

This was it! The thought of baring what little Josh hadn't seen of her body was exhilarating, and so was Jennifer's need to make this moment as memorable as possible. First she stretched her hands over her head, then purposely lowered them, taking time to caress her face, neck, and to brush the sides of her breasts on the way down to her hidden treasure. In total control of her man, her fingertips traveled past her waist and headed lower, to the waistband of her panties.

She wasn't sure why, but Jennifer felt the need to torture Josh a little more. It might've had something to do with his list of rules or how he'd ruined her Christmas, so Jennifer decided to brush her hands over her sex through the silky material of her panties. The look in Josh's eyes was so hot it made her halt and head back to safer ground; she'd pushed things too far! Josh was poised like a lion ready to pounce, so she gathered her nerve and unhurriedly slid her panties downward, pausing briefly at her hips before peeling them off. Now she stood in front of her husband completely naked and vulnerable, and a little clueless as to what to do next.

"You are so perfect, my love," Josh said in awe. He leisurely explored Jennifer's nakedness with his gaze until he couldn't control the rising need building inside. "I'm feeling a little overdressed," he added, before standing to carry his naked wife to the bed. "Now it's my turn to be in charge!" He gently laid Jennifer on the king-sized bed that was, ironically, covered in white rose petals to symbolize her virginity.

Jennifer stretched out in the middle of the bed, enjoying the exhilarating scent of fresh roses while looking at the best view she'd ever seen: her husband. Josh was standing far enough away to be in full view, but frustratingly too far away for her to touch. He didn't do a slow seduction scene like she had. *Thank goodness!* Instead, his clothes came off rapidly and he stood before her in his briefs. *Yikes! That was fast!* She swallowed hard, unsure of what to expect. She'd only seen a naked man in her art books and all those had been portrayed in a relaxed state, but in his black, fitted briefs she could see how excited Josh was to make love to her.

"I think I'd better wait until you're ready," Josh suggested with a lopsided grin.

"What?! Please don't tell me you're not going to make love to me," Jennifer said in a rush. "Why are you laughing?"

"I love a woman who knows what she wants! I was referring to removing my briefs. I wouldn't want you to faint at the sight of me."

"Is that what happens? Woman faint during—you know, during love-making? I admit, I've never seen a man before, but *faint?* Are you pulling my leg? Don't tell me you're laughing at me again. That does it, if you don't make me your wife this minute, I'm gonna scream!"

"In that case, allow me." Using his hands, he guided Jennifer down until she was on her back, then raised himself over her until he was looking down into her loving eyes and flashing her one of his best "this won't hurt a bit" grins.

Upon her shy smile of approval, he lowered his body until his full weight pressed her down—*there was no escaping now.* What Jennifer needed was a real man to claim her, and now that she was his wife he was finally free to partake of her innocence. Her seduction had caused the "rule book for virgins" to be tossed out. Instead, he'd use the clues she'd given him from her "stage show" to please her and send her into total ecstasy.

The weight of Josh's body made it so that Jennifer couldn't move even if she'd wanted to. A thrill went through her when Josh captured her hands in his and held her hostage while he kissed and sucked her neck, then entered her mouth to capture the tip of her tongue between his teeth. His action left no doubt in her mind who was in control! Primal instincts kicked in and her hips lifted, but Josh engulfed her hands in his and used them to press and hold her hips flat. His powerful move gave him full access to her breasts, while his private "ultra-spa" treatment included sucking until the delicious pain left her unhinged.

"Please, don't stop, I want you to do that some more," Jennifer pleaded, but Josh withdrew his mouth anyway. He moved southbound, trailing kisses along her stomach, waist, and hips. Her hands were useless in his vice-like grip and she was left subservient, begging for mercy. She cried out over and over, the likes of such begging she'd never before uttered.

"Please, Josh, *please* love me," Jennifer implored, trying to lift her hips and find relief. He was too strong and she was trapped under his muscular, hard body; a prisoner who was clearly receiving such treatment as repayment for her brazen performance.

"I've been dying to taste you, and now that you're my wife I'm free to enjoy every part of you." Josh took pleasure in the feel of Jennifer struggling underneath him and her shameless vocals. He openly took in her sweet, womanly treasures, inhaling her scent and knowing from that moment forward that he'd always recognize her wonderful aroma.

"Okay, but do you think you can enjoy me a little faster?" Jennifer begged desperately.

"Why Mrs. Smith, we must do something about your impatience; it seems to be getting worse. As this is your first time, I want to make sure you'll remember it forever."

Agh! But I want you to move faster! As if her thoughts had been heard, her hands were released and Josh took hold of her legs and spread them wide, giving him full access to her sex. *Finally!* She propped herself onto her elbows to watch what he was doing, and Josh looked up at her with a devilish grin before burying his head between her thighs. "Oh Josh…that feels…oh please…don't stop!" Jennifer called out when his tongue began stimulating her never-before-seen or touched sweet spot. Spasms scattered her senses in the most delicious way, and all she could do was tightly clench the sheets as she rode the wave of pleasure bringing her closer to the edge.

"Payback time, baby," Josh said, giving her an indication of what he thought of the way she'd tortured him with her exhibitionist undressing. With both of his hands under her butt, he lifted her hips for easy access and control over her sex. His tongue was relentless, and soon Jennifer's needy vocals filled the room.

"Please—I can't hold on—" Jennifer's words fell away. Unable to avoid the unknown she entered the mystical abyss that awaited, free-falling over the edge, embraced in ecstasy; she closed her eyes and gave in to the endless convulsing that freed her from all worldly bonds. When she'd thought it'd go on forever, her body subsided and she looked up at Josh, wide-eyed and in awe. She'd heard other girls talk about sex and orgasms, but their tales hadn't done justice to the event. As amazing as that was, she wanted all of him and was thankful when Josh stood and slid out of this briefs. Unable to turn away, she stared at his erection, open-mouthed and in shock of his manly perfection.

"Go ahead and take a good look—I'm all yours," Josh said, unable to wipe the grin off his face from her doe-eyed reaction. When she blushed and turned her eyes away, he laid down on the bed next to her and claimed her mouth, encouraging her to taste the sweetness still left on his lips.

Jennifer welcomed Josh's kiss and was treated to a sample of her arousal. *So risqué!* The naughtiness of tasting herself changed to lust as her need for him grew even larger. Twisting her fingers in his hair, she turned Josh into her hostage and deepened the kiss. His enlarged manhood rested on the cusp of her womanhood; she wanted and needed him, and if he moved a tiny bit, he'd be inside. With her inhibitions packed and sent on vacation, she begged for mercy. "Please, Josh."

"Please what, baby?" Josh waited to hear the words he longed Jennifer to say.

"Please take me now, my sexy husband." She felt him enter her cusp, giving her a small sampling of how large he felt. His foreignness was unfamiliar but pleasurable, and she was grateful when Josh paused and gave her a chance to adjust.

"This may hurt a little." Josh watched her expression while he eased slowly into her womanhood and felt her tightness ease and welcome him. When she winced, he stilled and gave her a chance to adjust once more.

"Are you okay?" he double-checked before resuming.

"Mmm, I'd like lots more of that, please," she begged. Josh's pace was slow as he moved in and out, rewarding her with the most exquisite sensations. Her hips instinctively raised to match each of his strokes as Josh filled her over and over, each time venturing deeper inside. A tidal wave of ecstasy grew in size as it headed to shore, and this time she had no hesitation.

"That's right, baby—let go." His words coaxed his bride to an explosive release. With one final thrust, hot pleasure ripped through Josh's body like a freight train as he emptied his very being inside his wife.

Jennifer laid in Josh's arms, savoring the feeling of him inside her and hoping he'd stay there forever. "Mmm," she murmured, her only coherent thought. Her mind was putty, and she only cared to concentrate on the euphoric state that encircled her. *I wonder if Josh feels the same.*

"Mmm," Josh concurred. He stayed inside his wife as long as he could, but now stilled, his manhood ebbed and withdrew. He couldn't help but chuckle at Jennifer's dejected look; clearly his wife wanted to hold him captive and had no understanding of what had happened. He needed to start with some basics. "I'll be ready for round two in a minute." He flashed her another one of his devilish smiles.

She took a deep breath and sighed contentedly. "Is it like this for everyone?" She gazed up through her lashes and flushed. "If so, how does anyone ever leave the house?"

"I can't answer for them, but if I were *you* I wouldn't make plans to go anywhere for the next five years," he joked.

"Okay," she agreed wholeheartedly.

"Now that we've settled your house arrest, are you sure you're not too sore?"

"Honestly, I don't feel sore at all."

"Must be because you're here, in Gisabella's domain." Josh's eyes lit up and his grin widened. "If that's the case, this is going to be one heck of a honeymoon!" When Jennifer squealed, he held her tighter.

Now married, she felt at ease to ask the question that'd been weighing on her mind. "Since we have a couple of minutes, I was wondering if you could tell me about Gisabella. I know she's your closest friend, but I'm having a hard time understanding it. From the little information you've shared, it sounds to me like *you're* the one who does all the giving."

"Jennifer, I owe Gisabella my life. I know it must seem to you like our friendship is lopsided or like we don't always care about each other, but nothing could be further from the truth. Gisabella can be a huge pain in the ass, but when you're down and out, she's the first person to rush to your side."

"Don't get me wrong—now that I've met her, I think she seems like a sweet person and the fairytale wedding she gave us was incredibly thoughtful. But you have to admit the two of you seem to argue a lot."

"That we do, and there are times I want to strangle her—but other than you, she's my only friend."

"You don't have any other friends? Not even a couple of guys you hang out with?"

"Not really; there are a few other protectors I hang out with once or twice a year, but none of us have more time than that unless we're between jobs."

"So you have no friends because you must watch over me." The thought made Jennifer sad. "You've given up so much for me."

"Jennifer, there's no one I'd rather be with then you. I know my lifestyle must seem unusual to you, but it's all I know. As for Gisabella, I'm certain she'll grow on you once you get to know her." Josh sealed his words with a gentle kiss and words of love.

"I'll be right back." Regretfully, nature called, and Jennifer had to get up. Now aware of her naked body's power and how she could effectively use it to her advantage, she gracefully climbed out of bed and gave Josh a full view of her nakedness. Thrilled by the hunger in his eyes, she posed on flexed, pointed toes, stretching and elongating her body before skirting away from his attempt to grab her. "Sorry, but you'll have to wait a few minutes before I'm ready for round two," she said with a sly smile as she walked away.

"What a minx you are, my wife!" Josh reclined with a huge smile plastered on his face. *My sweet little wife!* He noticed all the white roses in the room had transmuted to a dark blood-red, obviously as a way for Gisabella to let him know he'd successfully consummated their marriage. Looking back, he'd worried over nothing; while pure in the physical body, Jennifer was an amazing temptress and talented lover. Now married, it was clear that her many past lifetimes were shining through, along with her ancient soul's sexual desires. *I'm one lucky man!*

Across the room, Josh spied the wedding cake near the loveseat and headed over for a closer look. The cake consisted of three tiers of frosted delight, and he stood beside it naked, wearing a huge smile.

When Jennifer walked back into the room, she was stopped dead in her tracks at the sight of Josh's statuesque nakedness. It wasn't until he pointed that she noticed their wedding cake. A pang of hunger for frosted cake and her husband's body was all she desired. Together, they used the knife to cut their cake. Following tradition, she fed him the first bite, but when it was his turn to feed her, the look in Josh's eye and the huge piece of cake in his hand signaled "first fight."

"Don't even *think* about it!" Jennifer warned, eyeing the slice in Josh's hand.

"Think about what?" Josh said, playing innocent.

"Just so you know, smashed cake in my face is grounds for immediate divorce!" She was thankful when he offered her a small bite instead of a cake fight.

"That would've set a new world's record for the shortest marriage ever. Maybe now would be a good time to tell you that our 'forever' wedding vows can't be broken." Josh nuzzled Jennifer's neck until she moaned softly. "Do you like the cake?"

"Mmmmmm, delicious."

"Good, because I'll be feeding you more. I think I'd better remove this first," Josh suggested, before unclasping the blue diamond necklace she was wearing and placing it on the table. Then he skimmed his hand across the cake's surface, making his intentions obvious. "It's time for dessert," Josh grinned, holding up the glob of frosting. When Jennifer's eyes grew large, he deposited a finger-full on her lips and kissed it away.

"Mmmmmm, very tasty," Josh hummed, enjoying the taste of his sweet wife and her wide-eyed awe. *Frosted kisses are effective!* Gathering another finger-full, he spread it lovingly on one nipple, then the other, knowing it'd bring her to the brink. He trailed more frosting from the base of her neck between her breasts, continuing past her hips to her womanly triangle. The way she quivered under his touch proved she was succumbing to his tasty game. With his lips and tongue, Josh partook in his new favorite dessert: Jennifer and frosting. He worked his way back up her body to her breasts, taking one of her perfect orbs in his hand to lick it clean. Her soft cries of heightened pleasure made his game all the sweeter, and left him craving more.

"Please—Josh, I want you now." She'd never begged for anything in her life, but now that was all Jennifer seemed capable of doing. She watched as he placed a pillow down on the cool marble floor in front of the fireplace, the soft, flickering flames adding to the romantic mood.

Without saying a word, she willingly followed Josh's instruction to lie down face-up, with her head on the soft pillow. The tile was cool but it did little to diminish her heat or aching desire. To her relief, Josh lowered himself between her legs so that she was straddling him, his manhood full and ready to make love to her. She eagerly pushed her hips upward, giving him the indication that she wanted him inside her, *now.* Josh's answer was to leave a trail of frosting from her collarbone down her midsection as she helplessly watched him smear it all over. It felt so naughty and erotic! Her mouth opened in protest when he began smoothing a tiny bit between her legs, but it was when his finger began moving deep inside her that she doubled her vocal efforts. "I—need—you," she protested between ragged gasps.

Josh's eager wife was thrashing underneath him with such wantonness he feared it was beyond what she was capable of handling. Taking pity, he entered her fast and hard with one full thrust that rocketed her into a powerful orgasm. Without giving his wife an opening for words or thoughts, he took her again, setting an urgent pace as he was soon lost in the slick sensations of frosting and Jennifer. His release escalated closer, taking her to the edge with him. At the moment of their shared rapture, they called out the other's name, becoming one body, one heart, and one soul, for all eternity. Wrapped in each other's arms on the cool floor, they slowly floated back to reality.

From underneath him, Jennifer's soft curves roused Josh's need for her again. *I need to give the poor girl time to recuperate!* Josh's eyes met hers and his emotions took over. "I love you so much, Jennifer."

"I know," she said, flashing a huge smile before continuing. "My love for you is beyond anything I could've ever imagined possible. These past three weeks without you only proved that you're the only man for me and there's no one I could love more."

Josh stood with Jennifer in his arms, carrying her to the shower as she was too spent to do anything but stand. He squeezed shower gel on a sponge and washed Jennifer's young, flawless body free of frosting. "Baby, I don't think either of us will ever look at a wedding cake the same way again!" Josh said, with her answering giggle like music to his ears.

Once done, he used a fluffy bath towel and began to dry her, appreciating her body. A lump formed in his throat when he studied her closely. "I was so stupid for turning you away on Christmas—I caused you so much pain and so many tears. What can I do to make it up to you?"

"Please stop. I've never been this happy," Jennifer sighed.

"My angel, I know a way I can make it up to you—I can fatten you up!" When Jennifer groaned, he continued his mission of drying every inch of her body and took advantage of his closeness to inspect the gemstones surrounding her ankle. Many of them offered protection against evil in all dimensions, and were a useful addition in keeping her protected. Other stones would help Jennifer's third eye to develop, while increasing her psychic powers of intuition and her ability to communicate with spirits who, unlike him, existed on a lower energy plane. A few stones that helped to increase her sexual and physical pleasures were mixed throughout the anklet. *I'll have to remember to thank Gisabella for them!* There were more, but he needed to get Jennifer back to bed before she fell asleep standing up. He carried her limp figure back to the bed joining her under the soft, crisp sheets and down comforter. Gathering Jennifer into his embrace, Josh did something he hadn't done in years he closed his eyes and slept peacefully.

Gisabella put down the book she was reading and studied the roses on the nightstand, noting that they'd turned a wonderful shade of crimson. She was pleased things had turned out better than she'd anticipated. The fact that Josh and Jennifer loved each other as deeply as they had centuries ago brought a smile to her face, *especially* since the two of them had succeeded in forming an unbreakable bond. With the exception of Jennifer's temporary life-path marriage to another man, once they were reunited in heaven, not even the council could separate them.

Gisabella turned off the light and slept peacefully for the first time in years now that Jennifer was safely married to Josh. He was the only man who loved Jennifer enough to do *anything* for her—even if it meant giving up his very soul in exchange for hers.

CHAPTER TWENTY-ONE

Jennifer opened her eyes to find Josh studying her.

"Good morning, my beautiful wife." Josh's honey-dipped voice matched his "you've caught me watching you for hours" smile. "Did you sleep well?"

"Good morning, Mr. Smith."

"I was a little distracted last night—so much so that I forgot to give you this." Josh held up the delicate locket he'd made for her. "It's a wedding present for marrying me." *Why am I nervous?*

Jennifer gazed at the gold locket. "I love it!"

"I wanted to give you something that's yours and *only* yours forever." Josh opened the locket and showed Jennifer his photo, then placed it over her heart and held her hand over his own so she could feel how the two heartbeats were the same. "Jennifer, you alone hold my heart and my soul; I'll never love another—only you." He watched her eyes moisten. "The locket is protected and only you can open it. Once it's secured, the chain, like our love, can never be broken." Jennifer wrapped her arms around him and was soon kissing him passionately, and any doubts he may've had about his capabilities to love and be loved were cast aside instantly.

"My heart belongs to *only* you, and I, too, will never love another,"

Jennifer vowed, as if their marriage had been destined from the beginning of time.

"Are you hungry, Mrs. Smith?" Josh asked, doing his best to ignore the reality of Jennifer's predestined life-path husband. *Once her life on earth is over, Jennifer will be mine forevermore,* he reassured himself.

"Now that you mention it, Mr. Smith, I'm very hungry—*for you.*" She did her best not to blush or let Josh read her thoughts as she climbed out of bed and walked over to the cake. With an impish smile, she skimmed her hand across it until she'd gathered a bunch of frosting.

"You want cake for breakfast?" Josh questioned in surprise, unable to take his eyes off her. It was when she showed him her hand that he throbbed down below. *Will she or won't she?* Her seductive walk was enthralling, and he propped himself up so he wouldn't miss a thing. Jennifer crawled on the bed to stand over him, her feet planted on either side of his legs so that he all but drooled from the view. She lowered herself until her sex rested against his legs, but it wasn't until she placed her frosted hand at the base of his shaft that he was stunned into silence.

"What do you think I should do with all this frosting?" Jennifer asked.

"I'm all yours." Josh gestured towards his erection and watched intently as Jennifer wrapped her frosted hand around it. He bit the inside of his cheek and sucked in a breath as she began, haltingly, frosting him as if he were a cake. Her inexperienced moves were tentative and unsure, but her exuberance was refreshing and beautiful to behold. The tip of Jennifer's tongue stuck out as she concentrated on the serious job before her and the sight made his smile widen; somehow, she'd managed to save enough frosting for the tip of his hardness. Her eye contact never wavered even when she lowered her mouth and began flicking her tongue vigorously across his frosted tip.

"Damn, baby!" he said, fisting the sheets. What Jennifer lacked in experience she made up for tenfold by her eagerness. He closed his eyes and gave in to the enjoyment of the erotic sensation—but then she stopped! He opened his eyes to find her gazing up at him. His breathing was rapid and for the life of him, he'd no clue why she'd halted.

"Mmm—you and frosting taste yummy together." She purposely licked her lips and waited for him to subside.

That was it?! He'd had all he could take. "Damn it, Jennifer! If you don't hurry up and finish me off, I swear I'm going to sit you on top of me and fuck you so hard, your head will spin around!" To his dismay, his bluff didn't incite the response he hoped for as Jennifer sat back on her heels and chuckled. Any other time he'd have joined in, but leaving his gratification so close to being satisfied was no laughing matter.

"So help me, I mean it! Whatever frosting you haven't eaten will be inside you, and I *won't* be gentle." He was thankful when his threat succeeded to bring Jennifer's mouth back to him, moving up and down his firmness. He forced himself to absorb the hot pleasure as he held back and waited until she was ready for him to let go. Jennifer became creative, lightly skimming her teeth up and down his length. "That's right, baby. When you move up and down, it feels amazing! Remember how you used to suck lollipops, I won't be able to control myself if you do the same." Her mouth was over him, sucking, moving up and down and up again, harder and faster. "Baby, if you don't want a mouthful…" Before he was able to finish the warning, his love overflowed into her mouth. His breathing slowed and his only hope was that the experience hadn't shocked his new wife too much; but when he opened his eyes and gazed down at Jennifer, she was still holding him hostage in her mouth. *Had she swallowed it all?*

Jennifer finally sat back, licking her lips several times in an exaggerated display for his benefit. "Strawberry?" she asked, and was promptly pulled upwards until they were face to face and Josh's mouth was all over hers.

"I thought you'd enjoy a flavored version—it's a 'spirit trick.'" Frosting mingled with the strawberry-flavored essence on his wife's lips became Josh's favorite moment of all time.

"What other flavors are on the menu?"

"If you promise to do that again, you can have any flavor you want!"

"Pistachio and chocolate are two of my favorites!" Jennifer said hopefully.

"God how I love you, woman!" He could've easily made love to her, but it was getting late and her need to eat something—other than frosting and him—was made clear by Jennifer's famished look. "Come, let's go downstairs and see what there is to eat before you lose any more weight." Once in the kitchen, Josh pulled out a chair at the breakfast bar. "You should save your energy for later," he suggested, not bothering to hide his desire.

"Sounds good," Jennifer said, noting how Josh's words caused an instant response down below. *I'm ready to forgo breakfast in lieu of more sex, please.*

"Oh, how I love your comical, sexy thoughts," Josh exclaimed with a huge grin.

"Stop doing that!" *Agh, why can't I remember to block my thoughts?* "I think you should suspend your mind-reading invasions until after our honeymoon."

"I promise I won't *pry* into your thoughts, but I should explain how sexual thoughts come across louder and clearer than all others."

"In other words, I'm doomed."

"Yep! I probably should've told you earlier, but I was enjoying them too much."

"You, sir, are a scoundrel of the worst kind!"

"Thank you, I'll take that as a compliment." Josh's smile widened when Jennifer rolled her eyes in frustration.

"I hope you like egg white frittatas," Josh said a few minutes later, holding out two plates with identical meals on them. The look of delight on Jennifer's face told him she approved. As far as he'd seen, she'd never been exposed to different recipes, choices, and ingredients, so he looked forward to developing her palate.

"Thank you, this is amazing!" Her hunger wasn't shy, and Jennifer ate every mouthful while barely looking up at him. "You're elected to cook from now on."

"I think it's about time I teach *you* how to cook."

"Can you teach me how to make frittatas and your famous blueberry pancakes?"

"Absolutely! I'd enjoy showing you how to make them and other kinds of dishes. If you'd like, I can teach you how to bake as well. We'll have a lot of fun cooking together." He tried to keep the sexual undertones out of his comment. Someday he'd show his wife how sensual and erotic the feel, aroma, and taste of food could be when used to enhance each other's pleasure.

"Can we start right away?" Jennifer asked. Josh's offer sounded too good to pass up, as did the idea of cooking next to him.

"We can, but I thought if you weren't too sore, we'd go horseback riding." He'd barely finished the sentence before Jennifer was up the stairs, yelling out that she'd be right down.

It was a short walk to the horse barn and fields. Alone in the meadow stood an enormous, coal-black Friesian stallion with an extra-long, wavy mane and tail, who lifted his head when he noticed them approaching. With a look of recognition the horse galloped over, his massive hooves pounding the ground. The steed skidded to a halt mere inches from them, putting his mammoth head over the fence to nuzzle Jennifer.

"I've missed you so much, boy," Jennifer said, resting her head against the horse's thick neck. After a moment she looked at Josh with watery eyes. "This is my horse, D'Artagnan." She patted the horse lovingly, giving no indication of how odd it was that she knew this "heavenly" stallion. "Go ahead and say hello. Don't worry, he knows you're here with me so he won't try anything foolish."

"He's a beauty." Josh looked warily at the protective steed, but when D'Artagnan bowed his head, he scratched behind the horse's ears. *How does Jennifer know this horse? From a past lifetime?* Jennifer pointed to a dapple-gray mare, stating she was Josh's mount, and he casually asked for the mare's name.

"Misty," Jennifer replied immediately, acting as if she'd known their names all her life.

He'd seen it before—people remembering things from other lifetimes without thinking it odd. But this was different; D'Artagnan was in Gisabella's dimension, and this wasn't a place where people or animals came to be without the high priestess's permission. Since Jennifer gave no sign of anything amiss, he decided to wait and see if she exhibited any other signs that she'd been here previously. *Maybe being here has kicked Jennifer's intuition into high gear.*

Josh was buckling Misty's bridle when Jennifer began mounting D'Artagnan. His eyes were drawn in fascination as the large stallion lowered himself down to his knees, giving Jennifer easy access to his back. His wife grabbed ahold of a tuft of his mane and settled along the great horse's shoulders—riding bareback, much to Josh's horror. The stallion's back was so wide and his wife's legs spread so far apart that he feared she wouldn't stay on if D'Artagnan moved any faster than a walk. Before he could voice his concern D'Artagnan rose to his full height, dwarfing his wife by comparison.

"Are you ready?" Jennifer asked.

"Don't you think you should put a saddle on him?" Josh said warily from his position on Misty, reins in hand. Jennifer didn't dismount; instead she began saying something to the horse in a different language, but Josh wasn't close enough to hear which dialect she spoke. The stallion took a gigantic leap forward into a full gallop and Josh was left with his heart in his throat, fearing for her wellbeing. He'd watched Jennifer ride many times and she was skilled, but the sight before him was completely different; despite the fact she rode bareback, she did so with total abandonment, her long brown hair blowing in the breeze.

Josh urged Misty into a fast gallop and even though she was only slightly smaller than D'Artagnan, there was no way his Andulusian mount could catch the enormous stallion. Though worried about Jennifer's safety, he couldn't help but admire the two of them racing wildly across the field as though they were one. His libido overthrew his worried thoughts, and he wondered whether she'd ever ride *him* with the same reckless abandonment as she rode her stallion. *I need to get these thoughts out of my head and concentrate on catching up to my wife!* An impossible feat until Jennifer had brought D'Artagnan to a halt, who had no qualms about showing his displeasure by pawing the ground impatiently.

"Let's go this way," Jennifer called back to Josh. She guided D'Artagnan slowly down the rocky path, and when they rounded the bend, the thick foliage thinned to reveal a hidden oasis.

Josh watched Jennifer slide slowly off her horse, and it was one of the most erotic things he'd ever seen. *Damn, I want her again!* The truth of the matter was, he hadn't stopped wanting Jennifer since the first time they'd shaken hands. *How bad would it look if I accidently sexed my wife to death?* His ill-fated humor wouldn't have been so funny if Gisabella had been listening, although he had to admit that the idea of bringing Jennifer home with him now and forgoing the remainder of her current life-path was very tempting. Shaking the thoughts from his mind, Josh scanned the oasis's setting: one way in and out with rock ledges, dense foliage, and an impenetrable three-story waterfall that cascaded from a rock ledge into a pool below. The sound was soothing to his thunderous heartbeat and he began to relax, knowing Jennifer was safely by his side and they were protected by Gisabella's magic. He led the horses over to the lush grass so they could nibble on the succulent greens.

"Come with me." Jennifer took Josh's hand and guided him under the shade of a massive tree, where she sat down and urged him to do the same. She turned to her husband and pushed him down on his back, but his look of surprise didn't deter her from ravishing his mouth. Soon, her motivation to claim him overthrew her senses. She sunk her teeth into Josh's bottom lip, but the rich, coppery taste of his blood only increased her need as she fumbled to unzip his jeans and locate his readiness.

"Hurry—I need you now," Jennifer begged.

The taste of his own blood mingled with Jennifer's sweet lips skyrocketed Josh's desire, and he found himself getting caught up in the moment. He fought for control and rolled her over so she was underneath him, but she refused to have anything to do with his domination.

"Agh—give me what I want!" Jennifer commanded while struggling to retake the lead. Jennifer became as wild as a bobcat, waging an attack for control, but she was no match against his trained muscles. Jennifer's struggle escalated and so did Josh's passion; he scrambled to undo her jeans, pulling and pushing them until she was freed, then made fast work of her panties and boots. Before he knew it Jennifer was all over him, grabbing at the waistband of his jeans and begging for them to be taken off. Once he was bare-assed, her eyes became feverish and her need felt like hot lava flowing through the streets of Pompeii—and he was the city, engulfed by her power. He flipped her over face-down in the grass. There was no stopping him as he lifted her hips and forced her to kneel on all fours. With his hand, he checked to make sure she was lubricated before he plunged himself deep into her womanly treasure and filled her over and over again, spurred on by how she cried out for him to fuck her harder. Their breathing was no more than raspy gasps for air and her cries turned into screams when he felt her give way to ecstasy and shudder around him. With one final thrust, he poured himself into her sweet cavern and they collapsed in the grass, their hearts beating rapidly and their sated bodies locked together.

What came over me? Jennifer wondered as she waited for her breathing to slow. Her unbridled passion combined with her powerful lust for Josh had been greater than anything she'd ever experienced before. Now satisfied, she was left with the taste of Josh's blood in its wake, and a sense of uneasiness in the pit of her stomach.

"I'm sorry about your lip," Jennifer said, looking at the small cut on Josh's bottom lip.

"This?" Josh touched his mouth and smiled wide. "Baby, you can leave as many marks on me as you want. For the record, that was amazing!"

"I agree…it really was," Jennifer admitted, still confused about what had happened.

"So my wife loves rough sex. Mmm, I've married the perfect woman."

"Maybe it's because we're on our honeymoon…but I feel different."

"Really? How so?" Josh asked, ensuring his expression didn't give away the fact he'd been thinking the same thing.

"I don't know. I feel older, or something. Confident, even sexy…"*And a whole lot more experienced.*

"Older how?" Josh asked. Jennifer had failed to block her thoughts, but he was still left wondering what might've caused such a change in her behavior. The few times they'd kissed before marriage had suggested passion, yes, but nothing out of the ordinary, yet her recognition of D'Artagnan, Misty, and this hidden oasis, along with her immediate ardor for lovemaking was really beginning to perplex him.

"It's like I know things, but haven't a clue where I learned them," Jennifer replied. "You *have* to admit I'm different here—and it's more than just the honeymoon afterglow that's surely written all over my face."

"I happen to love that I had something to do with that glow."

"What about the other stuff?" Jennifer bit her lip nervously.

"Please don't worry, baby. I'll bet anything this is due to you being in another dimension; it's probably allowing you to access memories from your other lifetimes. For now, do your best to relax and go with the flow. If you run across other things that seem familiar or have the urge to seduce me like that again, let me know," Josh said, unable to suppress his huge smile.

"Oh great; I'm turning into someone from my past, and you're grinning like a fool!" Jennifer stood. "Now if you'll excuse me, I'm going skinny-dipping—and in case you were wondering—the water's heated!" She shook her head and looked skyward over this recollection, before taking off for the pool.

"Wait for me!" Josh said, scrambling to his feet to follow the trail of Jennifer's shed clothing to the water's edge.

Back at the house after dinner, they curled up together for a nice, quiet night of cuddling. If he wasn't on his honeymoon, Josh would've demanded Gisabella come forth that instant. He had a lot of questions to ask her about Jennifer: Had she lived there before? Who was she? How had she remembered D'Artagnan? He hadn't wanted to worry Jennifer with any of it, but there was far more to his wife than he'd been led to believe, and he would confront Gisabella as soon as possible and demand answers.

Josh carried his sleeping wife upstairs to bed and stayed with her until he was sure Jennifer was in a deep slumber. *It's time to ask Gisabella what the hell's going on,* he thought, surrounding the bedroom with protection and adding an invisible alarm in case Jennifer attempted to leave. The last thing he needed was for her to walk in on his discussion with the high priestess. If Josh's intuition about Jennifer's newfound knowledge was correct, she could be in serious trouble.

CHAPTER TWENTY-TWO

Once downstairs, Josh paced back and forth. *Of course Gisabella's taking her damn sweet time.* She'd always known how to get a rise out of him, and his temper heated with each minute that passed.

Gisabella watched Josh from her hovering position above the house and chose to let him stew a little longer. When she appeared, she did so behind him and took control before Josh could mutter one word. "Hello, Joshua. I trust you and Jennifer have been enjoying your honeymoon?" she asked, disappearing into the kitchen to put the teakettle on.

"Thank you for coming on such short notice," Josh ground out, forcing his anger down to a simmer. Gisabella was already perturbed about his earlier transgressions, so he needed to really watch himself now.

"I think we should have a nice cup of tea and a long conversation. I'm assuming you have some questions about your lovely wife." Gisabella poured two cups of tea and set them on a tray with a plate of cookies, then carried it into the family room and made herself comfortable. "How are you enjoying your new bride?" She couldn't wait to hear his response.

"As you can imagine, I am enjoying Jennifer's—er—*enthusiasm.*" Josh said, failing to disguise his smile. No doubt Gisabella already knew Jennifer's past lifetimes had begun to show themselves, and he had no complaints about his wife's old soul and overt sexuality making an unscheduled honeymoon appearance.

"Yes, I could see how her enthusiasm would come in handy." Gisabella hid her smirk behind her teacup. "Now, what was it that you wanted to know?"

"Jennifer has changed a great deal since we arrived here. She has, let's say, *opened* several of her abilities without being taught to use them. You could imagine my surprise when she remembered being here before." Josh paused and waited for Gisabella to fill in the blanks, but her only response was a silent sip of tea. "When we went to see the horses, I found it intriguing that D'Artagnan recognized Jennifer. Oddly enough, my wife blurted out both horses' names as if she'd known them her entire life. Her equine dexterity had greatly improved, which I witnessed first-hand as she rode bareback and led me to a secret, hidden oasis." His frustration grew with each second of Gisabella's silence. If he had any hope of getting answers, he needed to change his tactics. "Has Jennifer ever lived here?" He hoped the direct approach would earn him a response.

"Yes."

So this is how we're going to play the game. "How long?" He wanted to know if his hunch was correct.

"Five years—with time in between each of her many earth life-paths."

"Was her memory of those times shut down?"

"Yes."

"Is Jennifer gifted enough to reopen these memories on her own? Or do you think she had some outside help?" Josh leaned forward, waiting for Gisabella's response.

"Jennifer is gifted enough not only to open her memories, but to access all her gifts now that she's married."

"It's time to cut the shit, Gisabella, and tell me who Jennifer is to you!" Josh's patience had waned, and he knew of no better way to get his friend to spill her guts. "Start from the beginning and tell me everything."

"Fine—Jennifer is my granddaughter."

"Good to know," Josh said dryly. "Continue, please, and don't leave anything out."

"Have it your way—but I need to begin with my daughter Olivia's story for it all to make sense. I was on my last lifetime when I had Olivia, and after it ended and I took over the throne as the high priestess, part of my job was to watch over her as she carried out each of her many lifetimes on earth. As you may or may not know, every future high priestess is required to live a series of lifetimes. Once Olivia had completed hers, she was to join me as an apprentice. For her safety and that of the throne, Olivia's birth and her relationship to me were kept secret throughout all her lifetimes—only after she'd completed her final one would she have been introduced to the council as my successor."

"Go on," Josh encouraged.

"During her final lifetime, Olivia's lesson was to learn to tell the difference between who she could trust and who she couldn't. Much like myself, Olivia was a headstrong girl, but she'd never grasped how to distinguish who was untrustworthy. Since it was Olivia's last lifetime on earth and she'd expressed a desire for a child, I gave her one to rebirth."

"What do you mean by 'rebirth?'" Josh cocked an eyebrow.

"Everyone's soul goes through many lifetimes, and in each one their name is different. You can imagine how crazy it all gets with so many names over so many lifetimes, so, for the sake of simplicity, I'll use Jennifer's current name as I explain."

"Fine."

"Before you became a protector for me, you asked to have one lifetime with Jennifer, who'd originally been your lover nearly two thousand years ago. I helped you out by rebirthing Jennifer's soul after she'd lived several lifetimes, and by doing so gave Jennifer an opportunity to experience a lifetime as Olivia's child—all done in Jennifer's best interest, of course," Gisabella fibbed.

"Of course," Josh said. *In Jennifer's best interest my ass!*

"Olivia was due to give birth to Jennifer when her husband unexpectedly died; as far as we could tell it was after his passing when she became involved with a group of rebels. At the time, the council had let them be, thinking the group would fizzle and disband on its own. After Jennifer was born, Olivia seemed happy, but by the time Jennifer was one, my daughter had stopped answering my messages and ignored all requests to appear before me.

"Unbeknownst to me, Olivia had been appointed as their leader. I'm sure when they realized how psychic Olivia was, they decided to use her abilities for their cause. She somehow uncovered a plot to execute many council elders and myself, and instead of seeking my help, set a trap to expose them as the vile people they were. They killed her before she could."

"Do you know what happened?" Josh asked, squeezing Gisabella's hand warmly as she continued.

"Olivia's plan to trap them all in a cavern on earth and turn them over to the council was discovered by one of the rebels, who in turn set out to destroy her. By the time my protectors found her, she was already dead and her soul had been disintegrated." Gisabella wiped at her watery eyes and, once composed, went on. "Their numbers were larger than any of us had anticipated, and they were prepared for my force of protectors, ambushing them upon arrival. All but one of my protectors were disintegrated on the spot, and although he made it back, he was barely alive. Somehow he'd managed to get to Jennifer, who'd been less than a mile away at home asleep, and bring her safely here to my dimension. She was fourteen months old at the time, and was the tiniest, most delicate little thing I'd ever seen. She lived with me for five years before being sent back to earth to live a series of required life-paths. Josh—no one else knows about Jennifer's link to me, not even the council. I've kept her a secret for obvious reasons; face it, any living relative of mine is a target for those who wish to take over the universe."

Gisabella paused to compose herself before continuing. Although it'd been many centuries since Gisabella's daughter had been taken away from her, the rawness of the memory was still agonizing. "As you must've figured out, Jennifer is my only living soul connection."

"I'm sorry, Gisabella—I had no idea that happened. May I ask if they found out about Olivia's link to you?"

"Thankfully, Olivia never revealed to anyone she had a child. When her earth husband died four months prior to Jennifer's birth, I saw to it that all his memories of Olivia and her pregnancy were erased. He's had dozens of lifetimes since, so I'm positive all memories of Olivia and their baby are gone." Unsure of how to interpret Josh's quietness, Gisabella inhaled a deep breath and released the burdensome bomb she'd held on to for so long. "The protector who rescued Jennifer was the only one left who knew I had a blood relative." *Other than Jennifer's grandfather, but he doesn't count.* Gisabella prepared herself for Josh's reaction; she hadn't wanted him to find out this way, and especially not while on his honeymoon, but it would've been revealed eventually.

Josh's stomach tightened. "What happened to him?" *Can it be? Or does some other protector exist who knows that Gisabella has a granddaughter?* His breathing momentarily ceased while he anxiously awaited her response.

"*You're* that protector, Joshua." Regardless of the bad timing, it was a huge relief for Gisabella to finally tell him. "You'd sustained lethal injuries, and I wasn't sure if you'd pull through; the only option I had to save you had been outlawed by the council because it was considered to be black magic. If the council elders had discovered what I'd done, they would've disbarred and banished me to the outer darkness of nothingness. The potion I used works directly on the brain; in your case, it erased the injuries you'd suffered during the battle, and also all the memories that were associated with them." She didn't have the nerve to tell him how the potion had erased many other random memories as well.

"What the hell were you thinking, Gisabella? First you tell me about a daughter that in all our years of friendship you've failed to mention, and now you tell me that I rescued my wife many lifetimes ago. The next thing you'll tell me is that my wife is the next..." Josh froze midsentence, a look of horror on his face. "Holy fucking shit! Jennifer's the next high priestess, isn't she?!" Josh's nostrils flared and his eyes darkened with anger. "I can't believe you didn't have the decency to at least tell me *who* I was protecting!"

"I wanted to tell you, but my hands were tied. You can understand why, can't you?"

Josh shook his head, trying to grasp the full meaning of what Gisabella had done. When he reestablished eye contact, he did so with renewed purpose. "No wonder you didn't throw a bigger fit when I asked your permission to marry Jennifer or when we changed our vows. You *knew* this was going to happen all along! I'd even stake my soul on the fact you planned this entire thing centuries ago. What a jerk I've been to fall for your lies, all the while thinking we were best friends." Distress etched into the planes of Josh's face as the depth of Gisabella's betrayal became clearer.

"Please stop shouting and calm down before you wake Jennifer," Gisabella warned. "I did you a favor in matching you up with my granddaughter. If anything, you should be on your knees *thanking* me for my generosity." Gisabella held up a finger to stop Josh from speaking. "Secondly, marrying the girl forever was your *own* doing, so don't blame me for the fact you married the next high priestess. Thirdly, you're the one who asked me for a future lifetime with your former lover before you would agree to become a protector—all I did was take her soul under my wing and see to it that she was rebirthed into a position of power."

"You did what?" Josh sank into the closest chair and bent over with his head in his hands. "A position of power? How could you do that to the poor girl?" he moaned. "Wait a minute—you said that you promised me a lifetime with Jennifer, but according to you she must marry someone else in eight years. So you lied about that too!"

"I didn't lie!" *You were the one who failed to clarify how long of a life you wanted with the girl.* "Try to understand; at the time, we had just met and quite frankly, you were a pain in the ass—not that you aren't one still." Gisabella bit her lip trying not to smirk. "Now that we're related, let me be the first to welcome you into the family."

"Thanks; this just keeps getting better by the minute. Both my wife and my only other friend are in charge of my ass! As a member of your family, I'd like to say how appalled I am to have been unknowingly dragged into your circle." Josh exhaled wearily. "I guess I should ask if you think Jennifer will remember me bringing her here?"

"No. I'm positive she won't; when you brought her she was in a state of shock and wanted her mother. She hasn't remembered who *I* am and she lived with me for years, whereas you weren't with her more than twenty minutes. Plus, you were hurt so badly no one would recognize you as the same person. During the two weeks you spent here recovering, you had no contact with the child." In retrospect, Gisabella added, "Quite frankly, I'm shocked that Jennifer remembers anything."

"You can thank D'Artagnan for that. The bond between that horse and Jennifer is so great I don't think there's anything that could've stopped her from remembering him." Josh had so many more questions, and wasn't sure where to begin. *Why else was I placed in Jennifer's life-path? How many lifetimes have Jennifer and I shared together that I can't remember?*

"Josh, when you became the best protector in the entire galaxy, I had no choice other than to add you into Jennifer's life-path." Gisabella watched as Josh stood up, ran his hand through his hair, and began pacing as if in a cage; he didn't appear to be taking the information well. When he finally stopped walking and peered out the living room window into the darkness, she attempted a different approach. "Don't you get it? You asked my permission to marry Jennifer."

"Of course I asked to marry Jennifer!" He spun around with anger in his eyes and fists clenched. "Only to find out now that both our destinies were set in stone. Tell me the truth—did you tamper with Jennifer's life-path so she would fall in love with me?"

"You asked Jennifer to marry you *three years* earlier than written." Gisabella watched Josh try to register this fact. "Don't you see? You and Jennifer fell in love with each other long before destiny indicated you would. Together you changed your fates! The only way to do such an impossible feat is if both people share a soul connection of unconditional, true love. The fact that the two of you fell in love before the predestined time is nothing short of a miracle."

"Are you saying you had nothing to do with us falling in love?"

"I admit I may've uncloaked Jennifer so you'd notice she'd grown up and could access her thoughts, but I swear I had nothing to do with the feelings you have for each other. To be honest, I've never seen anything like it before. I can think of only one reason for it: your last lifetime on earth together. You'd both been so in love, and when you each died—less than an hour apart—it bound you two together. Don't you see? You and Jennifer are soulmates!"

"'Soulmates,'" Josh echoed, rolling the word around in his head several times to grasp its meaning. "I don't suppose Jennifer's the dark-haired girl who haunts my memory? I can't tell you how many times I've envisioned having breakfast with the same woman on a balcony in Rome. Now you tell me the partial snapshot of happiness that's tortured my soul for years exists with the woman I've married forever?"

"I'd say your chances are excellent that she's the same girl. Best of all, after Jennifer has completed her life on earth, you'll be together forever."

"Gisabella, would you please give me back Jennifer's paperwork and life-path so I may read them?"

"I've waited years for you to ask me about the lock on her life-path, since I *never* gave you access." Gisabella's wicked smile gave Josh a clue that he was still in trouble.

"Because I decided on the first day that Jennifer was nothing more than a sweet kid. Talk about eating my words now."

"Let's face it—when you began protecting my granddaughter, you decided not to take her or your job seriously. You thought Jennifer had not one *single* visionary gift in her procession!"

"Yep, my mistake." His irritation grew as he watched Gisabella laugh so hard she couldn't catch her breath. Her ridicule was doing nothing to improve his temperament.

"Talk about making a *big* mistake!" she cajoled.

"Yes, Gisabella, I get it—I screwed up royally and underestimated my wife's gifts and abilities. Ha, ha, you've had your laugh, Grandma. Do you think when you're finished shishka-bobbing my nuts over hot coals that you could find time to open Jennifer's life-path?"

"Consider it done. Now that you married Jennifer for all eternity, it's up to you to prepare her to assume leadership over the council and universe."

"Consider it done," Josh repeated her words back. "Gisabella, you never mentioned what happened to your relatives; I assumed you inherited the high priestess title from someone."

"Up until now, each of the high priestesses before me were victims of foul-play, and their souls no longer exist."

"Are you telling me that none of them lived long enough to retire?" Josh paled at the implication.

"Josh, why didn't you tell me we had company?" a voice called out from the upper balcony.

Josh and Gisabella whipped their heads around and watched in disbelief as Jennifer trotted down the steps to join them.

~I have no clue how Jennifer avoided setting off either of the alarms I put in place,~ Josh messaged Gisabella.

"Grandmamma!" Jennifer called out as she ran into Gisabella's arms. "I'm so excited you're here!"

"I'm happy to see you too, my dear." Gisabella hid her surprised expression and returned the embrace.

As if Jennifer had awoken from a dream, she backed up and shook her head in confusion. "'Grandmamma?'" *Why would I think Gisabella is my grandmother?* She turned and sought Josh's eyes, silently pleading for answers.

"It's okay, Jennifer." Josh hid his irritation with Gisabella and went to his wife's side. "Why don't you come sit down and let us explain." Josh kept his smile in place while he sent off a message to Gisabella. ~Now's your chance to come clean. If you don't, you may lose Jennifer's trust forever.~

"Josh is right, my dear—come sit on the couch with me while he pours you a cup of tea." Gisabella took a seat near the fireplace, leaving Jennifer no other choice but to join her.

"Here you go, baby. Be careful, it's hot," Josh said, setting the steaming mug on the coffee table before sitting in a chair to face them.

"Thank you." Jennifer picked up the cup and held it between her hands to warm her frozen nerves. "Well? Would one of you please explain what's happening and why things here are so familiar? Starting with my grandma—uh, I mean Gisabella." Despite her attempt to sound calm, Jennifer's voice came out two octaves higher than normal.

"I was just asking Gisabella the same thing. Do you care to explain?" Josh turned his attention towards the high priestess.

Gisabella glowered at Josh before she turned to Jennifer with a warm smile. "My dear, I'm so glad some of your memory has returned. I can't tell you how many lifetimes I've missed you. Now here you are, married to one of my closest friends and calling me 'Grandmamma.'" She reached over and lightly squeezed Jennifer's hand.

"Lifetimes?" Jennifer's eyes doubled in size. "What exactly do you mean?"

"You experienced many lifetimes on earth before my daughter Olivia gave birth to you over a century ago. I can't tell you how excited I was to have grandchild."

"Olivia? But my mother's name is Claire," Jennifer clarified.

"Olivia was the woman who rebirthed your soul—imprinting you forever as my granddaughter, and making you my only heir. Since then you've lived many lifetimes, and in this particular life, your birth mother is Claire."

"What you're telling me sounds crazy, and I should be flipping out," Jennifer said, blinking rapidly. "But for some reason, it just sounds *right* to me. Does it have something to do with being here in this dimension?" Jennifer stifled a nervous giggle, glancing from Gisabella to Josh and back again. "Who was my father back then?"

"I'm afraid his soul transitioned to heaven before you were born, and he never knew of you."

"How many different sets of parents, grandparents, and family members have I had?"

"If I had to take a guess, no more than a total of fifty different sets of souls have shared your lifetimes. Not at the same time, of course. It all depends on each of their life-paths and how long they were in spirit form before beginning a new lifetime on earth. It's a shame Josh hasn't found the time to explain all of this to you before now; if he had, it would be easier to understand." Gisabella glanced at Josh with annoyance.

"Gisabella's right—I should've begun your teachings earlier," Josh remorsefully added before sending a message to Gisabella. ~Don't you think it'd be a good time to tell Jennifer about her future? It'd sound better if it came from you.~

~Look at the poor girl; she looks like a deer staring directly into a pair of oncoming headlights. I'm afraid if I tell her now, it might ruin her honeymoon. Why don't we give her a chance to get used to being married for a month or two?~

~All right—I'll bring Jennifer back here in two weeks so you can tell her. Can we use the house again? I'm sure by then we'll need time alone to ourselves in a bed that's bigger than her child-sized one.~

~Fine. Same as last time—four hours earth time for four days here in your honeymoon house. I'll allow it on one condition: you agree to back me up when we tell Jennifer about her future title.~

"In Josh's defense about not having taught me these things, I gave him a hard time before we got engaged," Jennifer defended, thinking back to the time she'd refused to speak to him. "Why don't you explain it to me now, Grandmamma?"

"Sets of souls are born into each other's lives over and over, until each has reached the spiritual plane of higher knowledge. At that time they can choose to stay in heaven, or return to earth for additional lifetimes. This is the level which I believe Josh has told you he hasn't reached."

"Yes, Josh did explain that he'd given up his soul's journey when he became a protector. If I'm not mistaken, my husband holds the title of being your top elite protector, so I'd say his choice to forgo the remainder of his lifetimes was a good one, wouldn't you?"

Gisabella chuckled. "Jennifer, I've waited a long time for you to show a sign that you're from my flesh and blood, and now I can honestly say you remind me of myself when I was your age." Gisabella turned towards Josh and raised her cup in a toast. "All I can say is good luck old man!"

"I've gotta deal with *two* of you? What have I done to deserve such good fortune?" Josh's dry tone and worried eyes reflected his concern.

"You look absolutely petrified, Josh," Gisabella teased.

"You do look a little green in the face, honey. Maybe you'd better go lie down for a while," Jennifer added, before she walked over and climbed into his lap. "Somehow, I don't think two of us will present any difficulty for a strong man such as yourself." Jennifer sealed her words with a kiss.

"On that note, I think I'll let you two honeymooners have some time alone." Gisabella stood and headed towards the door. "We'll talk again soon."

"Gisabella, I think you should join us for dinner tomorrow night. I'm sure my wife will have more questions for you. Consider it our way of thanking you for everything you've done for us," Josh said.

"I'd love to have dinner with my two favorite people." Gisabella gave Jennifer a huge hug before leaving, and then turned to Josh. "Thank you for bringing my granddaughter back to me. I love you both so much," she whispered into his ear. The emotion in Josh's eyes mirrored hers. They'd been longtime friends, and unlike her, Josh had no relatives or close friends other than herself. She was thrilled that Josh now had Jennifer in his life. Best of all, once Jennifer's current lifetime was over, he'd never again have to watch his soulmate live another life from a distance as her protector.

CHAPTER TWENTY-THREE

"Come on in, Gisabella. Jennifer will be down in a moment," Josh said with a tight smile. The air between them felt thick, and his words had tumbled out a little too rapidly. The culmination of finding himself married to her granddaughter and welcoming Gisabella into her own house added to his discomfort. "Can I get you something to drink?" Josh asked, remembering his manners.

"I brought a bottle of my favorite vintage from a winery in France." Gisabella handed the bottle of 1961 Marques De Riscal Reserva to her host.

"I honestly don't have a clue how you're able to mingle so easily with the living." When he noticed the label, he chuckled. "Gisabella, you may not be able to cook or bake, but you never fail to please in the wine department."

"Something smells amazing!" A wafting, enticing aroma encircled Gisabella's senses, luring her deeper into the house.

"I can't believe you didn't tell Jennifer about her title last night," Josh said, immediately unloading his frustration.

"She'll find out soon enough."

"Jennifer needs to know the truth. You're not doing her any favors by hiding her destiny, especially now that she'll be joining me when her lifetime is over."

"Josh, this is none of your…" Gisabella halted when she noticed Jennifer poised at the top of the stairs.

"Grandmamma, I'm sorry to have kept you waiting," Jennifer said as she descended the curved staircase.

His wife's beauty stunned Josh into silence while his eyes traveled from Jennifer's pinned-up hairdo to the strapless, sapphire gown that showed off her slender shoulders to perfection. She was wearing the same ice-blue diamond around her neck that she'd worn during their wedding ceremony, paired with sparkling diamond earrings that added to her sublime elegance. *Is she really all mine?*

"You look breathtaking, my dear." Gisabella proudly watched her granddaughter approach with an air of confidence she hadn't seen in any of the girl's previous lifetimes.

"Remember," Gisabella whispered to the star-struck man beside her, "Jennifer will always be a woman first and a high priestess second. Most of all, she's your wife, and she loves you with all her heart. So close your mouth, Josh, and get a grip." Gisabella couldn't help grinning at his stunned reaction, almost as if he were seeing his wife for the first time.

Gisabella's words brought him to his senses, and with an appreciative smile for his wife, Josh walked forward to escort Jennifer the rest of the way. The view of the two women embracing stirred his emotions, and it was moving to see how Gisabella lit up around the granddaughter he'd never known she had.

"Josh, are we all set?" Jennifer asked.

"Yes." For the first time, he was at a loss for words. Though he was technically older and more experienced than she, Jennifer's appearance that night was so breathtaking that he felt nowhere near deserving of his high priestess wife.

An hour later they were seated in the dining room with soft music playing, candles flickering, Francesca china and white linen napkins laid out, and a table centerpiece made of red roses and the lilies from Jennifer's bridal bouquet.

"Joshua, you've outdone yourself this evening. No one can make a rack of lamb like you can," Gisabella cheered with her glass of wine. "Jennifer, you're a lucky woman to have married a man who knows his way around a kitchen. No matter what happens, you'll always have great food."

"What's that supposed to mean?" Josh challenged. "'No matter what happens?'"

"You know, regarding whatever happens; arguments, or finding yourself locked out of the bedroom, or if Jennifer's exhausted after you've kept her in bed all day and all night—she'll always be able to count on a good meal afterwards."

"What does that mean? 'Keeping me in bed day and night?'" Jennifer noticed how the two were struggling to maintain composure. "You're not implying…? Really? Is that possible?" When both sets of eyes danced with humor and their smiles widened, she had her answer.

"I don't know why you're so worried; most women would love to have a man with as much stamina as a spirit. Especially one that's of the protector kind, whose endurance training comes in handy for other things *besides* fighting."

"I'm not sure my wife is as pleased to hear about my stamina as I'd hoped," Josh said with a laugh. "Honey, I'd be happy to give it a go tonight if you'd like."

Mortified, Jennifer tried changing the topic. "How long have you two known each other?"

"I don't think my granddaughter is very happy with you," Gisabella chortled.

"If I end up locked out of our honeymoon suite it's *your* fault, old woman."

Jennifer's embarrassment morphed into irritation. "Please tell me you're both drunk and this isn't the 'norm' when you're together."

"Too much wine," Gisabella admitted with a snicker.

"Me too," Josh agreed.

Who's fooling who? "I'll ask again—how did you both meet?" Jennifer repeated before her dinner companions could restart their shenanigans.

"That's a good question—how *did* we meet?" Josh asked.

"Don't you know?" Jennifer looked confused.

"It seems to have slipped my mind." Josh shot an indignant look at Gisabella, who he now knew was responsible for his bouts of amnesia.

"It was long ago and not very memorable, so I can see how Josh forgot. From what I recall, he was brought to me by a protector who's since chosen to resume his life-paths on earth. When I met Josh he was known for his fighting skills in battle, and at one time had been a commander in Rome. I accepted his request to join my force of protectors, and now, many centuries later, we're close friends," Gisabella fibbed, doing her best to hide her lies behind a smile. The last thing she wanted was for Josh to figure out the truth; no telling what he'd do to keep Jennifer from marrying her life-path husband. It was a destiny Jennifer *must* fulfill before she could become the high priestess, and Gisabella couldn't risk Josh jeopardizing that.

Josh narrowed his eyes—none of what Gisabella'd said resonated with him, but he couldn't be sure she'd lied either.

They all headed to the kitchen, where Josh began preparing coffee and Jennifer made the frosting for the chocolate chip cherry cupcakes they'd baked earlier. Once his part was done, Josh joined Gisabella at the breakfast bar where they observed Jennifer's handiwork.

Gisabella couldn't help noticing how intently Josh watched his wife, and she didn't need to use her mind-reading skills to know that his craving went far beyond desiring to eat a cupcake. When Josh's expression changed from a mere longing to gluttony and he looked as if he was going to devour Jennifer on the spot, Gisabella took it as her signal to leave. A few warm hugs later she departed, leaving the honeymooners alone.

Josh walked up behind Jennifer and grabbed the hand holding the bag of frosting. "I haven't been able to take my eyes off you all night long. The way you insist on tormenting me with memories of wedding cake and frosting makes me want *you* for dessert." Josh took the bag of frosting from her hand and placed it on the counter. "You're sweet enough for my taste," he said, leading her upstairs for another night of passion.

The next morning, Jennifer woke up early and made breakfast for Josh. She was placing the finishing touches on the outdoor table when her eyes fixated on the manscape that stood in the doorway. Josh's hand was casually placed on the doorframe and he wore the slightest hint of a smile, a sign that he knew how much she was enjoying his half-nakedness.

His red pajama bottoms were slung low on his hips, providing Jennifer with the most inspiring view of his carved abs. Her mouth fell open in appreciation when Josh sauntered towards her in his bare feet, and there was little she could do to hide her change in breathing or her desire.

"This looks wonderful," Josh complimented, before taking Jennifer into his arms and planting a big kiss on her inviting lips. As far as he could remember no one other than Gisabella had ever cooked for him, often with inedible results. Thankfully, Jennifer hadn't inherited her grandmother's god-awful cooking skills.

Breakfast outside together was so relaxing that he found himself wishing the meal would never end, as it was their last morning alone before they transported back to earth and faced the reality of their situation. How would they pull off being married? They were nothing like a normal "earth couple." His concerns grew as the clock ticked, but he needed to force himself to focus on the matter at hand: their honeymoon.

"Jennifer, would you like to go see D'Artagnan?" Josh asked. He was rewarded by Jennifer's face lighting up as if he'd given her a key to a diamond mine. *Wow, what a woman like Jennifer could do to a man.*

"Would you come with me?" Jennifer asked hopefully.

"Just try to stop me."

A little while later, Jennifer was galloping by Josh on D'Artagnan at breakneck speed. Each time they raced by the fence, his heart lurched while the breeze the two made was strong enough to blow-dry his hair. It'd taken a few days, but he was finally capable of standing at the fence as she rode D'Artagnan without saying hundreds of prayers that she didn't fall off. Now that his fear for her safety was under control, the way Jennifer rode her stallion was creating lusty urges deep inside him.

Josh stood his ground when Jennifer pointed D'Artagnan towards the fence and whispered to her horse. D'Artagnan sprang forward and galloped full-speed to skid to a halt inches shy of where Josh stood, and for the first time their playful stunt didn't make him flinch. Too bad he didn't fare so well in the trance department, which only deepened when Jennifer slid seductively off her steed. His wife embraced D'Artagnan, then removed a lead rope from around his neck that Josh didn't recall her retrieving earlier. D'Artagnan pawed the ground and reared up in front of her, then rested his head against Jennifer's chest before galloping away into the field.

Josh's eyes never left Jennifer as she walked through the gate towards him, the lead rope in one hand as she used the other to pull his lips down to hers. Her kiss was urgent and hard, reminding him of their day at the oasis. When he forced himself to separate his lips from her captivating ones, he smiled wide.

"What are you planning to do with me, Jennifer?" Somehow during their kiss, his wife had managed to secure the lead rope around his neck and now held the other end. *This could get interesting.*

"So you like how hard I ride D'Artagnan?" Jennifer's voice was firm, her eyes unwavering as she stared into his.

"Yes. I do," he choked. *Had she read my mind?* He thought he'd guarded his thoughts. *Unless she breached them somehow…*

"Good, because you're next." She didn't give Josh a chance to respond or close his mouth before she led him to the barn. She had a plan that would exceed her husband's wildest fantasies, since for once she'd been able to read his thoughts unhindered.

He eagerly followed Jennifer into the barn, happy as a little boy on Christmas morning.

In another realm, Sarnia entered the well-known hangout for "lower level" protectors, one which her elite constituents refused to step foot in. It was a smoke-filled bar with drab walls, mismatched stools, and a few billiard tables that had seen better days many times over. Dark and dreary just like Sarnia's mood, the bar had a wide variety of hard liquor that made it the perfect place to lick her wounds.

The tables were filled, so Sarnia grabbed a seat at the end of the bar far away from anyone who had so much as a tiny smile on their face.

"What'll it be, hot stuff?" the bartender asked, leaning forward enough to catch a whiff of Sarnia's despair and a glimpse of her cleavage.

"If you want to live long enough to serve your next drink, you better get your eyes off my tits and fetch me a double of the strongest stuff you've got," Sarnia snarled, barely holding on to her temper.

"Can't blame a man for trying," the bartender shrugged, pouring her a double shot of bourbon. "This one's on me."

"Thanks," Sarnia replied, draining the entire glass. "I'll have another."

"Things that bad?"

"Why would you say that? Maybe I just want to get drunk," Sarnia said, hoping to chase him away with her scowl. He wasn't her type—blond hair, skinny, with thin lips and a weak jaw; the total opposite of Josh.

"Have it your way, honey. Here's the bottle, and I'll be at the other end of the bar if you need me." The bartender risked a wink before walking away.

"*Idiot,*" Sarnia muttered under her breath before draining the second glass of bourbon. She was finishing her third glass when a man sat down next to her and ordered a beer.

"Come here often?" the dark-haired protector asked with a chuckle. "I bet you must hear that cheesy line all the time. I'd wager you're the kind of woman who'd love to disintegrate any man who dares to say it to your face?"

"If that's what you want—I'd be happy to oblige by putting an end to your sorry ass," Sarnia replied, unable to stop her lips from curving up at the thought.

"Nah, I can think of much better things I'd rather be doing with you," the stranger said, leaning back on his stool and crossing his arms.

"My, my; you're a cocky one, aren't you?" Sarnia said without looking his way.

"That's what my friends tell me, but what do they know?"

"My guess is anyone who gets to know you wants to whip your ass," Sarnia murmured.

"Is that what you want to do to me? If so, I have no problem with that sort of stuff. Just remember, I give as good as I get!" The stranger leaned closer and whispered, "God, you smell delicious—good enough to eat and fuck for days."

"Who the hell are you?" Sarnia swiveled to get a better look, and froze when she saw his face. He looked…*familiar.*

"Better watch how much attention you give to Mr. Jim Beam, here; he's been known to cause one hell of a hangover. I'm sure the person you're drinking over isn't worth it."

"You think you're so smart, eh?" Sarnia snorted, squinting at the younger Josh lookalike, who was smiling back with carnal appreciation. "What's your name?" *If he says his name is Josh, I'm gonna give him the ride of his life!*

"It's Byron, but you can call me anything you like."

"Since you're feeling so brave, let's go to my place and get you naked. If you're anything like the man you resemble, you'll be in my bed for a long time."

"Works for me. And what should I call *you*?" Byron asked.

"Kitten." Sarnia's eyes sparkled.

"Lead the way, kitten."

Two hours and many orgasms later Sarnia smiled at the younger protector as he unfastened the leather cuffs that held her prisoner.

"You sure know how to show a girl a good time," Sarnia praised.

"Glad I could be of service, kitten," Byron said, pulling her to him for a kiss. "Now that I've curtailed your mood with a riding crop and made you purr so sweetly, what ever will you do to me?"

"Oh, Byron—a bad boy like you needs to be punished, then ridden hard until you have nothing left to give."

"I like your style woman! So that you know, I hold the man's record for the most orgasms in a day." Byron grinned widely at the naked redhead before him, one currently sporting a bright-red ass from multiple smacks.

"Seeing as though you're a protector and a spirit, if you're not able to fuck for twenty-four hours straight, I'd consider you a lousy lover!"

"No worries there, kitten," Byron said with pride. "I think you've talked enough now."

"Lie down on the bed so I can tie you up and make you hard—you're useless to me like this," Sarnia taunted, pointing to Byron's flaccid penis.

"Hey! No insulting my favorite body part!"

"Don't worry, I'll fix its condition," Sarnia said with a wink. "After all, it's my favorite part of you too."

When Byron was in place on the bed, Sarnia began fastening him spread-eagle to each of the bedposts. With both of his legs and one of his wrists secured, Sarnia held the final cuff and watched Byron's erection get harder and harder.

"Mmm, I haven't even finished and you're as hard as steel," Sarnia said in awe. Unable to resist, she lowered herself to take Byron into her mouth as deep and far as she could, sucking him until he begged for her permission to come. When he still hadn't finished and her jaw was aching, Sarnia lifted her head and Byron grabbed a handful of her hair with his free hand.

"You're not finished!" he growled, guiding the redhead back towards his cock. "Show me what a good kitty cat you can be. Suck me off!"

"I hope you're into teeth," Sarnia warned, opening her mouth wider. Her threat did the trick, and it wasn't long before she was lapping up his milky juice.

"Fuck, woman! You're going to be the death of me!" Byron watched as Sarnia climbed out of bed to retrieve the final restraint where she'd dropped it on the floor, a huge smile on her pretty face.

"What a good boy you are, Byron," Sarnia purred as she fastened the leather cuff around his wrist. "Now that you've had your fun, it's my turn," she said, rubbing her sore ass cheek. "I probably should've warned you before now, that I like to give *better* than I receive." Sarnia licked her lips as she walked by the riding crop that Byron had used on her ass earlier, instead choosing one of the whips hanging on the wall.

"Like I'm scared of a little girl like you!" Byron laughed.

"How dare you laugh at me, *Josh*! It's about time you paid for what you did to me!" Sarnia barked, her voice rising as her fury did.

"Kitten, I was only kidding," Byron said, swallowing hard as he observed the change in Sarnia's demeanor. Her once-cool expression had grown callous, leaving no sign of warmth behind. Worried, Byron began tugging on the restraints to no avail. "Did you use some kind of energy to make these unbreakable?" When his question went unanswered, a chill ran through his body.

"'Kidding?' *Kidding*?! Were you kidding when you came to me on earth and *stole* my virginity?!" Sarnia shouted, bringing the whip down hard across his chest.

"Agh!" Byron gritted his teeth. "Lady, I don't know what you're talking about! I've never seen you before tonight!"

"That's not true! You came to me under the full moon on my eighteenth birthday!" Sarnia cracked the whip just above the struggling man's knees, leaving an instant red welt in its place.

"Cut the shit, kitten. You're taking this too far!"

Sarnia briefly closed her eyes to bring everything into focus, reopening them to see *Josh* tied up in her bed.

"I swear I've never seen you before. Please let me go," Byron begged, until Sarnia grabbed her discarded panties from the side of the bed and stuffed them in his mouth.

"You took everything from me, then left before sunrise," Sarnia cried out, slashing the whip across the man she'd once loved over and over while he writhed to and fro, desperate for escape. "It's *my* turn to make you suffer! I waited in that field every night for you to return, but you never showed." Sarnia whipped him harder. "I vowed to find you after I died, but when I did so, you acted as if you didn't remember me! All these centuries I've tried to stir your memories. I thought for sure when you slept with me a thousand years ago you'd remember the past, but once you had your fun, you casted me aside like I was nobody." Sarnia unleashed a series of strikes across Byron's hard body, once or twice hitting his man parts and causing tears to run down his face. "That's right—it's your time to cry!" Sarnia delivered blow after blow, taking advantage of his helpless position before she sank to the floor, sobbing.

Byron kept yanking at his restraints, but it was futile; her energy was impenetrable. He laid there for an hour or two, waiting until the woman he knew only as "kitten" lifted her head to gaze up at him.

"Who are you?" Sarnia asked, emerging from her mental fog and scanning the bound, helpless figure before her. In the light of day, he looked nothing like Josh. "I'm sorry," she cried, touching one of the raised welts that covered his entire body. "Please forgive me—I, I thought you were Josh—I made a mistake…"

Byron's expression morphed, and she realized he'd guessed she was referring to Gisabella's highest elite protector. A tidal wave of fear gripped her soul. "I can't have you running to Josh or Gisabella. If they were to see what I've done, I'd be banished for sure!"

Byron's eyes widened at the words, and he tried with renewed vigor to free himself from the leather bindings. "No, no—wait—"

"I'll make this quick," Sarnia said, shooting a bolt of energy from her palms to hit Byron square in the chest and disintegrate him instantly.

She began to busy herself removing the "crispy" charred sheets and all other evidence of Byron's presence from her bedroom, humming to break the silence.

"All I have to do now is find the bartender and erase his memory," Sarnia said, hoping that talking out loud would soothe her nerves. "Damn shame—Byron was a good lay! This is all Josh's fault!" With an impatient swipe of her hand, Sarnia whisked away her tears. "Mark my words; if I ever get Josh in bed again, he'll receive the same!" She spun and left her house then, heading for the bar to finish cleaning up the last loose end she'd created.

CHAPTER TWENTY-FOUR

When it was time to travel back to earth, Jennifer stood in the clothes she'd arrived in, riding boots in hand and waiting to transport.

Before they left, Gisabella took Josh's hand in hers and transferred something deep inside the flesh of his palm. When she let go of his hand, Josh saw no trace of an implant. "You now hold the only other key to my personal transporting system, so you can transport Jennifer here without my assistance. The key will only work when you and Jennifer travel here together, and this house will always be here for Jennifer and you to use. Please bring my granddaughter here often, so her gifts develop in a safe environment. I know you'll make Jennifer very happy, and I trust you completely."

"I promise to bring her here as often as I can. Jennifer flourishes here, around you and her horse. We'll also need time alone together to keep our marriage *strong*," Josh said with meaning.

"Before you go, you're going to need these," Gisabella said conspiratorially to Josh, before handing him Jennifer's life-path and profile. "I think you'll find some of the answers you're looking for in them," she winked. Now that Josh had access to Jennifer's past lifetimes and most of her current destiny, he'd finally know how gifted and strong she was destined to become. Married to Jennifer forever, Josh was the only person who Gisabella trusted with her granddaughter's life.

"Thank you. I'll read them sooner rather than later," Josh said, looking abashed.

"I have no doubt it will be at the top of your priorities, right below Jennifer herself." Gisabella gathered him into her arms. "Take care of yourself, my friend, and I'll see you both in two weeks. As far as Jennifer is concerned you're the only man who matters, so don't do anything foolish."

"I'll try my very best," Josh quipped.

"My dear, sweet granddaughter," Gisabella continued, motioning for Jennifer to come closer. "Now that you know of me, you'll understand why you must listen and learn lots from Joshua. He's the best at what he does, and you'll be safe with him by your side. He loves you more than you could ever imagine!" Gisabella released Jennifer and gazed at the happy couple with unshed tears in her eyes. Then she stood back and watched Josh lower his lips to her granddaughter's, successfully transporting them to earth.

Once back home, Jennifer peered around in dismay; her previously adequate bedroom looked more like a walk-in closet after honeymooning in a luxurious, apartment-sized suite. Worst of all, her twin bed no longer looked big enough for one let alone the both of them, nor was there much room for Josh's clothes, books, and other stuff.

~I wish we were still on our honeymoon,~ Josh messaged, eyeing the bed.

~Months, not days, would've been my preference,~ Jennifer replied with longing. A warm, tingling sensation on both of her shoulders came from Josh's translucent touch. He'd been solid since Sarah's wedding, and she'd forgotten how different his energetic touch felt compared to his physical one. Time spent in the other dimension had been amazing, but now they'd have to deal with their abnormal lifestyle and his invisibility. The reality of their situation began to sink in, making her wonder if they could beat the overwhelming odds against them.

As a newly married woman, one thought in Jennifer's mind blared louder than all the others: *How will sex work when Josh is translucent?* She had no point of reference since Josh had been solid each time they'd kissed. Now at home, she, too, felt different; she was no longer as confident or uninhibited enough to take the lead, and felt shyer about discussing things of a physical nature.

How could his wife not be upset? Josh didn't have to read Jennifer's mind to know the reason why. He'd trapped her into an impossible marriage with someone who technically didn't exist in her world, then spent four days alone with her in another dimension playing house. Now back on earth, he needed his wife to act like nothing in her life had changed. How had he imagined he was doing the right thing by marrying her?

There must be things I can do to help improve Jennifer's life and be worthy of her. One of the first issues that needed addressing was a solution for their living arrangements, and his eyes immediately drifted towards the child-sized twin bed. *That will never do!* Before he could have a reassuring conversation with Jennifer, a glance at the clock let him know it was time to walk his new wife to school, presenting him with another item she needed: *a car.*

~Baby, I hate to say this, but it's time to leave.~ Josh noted his wife's sour expression, making him wonder how Jennifer would handle her first day in school as a married woman. He hoped no one would notice anything different about her; she'd graduate soon, and they'd have the summer to adjust as a married couple. As far as he was concerned, it couldn't come fast enough.

~I have something different in mind.~ Jennifer tilted her lips upward and was rewarded with her very first energy kiss.

~How bad was that?~ Josh asked warily. ~It's going to take some getting used to on both our parts.~

~Honestly, it wasn't as bad as I thought it'd be.~ When Josh cringed, she elaborated. ~Unlike when you're solid, in some ways it's more intense. Maybe because I'm not as caught up in how great your lips feel, I can direct my attention to the sensation of the energy between us. If I could please have another, it'll help me get used to the difference.~

His second smooch lasted much longer, proving how exceptional a kiss from her spirit husband could be. This time the kiss she received was burning hot, and felt as if Josh had poured every ounce of his passion into making sure her mind, body, and soul responded on a visceral level.

A rush of sensations traveled up and down her spine, before wrapping around to become a fireball of intense pleasure so great that she was engulfed in a mind-altering orgasm.

~How was that? Any better?~ Josh didn't bother to hide his smile as he used his energy to keep Jennifer upright.

~That was a little better. Don't worry, I'm sure with practice you'll get the hang of it,~ Jennifer reassured while she stumbled to the closet to get her coat.

~Mrs. Smith, you may wish to rethink your outfit,~ Josh snickered at her dazed expression.

Jennifer looked down and found she'd grabbed her bathrobe. Summoning up as much self-respect as she could muster, she turned back to the closet and exchanged the robe for her coat and her slippers for her boots. ~If you're waiting for me to tell you how amazing you are, you're out of luck. I wouldn't wish to inflate your ego.~ *Bravo, Mr. Smith!* A glance sideways told her that her sex-guru husband had read her unblocked, congratulatory thought.

Walking to school next to her husband was different, and after spending four days making love, Jennifer wasn't ready to let him forget all that they'd done together. ~I sure miss riding,~ Jennifer messaged. ~Do you miss it too?~

~I'm warning you, Jennifer, you'd better behave yourself.~ Josh turned away to hide his grin, while suppressing the urge to respond with a message that'd make her face go redder than a tomato. It was his job to set an example and some ground rules, beginning with explaining how her message was such that every teenage boy would be drawn to the sexual vibrations it carried, like fleas on a stray dog. They'd arrived at their destination, however, so he postponed the conversation until later.

~Okay, in you go, baby. Remember I'll be close at hand,~ Josh messaged with a "wait until you see what I have in mind for later" smile.

Mundane things like school and studies were hard to concentrate on knowing Josh was watching, and most of Jennifer's morning was spent daydreaming and glancing at the clock. *Will this day ever end?* When the lunch bell sounded, she was halfway through her first day in school as a married woman.

~I wish I could have lunch with you,~ Jennifer messaged on the way to the cafeteria.

~Me too, baby. If it's any consolation, I'll be with you in spirit.~ His humor didn't go unnoticed by his wife, who did her best to hide behind a blank facade. She would've pulled it off if not for the two splotches of color on her cheeks.

"Hi, girls," Jennifer said as she joined her friends.

"Hi, Jennifer," Elizabeth greeted, glancing up from the book she was reading. "How was your sister's wedding?"

"Did you meet any cute boys?" Mary added.

"According to this magazine," Colleen said, holding up the latest edition of *Cosmopolitan*, "weddings are one of the top places to meet your next boyfriend."

"*Next* boyfriend? Don't you mean Jennifer's first beau?" Mary chuckled.

"Knock it off—Jennifer's not dating until after college. Sorry," Elizabeth said, rolling her eyes.

"The wedding was really nice, and while I didn't meet any new boys, I danced with some guys I knew from previous family functions."

~Which other guy did you dance with that night?~ Josh inquired.

~If you were paying attention, you'd know I was referring to you. You attended my birthday party and the wedding, and in case you missed something, I only danced with you and my dad,~ Jennifer messaged back to Josh.

"Judging by the color of your cheeks, whoever you danced with made quite an impression," Mary said as she narrowed her eyes.

"No offense Jennifer, but you haven't exactly been 'Miss Sunshine' lately," Colleen commented.

"I'm sorry; I've had a lot on my mind." ~Falling in love with you, my sexy husband, while learning your self-proclaimed protector rules, decorating the Christmas tree, and enjoying our glorious wedding and honeymoon…~

~Hey Jennifer, you may wish to answer your friends,~ Josh chuckled.

Oh no! She'd been so busy messaging Josh that she'd lost track of her friends' conversation. ~What did they ask me?~ Another message from Josh reminded her of the question. "No, I didn't give him my telephone number." *No need for phones when Josh has a direct connection into my thoughts.*

~Jennifer, you should know that Elizabeth's thoughts indicate she's a little suspicious and is wondering if you're seeing someone in secret.~

~*Now* what should I say?~

~Nothing—just stick to your story and tell them you're happy because you're getting a car soon.~

~I'm getting a car?~

~Yep, one that comes with a copilot who'll make sure you don't break any driving rules.~

"You didn't give out your number?! *Honestly* Jennifer, how do you expect to go through the next four years without talking to the opposite sex?" Mary gawked.

Jennifer stifled a giggle over Mary's exasperation, and her other friends' thinly veiled confusion regarding her dating choices. Josh remained quiet during the remainder of lunch, which Jennifer was thankful for since she clearly couldn't maintain two conversations at once.

The afternoon dragged, but once school was dismissed, Jennifer hurried to join Josh outside.

~Am I ever glad to see you,~ Josh said, draping an arm around Jennifer's shoulders.

~I believe it's *I* who should be saying that, as you've seen me all day.~ Jennifer smirked at the wounded look on his face. ~What do you want to do when we get home?~ She was pleased when her question earned her a hungry, devilish look. ~Looks like I have your answer.~

~I love how we've been married long enough that we can read each other's thoughts,~ he teased.

With the knowledge that they had the house to themselves for at least three hours, they raced upstairs. Once in the bedroom, she felt Josh's heated energy coursing through her and watched in surprise as the buttons of her blouse popped open, one by one.

~Baby, I want you to remove all your clothes for me.~ Josh sat down on the bed and watched Jennifer tear her clothes off without a hint of modesty. *That's my girl!* Now naked, she stood before him and bit her bottom lip, looking perplexed about how to proceed. ~Don't worry, I promise it's not as impossible as it seems,~ Josh said, doing his best to sound confident. He told her to recline on the bed, and then undressed as fast as she had while Jennifer looked on in appreciation.

~I'm liking this part of your plan a whole lot!~ Jennifer leaned forward, not wanting to miss anything. ~Is it wrong to ogle one's husband?~

~Not in the least, especially since I plan on doing the same to my wife. Lie down face-up and I'll show you how we do things the spirit way.~ Josh's eyes filled with mischief as he watched Jennifer get into position. It was the best way to start, and would make it easier for Jennifer to see his expressions and feel his energy.

~Now what?~

~It'll be easier if you breathe, as passing out isn't on the agenda.~ When Jennifer giggled, he lowered himself until he rested on top of her without merging their bodies into one.

~Is that hard to do? I mean, how are you able to keep yourself on top of me and not go through?~ Jennifer asked in awe.

~It takes some concentration to keep my energy dense enough not to pass right through you and the bed. If that happens, don't panic. I'm kidding!~ Josh chuckled when Jennifer gasped in horror. ~I promise I'm not going to fall through you. That's why it's easiest if you stay on the bottom until we're used to how this works.~

~Agh! It feels like tiny zaps of energy when you laugh, so please stop before I jump up and make my escape right through you,~ Jennifer warned, hoping to put an end to his ticklish laugh.

~I'll have you know that I didn't build my reputation by letting anyone escape through me.~ Josh began kissing Jennifer lightly, until her breathing increased and she began mentally expressing her frustration. ~What's wrong, Mrs. Smith? Not giving you want you want?~

~No—you're frustrating,~ she groaned, trying to use her hands to pull him closer. They only passed through his arms, making her more agitated.

~I can't have my wife frustrated, can I?~ Looking into her eyes, Josh watched her expression as he slowly entered her.

~Oh! It feels—I mean, *you* feel…~ Jennifer's eyes rolled back and she was skyrocketed into a series of orgasms before she'd gotten the words out.

When he felt her body slowing, he began to move, giving and taking while setting a rhythmic pace. No longer worried about being too rough or her becoming sore, he sped up and didn't stop until they climaxed together. His breathing was soon back to normal a lot faster than his marathon-running wife, who was still glistening from exertion. The fact that she was the only one who looked as though she'd worked out made his smile grow wider. ~Well? Are you ready for round two?~

~Round two? Don't you mean round twenty-two?~ Jennifer's chest heaved. ~Now I understand your private joke earlier.~

~Sounds to me like you have no further complaints in the frustration department— but if you do, I'd be happy to take care of them. Best of all, in spirit form, I never get tired.~ His voice was dark and full of promise.

~So you and Gisabella weren't exaggerating?~ Jennifer verified, then squealed with delight when it was true. ~Again, please.~

Josh checked his watch before agreeing to her demands. ~Okay, but this round's more for me.~ He used his energy to make his hands dense enough to flip her over onto her stomach and before she could protest he playfully swatted her butt once, making her yelp. Without any warning he slammed into her, and soon Jennifer began to match his stride, pushing back to meet each of his forceful strokes. He made sure to keep his erection dense enough to give her pleasure, while answering each one of her callouts for more until he felt her tighten around him. He followed with his own release before withdrawing and squeezing in next to her on the narrow bed.

~That was amazing! All night long, huh?~ Jennifer's eyes lit up as if it she'd won the lottery.

~Just because I can, doesn't mean we should. To put it bluntly, Gisabella would have my head if I sexed you to death!~

~But what a way to die.~ Her remark earned her another butt swat and a giggle fit.

Later that night after Jennifer had fallen asleep, Josh reached for her profile and began to read. Oddly, it contained many blank spaces and omitted information; even Jennifer's previous lifetimes had signs of editing and obvious deletion of crucial information. Whoever had tampered with her paperwork must've had a reason for preventing him from knowing everything about her past, and he put his money on Gisabella. Even with the missing information, he could tell Jennifer's gifts and abilities were many. Now it was up to him to teach her how to use them properly.

Next he picked up Jennifer's current life-path envelope and noticed that the tamper-proof seal had never been cracked—*a stupid move on my part that I'll remedy now!* The lock was a new model that he preferred because it could only be opened with his fingerprint. He positioned his finger on it, but the lock flashed red and zapped him with an electric shock. He tried two more times, but each attempt resulted in his finger being shocked. ~Damn it, Gisabella!~ As if she'd been waiting for his burst of anger, the lock flashed green and popped open.

Like Jennifer's profile, her life-path contained limited information, and much to his dismay, Jennifer's future earth husband was one of the subjects missing. The thought of her marriage to another man, no matter how temporary, pained him more than he could've ever imagined. He spent the remainder of the night reading and memorizing every detail of his wife's current life-path, learning which items in her life he could change and which were part of Jennifer's destiny and thus set in stone.

Armed with this knowledge, Josh made a list of everything he wanted to alter. His wife had no idea her life was about to transform in ways she couldn't have dreamt possible as Josh spent the next two hours telepathically placing suggestions into the minds of the people who could make them happen. Now all he had to do was hope each person elected to follow his suggestions, thinking they'd come up with the ideas themselves.

On Friday when Jennifer arrived home, she found a letter stating she'd received an art scholarship from a prestigious organization. Best of all, her parents suddenly supported her decision to major in art as long as she obtained a second degree in business.

The next day Jennifer was lying on her bed doing homework with the radio blasting, while Josh watched for possible trouble from up above. *I bet it's only an excuse so he can read in peace.* The thumping beat of the next song began shaking the floor with its base, proving her hypothesis most likely correct. *Yep, reading in peace.*

"Jennifer, can you please come down so your dad and I can talk to you?" Mrs. Parker yelled.

Oh great, now what have I done wrong? With a groan, Jennifer closed her book and hurried downstairs to find her parents seated at the kitchen table with an opened three-ring binder.

"As you know, your mom and I always wanted to live on a lake, and we've attended open houses on occasion but never found one that'd make it worth our while—until now," Mr. Parker explained.

"You want to move before I finish my senior year?" Jennifer asked nervously.

"Promise to keep an open mind until I've explain everything." When Jennifer nodded, Mr. Parker continued. "We don't want you to miss out on your senior year, so we've taken all of that into consideration and have come up with a solution. The home is located twenty minutes from here, and you'd only have to drive to school for a couple of months. Of course, this means you'll need a car of your own."

"The house is closer to college, making your future commute easier. Plus we think you'll love all the extras it has to offer. Why don't you take a look?" Mrs. Parker added.

Jennifer looked down at the photo of the two-story white house with a brick walkway and double-door entry. She wasn't sure what kind of home it was, but it didn't look like a colonial or a raised ranch. The yard was lush and green with large pine trees that enclosed it completely, making it very private. The sketch of the floor plan showed all the basics: foyer, oversized family room with fireplace, study, kitchen, dining room, enormous master bedroom, and two smaller bedrooms.

"It looks like a nice house," Jennifer agreed.

"You may wish to look at this," Mr. Parker said with a huge smile as he passed another paper her way. "It might help make the move easier to accept."

Jennifer stared at the drawing labeled "recent addition," showing a staircase at the opposite end of the house that led to a separate bedroom suite over the garage. The addition was so large that if it'd had a kitchen, it would've been considered a small apartment. "Whose room is this?" Jennifer asked with crossed fingers.

"If you live at home until you finish college and agree to help around the house, it's yours," Mrs. Parker offered. "There's a lake with a beach and clubhouse, and a cafe with tons of stuff for you to do—boating, fishing, and dances with lots of people your age. Please tell your dad you love it so he'll agree to move!"

So that's *the reason for Mom's concern about my happiness.* "It looks amazing—like living at a year-round resort. How soon can we go?" Jennifer said.

"Our bid was already accepted, and there's a couple who wants to buy our house. All we need to do now is start packing, because the movers will be here in a month," Mr. Parker said gleefully.

"Wow...this is all so sudden. Too good to be true, almost," Jennifer mused. It was then that she noticed Josh leaning against the wall with his expertly delivered poker face, and began to grow suspicious that *he* was somehow responsible for some of her recent good fortune.

CHAPTER TWENTY-FIVE

~I'm sorry I can't help you pack,~ Josh said as Jennifer sealed another box.

~Funny how the full moon comes around the week after we move. If I didn't know any better, I'd think that you had something to do with the change in our moving day so you wouldn't be solid and able to help.~

~Maybe I can't help you pack, but I promise I'll make it up to you the next four days at our honeymoon house—which reminds me, we're leaving at midnight, so you should take a nap. You wouldn't want to spend the entire time sleeping.~

~How can I nap when my parents left me in charge of packing the entire house?~ Jennifer said in frustration. Her parents had decided that their social life was more important than packing.

~Why don't you invite your friends over next weekend for a sleep-over-slash-packing party?~

~You wouldn't mind?~

~Why would I mind? I'll even promise to stay away so you and your friends can have some privacy. Why don't you call them now and confirm it while I do another sweep of the perimeter?~

~Don't you mean while you escape from this mess?!~ Jennifer

motioned at the floor-to-ceiling stacked boxes that filled their small bedroom.

~I suggest you move the sleepover to the living room, and I think the phone is under that pile of newspapers.~ He pointed to the crinkled papers Jennifer had been using to cushion her collectibles. ~I'll catch up with you a little later.~

~Fine, but you'd better make me breakfast in bed while we're away.~

~Deal.~ Josh planted an energized kiss on Jennifer's lips and disappeared, leaving the claustrophobic room behind.

Later that night Josh's kiss woke Jennifer as he carried her to Gisabella's dimension, and when she opened her eyes they were standing in their honeymoon suite. Everything looked as it had before, minus the roses and wedding cake. In their place were numerous vases of aromatic lilacs, filling the room with a tranquil scent.

Jennifer's eyes traveled to the bed where Josh had made love to her, and she laid her hand on his solid chest. "I've almost forgotten how wonderful you feel." Now able to touch him, she unbuttoned his shirt and slid her hand underneath the fabric to caress his warmth. "I don't know if it's because you being solid is so rare, but all I want to do is touch you." She planted kisses all over his muscular chest while Josh carried her to the bed, where she became lost in his arms until the clock chimed a rude reminder that morning had arrived.

"Hit snooze again," Jennifer moaned as she pulled the covers over her head and rolled over. She'd only fallen asleep a mere five hours ago. *That's what I get for marrying a spirit who doesn't need sleep!*

The covers lifted and she was greeted by Josh's big smile and laughing eyes, making her burrow deeper under the comforter. "Go away!" Her warning was little more than a muffled, inaudible grumble.

"You can't be late for your meeting with Gisabella." Josh pulled back the blanket, but Jennifer's reaction wasn't the one he'd hoped for. "I'm going to make breakfast and bring it up so you can eat while you're getting ready." A quick kiss served as a peace offering for keeping her up most of the night.

As much as she longed to go back to sleep, Jennifer knew better than to give Josh an easy target to tease. Once showered, she was drying her hair wearing nothing but an oversized bath towel when Josh returned.

"You're a little overdressed for breakfast." He hugged Jennifer from behind, nuzzling her freshly scented hair and inhaling deeply. With a tug, the towel fell away and his hands were free to explore without restriction.

"Mmm…Josh, we can't, I'll be late for my meeting…" Her decline was halfhearted at best.

"She won't mind," he murmured, stretching the truth.

Jennifer's words faltered as she willingly gave in to his touch. After a cold breakfast with the promise of a hot lunch, they walked hand in hand to Gisabella's house an hour later. All her years of ballet classes and running couldn't have prepared Jennifer for her husband's endurance, and the walk felt good after a night of Josh's sexy workout routine.

"Welcome, my lovebirds." Gisabella noticed the guilty looks on their faces, answering the unspoken question of why they were late.

Right away Jennifer saw that unlike the house they were staying in, Gisabella's new home was contemporary. The floors were white marble, with the walls painted a soft pale gray. A floor-to-ceiling wall of glass made up the back of the house, providing a seamless, unobstructed view of the lake and its several long-necked swans. Jennifer admired the massive black marble fireplace, two cushioned couches, chrome and glass conversation tables, and spacious rug as Gisabella ushered them into an enormous kitchen. "I know dears—my kitchen is over the top, but the design in a magazine from earth was so nice I had to have the same one." Gisabella grinned indulgently, not caring what Josh would say about her chef-worthy, banquet hall-sized kitchen.

Josh couldn't refrain himself for more than a few seconds. "In all honesty, with your expert baking skills I'd say this is the exact size I'd pick for a huge trash bin!"

"Josh!" Jennifer scolded, unable to believe her ears.

"It's okay, dear. I wouldn't expect anything less from your ill-mannered husband. After all, Josh knows perfectly well what a great cook I am. You'd have thought I'd given him food poisoning once or twice." *More like ten or twenty times, but who's counting?* "Josh, I'll have you know that I slaved all day to make a cheesecake." Gisabella's eyes twinkled with the knowledge that Jennifer had never before been privy to hers and Josh's banter. She took pleasure in his discomfort, and his valiant effort to temper his sardonic humor in front of Jennifer.

"A cheesecake? God help me! Did you cook it fully, woman? Or are you planning on me spending my time here with Jennifer doubled-over?" Josh wasn't about to let Gisabella use his wife as a pawn. Maybe he wouldn't earn any points with Jennifer, but he couldn't let his friend off the hook.

"With any hope, you cad!" Gisabella's retort flowed easily as she was no longer putting on airs in front of her granddaughter.

"Considering your cooking abilities, I'm sure you'll get your wish," Josh shot back, forgetting Jennifer was in the room until he heard her gasp. Afraid of her reaction, he turned to see Jennifer starring at them with her mouth open and her eyes large and humorless.

"Jennifer, we're sorry—I should've warned you ahead of time. I speak for Gisabella and myself when I say we've been friends for so long that sometimes our humor is a little off the cuff. In my defense, I wouldn't expect anything less than Gisabella feeding me something to make me ill on purpose. All these years, I thought she couldn't read a recipe—*now* I find out that she purposely fouled up to make me sick!"

"My dear girl, your husband speaks the truth. Our humor can be in bad taste, but as you can see, it's my only weapon to keep Josh in his place." Gisabella flashed Jennifer a warm smile in an effort to come across as nicer than her counterpart.

"Grandmamma, you poor woman. My husband can be a handful, and I imagine you're right—he's hard to control. I'm looking forward to your delicious cheesecake." Jennifer cracked a smile. "However, if I end up doubled-over or ill, I'll lead the way in tormenting you with *my* kind of humor."

"If I were you, I'd watch out—I believe my wife means business!"

"Maybe I'll serve the lemon meringue pie from the bakery." Based on her history of unsuccessful baking attempts, Gisabella wasn't about to take any chances of alienating Jennifer, no matter how temporary. Though she and Josh bantered in fun, she wasn't so sure Jennifer's comment had been made in jest and this visit was too important not to have the girl on her side.

"Good. Now if the two of you would be so kind as to holster your sharp tongues, maybe we can have a nice chat." Jennifer turned her attention solely to Gisabella. "Grandmamma, I believe you wish to discuss something important with us?"

"I promise to holster my tongue—until later tonight." Josh said the salacious comment meant only for his wife's ears a little too loudly, causing Jennifer to blush a near-scarlet as Gisabella cackled.

"Okay then—Grandmamma, let's go make tea and enjoy our talk." Jennifer hooked her arm through Gisabella's and headed into the gourmet kitchen. A little while later, Josh sheepishly walked into the room to join them.

"Jennifer, I assume you've figured out that I am the High Priestess of the Universal Council," Gisabella said. "What you may *not* know is that since the beginning of time, our family has held this position, and it's your birthright and destiny to take over the throne when I step down. That's the reason I assigned Josh as your protector: because he's the best at what he does. There's no other in the entire universe who's more equipped to teach and watch over you than him." Gisabella paused and nodded respectfully towards Josh. "If you refuse to accept your birthright, the future may fall into the wrong hands when another family takes over."

"So *this* is why I have a protector? And why Josh was around for so long?" Jennifer asked, her face darkening with understanding.

"By Josh's own choice he asked to marry you, and even changed your wedding vows to bind you for all eternity. In doing so, he unknowingly married the next high priestess—and I'm pleased to say that he'll now always be by your side. You'll have Josh to confide in, and he'll be your pillar of strength when you're faced with tough decisions," Gisabella explained.

"Josh, did you *know* any of this before you proposed to me?" Jennifer asked, praying her future title hadn't had anything to do with why he'd married her.

"I swear on my soul I had no knowledge of your title, or that Gisabella was your grandmother. I asked you to marry me forever because I knew I never wanted to let you go," Josh promised, bringing Jennifer's hand to his lips.

"In Josh's defense, *no one* knew I had an heir; keeping your existence a secret was the only way to keep you safe. Not even the council members know that my daughter, Olivia, had a child."

"So *I'm* the next high priestess? I don't even know what that means, or how I'll be able to run the, what, the *universe*? Please tell me I have a few years to learn how to do this," Jennifer rambled.

"I hadn't planned on retiring for another four hundred years or more, but now that you and Josh have married each other for all eternity, this has become your final lifetime on earth. Once it has ended, you must assume your position and title." Gisabella scowled in Josh's direction.

"But I'm not ready!" Jennifer cried.

"The council law states that each high priestess or priest must pass the title to their direct descendant within six months after their descendant's final lifetime death—otherwise the title will be forfeited to the next family in line," Gisabella continued evenly, having no pity on the two who'd taken it upon themselves to change their destinies and end her reign of power. "You'll continue training with Josh, and once you come home to heaven, you'll be my protégé. That will entail shadowing me and holding council meetings under my watchful eye before you're finally ready to be left on your own." Gisabella couldn't be mad at the girl, as it wasn't her fault—it was Josh's! *Looks like I need to update my plan.* She couldn't afford to waste time, not if she hoped to ensure her family's legacy.

"Don't I have any say?" Jennifer's voice shook with emotion. "I don't wish to run a country!"

"Correction—you don't wish to run heaven, earth, and all other dimensions," Gisabella explained.

"As far as I'm concerned, I don't want to run anything!" Jennifer closed her eyes momentarily. "What happens if I refuse?"

"Heaven, earth, and every dimension would fall under the leadership of my second-in-command, Garth." Gisabella tried her best to keep from lashing out. *How are we ever going to get Jennifer ready before her lifetime ends?*

"Garth is the vilest person in the entire universe! Jennifer, I know this is a shock to you; it was to me too, but all Gisabella's asking is that you study hard and not make any rash decisions. I've given my entire afterlife to guard against someone like Garth taking over. I promise I'll be by your side the entire time, teaching and training you so that you'll be ready. Please just tell us you'll keep an open mind," Josh pleaded.

"So what else are you two keeping from me?" Jennifer asked suspiciously.

"Not much, dear. Josh will begin by teaching you to use your innate gifts as well as keeping you under his protection." Gisabella summed it up neatly, hoping Jennifer wouldn't ask for details.

~Really, Gisabella? Not keeping "much" from Jennifer? What about how you locked her into a life-path stating she must marry another man? Or maybe you should tell Jennifer how, once found out, she'll have a huge bounty on her head from the same kinds of rebels who killed her mother?! While you're at it, you could explain that they'd do anything to kill and evaporate her soul while she's untrained and unable to defend herself. Maybe you should start by sharing those small facts with your granddaughter,~ Josh messaged. The look in Gisabella's eyes let him know she was not pleased.

"I have more gifts?" Jennifer said excitedly.

"Yes, baby, you have many gifts and I'm looking forward to teaching you how to use them. I thought we could start while we're here," Josh said, quickly volunteering his help in an effort to appease his high priestess friend, whose glaring eyes were fixated on him.

"Wonderful idea, Josh. Take advantage of the time you're here to help teach Jennifer what she needs to know," Gisabella stated aloud, before sending him a private message. ~I'd keep your mind on your job instead of on the things you wish you could change in Jennifer's life-path.~ Gisabella turned her gaze towards Jennifer. "Jennifer, would you like to come and visit here once a month? It will give you and Josh a chance to be alone as newlyweds, and will provide Josh with some much-needed time off from guarding you on earth."

"I'd love that!" Jennifer exclaimed. *Time alone with Josh in solid form* and *an entire house to ourselves? What could be better?*

~Consider yourself lucky, Josh, that you're my friend and I'm not one to hold grudges,~ Gisabella messaged with a smile. "I take it *you* also find my offer acceptable, Josh? Feel free to bring Jennifer here whenever you wish. The honeymoon house is yours to use whenever you want, and I'll see to it that it's kept stocked at all times for my granddaughter's comfort."

~I'm sorry for speaking out of line, Gisabella. I know you love Jennifer and are only doing what's in the best interest of the universe. I consider myself lucky to have a house in this realm where I can fuck my wife.~ Josh was pleased when his uncensored message made Gisabella choke on her tea.

~For the life of me, I don't know what my granddaughter sees in you, unless you've been hiding your scurrilous side from her.~ Gisabella shot off the sarcastic message to Josh before turning back to Jennifer. "I've taken the liberty of filling your closet with everything you could possibly need while staying here. Feel free to sneak a few things home to wear—Josh will show you how to remove an object's duplicate energy and transport it down to earth. I'll see to it that you also receive a wardrobe update for college. Consider it my graduation gift, dear."

~I'll have you know my wife likes my crude humor and wicked ways. I'm sure if you asked Jennifer, she'd confirm how much she enjoys being with me,~ Josh messaged smugly.

"Thank you, Grandmamma." Jennifer noticed a suspicious glance pass between Josh and Gisabella. *They must be messaging each other and blocking me out of their conversation.* "Josh, would you care to tell me why you just shared such personal information with my grandma?"

"I didn't think the fact we enjoy cooking together was too personal to mention, do you?" Josh said quickly. If his wife thought he'd fall for such a general comment, she was mistaken.

"Yes, I do enjoy that, and the *other* things you spoke of in your messages." *You're hiding something.*

"See, Gisabella—I told you my wife loved everything about me!" Josh said, shifting under Jennifer's displeased expression. He held back from sending a message to Gisabella about how they'd better enjoy their private messaging now, before Jennifer became a "message spy." They'd have a hard time evading Jennifer's stubborn persistence then.

An hour later Jennifer and Josh said goodbye to Gisabella and walked back to the house in silence.

"What do you say to a little exploration?" Josh asked once they'd made it back, hoping his wife was no longer cross with him.

When Jennifer enthusiastically nodded to his suggestion, they began with the main floor past the dining room and staircase, soon coming upon a door on the right. Like a couple of excited kids, they turned the knob in anticipation.

"Are there cars in heaven?" Jennifer said, looking at the empty two-car garage.

"Nope, but garages come standard; good place to store junk." Behind the other doors they found a bathroom, an art room for Jennifer, and a spacious study that thrilled Josh. At the end of the hallway, a set of double doors awaited their exploration. When Josh opened them, Jennifer squealed and darted inside.

The smooth wooden floors invited Jennifer to twirl around and around, her impromptu moves reflected in the floor-to-ceiling mirrors spanning the wall opposite the entrance. She kicked her shoes off and did a three-turn pirouette into an arabesque to test the feel of the floor's surface, before beginning to dance openly. Several times she went into her learned ballet positions, adding many new ones she was only able to do because of her presence in Gisabella's realm. As she gained more confidence, Jennifer increased her speed and leapt into a grand jeté, landing it perfectly. She felt free and uninhibited once again, and found it easy to give herself over to the music in her head while doing chaînés on-point spins down the entire length of the room.

Josh watched Jennifer in amazement. Where had she been hiding this talent? *Was this another benefit from a past lifetime?* Through the years of protecting Jennifer he'd suffered many a dance class and boring recitals, but she'd never danced like this before; it was so mesmerizing that her moves held him captive. When Jennifer flew through the air with her legs outstretched and toes pointed, he also soared. The way the sun streamed in through the wall of windows at the far end of the room outlined her slim curves, holding him spellbound while she quickly covered the span between them. His outstretched arms welcomed her as she tossed her head and leaned back, supported by his hands around her waist. In one swift motion, he pulled and she was brought upright. When their lips touched, he found himself silently imploring Jennifer never to leave him.

"Please…" Jennifer pleaded after feeling the desperation in Josh's kiss that had caught her off guard. In response, Josh's hands brought her so hard against him that it was comparable to a fusion of steel, molding and merging their bodies into one being. Every cell in her body reacted to his feverish need to become one, and she responded with the same intensity. She needed him to make love to her there, on the wooden floor in front of all the mirrors. Her breathing was harsh and her hands demanded him, but suddenly Josh broke away and released her without warning so that she ended up seated on the floor.

"What the hell was that?" Jennifer waited for an answer, but none came. Josh paced, clearly trying to cope with some unseen torture occupying his thoughts. Even from a distance, she could feel his torment, and his actions indicated that whatever was bothering him was so fierce that it went beyond anything he'd dealt with in the past. The question *now* was what had set him off? *All I did was dance.*

The intensity of his feelings for Jennifer as he watched her dance had frightened him to his core. If watching Jennifer dance made him this crazy, what would happen when she married another man? What would he be capable of doing then? Josh ran his fingers through his hair. *How have I fallen so hard for this girl?!* His feelings went deeper than anything he'd ever experienced. He loved Jennifer with all his heart, but what he felt at that moment went deeper than ordinary love. He'd have to figure out later, in the meantime, he had a bigger issue: his love was sitting on the floor with smoke coming out of her ears.

He needed to diffuse his wife's hostility and give her an explanation, but wasn't sure where to start. He walked over to the stereo and turned it on, and as the music drifted throughout the room, Josh returned to stand before his wife with his arm extended. *Please don't refuse.* His inner fears ran rampant until Jennifer acquiesced to reach for his hand; once she stood, he brought her into his arms with one unexpected, swift pull, holding her tightly against the length of his body and beginning to sway.

Jennifer relaxed as Josh spun around, dancing as if they were one. Josh slowed and stopped in the middle of the room, but didn't say a word as he held her. She could tell he was full of mixed emotions, and for the first time ever, her strong husband seemed confused as to what to do next. She began to unbutton his shirt, but he still looked somewhat unsure as she lifted her sweater over her head and dropped it on the floor, followed by her bra, jeans, and panties. Naked, she pressed herself against his muscular body, and when Josh sighed she took it as a sign to begin undoing his jeans. She needed him to quench the ache that had become unbearable within her.

Josh found himself smiling at how quickly she'd managed to remove both of their clothes and successfully mold herself to his form. "Not here," he murmured, carrying her from the studio to the fur rug in front of the fireplace. The fire was still robust and warming even though it hadn't been stoked in hours, leaving him to wonder if it was a sign that despite his concerns, their love would never die. He laid Jennifer down and gently explored every part of her sweet dancer's body, and was rewarded when she shuddered and climaxed underneath his touch—yet he still couldn't dispel the thought of losing her to another man one day. With a throaty groan, he wrapped Jennifer in his arms and held on to her tightly while he breathed in her scent.

"What's wrong?" Jennifer asked.

"Nothing." *I just want to hold you forever and never let go.*

When Josh diverted his gaze, she clasped his face and looked into his eyes, where she caught the briefest glimpse of something that was gone so fast, she wondered if she'd imagined it—*despair?*

So far Josh had only touched her with his hands, but she needed all of him deep inside her. She pressed her nakedness against him and moved rhythmically, indicating that she wanted more. When his hands steadied her hips, she became frustrated and sat up. She was *not* going to give up, so she pushed him flat on his back and got on top. *Is this what he wants?* She claimed him hard, then slowed the pace until his expression changed from a wan smile to frustration. Abandoning her steady pace, Jennifer rode him harder and faster until they were both satisfied, then collapsed on his chest, breathless and damp. *How did Josh make it look so easy?*

Josh rolled her over until he was on top, pinning her under his body. "Determined little wench, aren't thee?" he asked with a smirk. His eyes clouded over once more, and his expression became serious. "Promise me one thing, Jennifer." He hesitated as he tried to think of a way to phrase what he needed to say. "Promise me you won't dance for anyone else—not like that, so unbridled and passionate. I couldn't bear it if you did."

"May I inquire why?" *Perhaps this was the cause of his distress?*

It took a moment and a deep breath before he replied. "When you dance that way, it's from a place of purity and powerful love, and I was overwhelmed by the energy you created…it was hypnotic and intoxicating. I found myself wanting to literally possess you—mind, body, and soul. The power of my desire was overwhelming, and my reaction so extreme that it frightened me." Josh looked down; he didn't want to see the look in Jennifer's eyes as she found out her "protector" had his own form of weakness.

"Josh, I am yours and only yours forever. I promise that I'll do my best not to dance like that for anyone else," Jennifer said, determined to express how strongly *she'd* felt in the dance studio. "I admit that I got caught up in the moment as well, and craved you with the same intensity you've just explained. It scares me too…"

"I guess we still have a lot to learn about each other, don't we? Let me start by saying how sorry I am," Josh said, looking into her eyes as he said the meaningful words.

"I'll forgive you on one condition," Jennifer baited. "Kiss me."

"I hope all our future fights are this easy to solve," he replied, kissing her many, many times over.

CHAPTER TWENTY-SIX

The next day after lunch, Josh strolled into the family room with a massive book in his hands.

"Hey baby," he said, joining Jennifer where she was curled up on the couch.

Jennifer blanched at the publication he was already rifling through. "Oh no..."

"Today I thought it'd be fun to teach you a little about one of my favorite healing tools. What you may not know is that as a protector, I've studied many kinds of natural healing techniques, and like Gisabella, I also favor using gemstones and crystals because of their invaluable properties. As the next high priestess you must be well-versed in their meanings and uses, because someday they may save your life."

So much for a vacation! Jennifer hid her thoughts behind an innocent smile.

"I thought we'd get started with the gemstones on your anklet. Why don't you lift up your foot so I can get a better look?" Josh knew most of the gemstones and could've rattled off a synopsis about each one, but for Jennifer's sake he wanted to look up each in the book he'd brought and read the highlights.

"This first gemstone is adularia," Josh said, pointing to the clear crystal. "This is better known as the 'goddess stone.' It provides tranquility and helps to hone your psychic abilities and develop your medium skills—you know, talking to spirits." Josh paused to look at Jennifer, and she nodded mutely.

"The purple one is amethyst. Many use this to shield themselves from bad energy and negative spirits, like when I have you imagine white light around yourself. In case you get any ideas, I'm immune to its power." Josh glanced over and Jennifer blinked, her eyes already glazing over. Three more gemstones and head nods later, he was tired of his student's uninterested responses.

"This orange-hued stone is tangerine quartz. It helps with creativity and playfulness." Once again, Jennifer nodded. With a playful grin, he continued to read off his favorite benefits. "It's best known for stimulating sexual desires, making the wearer creative during sexual exploits." He was pleased when Jennifer's eyes widened and her cheeks turned a sweet shade of scarlet. "I speak from experience when I say I love how tangerine quartz affects you. A very enjoyable gemstone, indeed.

"Red jasper is my personal favorite. It's linked to the root chakra and gives the wearer the physical strength and stamina to make love all day and night without a break." This time his student leaned forward, showing a little interest. *I should exaggerate all the stones' properties, apparently!* He continued with his embellished version. "This stone is a great one for virtuous ladies to wear on their honeymoon night. It sure opened you up to intimacy with your husband." He looked into her eyes, challenging her to nod again.

"For a while there I thought *you* had caused all those wonderful orgasms, but now I know the truth—the gemstones played a major role." Jennifer sighed with fake disappointment and hoped her sarcastic comment wouldn't be accepted lightly. She was pleased when Josh gazed at her in disbelief and slammed the book shut with a bang, then set out to prove how *he'd* been the one responsible for her pleasure. After Josh's torrid lovemaking, he sat up and continued reading, much to Jennifer's dismay.

"This stone is yellow sapphire." Josh forced himself not to laugh at the sight of Jennifer's displeased expression. "I'd have never chosen this stone for you; it strengthens a person's will. A department you need *no* assistance in." He ignored Jennifer's icy stare and continued. "Oh, wait a minute—it says something about enhancing sexual energy. Looks like it's a good stone for us after all." He didn't bother telling her that most gemstones, even those meant for healing and protection, offered some sort of sexual benefit.

Six stones and six exaggerated sexual meanings later, Josh closed the book, leaving moldavite for another time. To describe it could take days, if not months. Instead, he pulled his true love into his arms for a second and third round of sexy, creative lovemaking.

Later that night, much to Josh's amazement and horror, his student described every single gemstone's qualities to Gisabella without faltering. When Gisabella turned and gave him a fake smile, Josh knew the high priestess wasn't pleased with his dramatized descriptions.

When Jennifer excused herself for a few minutes, Gisabella turned to Josh. "I commend you for teaching Jennifer so well. Her knowledge of the *sexual* benefits of each gemstone is masterful, and I'm not surprised that red jasper is her favorite stone based on what you told her! You'd better make sure Jennifer reads the entire gemstone dictionary so she knows all the benefits of the anklet she's wearing, and not just the ones that benefit *you*! If you don't teach her properly, I'll make you both sit through my gemstone class," Gisabella threatened, eyes twinkling with humor.

Before dessert was served, Gisabella handed Jennifer a box tied with pink ribbon. "Now that you know your destiny, I think it's time to give you something I've been saving since you were a little girl."

When Jennifer opened the box, she found a large crystal ball amidst royal blue velvet inside. "It's beautiful!" There was no hiding the awe in her voice as her gaze transfixed on the glowing orb. "It looks like the one that Professor Marvel used—you know, in *The Wizard of Oz*."

"Go ahead dear; pick it up and have a look," Gisabella encouraged, having no idea who or what the girl was referring to.

Jennifer gently lifted the seemingly clear orb and held it up to the light, making out mountains and crevices that looked to be disguised under wispy waves of smoke. Upon closer examination she noticed the various shades of lavender, indigo, and pink in the mountains, and felt herself being drawn to its powerful core.

Josh and Gisabella carefully observed Jennifer's reaction, both aware of the fact that Jennifer's status as a married woman now allowed her to see images and signs of both the past and future inside the orb. Jennifer would first need to merge her energy with it, achieved by holding it, carrying it, and sleeping with it under her pillow. Once on the same wavelength, she'd be able to receive accurate answers to any question asked, as well as to view future events.

"Thank you, Grandmamma. How did you know I've always wanted one?"

"Simple, my dear. Every future high priestess is given a special orb, also known as a crystal ball or sphere, when they come of age. Your subconscious has been waiting for your orb since the day I selected it, and it's the one you'll carry with you forever. No one else should ever be allowed to hold it or use it, because the energy link could be damaged."

"Does this mean my crystal ball will tell me when you or Josh are playing a joke on me?" Jennifer innocently inquired with a straight face.

"No, dear, as you'll find the protection I hold in place around myself is too powerful for your orb to detect. As for your husband, I'm sure it'll be a useful tool in making sure he isn't causing any trouble."

"How does it work?" Jennifer said with a wink in Josh's direction. She'd surmised that her husband also kept powerful protection in place that'd guard against the orb's powers.

"An orb is fairly easy to use. Now that you're aware of your future, you'll be spending a lot more time working on developing your gifts. Currently you're somewhat behind, so Josh and I need to get you caught up. Josh—I think you should start on protection against energy attacks and other basic development skills."

"I'll get started right away," Josh promised.

"Maybe next visit we'll play some games designed to help improve and test your skills," Gisabella offered.

Oh joy! Jennifer groaned inwardly.

Later that night Josh found Jennifer in bed, reading his book about gemstones. "Tell me something, Jennifer. Why did you act so disinterested when I was teaching you earlier, yet you were able to recite everything I taught you to Gisabella?"

"I enjoy learning things that you're passionate about, but it was more fun watching your growing frustration when I acted disinterested. The best part was when you slammed the book shut and did your best to prove..." She was interrupted when Josh grabbed the book out of her hands and closed it to leer at her.

"I think it's time to teach you a lesson in good studenting."

"'Studenting?'Is that even a word?"

"It is, and I guarantee you'll remember it when I'm done. By the way, in the future you may wish to avoid nodding or feigning boredom if you don't want to end up across my knee."

"*What?* You wouldn't dare!"

"Oh baby, you know I'll never back down from a dare. Maybe now would be a good time to tell you that as your protector, I'm allowed to carry out any teaching method I choose, including a wide variety of reprimands."

"Do it and I'll scream!" Jennifer's effort at sounding indignant came across as flatly as her singing.

"Consider your butt safe for tonight—but be warned you may not fare so well next time."

She didn't miss how his threat came with a sexy grin and twinkle in his eyes, making it so hot in nature that she was almost tempted to act bored right then and there to see what he'd do.

When morning arrived, Jennifer opened her eyes to find a note from Josh:

Jennifer,

I have breakfast waiting for you, but first you'll need to find me. Unlike the child version of "hide and seek," the spirit version requires all your senses to locate what you're not able to see. Let the games begin!

Love, your protector

How am I going to find someone I can't see? ~What happened to breakfast in bed?~ She messaged, but received no response. ~I could always make my own breakfast while you hide all day.~

~If I were you, I'd think twice before you opt out of playing. Remember, a protector has many devious ways of showing displeasure.~

~Funny, I was thinking the same about my husband.~

~Know what's even funnier? My obligations as your protector outweigh those that come with being your husband.~

The laughter heard inside her mind was as irritating as Josh's messages, and Jennifer stomped off to find Josh and give him a piece of her mind. It was a mission that proved to be a lot harder than she'd anticipated.

~What's keeping you? Your breakfast is getting cold.~

It's bad enough that he's hiding, but does he have to be so annoying?! ~The least you could do is give me a hint on how to search for you.~

~All right, I'll take pity on you. I'm not upstairs or in the kitchen or garage, and it helps if you close your eyes and concentrate on feeling my energy.~

Jennifer shut her eyes and did exactly that. Once she'd located him, she began walking in that direction, stopping once or twice to close her eyes again. Unlike before, she easily found that he was hiding in the study, but couldn't figure out exactly where. She briefly shut her eyes to block out the rational thoughts interfering with her intuitive side, and concentrated on feeling the energy she'd come to know so well.

She walked over to the desk and ran her fingertips along the edge, sitting sideways in a tall armchair—hoping she wasn't making a fool out of herself as she caressed and kissed the smooth leather. *If I'm wrong, Josh is never going to let me live this down.*

~Job well done.~ Josh steadied Jennifer as he solidified beneath her. "Next time I hope you're quicker."

"Where are you hiding my breakfast?" Jennifer ignored his dig and gave him a playful nip on his neck.

"Right here." Josh held up a muffin.

"What happened to it?" Jennifer asked, pointing to a large bite mark.

"It took you forever to find me."

"What was the purpose of this so-called 'game' of yours?"

"You need to be able to recognize my energy even when I'm invisible. If we're ever in a situation when I need to disappear from sight and there are other spirits in the room, you'd better know which energy is mine."

"Has that ever happened? You fighting other spirits in an invisible form while protecting someone?"

"Yes, several times. It takes more energy for me to be translucent, meaning doing so during an attack would leave me at a disadvantage."

"Do attacks happen often?" Jennifer asked nervously.

"Not since the rebels have been extinguished, but there are a few rogue spirits who'd think nothing of attacking for the fun of it. Some of them are strong enough to inhabit humans—they're the most dangerous threat of all. But, don't worry, baby, that's my job. I wish I could bring in a few other protectors to give you a chance to practice sorting through a bunch of different energies to find me, but I can't risk anyone discovering our relationship or who you are."

"That's okay, I think I got it."

"I'll be the judge of that," Josh warned, standing with Jennifer in his arms. "Now let's go eat a real breakfast."

Though she was held securely in Josh's strong embrace, the "rogue spirits" Josh had mentioned stirred something deep inside Jennifer's psyche, alerting her to how dangerous these rebellious individuals could become.

After breakfast and a shower, Jennifer trotted down the staircase with a big smile, ready to head to the stables.

"What are those?" she asked warily, pointing to the four stacks of books on the table in the kitchen.

"Just some books I thought you'd enjoy reading," Josh said as he set another huge stack beside the others with ease.

Jennifer glanced at the one on top. "*Numerology for the Beginning Psychic*; what's that?"

"It's the study of how a number or combination of numbers bring the same results. Birthdates, addresses, and even letters have a number attached to them. All can be used to forecast outcomes, or if combined can bring forth a desired result. Before the birth of Christ, Pythagoras and other philosophers discovered a correlation between numbers and consistent outcomes." When Jennifer looked at him with a frown, Josh added, "I'd better find a book about Pythagoras for your reading material too."

"Chakras?" Jennifer held up the next book.

"Everyone has seven chakras. Each energy has a different color, and they're what keep your body, mind, and spirit working optimally. For example, if your throat chakra is out of synch, it could mean your thyroid is off. Either that, or you have something to tell me that you're afraid to say," Josh said, turning around expectantly.

"Nope, nothing to say," she quipped, picking up the next book. "*The Law of Attraction.* I think I know what that is."

"The law of attraction involves using thoughts and intentions to attract the life you wish to live. Unfortunately, a person's negative thoughts will induce the opposite, bringing forth unwanted results, and that particular book discusses real-life examples of this. One story's about a woman who attracted a man who matched everything on her list with one exception: she'd never put forth the intention that he be heterosexual. Even though the result wasn't what she'd expected, the two became the best of friends, and opened an international travel company together."

"That's a nice example. Can someone use this 'attraction law thing' to change their destiny?" Jennifer asked hopefully.

"If you're inquiring as to whether you can change your high priestess obligation, the answer is no," Josh said with a sympathetic quirk of his lips.

"I didn't think so." Ignoring the heavy weight of responsibility, Jennifer picked up another book. "*Astrology 101—finally* a fun book. I'd love to read more about zodiac signs." Jennifer flipped through the pages and looked up with a scowl. "What are all these charts and junk?"

Josh quelled the urge to grin. "I find it easier to think of astrology as the study of how the positions and movements of celestial objects affect people and events on earth. The charts are used to map out the sky at a particular moment in time, and decipher its meaning."

"Why would I want to know that?" Jennifer demanded, turning to face Josh in time to catch him biting his lip and trying not to laugh. "What's that look for? Tell me!"

"A big part of your position revolves around you becoming an expert astrologist."

"And I suppose *you're* an expert?"

"I know a lot about astrology, but Gisabella's the expert."

"What about all these other books?" She gestured towards the stacks of reading material. When Josh nodded, Jennifer's mood darkened. "Don't tell me I have to read all these! How am I going to have time for anything else?!"

"Sorry, Gisabella's orders. I was thinking of adding bookcases and a table to our bedroom. There's plenty of room, and it'd give you a place to store the other books when they arrive."

"There's more?" Jennifer's mouth dropped open. "How am I going to go to college and get a job if I have to learn all this stuff?! Wait a minute —you want to clutter our bedroom with books?!"

"We can talk about that another time. For now, why don't you start with one of these?" Josh selected three and handed them over. "I think you'll enjoy them."

"Animal totems, tarot cards, and zodiac signs. Finally, something more fun than meditation, white light protection, and rocks!"

"Gemstones," Josh corrected.

"Same thing," she baited.

"What should we do about your foul mood?" Josh sauntered over and grabbed Jennifer by the waist. "We have nowhere to be, which gives me plenty of time to give you an attitude adjustment."

"Agh! Put me down, you big lug!" Jennifer commanded between laughter, only to feel Josh's hand landing solidly on her butt. "Hey! What do you call that?"

"An adjustment. Better stop laughing—and squirming, for that matter." Josh landed another swat with a chuckle, tightening his hold on his giggling wife. "To bed with you, woman! The sooner you get naked, the better."

Much later that night, Jennifer curled up contentedly next to Josh on the couch with her zodiac book. After opening the cover, she immediately flipped to Josh's sign: Aries, the sign of the ram.

Josh was concentrating on the rise and fall of Greece when Jennifer's spirited laughter piqued his interest. He peered over her shoulder to see what all the fuss was about, only to see that it was his sign causing her slapstick-level cackling.

"What, exactly, is so funny about Aries? I'll have you know it's the birth sign of many great warriors!" Josh cried.

"Oh, nothing really. I was just reading about your characteristics," Jennifer said, purposely keeping her response vague.

"Okay, I give. What does it say?"

"That you can be a little controlling, and very protective. I honestly haven't noticed that about you," she said, failing to control her sarcasm. The look on Josh's face made all her efforts to keep a straight face futile, and she covered her coquettish grin with a hand.

"So you think I'm funny?" *Two can play this game.* He grabbed the book away and flipped to her sign: Sagittarius. "Let me see what it says about you…imagine this! You're unable to sit still, and always fidget." He glanced up to make sure he had her attention before continuing. "Just as I suspected. Your sign says you take too many risks, such as galloping very large horses wildly across fields! No wonder I have to be so controlling and protective!"

"I recall the book also saying that Aries are moody, quick-tempered, and impatient. Yep, I'd have to agree," Jennifer replied, challenging him right back.

Josh flipped to another page, pretending to read its contents. "According to this, you can be a little risqué, and crave someone who isn't afraid to take you over his knee. I'd say we're a good match, wouldn't you?"

The look on his face let Jennifer know this time she may not be so lucky if she continued to tease him, so Jennifer gently retrieved her book with a look of demure acceptance and continued reading. Ignoring Josh proved to be a lot more irritating to her warrior man than anything else, however, and before long she found herself being pulled into his arms while he took his time exploring her mouth and more.

CHAPTER TWENTY-SEVEN

SEVEN MONTHS LATER

"Hi Mom, what are you making?" Jennifer asked, joining her mother in the lake house's kitchen.

Since marrying Josh, her life had been a whirlwind. She'd moved to the lake house with her parents, graduated high school, spent a summer traveling back to Gisabella's realm for her high priestess lessons, learned to cook, and had begun sailing. Other than being overwhelmed by all that she needed to learn, everything between her and Josh had been great, except for one small detail—her secondhand, five-speed red sports car that her dad picked out. There was absolutely no doubt in Jennifer's mind that Josh was overprotective and had a volatile temper after several months with him in the passenger seat.

Even Jennifer's relationship with her mother had improved, with Mrs. Parker becoming a little more attentive and caring. Jennifer attributed it to the "lakeside style of life"—who wouldn't find sitting on a sandy beach watching colorful sailboats float by relaxing? Not that things were perfect, or that her parents had cut down on traveling; on the contrary, they traveled more frequently than ever. But when they *were* around, they all got along for the most part.

"Gnocchi and tomato sauce for our dinner guests tomorrow night.

You remember my friend Jane and her husband, don't you?" Mrs. Parker answered, wiping her arm across her forehead leaving a trail of flour in its wake.

"I'd love to help," Jennifer offered. Her mom looked tired, and now that she'd become Josh's "sous chef," Jennifer had the skills to back up her offer.

"Are you sure you wouldn't rather be out with your friends? After all, it *is* Saturday night. Or, should I say 'date' night? Which reminds me—have you heard from that nice boy who sang at Sarah's wedding?"

Her mother's hint was as subtle as a bull skateboarding blindfolded through an overcrowded china shop. "We talk," Jennifer said, keeping her expression as vague as her answer.

"Funny, you haven't mentioned him in months—seven to be exact."

"Sorry, Mom, not much to report." *Other than that we're married.* "The thought of a nice, quiet evening with you and Dad sounds perfect."

"What a nice thing to say. I don't suppose you'd mind dicing the onions for the sauce?" Her mom pointed to several yellow onions on the counter.

"How'd you know dicing onions was my favorite thing to do in the whole world?!" Jennifer's sarcasm accompanied her crinkled nose. Within a short time she'd finished cutting up two, and had started on the third.

"What a great job you're doing with those onions. I guess your Home Ec classes paid off," Mrs. Parker said.

"Yep." Jennifer hid her smile. "I learned all sorts of kitchen skills. If you wouldn't be offended, maybe I could take over cooking some of our meals. You work so hard, Mom, and I *did* agree to help you more around the house in exchange for my amazing bedroom. Plus, it'd give me a chance to practice what I've learned." She hadn't *exactly* fibbed.

"You wouldn't mind? I must admit, it's a great idea. Some man is going to be lucky to have you. A beautiful, smart girl who can cook is a hot commodity."

"Oh, Mother," Jennifer sighed.

"You can't be mad at me for wanting to see you happy like your sister is with Dave. I only wish there'd been more time to plan a nice wedding," her mom said wistfully. "Please tell me you'll elect to have a long engagement so I can plan a big wedding for you, with all the bells and whistles. You know how much I love parties."

"Yes, of course." A tear landscaped its way down Jennifer's cheek and landed on the cutting board as she spoke. *I wish you could've been there to see me marry Josh. I felt like I was a fairy princess and Josh was Prince Charming. My grandma from many lifetimes ago was kind enough to walk me down the aisle and give me away on Dad's behalf. Please don't be upset with me, Mom. I wish I could tell you everything, but Josh and I could be killed and our souls disintegrated if I did so.*

"Have you found anyone you want to date that lives in *this* country? Maybe when you start college you'll meet a nice boy, but don't wait too long; before you know it, all the eligible bachelors will be taken. While we're on the subject, I don't believe I've had the 'talk' about the birds and the bees with you." Her mom flushed from embarrassment.

Been there, done that—many, many times. If it's any consolation, we waited until our wedding night. Josh was so gentle and loving. Why didn't you tell me how wonderful birds, flowers, and a bee are when they're together? Jennifer cleared her throat. "No, Mom. I want to wait until I'm out of college and have my career up and running before I date. Don't worry, I'm sure there'll be plenty of bachelors around when I'm ready; if not, I think there's still a need for mail-order brides in Alaska." Jennifer snickered, then added, "As for sex, I think I've seen enough animals on television to get the basic idea of what transpires."

"Oh, Jennifer, really!" Her mom spun around and stared, then noticed Jennifer's eyes. "Do you need a tissue honey?"

"No, I'm almost finished." Jennifer turned her attention back to the onions, thankful that they hid the real reason for her tears. *Someday, when we're all together in heaven, you'll see Josh again. By the way, I found out everyone goes to heaven unless their soul is evil, in which case it's disintegrated.*

"There's a young man where I work who seems eligible; maybe I'll ask him over for dinner next week. You'd like him, Jennifer—he's an avid photographer and has had several of his photos published. I can make chicken pot pies! I'll ask him on Monday."

Oh Mother, is this any way to treat your son-in-law? Jennifer shook her head over her mom's plan to find her a man. It wouldn't pay to outright refuse her gesture, as that would only cause an argument. From her mother's expression, she was determined to push the two of them together. *Maybe Mom's chicken pot pie will sicken the poor guy and he'll need to leave immediately after dinner.* For once her mother's horrid cooking might turn out to be a good thing.

It wasn't Josh's intention to listen in on Jennifer's private conversation with her mom, but she'd failed to block her thoughts and he'd heard every word, and saw his wife's tears. Since their wedding day, she hadn't said much about the rushed ceremony or indicated any remorse or guilt, so learning she felt that way came as an eye-opening surprise to him. There wasn't much that could be done about it now, but maybe he could find a way to make it up to his wife in the future.

"This was always my favorite part." Jennifer left a thumbprint in each gnocchi. "Mom, you look tired. After we put these in the fridge for tomorrow night, you should take a break and lie down. I've watched you make sauce dozens of times and I know how to follow a recipe. Plus I can put together a quick meal for tonight's dinner."

"Are you sure? I *have* been doing a lot of overtime."

"I got this, Mom. The kitchen is officially off-limits—now go and relax!" Jennifer hurried her mother out of the kitchen and went to work. Soon Josh was by her side and they were searing pork, browning sausages, and steam-peeling fresh tomatoes.

~Can you imagine the look on my parents' faces if they walked in now? All they'd see was food flying about and spoons and spatulas stirring with no trace of you in sight!~

~That is something I'd like to avoid. Can you please hand me that potato?~ Josh messaged, pointing to the peeled Idaho nearby.

~What are you going to do with this? Jennifer asked as she handed it over.~

~Add it to the sauce. It's a trick I learned years ago that helps reduce the acidity.~

~Cool—what should I do next, boss?~

~Hmm...boss, huh? I can think of lots of things you can do for me!~

~I meant in the kitchen.~

~So did I!~

His suggestive expression and the color of his eyes let Jennifer know he intended to make good on his threat, and she hightailed it out of there. ~Since you don't need my help with the sauce, I think I'll set the dining room table for tomorrow night.~ It would've been bad enough for someone to see some spoons stirring on their own, but the two of them fooling around? The thought was disturbing!

When dinnertime arrived, Jennifer pulled the lightly browned rolls out of the oven and transferred them to the basket on the kitchen table.

"Oh my goodness, Jennifer. I can't believe you did all this by yourself," her mother exclaimed as she gazed at the meal before them. Meatloaf, mashed potatoes, hot rolls, and a salad spanned the table, not to mention the sauce, antipasto, and cheesecake Jennifer had made for the next night. Her daughter had even set the table in a manner befitting of a royal ball. "It smells incredible!"

"Mangia!" Jennifer raised her glass of iced tea in a toast while she messaged a quick thank you to Josh for all his help.

The next night, Jennifer couldn't escape her mom's plan to marry her off to the first available bachelor she could find.

"But Jennifer, the table is already set for six people. You *must* join us! It'd ruin everything if we had an odd number of bodies," her mother insisted for the fourth time.

"All right. I'll join your company for dinner," Jennifer begrudgingly accepted, ruining the plans she and Josh had made for the night.

"It's not like you had any plans, right? Besides, Jane and Frank's son Gary is in town and he's all grown up now. I hear he's gotten pretty cute, *and* he's in med school," Mrs. Parker said conspiratorially.

Her mother's words filled Jennifer with dread. *I bet she set this whole thing up from the beginning!* Sarah had warned her that "she was next." At the time Jennifer hadn't given it much thought, but now it all made sense. *I only know of one way to change my mother's matchmaking agenda: behave in a way that ensures she never fixes me up with one of her friends' kids again.*

Alone in their bedroom, Josh narrowed his eyes as he watched his wife getting dressed for dinner.

~Josh, for the third time, I'm sorry. I had no other choice.~ Jennifer slipped on one of her new tailored dresses with matching heels—compliments of Gisabella—while her husband watched.

~That may be the case, but it doesn't mean I have to be happy about you having dinner with a blind date,~ Josh huffed, not bothering to disguise his anger.

~It's a dinner party, not a date! Do I look all right?~

~Better than all right. Maybe you should change into your green pantsuit.~

~That ugly thing? You're joking, right?~ Her lime green, frog-colored suit had been a hand-me-down from her sister's closet, and though it went perfectly with Sarah's blonde hair and blue eyes, Jennifer thought it made her look like a reptile.

~Please forgive me if I don't support you looking gorgeous for your blind date,~ Josh growled.

~See these rings?~ Jennifer held up her left hand. ~They mean I'm all yours, and no one else in the world matters to me but you.~

~Too bad no one else can see them! I'm sure you'll understand that I won't be taking my eyes off you all night!~

~I expect nothing less, sir!~ She flashed him a smile on her way out of the room. *I'm so going to pay for baiting him!*

That night as Jennifer fiddled with her napkin and avoided curious staring from the attendees, she decided that it was by far the most uncomfortable dinner she'd ever sat through. Her mother and Jane took every opportunity to tie Gary and her together, and resembled the epitome of two marriage brokers in desperate need of a commission check. Gary seemed nice enough, and in his defense he looked as uncomfortable as she felt having dinner with someone other than her husband. Josh's frigid stares and indignant stance did nothing to lessen Jennifer's distress as the seconds ticked by.

When one of her mother's comments sounded like the offering of a substantial dowry, Jennifer realized she'd need to end the negotiations before she unwillingly became a polygamist. She turned to poor, unsuspecting Gary, whose uneasiness was about to become a whole lot worse.

"I'm sure my mother has already given you a resume of all my attributes, regarding the fact that I made tonight's meal and know how to entertain. Just think what a valuable commodity I'd be to your career as a surgeon, Gary! Even though I told my mom that I wanted to wait until I'd finished college and established a career before getting married, she reminded me that by then, I'd be hard-pressed to find a man. After all, the worst future I could ever experience would be as a twenty-three-year-old spinster, so I must do everything possible to counteract that. Wouldn't you agree?"

Gary's jaw dropped along with the rest of the guests' as Mrs. Parker's eyebrows rose to her hairline. The only one in the room who seemed pleased with Jennifer was her invisible husband, who grinned from ear to ear. It was the first pleasant expression she'd seen on Josh's face all night.

"I agree, Jennifer." Gary raised his glass, smiling before he continued. "I'm with you! I'm tired of being set up on blind dates with all mother's friends' daughters. If I was looking for a wife, rest assured that you'd be the sort of strong woman I'd want by my side. Why don't you and I make a pact that if we're still single in six years when I graduate, we'll go out for coffee?"

"It's a deal." Jennifer didn't bother to tell Gary that it'd never happen.

Her soft-spoken, mild-mannered father caught her attention when he stood up to address the table. "Well I, for one, am glad. I'm not ready to share my little girl's heart with another man," he said, blowing Jennifer a kiss.

"Thank you, Daddy." Her heart ached with the knowledge that he unknowingly shared a place in her heart with his unseen son-in-law.

"This cheesecake is the best I've ever tasted," Gary said, smacking his lips in approval. "Maybe we should reconsider the time limit on our agreement to three years."

"Oh, I don't know, Gary. I think six years sounds better." For the second time that night, Jennifer managed to quiet the room—except for Josh, whose enjoyment came across loud and clear.

~Way to go, baby! Like the man said, you're one heck of a "say it as it is" kind of woman. Looks like your friend Gary can't wait to leave now that you made him look like a fool.~ Too bad Josh was unable to convince himself about such a statement. *Is this a glimpse at Jennifer's future husband?* The thought sliced through him like a sword. No wonder his wife's documents had been edited; Gisabella must've known he'd fall so hard for Jennifer that he'd stop at nothing to change her destiny, even if it meant risking his own disintegration in the process.

~I'm glad you enjoyed the show. It appears you're the only one who's appreciated my humor—I think you've rubbed off on me. Thanks to you, I'm officially lacking in decorum and have ruined my "coming out" debut and any chance for a successful and profitable future. I'm not worried though, because I've already found my Prince Charming,~ Jennifer messaged.

~Now to convince your mother,~ Josh answered wryly.

After their guests left Jennifer received an earful from her mom, who wouldn't hear any excuses for her outlandish behavior. The one good thing that came from Jennifer's outspokenness was Mrs. Parker's agreement to stop pressuring her to date until her final year of college. *Mission accomplished!*

That night they laid in each other's arms, placated and consumed with love. ~What are we going to do, Josh?~ Jennifer asked. ~My mother agreed to back off for a little while, but it's only a temporary situation. Between my well-meaning friends, my mom, and who knows who else, how long will they accept my excuses before digging deeper into what's going on?~

~Jennifer, please don't worry about this now. Let's enjoy our night and discuss it tomorrow. For now, I only want to enjoy the feel of you in my arms,~ Josh said as he kissed her softly.

~It's not fair how quickly you change the topic using unscrupulous methods. You know how lost I become with your kisses. If you don't stop now, I won't be able to think.~

~That's the whole point, baby. I'd rather make love than talk about what others think.~ Josh increased his energy's density and pulled her on top, watching her face as he buried himself deep inside her womanly heaven.

Jennifer tilted her head back and allowed a deep moan of pleasure to escape. Josh had her hands locked in his, steadying her over him as he brought his hips up to meet hers over and over. Soon her body clenched and embraced him with ripples of ecstasy. With one last deep thrust, Josh's hot love filled her once more.

Breathless, she collapsed on his chest, lost in Josh's love and the feel of his energized fingertips lightly brushing her back. She hadn't missed how Josh had once again managed to distract her from their serious conversation, nor that Josh's version of "tomorrow" didn't necessarily mean the next day. Either way, it was something they'd need to discuss soon, before it became an even bigger problem.

CHAPTER TWENTY-EIGHT

~Where do you think you're going?~ Josh eyed his fully dressed wife as she stretched her arms over her head.

~Where does it look like I'm going?~Jennifer grabbed her hair tie, doing her best to escape before Josh reminded her that she was under house arrest. Ever since finding out that she was the next high priestess, his protectiveness had become more smothering than anything. Before she reached the door, she felt his hand wrap around her wrist. *Agh!*

~Don't think you're leaving the house without me. You know the rules; twenty-four-hour protection is mandatory for a high priestess,~ Josh recited, ignoring Jennifer's groan.

~They weren't the rules when you first began protecting me. Can't we go back to the old way?~

~If I didn't know any better, I'd get the impression you weren't enjoying my company. Not a good beginning for our "forever marriage."~

~Maybe if you didn't spend so much time complaining about how far or how long we jog, I'd *welcome* your company. Running used to be peaceful, and it gave me time to declutter my thoughts without any distracting voices in my head.~ Her attempt to pull open the door was thwarted, and Jennifer found herself being carried back to bed. ~Oh no you don't, not this time!~

~Relax, I only wanted you to wait until I'm wearing something. Unless you'd rather I ran next to you like this?~

Jennifer glanced at his naked body and gulped. She was tempted to dare him to, but he'd jump at the chance. ~You'd like that, wouldn't you? ~

~Running like this? Not particularly.~ Josh gestured towards his relaxed male parts and scowled.

~In that case, I'll wait,~ Jennifer said, failing to stop the color from rising in her cheeks.

They'd just hit the pavement when Josh began messaging her questions and information she needed to know in the future. ~A better method of clearing your mind would be to practice your morning meditations. They're supposed to be done daily.~

Jennifer stopped and glared. ~I'd appreciate it if you'd let me run in peace.~

~What's so horrible about meditating?~

~What's there to *like*? No talking, keep my mind blank, don't fall asleep, sit still, ignore my itchy nose, and so many other rules that make it impossible to relax and quiet my mind at all!~

~I'll make you a deal; if you meditate for at least a half hour in the morning without complaining, I'll keep quiet while you run around the lake.~

~Does that mean you'll let me run by myself?~

~Not quite, but I can follow you from above so you'll *feel* like you're alone.~

~I take it I don't have much choice in the matter.~

~Nope. We'd better get going before someone stops and asks if you're in a trance.~

~Oops!~ Jennifer giggled when she realized how silly she'd look glaring at her translucent husband to everyone else.

~How about next week we escape to our honeymoon house? It'd give us a chance to relax before you start school,~ Josh suggested.

~On one condition—you let me finish my run in peace.~

~I know you're up to something, Jennifer!~ Unable to read Jennifer's blocked thoughts, Josh could only surmise she was up to no good.

~Who, me? Looks like you're already in breach of our agreement. Not another word, or you'll be visiting our honeymoon house without me.~

~*That will be the day!*~ Josh blasted.

Jennifer received Josh's blaring message and sped up the pace, something she knew would irritate him more than a retort. *Today's a perfect day to run around the lake twice!*

A week later they were in their honeymoon home, celebrating the last weekend before Jennifer began college.

Jennifer woke up early and planted a quick "see you later" kiss on her husband's lips, enjoying the normalcy of Josh's slumber when in Gisabella's domain. Even though he was a tireless spirit, there were traces of stress on his face that had begun to appear after he'd learned of her impending title.

Since Josh had mentioned his plans to visit Gisabella that morning, Jennifer headed out the back door to the barn, skipping like a little girl who'd just heard the ice cream truck's bell ringing. In this case, the celebrated "treat" was freedom; something that only existed when they were away from earth and under her grandma's protection.

D'Artagnan was waiting by the fence, eager to help her escape her protector's worsening vigilance. Once on board, they galloped in the direction of the oasis, where she planned to revel in her solitude for the next two hours. After dismounting, Jennifer sat in the grass and listened to the water making its way down the rock facade and into the pool. With the birds chirping above and D'Artagnan grazing nearby, Jennifer reclined on the cushiony grass and closed her eyes, savoring the soothing sounds of tranquility. *Ahh, freedom at last.*

"I'm glad to see you've given my granddaughter a break," Gisabella said opening her front door wider. "Why don't you have a cup of tea and some baklava with me?"

"Yeah, I figured Jennifer was getting a bit sick of me," Josh sheepishly replied.

In the kitchen, Gisabella poured the tea and placed a plate of bakery-made baklava before him. She was glad Josh had loosened the reins, until his guilty expression let her know he was hiding something. "What have you done?" she snapped.

"I haven't done anything." Josh reached into his pocket and withdrew a rounded glass object before placing it on the table. "What? You didn't expect me to let Jennifer out of my sight without knowing if she was okay, did you?" Gisabella answered with a visible eye-roll. "You should be thankful I take my job and your granddaughter's safety seriously!"

"Yes, you're right, but I don't advise mentioning your spying tactics to Jennifer. It'd be better if she didn't find out that the freedom you gave her *wasn't* so free. Many moons ago, when I was her age and living my final life-path on earth, if I would've found out that my protector was spying on me, I'd have had his balls on a silver platter—so if I were you, I'd watch out!" Gisabella watched as Josh picked up the orb and studied its smooth surface again.

What was that? Jennifer opened her eyes and glanced nervously towards a rustling sound on her left. She'd dozed off at some point, and now D'Artagnan was anxiously pawing the ground as he gazed in the direction of the noise. If she'd been on earth instead of in another realm, she wouldn't have been so jumpy—it was the unknowns of Gisabella's realm that heightened her fear. Immediately, she surrounded herself and D'Artagnan with protective white light as Josh had instructed many times. *What an idiot I am for putting off Josh's self-defense lessons!*

"Whoa, boy—easy, D'Artagnan," she said, stroking the skittish horse's neck. "You heard it too, didn't you?" Her words did nothing to calm D'Artagnan's flight instincts, and recollections of the rogue spirits Josh had spoken of filled Jennifer's mind. "Let's head back!"

Before D'Artagnan was in position, another noise caught their attention, and Jennifer spun around in time to see a streak of red flash among the trees before disappearing. *A cardinal or some other bird?* she guessed, though something deep inside objected to such a harmless explanation.

Josh was enjoying his third triangle of pastry when a movement in the orb captured his attention. He took a closer look, but couldn't find anything suspicious that would've caused his wife's frightened response.

"What is it?" Gisabella didn't like his worried look.

"I'm not sure. Something scared Jennifer, and D'Artagnan is fidgeting too." He looked up with concern. "I need to go to her."

"Don't you dare—Jennifer's safe here. If she's to run the universe, she must become strong enough to stand on her own. Please tell me you've begun to teach Jennifer how to defend herself?"

Josh studied the vision in the crystal sphere, then glanced up with a smile. "I think I may've found the source—peacocks! Looks like they were walking through the fallen leaves."

"Joshua, if you don't wipe that smile off your face this instant, *I* will! Jennifer's a strong woman who just so happens to need your protection and guidance, but be forewarned; if I find you've made my granddaughter fearful of being alone or codependent on you, I'll kick your butt to the curb!"

"I understand." He smoothed away any trace of glee from his face. "No butt-kicking needed; I'll see that the two criminals are removed from the oasis. We wouldn't want Jennifer needing my services—the protector-related ones, anyway!"

"You better not have had anything to do with those birds being there in the first place." Gisabella's voice was stern, even though she didn't really suspect him of trying to scare Jennifer on purpose.

"Wasn't me!" Josh swore, raising his hands in surrender.

D'Artagnan sensed Jennifer's nervousness and picked up the pace down the treacherous, rocky trail, losing his footing several times. Once in the clearing, he lunged into a gallop towards the barn. Jennifer looked back over her shoulder in confusion, but saw no one following them. Once home, she quickly dismounted and set D'Artagnan loose, then hurried back to the house. *What's gotten into me?* She'd never been afraid to be by herself before. *It's all Josh's fault for making me so jumpy from all his excessive precautions and needless warnings!* She couldn't completely discount the noise that had caused D'Artagnan to become alarmed, but mentioning it to Josh would mean kissing any semblance of freedom goodbye.

The combination of only having shared an apple with D'Artagnan for breakfast and her adrenaline had left Jennifer with a case of rubbery legs. *Hopefully I can sneak in without running into my overly protective sentry,* Jennifer thought wryly as she opened the back door.

"Have a nice ride?"

Oh no. She turned around to find Josh leaning against the doorframe. "Good morning," she stammered. Recovering, she flashed a warm smile and wrapped her arms around him.

"Good morning to you too, my dear." He hadn't missed how Jennifer had jumped when he'd greeted her, nor the brick wall she was using to block her thoughts. "Did you have a nice ride?" he repeated, hoping she'd mention the scare on her own.

"Very nice—the oasis is always so peaceful, and it was nice to spend some time alone."

"Anything you want to share?"

"Nope. How about you? How was your visit with the high priestess?" Jennifer asked, unable to resist reminding Josh who her grandma was.

"My visit with Gisabella was pleasant, thank you. She gave me instructions to begin your energy protection lessons immediately, in case you ran into any *trouble*," Josh sneered.

He knows! "I'm going upstairs to take a shower." Before she was able to turn and walk away, Josh tightened his arm around Jennifer's waist.

"That can wait until later." *Now that you opted to break all protocol and hide what happened at the oasis from me.* As Jennifer's protector, he needed her to be forthcoming when it came to her safety, especially back on earth.

Geez, sometimes he's such a pain! Maybe I can change his annoyance into something a little more fun. Jennifer began messaging him a stream of provocative images.

"Sorry baby; even though you're delicious, your very descriptive thoughts will have to wait," Josh said, enjoying Jennifer's unrestrained display of irritation. When her eyes darted to the refrigerator, he couldn't resist adding another distraction she'd have to overcome. "Since you've already eaten breakfast, let's get right to your energy protection lesson."

What? That's not the game I wanted to play! "How about we play your game tomorrow?"

"Now that you know who you're destined to be, you realize how important it is to work hard so you can protect yourself. If you and I were attacked by a gang of rogue spirits or rebels, you should know how to defend yourself."

What if it hadn't been a false alarm at the oasis, but a rogue spirit? Jennifer wondered. Now that she was safe with Josh—well, "safe" might've been stretching it, based on the way he was regarding her—it seemed far less probable.

Her empty stomach began to complain loudly, making matters worse and earning her an additional scowl from her husband.

"Okay, let's get started," Josh said with overt enthusiasm. "The only thing you need to accomplish is to make us each a cup of cocoa." He blocked his thoughts and kept his expression vacant as not to give anything away.

"I just have to make some hot chocolate?" *What's he up to?* To her dismay, Josh easily thwarted each of her inexperienced attempts to read his mind; it was like a steel trap, unwavering and non-disclosing.

"I almost forgot—while you're making our drinks, I'll be trying to distract you." He flashed her a pirate-worthy, wicked grin, giving her a hint of what was to come. "All you need to do is block my energy the same way you blocked me from reading your thoughts." ~Starting now!~ Josh took aim and hit his intended target with a dead-center bull's-eye.

Agh! Before Jennifer had a chance to prepare, she found herself a sitting duck for Josh's unfair play. The objective of his game became apparent the moment his energy bolt hit with such force that she needed to grab hold of the counter to stay upright.

Josh snorted; even if Jennifer wasn't ready, she should've used *some* method of protection. *It's not like I didn't warn her.* He spared his wife the normal humiliation and ridiculing that usually accompanied this well-known protector game.

"Hey! I wasn't ready!" Jennifer yelled in a husky voice while she tried to equalize her defenses after the energy-induced orgasm.

"What's your point?" Josh taunted with a shameless smirk. *At least I'm not employing the electrical-shock kind of energy strike.*

"So that's your game?!"

"Baby, you should thank your lucky stars I'm such a nice guy. If you were any other protector's charge, you'd be lying on the floor in pain," Josh said, using yet another form of intimidation to throw her off-balance.

"If you were such a nice guy, you wouldn't have started before I was ready. And you *wouldn't* have spied on me earlier!" Jennifer spat.

"So you're saying you don't think I'm a nice guy? Okay!" Josh fired a shot of pleasurable energy her way, and was proud when Jennifer successfully diverted it towards a wall of hanging decorative plates and sent several crashing to the floor.

"Are you planning on destroying the entire house, or are we done playing your silly game?"

"Prepare yourself, woman! You're about to be *toasted*!" He propelled another bolt at her.

Now that Josh's intended target was clear, she placed all her concentration on envisioning a creature that was powerful enough to ward off Josh's energy. She successfully deflected another one of his shots, causing a silver tray to clatter to the ground.

"Is that the best you can do?" Josh asked. He stared in disbelief at the juncture of Jennifer's thighs, where the enormous, gaping jaws of a great white shark stared hungrily back at him. When it faded and disappeared, he chuckled. "I think you've watched *Jaws* one too many times!"

"It worked, didn't it?" With Josh's defense lowered, Jennifer aimed and fired a retaliatory bolt in his direction. Even though she'd scored a direct hit, her husband only looked mildly affected. Josh's stance and whole demeanor changed, however, and Jennifer gulped. *What have I done?*

His honed reflexes had automatically shielded the attack, leaving only a slight discomfort in its wake, but the sample was strong enough to prove that Jennifer was out for blood. No student had dared to carry out an offensive move against him in the past. *Leave it to my wife to be the first!*

I'm not going down without a fight, Jennifer thought, even as Josh's bloodthirsty expression made her knees quiver and her heart beat in double-time. She encircled herself with the strongest energy wall she could muster, mirroring each one of his moves so that she was facing him at all times.

Josh continued to dog his student until her concentration began to falter, waiting for fatigue to weaken her protection field. "Getting tired, baby?" His voice was dark and merciless—another tool commonly used to distract an opponent.

"Not at all," Jennifer lied. "What I *am* getting is a lock for our bedroom door!"

"I guess you plan on sleeping in the barn with your horse." He paused and pretended to study her. "I believe it's hunger I see in your eyes."

"The image you *see* in my eyes, Mr. Smith, is what I intend to do to you after we're done playing your little game." She sent a photo of him tied to the bed. *See, I can play as dirty as you.*

"I think you have your facts mixed up, Mrs. Smith." Josh's level of enjoyment rose higher now that his wife had stooped to his level of unfair tactics. "I'm picturing the scene more like this."

An image popped into Jennifer's head of herself naked and spread-eagled on the bed, tied to the bedposts with Josh holding a black leather whip. The sadistic photo was clearly designed to distract her so her shield would falter. "If that's what you want, it can be arranged. In fact, I'd *love* to give it a try." Jennifer bent over seductively, sending off a bolt of energy at the same time and hitting Josh in the groin.

"Nice shot, my love," Josh growled in a disturbingly low tone. *I can't believe she hit me in the nuts! If I hadn't blocked most of the impact, she'd be spending the night shackled naked to the wall!* The intense energy his wife was throwing around was only used for enemy assaults, not gameplay, and it wasn't the least bit pleasurable.

"Thank you, dear," Jennifer exclaimed. "Now that I've proven I'm able to fight off the best protector in the universe, I think we can forgo the rest of this lesson." As she spoke the playful, egotistical words, all of her protection suddenly faded away. *What happened?* As hard as she tried, she wasn't able to raise her protective shield, leaving her helpless as Josh prepared to deliver his "take no prisoners" shot.

Josh's lips curled as he sent a super-sized, pleasurable ball of energy into her unprotected sex root chakra.

"Agh!" She was stopped dead in her tracks when his energy hit her with a vengeance that dropped her to her knees, dissolving her into nothing but a quivering mess.

A look of pure, euphoric wonder covered Jennifer's face, but Josh was aware that after the tenth straight orgasm, her bliss would become intolerable. *I think she deserves eight or nine before I make them stop.* When done, Jennifer collapsed into his arms, gasping and trembling all over.

Jennifer blinked to find Josh gazing down with a concerned look on his face. "Can you do that again? Please!"

"Absolutely!" he said, dumbfounded at her stamina.

Ten minutes and nine orgasms later, Jennifer found herself seated at the table with a much-needed breakfast. Josh watched her eat in silence, wondering whether he should share with her how treacherous an encounter with a rogue spirit could really be. Not only would she have lost her current lifetime, but her forever afterlife with Josh if they were strong enough to disintegrate her soul. It was a truth that wholeheartedly took away his appetite, and only served to increase his concern for her safety.

CHAPTER TWENTY-NINE

~You look very nice, baby,~ Josh messaged, purposely leaving out how sexy Jennifer appeared in the sapphire sweater and jeans that accentuated her figure to perfection. *Now how do I hide her?* The last thing he wanted was guys thinking his wife was available.

Jennifer entwined her arms around Josh's waist and rested her cheek against his broad chest. ~I love you and only you, Josh.~

~Try to understand that the thought of you in college surrounded by other men your age makes me crazy.~

~Don't you mean "jealous?" You really shouldn't be.~ Jennifer gazed up into her husband's apprehensive eyes. ~I know part of your uneasiness is because you're worried about keeping me safe. You needn't be—thanks to you, I know how to handle both offensive and defensive energy attacks.~ When her statement didn't do much to ease his worrisome look, she tried a different approach. ~Josh, you're my knight in shining armor, and a sexy one at that. Besides, it's not like you won't be watching every move I make anyway.~

~You got that right—my eyes will be on you at all times.~ *So what if I keep the entire male population of students away from my woman?*

Yikes! Josh's instant switchover from "worried" to "domineering" made Jennifer's head spin, so much so that she sent him a private message expressing what she planned to do to him after school. Then she headed for the door, leaving her aroused husband to stand there, unsure of what had just happened. It wasn't long before Josh was seated in the car next to her, tightly securing his seatbelt. ~Honestly, Josh? Don't tell me you still don't trust my driving?~

~Oh, I trust the driving part. I just don't trust your ability to see other cars, red lights, stop signs, construction cones, or speed bumps! Remember the orange construction cone you brought home that I had to pry off your front bumper?~

Jennifer snorted a laugh. ~That was hilarious.~

~I rest my case!~

~Perhaps I should purchase you a crash helmet to go with the seatbelt you're wearing. No offense, Josh, but you wearing a seatbelt seems a little pointless.~ His stormy glare was proof enough that she had better watch her step, so in an effort to enjoy the lovely fall day and scenic ride, Jennifer kept her speed down and made sure to obey every traffic rule in the driver's manual—even the unwritten additional ones Josh had created.

~My job is to watch over you and ensure you stay safe,~ Josh lectured.

So much for our enjoyable ride and a normal college experience, Jennifer thought, hiding her sarcasm under a blank facade.

~Try to understand that I need to survey everyone who's near you,~ Josh explained. ~It's a fact that higher percentages of all attacks on earth are carried out by males. In addition, you come with a set of problems all your own; you're married to *me*, a spirit from another dimension, and you're the next high priestess! If anyone intending to do you or your grandma harm discovered even one of these items, you'd become the most sought-after visionary of all time. While you've learned a lot, you were assigned to me because no matter how experienced you become, not being a spirit means you'll never be strong enough to handle a full energy attack on your own. Sure, you can protect yourself and launch a few offensive moves, but you wouldn't have the strength needed to keep yourself alive for more than a few minutes.~

~Josh, I appreciate your concern and the wonderful job you do protecting me, but as for your worries about college boys—our marriage must be based on a foundation of trust and love. There might be times that I'll need to talk to other men. For instance, when my friends' boyfriends hang out with us from time to time.~ Jennifer held her breath, wondering whether *something* she said would sink into Josh's thick skull.

~I do trust you.~

She hesitated a moment before approaching a riskier topic. ~We both know that people are going to expect me to start dating, and I need you to trust me to handle their questions. Let me remind you that I never want to go on a date with anyone other than you.~ Jennifer fought back the thought that it'd be easier said than done to deal with well-meaning outsiders, her mother, and her overprotective husband. Silently, she implored Josh to give her a little more freedom so she could experience all that awaited her.

~You made your point, Jennifer. I know I have to let you finish growing up and give you a little more freedom. I'll still be watching over you, but I agree to do so from a distance as long as you still share my bed every night and wake up next to me each morning.~ Too bad his wife didn't know that his fear was real, or that in the future she'd be unable to deny her attraction when destiny brought her life-path husband to her. The love his wife had for him now wouldn't matter then, and all he could do was hold on to a glimmer of hope he'd find a way to change Jennifer's life-path.

~For the record, I'm only going to school during the day, and there's *nobody* I'd rather spend time with than you. I'll be sleeping with you every night, and you better be lying next to me when I wake up—otherwise there'll be hell to pay!~ Jennifer messaged. The energy in the car had become overbearing, and she needed to lighten the mood. ~After all, what would I eat for breakfast if you weren't there to cook?~

~So *that's* why you like waking up with me in the morning? For my breakfast skills? That's it, young lady, you're cut off—no more blueberry pancakes for you! From now on, you'll receive cold cereal. Then I'll know I'm in your bed because you want me there, and not just for the breakfast I make.~

~Cold cereal sounds great as long I wake up with you.~ Discarding all humor from her voice, Jennifer continued: ~I promise tonight I'll prove just how much I desire you in my bed. I suggest you get a lot of rest today, because you'll need all your stamina for later.~

~I'll be looking forward to it, my wife. I hope you're not planning on getting any sleep either.~ Josh's desire was reflected in his emerald green eyes.

~*Now* how am I going to concentrate? All I'll be thinking about is you. Can you imagine the notes I'll be taking and the suggestive pictures I'll be drawing?~ One glance at Josh's carnal, hot expression nearly had Jennifer turning the car around to bring them back home to bed.

Once she pulled the car into the parking lot, she took extra care to avoid her nemesis: the speed bumps. One thing Josh couldn't fault her for was how well she maneuvered her car into tight parking spaces. After parking, it was time to leave the car and begin her college adventure.

~I wish I could kiss you goodbye,~ Jennifer messaged, afraid that someone might see her kissing what looked to be empty air. With a nervous smile and a quick wink back to Josh, she went off to begin a new chapter of her life.

Josh watched his wife walk away, knowing that spending an entire day swimming and sailing with Jennifer was far different than protecting her from above. Regardless of his preference, he had a job to do, and became fully invisible before setting off after his charge.

Jennifer scouted the "new student" line until she caught sight of three hands waving. "Hi, girls—I can't tell you how happy I am to see the three of you," Jennifer said as she joined her friends. "I wonder if we have any of the same classes."

"Me too! I'm so happy the four of us are together," Mary replied with a flip of her blonde hair.

"Me three," Colleen added.

"I'm glad we're together too," Elizabeth agreed.

They chatted until they'd reached the front of the line, where they were given nametags and told to wait for their tour guide. Before long, a tall, handsome boy with sandy-colored hair and blue eyes similar to Mary's came walking over. Even though Josh wasn't visible Jennifer could feel his energy, and at that moment she was sure he was cringing. She wanted to message him to calm down because she wasn't interested in the beach boy, before realizing that even acknowledging the issue at all would be a mistake.

"Hi girls! My name is Fred," the young man said with a cheerful smile. "I'll be your tour guide around campus today. Feel free to ask me any questions, and let me know if you need anything."

As they introduced themselves, Jennifer noticed her three friends vying for Fred's attention. They were full of smiles and flirtations for their personal tour guide, one who didn't look as if he minded the attention. *Hopefully my husband isn't having a cow!*

"Right this way," Fred said, motioning for the group to follow. "First stop is the cafeteria, where most of the students hang out." Fred continued their tour, pointing out the library, auditorium, counselor's office, and numerous other buildings. He'd even taken the time to map each of their classes out for them.

At the end of the tour, Jennifer saw Mary give Fred her number. She couldn't help noticing how enchanted Fred looked by her gorgeous friend, and how Mary was listening to each and every word coming out of Fred's mouth as if it were chocolate-coated.

Phew! Josh breathed a sigh of relief when Fred's attention was directed towards one of Jennifer's friends, but it served as a rude awakening that his job had gotten a whole lot harder. When he read some of the boys' minds he found that girls were their top priority, with a *distant* second being the obtainment of a diploma.

It was three o'clock when Jennifer reached her car. Even though she'd had an easy day, she felt worn out. There were so many new faces, and the campus was much larger than she'd originally thought.

~I've been looking forward to this afternoon's activities all day,~ Josh purred after she'd closed the car door.

~Only after we pick up a couple of hotdogs from the lakeside cafe,~ Jennifer said, her stomach growling in protest of any romantic plans.

~I see where your priorities lie, woman. I guess I should be thankful I'm second and not close to the bottom of the list.~

~Don't worry—after you feed me, you'll be my first priority.~ She quickly started her car, shifting into first gear and trying to keep from speeding to the first fast food restaurant she saw.

By the Friday of her second week of college, balancing an unseen husband, classes, homework, and her friends' prospective date recommendations had taken its toll on Jennifer. Frazzled and distracted, she hurried between classes, winding through hallways of scattered students who blocked her way. As she rushed around a corner, Jennifer crashed headlong into her history teacher and sent his papers and books scattering.

"Oh! I'm sorry, Mr. Burk, let me help with those," Jennifer mumbled, bending down to gather the jumbled books from the floor.

Mr. Burk's first reaction was to lash out at the clumsy student for not paying attention to where they'd been going, but when the klutz turned out to be one of his newer students, he held his tongue and searched his memory for the girl's name. She was on the list of "attractive female students" he'd been admiring in his class.

"That won't be necessary, Jennifer. Don't worry about knocking into me." He silently added, *it's totally my pleasure,* as it was too soon to say something like that out loud. "I'm sure you have a good reason for rushing down the hallway. Late for class, perhaps?" He flashed her a warm smile in the attempt to keep her from running off.

Even though Mr. Burk's words seemed harmless on the surface, something inside Jennifer became alarmed. After a quick goodbye and another apology, she briskly walked away.

Mr. Burk's eyes followed Jennifer intently, enjoying the way she sashayed down the hall until disappearing from view. Jennifer was one fine-looking girl, and her shyness was welcome. He liked his girls meek and unassuming; they were easier to handle and more willing to please. Often, they welcomed his attention and loved their lessons with him. He, in turn, taught them things about becoming a woman and pleasing a man. What Mr. Burk didn't realize as he fantasized about Jennifer's education was that his thoughts were being read by Josh, who loomed close by and was watching the teacher's every move.

Josh hung back, not wanting his presence to be known until he'd scouted the teacher's behavior a little longer. He wanted to uncover the depth of Mr. Burk's depravity before he took action. In the meantime, he'd make sure there was no way Jennifer's perverted teacher got within ten feet of her again except for in class. He was prepared to take aggressive action to rid Jennifer and the whole school of Mr. Burk's evil presence as soon as he'd gathered enough proof to justify his reasoning. Josh's smoky eyes flared as he thought of all the things he could do to the unconscionable man, with no one the wiser. In his gut, he felt the teacher had done this many times before—but *this* time, he'd picked the wrong girl to lust after.

There was nothing Josh could do about it at the moment, however, as Jennifer was on the move and he had to hurry after her.

CHAPTER THIRTY

Mr. Burk walked up and down the rows of seats, passing out the graded midterm essays and saving Jennifer's for last.

"Miss Parker, I'm very disappointed with your theories of how the collapse of the Roman Empire could've been prevented," he chastised, tossing it on her desk before shuffling away.

Jennifer gazed down at her grade and cringed. *How can I be doing so poorly?* She knew the answer must lie in trying to balance school, her high priestess lessons, and the growing number of books Josh assigned to her all at once.

After class Jennifer joined her friends for lunch, where once again she was subjected to their favorite topic: her dating life!

"Jennifer, don't tell me you're not coming to the costume party? Fred and I are going together and Elizabeth and Colleen have dates too—Fred has a friend we can set you up with, and you can even wear my ballerina costume from last year! It'll look amazing on you," Mary rattled off in one breath.

"I'll actually be out of town visiting my sister then," Jennifer said, trying to appear disappointed. Her friends' persistence had grown considerably worse over the past month, and with each refusal their efforts to find her a man seemed to double. *Things would be a whole lot easier if I could tell them about Josh.*

"Colleen, explain to Jennifer that this is the highlight of the year, second only to the Christmas formal!" Mary demanded. "If you don't attend, you'll be committing social suicide!"

Jennifer could barely contain her laughter over Mary's melodramatic performance. "Sorry, but I haven't seen Sarah since she moved and I want to spend the weekend with her," she fibbed, even though it'd been less than a week since she'd seen Sarah last.

"I guess I can understand your reasoning," Mary mumbled, her face brightening a moment later. "Mark your calendar now so you won't miss the Christmas Ball." With renewed determination, Mary switched gears. "Fred and I are going to dinner on Friday night. You should join us!"

No doubt this is another one of her blind date attempts. "I'm leaving after my last class to avoid the traffic. If I don't run, I'll be late for class—see you Monday," Jennifer called out as she hurried away. She hated lying to her friends, who only wanted to see her happy and had no idea that their matchmaking tactics were only complicating things. *Maybe Josh can help me come up with a more effective solution than simply dodging their invites left and right.*

Once home, it was clear that Josh wasn't in a good mood. Instead of talking their quandary over, Josh carried Jennifer to bed and did what he did best: took away all thoughts of anything but him. Jennifer found his way of dealing with emotionally charged issues very pleasurable, but even *she* knew it wasn't going to work for long.

Later that night across town, Mr. Burk was trying unsuccessfully to stop the murderous thoughts from running rampant inside his head. He'd been through it before, and knew if he didn't feed the demon inside him soon, he'd be forced to do something horrible. Mr. Burk's craving for flesh made his mouth water and his pupils dilate, but his carnal need to make his victim submit to him was even greater.

Mr. Burk opened the fridge and pulled out his least favorite meal—a pint of ruby liquid. "This should quiet you for a while," he said aloud in the vacant room. Closing his eyes, Mr. Burk lifted the bag of blood to his lips, guzzled the contents, and swiped the back of his hand across his mouth to leave a streak of red in its wake.

"We need to be patient and careful—I'm not going to allow what happened last time to occur again. No fingerprints, no slipups. If Jennifer were to suddenly disappear so soon, I'd be the first person the police would question." Mr. Burk listened to the response, one that would've gone unnoticed to the untrained ear. "Glad you agree! Now leave me alone so I can think." The voice inside his head quieted, but Mr. Burk knew it was only a temporary fix, and that he'd be forced into action soon enough.

By Friday afternoon, Jennifer's nerves were frayed to the point of breaking.

"I need a vacation!" she moaned as she dropped a new pile of books on the table.

~Are you talking to yourself?~ Josh messaged from his position above the house.

~Why are you eavesdropping?~ *Ugh! Why can't I just have a little space!* Jennifer's irritation rose higher with each message from Josh.

~For the record, I *will* hear you if you shout. What's going on down there?~ Josh asked, knowing better than to get in Jennifer's way during her monthly hormonal disturbance. He'd tried using reiki and other energy work the day before in the hopes they'd help Jennifer relax, but saw no improvement.

~Nothing!~ Jennifer snapped, then burst into tears. ~I mean—*everything...* You not being solid or acting like a normal husband doesn't help!~ Before she could mutter another word, she was cocooned in Josh's energetic embrace.

~Shhh, baby, please don't cry,~ Josh soothed. ~Let's go away for the weekend. It'll give us time to relax, and with your parents away and your friends thinking you're out of town, no one will be looking for you. What do you say? We can leave Saturday night and come back Sunday morning before your parents' plane lands, which will give us ten days in the other realm.~

~Ten full days of you and I in the same dimension—I'd love that! But only if you promise not to bug me about my lessons. If this is a vacation, there'll be no energy warfare games or any other high priestess lessons. Got it?!~

~Okay—I promise none of *those* kinds of games.~

Yikes! Jennifer thought as Josh's salacious intentions became obvious by the change in pigment of his irises. ~So help me, if you break your promise, I'll transport myself back to earth!~

~And how do you plan on doing that?~ Josh chuckled.

~Don't you dare laugh at me!~ Jennifer stomped her foot in frustration, knowing full well Josh was right; she had no clue how to transport.

~I could teach you, but it's illegal for you to transport without me. Any attempt to do so and I'll be demoted.~

~That's insane! As the next high priestess, I *should* be learning how to transport myself! It sounds a whole lot more fun than you shooting bolts of energy at me.~

~You don't seem to mind the energized orgasms. I've noticed how you've been missing a few easy shots on purpose.~ Josh flashed Jennifer a knowing smile.

~Have I?~ Jennifer played innocent, then attempted to change the subject before Josh could get any ideas about firing a heated bolt her way. ~Should we order a pizza?~

~Sure,~ Josh agreed, avoiding any risk of irritating his wife again.

Three days later, Josh's kiss whisked Jennifer away to their honeymoon house, giving them both a much-needed ten-day vacation in the other realm.

When Josh pulled away, Jennifer opened her eyes to find them standing in their honeymoon bedroom. "Ahh, I can think of no better place to vacation than here in your solid arms," Jennifer sighed. "I'm looking forward to curling up on the loveseat in front of the fire with a good romance novel." Jennifer looked towards her destination of choice, but instead spotted the new addition to the room and immediately went red with fury.

"Don't tell me you were serious?" Jennifer said, examining the round table, four chairs, and wall of bookcases that were now tucked in the far corner of their bedroom.

"They come with a special present," Josh appeased.

"And what would that be? A *torch*?!"

"Weren't you saying the other day that you wanted to know how to transport?" Josh said, leading Jennifer over to the table and pulling a chair out for her. "Well, if you read the entire high priestess manual and code of conduct, you'll learn that and more. As it happens, I have a copy with me." Josh reached into his pocket and pulled out a tiny book the size of a quarter, placing it in front of her.

"How am I supposed to read this?" Jennifer watched as Josh tapped the book three times and said something, then leaned back as it grew into a gargantuan tome that caused the table to groan under its weight.

"Is that better?" Josh grinned.

"How many pages are there?" Jennifer lifted the oversized, gilded cover and peeked inside at the miniscule lettering.

"I'd say there's enough reading to keep you out of trouble."

"Josh, you promised me a vacation with no high priestess lessons."

"*You* were the one who said you should be learning how to transport. I'm gonna run over and check in with Gisabella; I'll catch up with you later," Josh said before hightailing it out of there.

Once Josh disappeared, Jennifer flipped to the table of contents, searching the tiny print until she located the information she wanted. *Hmm, here we go…page 3,231.* After a quick double-check to make sure she was alone, Jennifer found the desired page and began reading the chapter: "How to Transport To and From Other Realms."

An hour later Jennifer closed the book. *It sounds easier than I thought.* Vowing to pay more attention next time Josh transported her, Jennifer concentrated on finding a better book to read. *I hope there's a Harlequin romance!* Upon scanning the four floor-to-ceiling shelves packed with books of every size to no avail, she sunk to the ground in a puddle of despair.

This was supposed to be a vacation—not a trip to the library! Why did I have to be born a high priestess?!

CHAPTER THIRTY-ONE

Two months had passed since Jennifer's first day of college, and she was doing well in all of her classes except one: history. Even though she always studied and had done okay on the exams, several of her written papers had lowered her grade and she was barely holding on to a "C" overall. A few of the other girls who'd taken Mr. Burk's class previously had mentioned that he liked it when his students asked for extra help, and how doing so had increased their grades significantly—and Jennifer was desperate.

~Where do you think you're going?~ Josh bellowed into Jennifer's mind. ~Jennifer I don't want you going in Mr. Burk's office.~

~But I need to discuss my grade.~ Jennifer squared her shoulders and knocked.

~Jennifer—stop this instant!~

"Come in," Mr. Burk instructed.

Jennifer entered to find him seated behind a large ornate desk. "Mr. Burk, I'm sorry to bother you, but I wanted to discuss my current grade. Your class is the only one I'm doing poorly in, and I'm concerned about my scholarship."

At last, sweet Jennifer is knocking on my door looking for me, Mr. Burk thought, unaware that his mind was being read.

Josh stifled a disgusted groan from where he stood against the wall. *If this jerk tries to lay one finger on my wife, he'll be wishing he was dead by the time I'm done with him.*

"Please have a seat so we may discuss your concerns. Maybe I can come up with a way for you to bring up your grade." The professor remained seated, motioning Jennifer to sit in one of the medieval-looking chairs across from him.

Leaving the door open, Jennifer walked over to the chair but remained standing.

Mr. Burk noticed Jennifer's defiant pose, and although he usually liked his prey shy and mousey, he found the girl's gumption refreshing and relished her spunk. She didn't look nor act like his normal targets. This time, he'd need to use his brain and remain levelheaded if he had any chance of bedding her. *Let the cat-and-mouse game begin.*

~I got this, Josh,~ Jennifer messaged, approaching the professor and trying not to vomit at his self-indulgent air. "Mr. Burk, let me see if I have this correct," Jennifer said in a confident voice that even her grandma would think befitting of her royal status. "I don't appreciate how you've been purposely marking my work lower so that I'd become your willing sex partner." *What disgusting thoughts he has!* She ignored Josh's groan and held her ground.

Oh no! Josh groaned. *What is Jennifer doing? More importantly—how did she read Burk's mind?*

Mr. Burk stood, his face hard as stone as he walked around the desk to approach Jennifer. He gave the girl credit for her unwavering eye contact; it was this defiant act that made Jennifer even more fun than he'd expected. "Jennifer, your grades are indeed that bad. Judging by your attempt to discredit me, you're more desperate than I thought—but I'm willing to overlook your outburst and your accusations, and will even let you do extra credit to pull up your overall grade." Mr. Burk challenged Jennifer with his eyes, deploying a method he'd designed to make girls cave in to him. If she didn't succumb, he'd keep failing her until she grew desperate enough to bow down before him.

Josh flexed his hands, ignoring the way they itched to throttle Mr. Burk until his face turned a lovely shade of purple.

Jennifer hesitated; she'd read Mr. Burk's thoughts clearly, but was too busy concentrating on holding her ground to question how she'd done so. *Maybe it's time to pull the rug out from underneath him?* "Mr. Burk, I know what you've been thinking." Jennifer waited for his response, and when none came, she continued. "You think there's no way I can prove anything, but what you haven't figured out is that I can get your *former* female students to step forward. Together, we'll press charges against you." Throwing down the gauntlet, she leveled her eyes to stare into his beady, deviant ones. If Mr. Burk didn't believe her, then he'd soon be up against a greater force—her protector, who'd positioned himself within striking distance of the professor. Jennifer didn't know about Mr. Burk, but she'd rather face anything other than Josh's fury!

"If you feel it necessary to speak to the other students, I can't stop you. But if you do, prepare yourself for a retaliation you'll never forget."

Mr. Burk's evil threat made Jennifer recoil and step back. Goosebumps spread up and down her arms from the change in atmosphere now that Mr. Burk had shown his true, hateful colors, and she immediately felt out of her depth. Her fear rose higher when the teacher balled his hands into two fists, and if not for Josh standing nearby, she would've feared for her safety. It was time to admit defeat and let her bodyguard take over. Jennifer glanced towards Josh and nodded. ~Give him hell, Josh.~

It's about time! The second he received Jennifer's message, Josh rocketed a bolt of energy at his victim. It slammed into the professor's crotch and dropped him instantly to the floor; when effectively delivered, Josh's protector energy was more lethal than a pitcher's fastball. Josh smiled down at the helpless excuse for a man, making it so that Mr. Burk couldn't speak or move.

~Now you won't be able to plead to Jennifer for leniency. Once I send her away, there will be no one here to stop me.~ The message he placed in Mr. Burk's mind caused the teacher's eyes to widen in terror. ~Best of all, asshole—you'll never know who was responsible for your excruciating pain or your inability to move even a millimeter. Pardon me a moment while I send my wife away. Jennifer—you're to leave this instant and close the door,~ Josh commanded.

~Yes, sir.~ Jennifer hastened out of the room, leaving her protector to clean up the mess she'd made. Shaken from the encounter with Mr. Burk and from observing Josh in action, Jennifer scurried to the ladies room. She was sure that when Josh was done, the horrendous Mr. Burk would never sexually assault or harass another woman for the rest of his life.

Jennifer crouched down in the bathroom stall, wondering whether Josh might be saving a little of his wrath for her. He hadn't looked happy —in fact, he'd seemed furious when she'd tried to take matters into her own hands. *In my defense, how was I suppose to know the teacher was such a scumbag?*

Once Josh was done torturing the snake, he placed a thought in Mr. Burk's mind that he must never touch another student again lest he die a gruesome, violent death. The sight of a large wet spot appearing on the teacher's pants made Josh laugh so loud that the teacher's eyes bugged out. ~Oh—and resign immediately, you slimy fucker,~ Josh added.

Josh laughed when the teacher's eyes began darting to and fro, frantic to find the source of the voice inside his head. Once Josh had made sure that "Mr. Burk Shit" wouldn't blame Jennifer in any way for his distress, he released his hold, leaving the teacher lying there in his own filth. He had no doubt the man would be crawling to the principal's office to hand in his resignation by the end of the day. *Looks like my work here is done.*

Mr. Burk opened his mouth as Josh stepped over him, emitting a black cloud of smoke that caught Josh off guard. The smoky substance congealed into a faceless, manlike-entity whose only sign of life was a pair of red, menacing eyes. *What the hell?* Josh thought. Without warning, the creature's eyes flashed and released a bolt of energy aimed at his chest, one that traveled faster than the speed of light. Josh dove to the side, but not fast enough to avoid it completely. He gritted his teeth as the bolt of energy blazed a trail along his ribcage, shooting across the room to burn a hole in Mr. Burk's desk. He fought off the sickening pain and the desire to double over, knowing that if he did, it'd be his last move before his soul was disintegrated. *Now I'm really pissed!*

~Go ahead and take your best shot before I blow you to smithereens!~ Josh messaged, hoping the faceless spirit would understand him and surrender. This time when the creature's eyes started to glow, Josh's cat-like reflexes kicked in and he launched himself upward to fire a massive bolt of energy at his attacker. Josh covered his eyes as the dark figure exploded in a flash of blinding light and flying sparks of color, vanishing from existence forever.

Holy fuck! Was that thing inside this dickhead teacher the entire time? Josh studied the man where he was curled in the fetal position, before taking off in search of Jennifer.

~Hiding are we?~ Josh asked as he joined Jennifer from up above her bathroom stall. His energy hadn't calmed yet, so his irritation with her sounded more threatening than he'd intended.

~Why would I be hiding from you? You *are* my protector, aren't you? I'm thankful you were there to take over the unfortunate situation.~ Jennifer kept her voice calm and forced herself to look up into his eyes, knowing Josh would respect her more than if she shirked away from him and his anger.

~Maybe you're hiding because you realize that you could've been walking into a trap when you went to that weasel's office. All you had to do was ask for my opinion or give me a heads up and I'd have been there for you—I can't believe you did such a stupid thing.~ Josh didn't miss Jennifer's recoil, a reaction that did little to appease him. But this wasn't the time nor the place to tell her about the demonic spirit that'd been in possession of Mr. Burk; Josh would wait until after he'd seen Gisabella. She could provide some guidance on what was going on, as well as to treat the slash in his side that was currently burning like an inferno.

~In my defense, I never thought…~ Jennifer's voice trailed off when Josh's hardened-steel eyes hadn't softened. There was no use trying to defend herself when he was in protector mode.

~I'll be watching you the rest of the day—see if you can manage to keep out of trouble until then, okay? I'll see you at home.~ *For fuck's sake!* Josh clenched his teeth fighting off the searing pain. *Fucking beast!* As an extra precaution, Josh surrounded Jennifer with tons of protective white light and cloaked her aura, before cloaking his energy. Doing so served two purposes: he'd have an advantage if any further trouble showed up and it'd teach his wayward wife a lesson.

Geez, what's his problem? To discuss anything now was pointless; Josh was far too mad. All she could do was stare up at him and watch him fade away until he was completely invisible. Even his intense energy had disappeared. She swiped at the tear trickling down her cheek—the last thing she wanted was to appear weak. When she faced him later, she'd do so as his equal, with her head held high and no trace of tears in her eyes.

After splashing some cold water on her face, Jennifer made her way to her last class of the day: art. Once inside, she glanced around for Josh, but neither he nor his energy were in the room. She opened her notebook and used her messaging pen to draw a heart before writing, "I'm sorry." When the words "message refused" became visible, Jennifer stood and picked up her belongings to make a quick exit; she wasn't in the mood to draw the bowl of fruit arranged on the table.

Jennifer climbed into her car and shut the door, giving in to a full-throttle crying jag. She couldn't feel Josh's energy anywhere around her—not that it was such a bad thing, considering how angry he was. Didn't he know she was already beating herself up over this? *I couldn't even face one dumb, weak teacher without my protector having to come to my rescue.*

She had no clue how long she sat there crying, and the thought of Josh watching over her didn't make her feel better. He was surely laughing or gloating over her self-indulgent sob-fest, and he probably felt like she deserved all she'd gotten.

She was tired of it all! Tired of trying to be everything that Josh and her grandma expected. Jennifer questioned whether she was cut out to be a high priestess at all. *Her* leading the masses in heaven and earth? *What were they thinking?!* How would she ever be ready for such an enormous responsibility when she wasn't even able to please her husband with her driving abilities?

Jennifer's pity party had hit rock bottom, forcing her to face the facts. The truth of the matter was, she shouldn't have placed herself in such a precarious position without forewarning her protector. Coming to her senses, she knew it was time to find Josh and thank him for helping to fix the dilemma she'd caused. Jennifer dried her eyes and started the car; it'd be a long ride home without the company of her copilot.

Josh added more protection around Jennifer and her car to keep her safe before he summoned Gisabella.

It was a rarity for Gisabella to transport to earth with the sole purpose of meeting with a protector, but Josh's message had her doing so without hesitation.

~Thank you for coming, Your Excellency.~ Josh bowed to kiss Gisabella's ring, then fell to the floor.

~Josh!~ Gisabella shouted, crouching beside him. ~What's wrong?~

~My side,~ Josh gasped.

Gisabella pulled up his torn shirt and shrieked. ~Who did this to you?~ She glanced around the room. ~Where's Jennifer? Please tell me she's safe!~

~Check my orb.~ Josh pointed to the black crystal ball just out of reach.

Gisabella gazed into the orb and once she'd confirmed Jennifer wasn't in any danger, she went to work on Josh using both healing energy and gemstones while he recounted everything that'd happened.

~I'm sorry—I destroyed it before we could find out anything,~ Josh confessed.

~Nonsense. If you hadn't, there'd be nothing left of you. Since you haven't seen any others around, maybe it'd been harboring inside the teacher for years. There's no way of knowing how long it was in possession of the man's soul or if it was the reason the teacher sexually abused women; it may've been drawn to his bad energy.~

~I should've stopped Jennifer before she confronted Mr. Burk. She could've been hurt or worse.~

~Joshua, you of all people know that she must learn to handle things on her own. Speaking of Jennifer, she's pulling in the driveway—and now that I've fixed you, she'll never know what happened. I think it's best for now if you hide these details from her, at least until we have a chance to figure out why it was here.~

~Gisabella, I disagree; my wife needs to know what happened! It'll be easier to protect Jennifer if she understands why we're on high alert. No offense, but your granddaughter is harder to protect than you ever were.~

~I command you to keep your trap shut! I must go before she sees me —we'll talk further when you and Jennifer visit.~ Before Gisabella transported back home, she converted Josh to solid form as a peace offering for following her orders.

Jennifer pulled into the driveway and went up to her room, preparing herself for the worst. What she *didn't* expect was to find her husband standing in the middle of the room, arms crossed and fully solid.

They stared at one another for a full ten seconds before Josh opened his arms, offering Jennifer sanctuary in his loving embrace. She ran across the room and he held her tightly, intermittently stroking her hair and kissing the top of her head.

"You're not mad?" Jennifer asked hesitantly.

"I never said I wasn't still mad. Finding you trapped and at a distinct disadvantage with a sexual predator and then watching you *tell* him you'd read his mind was not the best part of my day."

"You're right; I read Mr. Burk's thoughts! That's never happened before. Do you think it's one of my gifts? You know, to read people's thoughts?"

"This is not the time to discuss your newfound abilities!" Per Gisabella's instructions, Josh forced himself to hide the truth from Jennifer. "What we *should* be discussing is your punishment." He breathed in her sweet, fragrant scent and gathered her a little tighter. "Jennifer, I love you and I'm thankful you're safe, but the dilemma of being your protector and your husband causes me to feel very divided."

"I love you so much too." Her lips searched and captured Josh's mouth, silently begging him to let her inside. She was rewarded when he carried her over to the large, overstuffed chair in the corner of her room and sat her down, moving his hands under her blouse to unclasp the front of her bra. Josh took turns bringing each of her nipples to attention with firm, harsh pinches, serving as a reminder that she was not out of the woods from his rebuke. She cried out for mercy as he forcibly took turns, stretching and squeezing each one.

"These are mine," Josh said harshly, before lowering his mouth and sucking each one hard while he held her in place.

Jennifer gave into his creative, well-deserved punishment, laying herself all the way back with her head on the soft armrest and granting him full access to her whole body. She was his, all his, to do with as he pleased.

Her parents were thankfully away in the Hamptons until the next Monday, making it possible to enjoy Josh's solidness all night long and to question him without fear of being interrupted.

"When are you going to tell me how I read Mr. Burk's mind?"

Jennifer asked Josh an hour later, both naked and sated as they cuddled in bed.

"When someone like yourself begins to try and read minds, it helps if they increase their energy to a heightened state of awareness. Given the circumstances, you must've achieved that state unknowingly."

"So what you're saying is if I want to read someone's mind, I simply have to become super excited or scared?"

"That's *not* what I said. Yes, that's probably how you were able to read the slime-bucket's thoughts, but I haven't given you permission to try and read the thoughts of anyone else. In fact, I forbid you to attempt to read anyone else's mind until I've decided you're capable of understanding the rules involved."

"Can I practice reading your mind?"

"I dare you to try, little girl!" Josh quirked his brows and grinned wickedly. "I'd welcome the chance to reconsider my decision not to punish you earlier."

Yikes! "How do you manage to make punishments sound so tempting when they're obviously not?! If it's okay with you, I'll forgo all forms of mind-reading until my protector decides I've become worthy enough to partake in them."

"Good choice." Josh chuckled before he flipped her over and swatted her butt.

Ouch! "What was that for?"

"A sample—in case you're thinking about breaking my rules," Josh warned lightheartedly, before sinking his erection into his wife. "Mmm, being inside you is better than wasting my time punishing you."

"I agree—much better—this—way," Jennifer said between Josh's deep thrusts. True to his word, he made love to her long into the night.

At school the next day Jennifer pretended to be surprised when the other students spoke of Mr. Burk's sudden departure, stifling her smirk at the thought of him cowering in his home, afraid of another unseen attack.

The class settled down when their new history teacher called their attention up front—she was a middle-aged, dowdy woman who immediately began walking the class through the social hierarchy of ancient Greece.

With messaging pen in hand, Jennifer wrote, “I bet you’re pleased with your new teacher selection.”

Josh’s message read: “Eyes up front and pay attention, wife. Otherwise I promise I’ll personally teach you a lesson on one of the most effective uses for a wooden ruler.” Jennifer blushed fuchsia, closing her notebook and turning her attention promptly towards the blackboard with a big smile.

CHAPTER THIRTY-TWO

After Gisabella left Josh, she hurried home and went to her mystical pond to gaze into its stilled surface, summoning the only person who'd know what to do.

~Merlin, I need to talk to you—alone,~ Gisabella messaged, waiting for his image to appear in the water.

~What is it, lass?~ Merlin answered seconds later.

~Is it safe to come to you now?~ Gisabella asked the blue-eyed, bearded wizard currently looking up at her from the watery surface.

~Yes; will you be arriving without an escort?~ Merlin asked in surprise.

~Just me. I'll explain when I get there.~ Gisabella waved her hand over the pond, transporting herself instantly to Merlin's woodsy domain.

"Gisabella, what's happened?" Merlin questioned, pushing back the hood of his cloak to get a better look at her.

"Oh Merlin, I don't know where to begin," Gisabella fretted. "Josh was attacked by a demonic entity who may've been after Jennifer. They're both okay, but I'm worried this may not be an isolated occurrence."

"Does Josh agree?"

"No, but I told him the thing was gone so not to worry. Merlin, if not for Josh's honed reflexes, the slash he received on his side would've sliced him in half and disintegrated him."

"Josh sure is one lucky guy," Merlin agreed. "But attacks happen all the time, and as long as Josh annihilated the demon, that should be the end of it."

"There's more," Gisabella swallowed. "As you know, I've done some terrible things in my life—"

"That you have, love, but nothing I'd change," Merlin grinned. "If it weren't for your trickery, I would've never become a father. Speaking of which, other than the attack, how is my granddaughter?"

"She's well, and Josh has begun to work with her. Jennifer's a promising student, and Josh sees much potential."

"I should hope so! She has our genes, after all," Merlin said with pride. "You couldn't possibly have done something as terrible as when you created the first interdimensional child. To this day I don't know what you put in that wine; imagine, *me* a spirit and you alive on earth, somehow successfully creating a child." Merlin's voice cracked. "I don't know what spell you used or how you were able to trick me into doing such an illegal thing, but I'm sure glad you did. Olivia meant the world to me."

"I know. Me too, Merlin." Gisabella placed a comforting hand on his shoulder. "But I'm afraid it's even worse this time…"

"Let's go inside where it's not so damp." Merlin wrapped an arm around Gisabella's waist and guided her over the rough terrain until they reached his small cabin. "Go ahead and sit by the fire while I fetch us some hot toddy."

Gisabella did as told and sat down with her hands clasped, until Merlin reentered the room with two steaming mugs on a tray.

"Go ahead, drink up—it'll chase away the chill while you tell me everything. If it's as bad as you say, then you've come to the right place. There's nothing I wouldn't do for you, my love," Merlin vowed with a twinkle in his eyes.

"Oh Merlin, if only things could've been different." Gisabella did her best to hide the sadness in her voice; it'd been many years since Merlin had mentioned his love for her or their relationship, and she'd always hoped someday he'd come back to her.

"Me too, lass—we can talk about all that later. First, tell me about these supposed 'horrible' things you're so worried about."

"As you know, Jennifer's soul was rebirthed as Olivia's baby." Gisabella waited until Merlin nodded. "What I *didn't* tell you was where I'd gotten Jennifer's original soul."

"You told me she was a new soul who'd only lived one brief lifetime," Merlin corrected.

With a deep breath, Gisabella began: "I may've misled you. Josh and Jennifer were former lovers many centuries ago, sharing other lifetimes before that. During their final shared lifetime, their love affair was discovered by Jennifer's husband, who in turn tried to force Josh into testifying against Jennifer. When Josh refused to expose her, he was forced to fight in the Colosseum; even though he won, Josh was met with foul play when Jennifer's husband had him murdered. In that lifetime, Josh was known as 'Demetri' and Jennifer as 'Astraea.'

"I'd waited centuries for Josh, and he was primed to become one of the greatest additions to my newly formed elite squad. But when I was speaking to Josh, Astraea killed herself, and he became inconsolable, wanting only to join her. With Josh being so in love, it was easy to convince him to work for me in exchange for a lifetime with his lover."

"Is that all?" Merlin asked.

"Not even close. After Astraea finished serving one lifetime of her suicide penalty, I took her soul and gave it to Olivia to rebirth as Jennifer. When Olivia was killed, Josh rescued Jennifer and brought her to heaven to be cared for until she was ready to begin her required high priestess life-paths. When Josh was well enough he returned to his apartment. That's when I contacted you. You remember chasing after Jennifer with me." Gisabella smiled at the long ago memory before continuing. "During the time Jennifer was with us, I secretly advanced Jennifer's soul faster than permitted by law and gave her many psychic abilities, so she'd become as powerful as me. Of course, when Josh found out his new bride was destined to become the next high priestess, he wasn't pleased." Gisabella sighed before adding, "I never expected them to marry each other for all of eternity!"

"They did what?!" Merlin jumped to his feet and began to pace. "If anyone finds out, we'll all be banished! How could you let this happen?!"

"Think about it, Merlin; since Josh married Jennifer forever, the moment she dies, she'll transcend to heaven and my final days as a high priestess will be numbered. Don't get me wrong, at first I wasn't pleased, but the more I thought about having my freedom, the happier I became. With Josh by Jennifer's side, we won't have to worry. Don't you see? We can finally have a life of our own!"

"I could think of nothing better than to finally have our love out in the open," Merlin agreed. "But in the meantime, if we don't figure out a way to keep this a secret, none of us will live long enough to *experience* that." Merlin thought for a moment, before turning his attention back to Gisabella. "You said that Josh and Jennifer were lovers who died on the same day? Do you remember the year?"

"180 AD. Why?"

Without answering, Merlin leapt to his feet and rushed to a wall of books where he grabbed a bronze-covered tome. "If I can find what I'm looking for, it may give you a reason for doing what you did." After a few minutes, Merlin gave a little yip of victory. "Here it is! In the 1500s, Nostradamus made a prophecy that included details of how the world would end. When I researched his theory, I stumbled upon a story written by a group of wizards that spoke of a dagger used to murder a senator from a powerful family who'd fallen in love with the wife of the emperor's cousin. It went on to say how the dead man's lover was so distraught she'd used the same dagger to kill herself."

"So far it sounds like Demetri and Astraea."

"According to the legend, the girl's husband will return to earth centuries later, only this time he's invincible. If he's not stopped, it's prophesied he'll destroy every dimension except the one he's chosen to rule. Whoever he is, if he were to find out who Josh and Jennifer are, he'd stop at nothing to destroy them."

"How can we stop him?"

"Prophets claimed that the dagger that ended the scorned lovers' lives is the only weapon that can kill him, thus putting an end to the foretold war. If we fail, every earthbound soul will be destroyed indefinitely," Merlin explained. "Gisabella, do you know what happened to the dagger?"

"I have it. Don't ask what possessed me to retrieve it from Astraea's corpse."

"Please tell me you never cleaned the blade. The lovers' mingled blood is the only poison strong enough to kill such an evil man."

"I kept it as it was, planning to use it during Jennifer's psychometry lesson to see if she might pick up any information from the past."

"Excellent, lass!" Merlin cheered. "Here's what you need to do…"

An hour and much explanation later, they agreed it was best to wait until after the elite protector meeting and Christmas to enact their plan.

"Whatever you do, make sure Josh doesn't learn about the dagger. If he acts sooner than the appointed time, he'll fail, and all of us will be disintegrated," Merlin warned.

Armed with Merlin's instructions and a kiss, Gisabella headed back to her domain to wait for the appointed day to hand Jennifer the dagger, and to cast the spell that'd hopefully change the foretold prophecy.

CHAPTER THIRTY-THREE

Now that Jennifer's final exams were finished and she'd received a "B" on her history final, she was done with classes until the new year.

~I promise I won't be too long,~ Josh said as he buttoned his shirt. ~All I ask is that you stay put and don't leave the house.~

~You know how much I love to run around the lake at midnight,~ Jennifer joked.

~If you attempt to leave the house or anyone tries to break in, the silent alarm will sound. Break my rule and you'll be dragged back into the house before you get more than three feet out the door,~ Josh warned with an "I dare you to disobey me" grin.

~You don't scare me! Jennifer's stomach clenched in the most delicious way.~ *Great, nothing like wanting Josh's darker side to come out!*

Josh walked over and lightly kissed the top of Jennifer's head. ~You *should* be afraid! I mean it, Jennifer; don't leave the house. If this meeting wasn't mandatory, I'd stay here and give you what you crave—a taste of something a little darker.~ Jennifer's sharp intake of breath put his mind at ease that she wouldn't be attempting any midnight escapades. After their experience with Mr. Burk, Josh wanted nothing more than to skip the annual elite protector meeting. At Gisabella's insistence, however, he'd agreed; it would've attracted too much attention if he wasn't in attendance.

~Aren't you going to be late for the meeting?~ Jennifer asked, doing her best to look unaffected by his warnings.

~Are you trying to get rid of me, my love?~ Josh chuckled. ~Don't worry, I'm leaving; I have to pick up Gisabella on my way. Remember, if you run into any trouble, message me.~

~Josh, I've spent most of my life alone in the house. Stop worrying, I'll be fine.~ After receiving a chaste kiss, Jennifer watched as Josh transported away.

Josh took his position to the left of Gisabella while she began the meeting, doing his best to ignore Sarnia. The redhead continued to glance his way, smiling flirtatiously and acting like the incident at his apartment had never happened. *Such odd behavior for a woman who'd promised I'd burn in hell.* Josh forced himself to listen to Gisabella's phony, rosy speech without scowling. *She should remind them to watch out for demonic spirits harboring inside people on earth!*

"I am pleased to pass out this final award to one of the first protectors inducted into this prodigious group. In addition to being my personal guard, he holds the record for the highest number of successful visionaries who have gone on to complete their purpose. I think he'll be the first to tell you what a pain in the butt I can be to work for…" Gisabella paused, waiting for the laughter to die down. "I'm sure he's called me many other things under his breath, but through thick and thin, I know I can always count on him. Please join me in congratulating Joshua." Cheers and catcalls rang out as Gisabella turned and motioned for Josh to step forward.

Josh begrudgingly joined Gisabella at the podium and took the award.

"Congratulations, Joshua. This is long overdue. Thank you for your devoted service, *my friend*," Gisabella added quietly, before pulling Josh into a congratulatory embrace. "The microphone's all yours!"

"Thanks," Josh said sardonically. When the applause had died down, he stepped forward. "Thank you, Your Excellency, for your faith in me and the chance to make a difference in so many lives. What Gisabella failed to mention, though, are all the names *she's* called me! In her defense, I probably deserved each one of them. I'm honored—thank you all!" Josh cleared his throat and quickly removed himself from the podium, ready for Gisabella to dismiss the meeting.

"I promised a few people I'd meet with them as soon as we were done," Gisabella said as she and Josh left the stage, heading in the opposite direction of Sarnia. Gisabella had caught a few glimpses of the protector mooning over Josh like a lovesick puppy, and felt it best they didn't interact. "Don't look now, but Sarnia's trying to get your attention."

"Just ignore her and hopefully she'll get the hint," Josh said, glancing down at the gold band on his left hand. "I wonder what she'd do if she could see my wedding ring?"

"I, for one, am glad we'll never find out," Gisabella said with relief. Josh escorted her to a group consisting of five protectors—three men and two women. "I'll be a few minutes, if you'd like to say hi to your friends."

Josh nodded, and started to head in the direction of Lancelot and a few other guys who looked to be in a heated discussion.

"Hey Josh!" someone called from his left, and Josh turned to see his neighbor Richard approaching.

"Oh hey, how's it going?" Josh forced out a polite response.

"Haven't seen you around since the night that sexy redhead showed up at your door," Richard continued. "Why didn't you tell me she was the second-highest protector? Geez, Sarnia must've thought I was an idiot for not recognizing her! Are you two dating? I'd love to ask her out..."

"Sarnia and I? *God* no! You're welcome to her!" Josh said, flabbergasted by Richard's ability to remember her even after his inebriated state that night.

"Cool!"

"Just watch yourself; Sarnia's a little hot-tempered, and she didn't become the second-ranking protector without learning how to inflict some serious damage."

"Are you just saying those things because you want her for yourself?" Richard accused.

"Absolutely not! Look, Richard—you're a nice guy, and Sarnia...well, she's trouble with a capital 'T!'" The noise level in the room had grown louder as protectors all around them converged to catch up and embrace, and Josh had to practically yell his last words to be heard.

"I didn't see you turning her away the night she showed up at your apartment!" Richard said above the noise.

"I've been trying to get Sarnia off my back for years, and you broke into my apartment to let her in! Would you believe she was waiting in my bed, *naked*?! Thanks for that!" Josh roared, his voice level catching Gisabella's attention.

"Lucky bastard! You *should* be thanking me! Sarnia would've been the fuck of your life! For such a smart guy, you're a fool!" Richard shouted, doubling Josh's volume. Neither he or Josh noticed the room had quieted and heads were turning their way.

"Will you all please excuse me?" Gisabella said to the group she'd been conversing with, before hurrying past Josh and Richard with pursed lips. *I'll deal with each of them later.* By the time she reached Sarnia, Gisabella's fury was boiling over.

"Your Excellency—I'm sorry, I didn't see you..." Sarnia began.

"I *warned* you of what would happen if you went near Joshua again! Pack your things and get out! Consider yourself lucky that's all I'm doing to you!" Gisabella bellowed in the protector's face.

"Josh told you?" Sarnia croaked. "He said he wouldn't say anything as long as I left."

"Well he *lied*!" Gisabella said, not bothering to inform the redhead of the real reason she'd become aware of the escapade.

"You and Josh deserve each other! Looks like he'd rather sleep his way up to the top than be with a woman closer to his own age!" Sarnia spat out.

Gisabella slapped Sarnia's face hard enough to leave a reddened handprint in its wake. "You have exactly twenty seconds to remove yourself from my presence before I disintegrate you on the spot."

Clutching her cheek, Sarnia ran from the room.

The room was completely silent as Gisabella walked back to where Josh and Richard were standing, everyone's eyes fixated on her.

"Richard, you're demoted back down to a basic protector for letting someone into another protector's apartment. Remove yourself from my sight now before I reconsider my leniency," Gisabella commanded, loud enough for everyone to hear.

"Yes, Your Excellency," Richard murmured, hurrying from the room and looking relieved to be out of Josh's range of fire. If Josh was demoted, there'd be no place safe enough for him to hide.

Gisabella stood in front of Josh with her eyes blazing. "If you weren't so important to our cause, I'd send you packing! If I were you, I wouldn't plan on being able to service any woman for a while, because when I get done torturing you, you'll be of little use to them." She gazed into Josh's worried eyes, pleased her words had hit home. "Let's go before you make a bigger fool out of yourself!"

"Yes, Your Excellency," Josh said quietly with his head bent in shame, keeping it lowered even after they arrived at Gisabella's home.

"If my granddaughter wouldn't hate me, I'd make good on my threat! Since the option to castrate you is off the table, I have no other choice but to demote you to second. You made me look like a fool in front of everyone!" Gisabella berated loudly. "Not only that, but you've put me in the horrible position of losing my two top protectors in one day! I don't know who I'll find that's capable of replacing you." Gisabella's lips trembled, but her eyes were void of all emotion.

"Gisabella, please, let me explain…"

"Save it, Josh!" Gisabella yelled, beginning to pace. "What possessed you to keep such a secret from me?"

"The only reason I didn't say anything was because I felt sorry for Sarnia. She made a stupid decision showing up at my apartment, but no harm came of it."

"A stupid choice would've been if Sarnia had knocked on your door fully dressed. How do you think Jennifer will feel when she finds out?"

"Please don't say anything. Nothing happened—honest!"

"When *exactly* did this occur?"

"When I went back to my place to get dressed before picking up Jennifer."

"What day?"

"January thirteenth, 1979—a half hour before I was scheduled to transport Jennifer here," Josh mumbled.

"The eve of your wedding?! Good luck explaining *that* to your wife!" Gisabella let her words sink in before adding, "That will be your punishment for making me look like a fool in front of everyone. You must tell Jennifer about Sarnia and how she was naked in your bed. If Jennifer forgives you, then I will too."

"Please Gisabella, don't ruin Jennifer's holiday; she's been looking forward to our first Christmas together for months."

"For Jennifer's sake, I'll give you until New Year's Day to fess up."

"Thank you," Josh said blandly.

"Doesn't feel so good, does it? Now that the shoe's on the other foot," Gisabella baited. "Maybe you should've thought twice about chastising me for not telling Jennifer about the demonic spirit attack."

"Wait a minute—withholding information from your granddaughter about a direct attack is *entirely* different than Sarnia waiting naked for me in bed." The realization of how bad that sounded made Josh blanch.

"Looks to me like you've answered your own question," Gisabella laughed. "Like I said—good luck, old man."

"Thanks," Josh said dryly. "Are we done here?"

"Enjoy Christmas dinner with your in-laws," Gisabella taunted, knowing that doing so was like rubbing salt into an open cut.

Without another word Josh transported himself back to earth, grateful to find Jennifer sound asleep. *How am I going to tell her about something that happened almost a year ago? For Jennifer's sake, I must put it out of my mind until after Christmas. It'll be easier to explain how I've been demoted then too. It's not like I was ever worthy enough to be Jennifer's husband to begin with.* Josh sat down in the closest chair to the bed, watching the only woman he'd ever loved sleep. Every so often he'd swipe a tear or two from his cheeks, ones that fell due to the possibility of losing Jennifer years earlier than expected.

Excitement built as their first Christmas as a married couple drew closer. With her parents gone for the week prior, Jennifer was in charge of all the decorations and planning the family get-together. Josh and Jennifer enjoyed basking in each other's company while picking out the perfect tree, ornaments, other decorations, and presents for her family and Gisabella.

By Christmas Eve, everything was in place. The Christmas supper menu was planned and cookies were baked for the special day, while presents for both dimensions had been wrapped and hidden out of sight.

"Jennifer, what a beautiful job you've done," Mrs. Parker exclaimed on Christmas Eve, surveying the elegant decorations of gold, silver, and red around the house. Lit candles glowed and wreaths of pine with fruit served as accents, giving a look of warmth to each room. The dining table was set with fine china and crystal, and was adorned by a pine-and-fruit centerpiece glowing with candles.

Alex was visiting from college and Sarah had flown in with Dave to celebrate, so the Parkers sat around talking into the wee hours before hitting the sack. On Christmas morning while her entire family was at church, Jennifer worked with Josh to prepare a memorable feast for everyone.

Even though Jennifer had grown used to Josh's exclusion from her daily social life, she wasn't prepared to cope with him being left out of the festivities. Balancing conversation between her family and Josh under normal circumstances was hard, but with her sexy husband in plain view only to her, it was impossible to concentrate. Her valiant effort to keep her facial expressions under control didn't go unnoticed by her husband, who looked to be enjoying her predicament.

~Only five more hours,~ Josh messaged.

~Five more hours?~ She couldn't resist his suggestive bait.

~Five more hours until I unzip the back of that velvet dress you're wearing. I've been dying to remove it since the moment I saw you weren't wearing a bra.~ Josh didn't bother to hide his salacious grin in anticipation, making sure his wife saw his exaggerated expression. ~Remember, no blushing, sweetheart,~ Josh added with a chuckle when he saw the way her cheeks grew pink. She was doing better than he'd expected, until she started to giggle and everyone in the room turned to look at her.

"What a klutz I am! I almost tripped and fell," Jennifer falsely claimed, pointing at her heels as evidence.

"You are kind of a klutz," her brother teased, adding to her embarrassment. Everyone in the room had a good laugh about it—*including* Josh.

~Just so you know, Mr. Smith, I intend to repay you later for this episode.~ She flashed her mischievous man a dirty look and watched him laugh harder. ~Go ahead and laugh now, but I can assure you I'll make you suffer greatly later,~ Jennifer threatened, thankful when it tempered his boisterous cackling. Too bad it didn't deter Josh from messaging her more comments meant to make her squirm, especially his last one: ~I'm looking forward to it, my lady.~

After that, the gloves were off. First came Jennifer's provocative game designed to push Josh over the edge. Once she discovered how enjoyable a simple game of teasing Josh could be, she took every advantage to make it happen. A few items dropped on purpose gave her the opportunity to lean over, giving him a full view of her braless cleavage. She took joy in watching his desire visibly increasing with each of her playful acts. She wasn't worried about how he'd repay her, and soon began to look forward to it. By the look in Josh's eyes, it was sure to be creative and torturous.

Two can play this game, my dear. Josh couldn't help but be amused by his wife. It was clear she was purposely pushing for his darker side to come out—an invitation he couldn't resist. He waited until Jennifer was leaning over to move a low-hanging ornament to send her a much-deserved warning: ~Jennifer, you're playing with fire.~ He followed it with a bolt of energy up her dress.

"Oh!" Jennifer yelped as the unexpected bolt hit.

"What is it dear?" her mom asked.

"Oh, nothing. I just noticed…" *Oh no!* Jennifer's mind went blank.

~There are too many red ornaments on the tree,~ Josh said, offering an explanation also designed to win an earlier argument they'd had.

"I noticed there aren't enough red ornaments; in fact, I should've done the *entire* tree in red," Jennifer said brightly. ~Josh, did you really think I'd concede to you so easily? Geez, talk about stooping to an all-time low!~ She was thankful when everyone accepted her explanation and went back to talking. Too bad her husband didn't look like *he* was ready to let go of their game, especially now that she'd scored the winning point.

~I'm sure I can think of other ways to score a win.~ Josh sent his message with a side of heated energy designed to bring color to her already flushed cheeks.

~Please, sir, take mercy on me,~ she messaged, flashing her widened eyes his way.

~Okay Jennifer, you win. I'll behave myself.~ *For now.* He wasn't the least bit fooled by her frightened act, but they'd need to be more careful before someone began questioning her exceptionally odd behavior that night.

A bit later, the Parkers were in the middle of their family dinner and all was quiet on the playful Christmas warfront when Sarah's husband stood up and clinked his wine glass.

"May I please have your attention? Sarah and I have an announcement to make." The room hushed and everyone's attention turned their way. "Sarah, would you like to do the honors?"

"I'm pregnant!" Sarah blurted out in excitement. "We're having a baby!"

Her sister had always talked of having lots of children, but as happy as Jennifer was for Sarah, it didn't halt the pang of envy she felt. She leapt up to join the others in giving Sarah and Dave a big hug, doing her best to hide the tears that pricked her eyes.

"I can't believe I'm going to be a grandmother!" Mrs. Parker gushed. "When are you due, honey?"

"The middle of June. Not much else to say other than I've been a little nauseous and tired," Sarah sighed as Dave rubbed her back.

"If only you two sisters were closer in age, you could be pregnant together. Then your children could play with each other like you did with your cousins," Mrs. Parker said wistfully.

"Jennifer looks as if she's seen a ghost!" Alex cried, pointing at Jennifer's pale expression.

Great choice of words, Alex! Jennifer tried to think of a comeback that wouldn't crush her mom, but came up empty.

Josh didn't miss the look in his wife's eyes. If he were alive on earth, he'd be sitting next to Jennifer holding her hand, talking about *their* future kids together. He only hoped he could pull off his plan for a special Christmas with her grandma, knowing he had to explain about

Sarnia afterwards. He'd worked out all the details with Gisabella, and soon the three of them would be enjoying a holiday feast. It wouldn't make up for him being invisible to her family on earth, but hopefully it'd make Jennifer happy enough that she was married to him, regardless of his neglect to tell her about Sarnia earlier.

Sadly, he'd now seen one more reason why Jennifer's best interests might include her marriage to someone else. When the time came to let her go, he'd need to do so without a fight in the hopes that when Jennifer's life ended, she'd return to his side.

After Sarah's announcement, Jennifer became wrapped up in her family and Josh silently watched from a distance. Jennifer tossed her head back, laughing and talking animatedly with her siblings over memories of some of the disasters that had occurred during former family holidays. It'd been so many centuries since he'd been part of a real family, and he'd forgotten all but a few special memories of what it was like to be surrounded by so many loved ones. The longer the night went on, the more Josh realized he'd never fit in. It wasn't like he could head over and engage Jennifer's dad in conversation or help his mother-in-law clear the table to serve dessert. If he hadn't been on high alert during the holidays, he'd have retreated to the other room with a glass of brandy and a good book.

Jennifer was laughing so hard from one of Alex's jokes that tears ran down her face. *I haven't laughed like that since Josh—oh, no.* She sought out her husband. *How could I have gotten so caught up with my family that I failed to include the man I love?* When her eyes met Josh's, his heart-broken expression made her ache.

"If you'll excuse me, I'll be back shortly," Jennifer offered, before she went upstairs to their bedroom. ~I'm sorry, I didn't mean to leave you out! I wish you could be solid all the time so the others could see you. After all, you're a member of our family now,~ she messaged as Josh joined her in the doorway.

Josh was unsure of what to say about the impossible wish that could never come true.

~Please, come back to the party and sit with me. That way you'll be part of the celebration. It'd mean so much to me if you would.~

~Jennifer, you know what that means, don't you?~

~Yes—I believe it's only possible if the chair aligns together in both of our dimensions to occupy the same space. Meaning that when we sit in them, we'll *also* be occupying the same space and our energies will mingle together. Am I correct?~

~Do you think you'll be able to hold yourself together? It'll be one hell of a powerful combination to concentrate on anything else but you and I.~

~My dear, sweet husband—let me remind you of who I'm to become. Surely I should be able to handle us in the same chair.~ With Josh's hand in hers, Jennifer led the way back to the party where she sat down with Josh. When their energies first merged together, it was hard to adjust to their combined essences, and the feeling of Josh squirming beneath her didn't help. It took much effort to eat dessert and hold a halfway coherent conversation with the others, never mind sending and receiving messages with her playful man.

~I don't know about you, baby, but your energy is doing wicked things to my body—in all the right ways,~ Josh messaged before lightly kissing her neck.

~Umm, deliciously wicked. *Oh my god*—I almost moaned and begged for more out loud!~

~I bet that'd have turned a few heads,~ Josh laughed. ~I wonder if anyone would notice if I began unzipping this zipper staring me in the face. So tempting...~

~Don't you dare touch my zipper! As if our combined energy isn't hard enough to handle, you have to send corrupt messages! I promise that you'll be at my mercy later, and I'll take great pleasure in making you beg me for relief.~ Jennifer's retort caused a surge of energy to rush through them both, making her lightheaded. She might've fallen out of her chair if not for Josh's quick actions, but his mirth over her dilemma didn't go unheard.

~What happened?~ Jennifer asked, a bit dazed.

~You can't play with the big guys when you're still an infant.~

~Come again?~

~You have much to learn before you can attempt to message sexy thoughts while our energies are merged. Let me add how proud I am that you've managed to stay sitting together. Now we can do this during family meals, parties, movies with your friends, and all the other times I've stood off to the side.~

~You've got to be kidding!~

The moment her mother mentioned moving the party into the living room to open presents, Jennifer was on her feet making a beeline away from her energy-charged "chair" and to the safety of a different seat, causing Josh to snicker some more. Ignoring him, she positioned herself at the end of the couch so he'd have a place to sit next to her on the armrest, and a quick glance up at Josh's smile and twinkling eyes made her Christmas complete.

Presents were opened with a flurry of flying paper and bows. After several hours of celebrating, hugs, and kisses, loud goodbyes rang throughout the house. When the last guest left, Jennifer helped clean up and put the food away before escaping to the bedroom where her naughty husband waited, now solid for the holidays.

"Remind me to thank my grandma for letting you be solid for Christmas—being able to kiss you is the best present I could ask for," Jennifer said as she gave herself over to her husband, who lived up to each and every one of his earlier coal-deserving messages.

"Merry Christmas, baby," Josh said to his exhausted wife when they were done.

"Mmm. Merry Christmas, darling—I love you now and forevermore," Jennifer said sleepily, before drifting off in his strong arms for the night.

"That's right baby—sleep while I stay awake and watch over you. Get all the rest you can tonight, because tomorrow we start our celebration in my dimension!"

Jennifer had put up with a lot of extra protection since her run-in with Mr. Burk, and thanks to Gisabella's handiwork, she'd never noticed the wound Josh had suffered during the attack. It didn't change how uncomfortable he still felt about keeping her in the dark, and he'd vowed to tell his wife about any future attacks *regardless* of what Gisabella commanded.

Josh couldn't ignore the pang of regret for not telling Jennifer about

Sarnia sooner. Before they'd been married, Jennifer had told him that she'd forgive any previous women in his life as long as he pledged his full heart to her. *I owe Jennifer an explanation about Sarnia and how she paid me an unexpected, unclothed visit—but* after *we celebrate our first Christmas together in the other realm.*

CHAPTER THIRTY-FOUR

Josh and Jennifer arrived in the other realm with their hands full of packages to find an explosion of holiday decorations in their honeymoon house.

"Wow!" It was the only expression Jennifer could think of when she saw all the stuff that'd been crammed into every nook and cranny. Floor to ceiling and everywhere in between, there wasn't a spot left untouched by the Christmas spirit. It was as if they'd walked into Santa's workshop itself!

"Ditto!" Josh stifled a snicker when he saw Gisabella's extreme decorating style. All he'd asked his friend for was a Christmas tree with lights, ornaments, and a wreath over the mantle so Jennifer would feel more at home—what they'd gotten was an over-the-top Christmas extravaganza.

Jennifer's eyes couldn't take it all in as she scanned the room. A Santa Claus here, a reindeer there, and some snowmen peeking from behind tiny evergreen trees decorated with twinkling red lights on the mantle. Two life-sized nutcracker men stood guard in the front entry, watching over the many decorations her grandma had managed to fit into the house. A twenty-four-foot-high tree stood in the corner of the family room again that year, but this time it was covered in huge white glass ornaments and dazzling, frosted crystal icicles with peacock feathers nestled in between the branches. Underneath the tree were piles of colorfully wrapped gifts that gave little doubt Santa had found his way there.

In truth, it was the most beautiful Christmas tree she'd ever seen. "Grandmamma really outdid herself," Jennifer said in approval. As if on cue, the doorbell rang.

"Merry Christmas," Josh and Jennifer greeted Gisabella in unison.

"Merry Christmas, my newlyweds." Her voice reflected much emotion as she hugged them. The next hour was spent with Josh cooking up a Christmas feast, while Jennifer and Gisabella looked in on anticipation.

"Would you like some wine, Gisabella?" Josh began pouring three glasses when they were seated at the dinner table.

"Please," Gisabella said, immediately digging in. "Everything tastes stupendous. I must ask for your recipes."

"I'll give them to you, but don't expect miracles," Josh retorted, trying to appear as if everything between the two of them was normal.

"Admit it, Josh; you always leave out a few ingredients on purpose," Gisabella winked.

"More like you can't cook to save your life."

"How long have you two been like this?" When Jennifer's question earned her confused looks, she rolled her eyes. "Why do I get the feeling you've been bickering since the day you met?"

"That's because Josh has been obnoxious since the moment he opened his mouth."

"I've always had a valid reason!"

"You've never told me what Josh was like when you first met him," Jennifer cut in, trying to sidetrack Gisabella before their bantering escalated.

"Be nice, old woman—I know where you live," Josh warned with a hearty chuckle.

"To begin with, Josh was as he is now: a handsome man's man who didn't take crap from anyone."

"I know he's sexy, but I'd like to know if he was always so controlling." Jennifer didn't acknowledge Josh when he snorted in protest.

"He's always been kind of a pain in the ass, but I think that's why we've become such great friends. I trust that he'll always be *honest* with me, even if he knows I won't agree. As a high priestess, you'll be hard-pressed to find someone who'll be forthright enough to disagree with you. With Josh, I never worry he'll be too afraid of my title to speak up for what he believes is right." ~Too bad you're not as *honest* as I thought you were, Josh,~ Gisabella tagged onto the private message, with an accompanying glower for his eyes only.

"What was Josh like when he was first a protector?"

"He was the worst!" Gisabella groaned.

"Hey! What do you mean by that?" Josh roared, doing his best to ignore Gisabella's private message.

"Josh, you can't deny you had very little patience with your charges' abilities to follow instructions." Gisabella turned to Jennifer to explain. "Unlike you, all his other charges required subtle hints to be given through their thoughts. Too bad Josh had a hard time grasping the concept of their 'free will' when they didn't follow his demands. I can't tell you how many nights I got long, ranting messages and needed to calm him down. Thankfully, within a relatively short time Josh figured out how to persuade his charges to do what he needed in order for them to move forward and complete their purpose. Once he learned this trick, he skyrocketed straight to the number one spot and has held the title ever since."

"How many times did you have to save someone's life?" Jennifer asked Josh.

"I lost track of the number, but there were a few cases when I needed to step in." ~The latest being you and your episode with Mr. Burk!~

Jennifer received his private reprimand and responded. ~It wasn't like you *actually* had to save my life that day.~ When her message caused Josh's eyes to narrow, she quickly diverted her gaze away. *Don't tell me I'm in trouble again. Why does this always happen whenever Mr. Burk's name comes up?*

"Don't let Josh fool you; he's being modest. Centuries ago, things on earth weren't as civilized as they are now and I needed my protectors to go and help. Josh fearlessly led the way into battle and victory many times, as this was before Merlin's energy warfare teachings. Back then, they'd convert to solid and fight hand to hand with crude weapons.

Thanks to Merlin, my elite protectors are now able to handle anything thrown their way."

"I think we've heard enough about me. Why don't we go open presents?" Josh stood up and pulled out each woman's chair before leading the way into the family room.

"Since Gisabella mentioned our friend Merlin, I'll go grab the special gift I had him create for Jennifer." Josh's eyes danced as he darted from the room and returned shortly with a leash in his hand. "I hope you like *him*."

"Him?" Jennifer said warily, taking the end of the leash that was so long she couldn't see what was attached to the other end.

"Well? What are you waiting for? Reel in your gift," Josh prodded.

The look on her husband's face made Jennifer more worried than before. *Who knows what he's conjured up now*? Slowly, she did as Josh instructed and was soon met with resistance. Giving the lead a tug, she found the source of the stubbornness and her eyes grew huge with alarm. She didn't know what to make of the stealthy panther slinking into the living room, one with fur the color of a starless midnight sky, piercing, hungry eyes, and sharp fangs.

"What the hell do you call that?!" Gisabella demanded in a shrill voice.

"Jennifer's Christmas present," Josh answered matter-of-factly.

"Did it ever occur to you that Jennifer may not want to be eaten alive?!" Gisabella said, following it up with a private message: ~Great gift, Josh—after all, nothing says *"Christmas"* like a deadly animal!~

"You have it all wrong. He's been trained to protect Jennifer and to message me if she's ever in trouble."

"Honestly, Josh, are you really planning on bringing this beast down to earth?" Gisabella stared in disbelief.

"Actually, he'll be accompanying us back and forth. Stop looking at me like I've lost my mind. On earth, he'll look like a normal black cat. It's the perfect gift for her. Not only will Jennifer have a little more freedom, but I'll be less worried knowing I have a backup I can count on."

"What's your name?" Jennifer said, sitting on the floor to rub the large cat's ears.

"Well, I'll be darned," Gisabella exclaimed, watching the beast and her granddaughter bond.

"I thought we could pick out a name together." Josh knelt down and began to scratch the cat's other ear.

"What about something like Zeus or Adonis?" Jennifer asked, then looked a little longer at the big cat before adding, "I suppose a name like Demetri would be nice, too." Neither she nor Josh noticed the look of terror on Gisabella's face at the name's utterance.

Gisabella stood frozen in place, waiting to see if Josh would react; when he didn't, she exhaled. "He looks more like a Zeus or Adonis to me."

"I wish I knew what he wanted to be called," Jennifer said quietly.

~If you don't mind, I'd prefer to be called Talos.~

"Oh! You can talk—I mean message. That's so cool! We shall call you Talos, then," Jennifer exclaimed.

"Talos, like the giant Zeus created to protect his lover. What an appropriate name," Josh agreed.

"What else can he do?" Gisabella said, looking at the cat through narrowed eyes.

"I'm not sure. Merlin only mentioned the messaging thing, plus the ability for me to look through Talos's eyes and see what he sees if I need to."

"I guess we'll all find out what Talos can do in time as he shows us," Gisabella said with a side of irritation. ~I can't believe you didn't question Merlin in detail. Who knows what this beast is capable of doing? Whatever mess Talos creates, *you'll* be held responsible, she added in Josh's direction.~

~Would you relax, old woman? Look how much your granddaughter loves him. I'm sure Merlin would've mentioned it if Talos had any detrimental behaviors. More importantly, when I need to attend one of your meetings or my wife requests a little space, Talos will help keep her safe.~

~You'd better hope that cat doesn't do anything stupid.~

"Jennifer, this is for you," Gisabella said as she gave her a box tied with silver ribbon.

Jennifer unwrapped the present and discovered the blue diamond pendant she'd worn on her wedding day inside. "Oh my goodness, I couldn't possibly accept something this priceless!"

"I insist, dear; I want you to always remember that special day."

"Thank you Grandmamma," Jennifer said, giving Gisabella a hug.

"And *this* gift is for both of you," Gisabella continued, smiling wide as she handed another box to Jennifer.

"Why don't you go ahead and do the honors, Jennifer?" Josh said, wondering with discomfort whether Gisabella had felt obligated to include him in the gift.

Once Jennifer unwrapped it, she held it out so Josh could open the top of their first-ever Christmas present together as husband and wife. Inside was an unusual key.

"Go ahead, take it out," Gisabella instructed with a glint in her eye. "I wanted to make the house officially your home! That is, if you don't mind living next door to an old lady." Gisabella cracked a smile at Josh's impromptu coughing sound, knowing he'd gotten her joke. She'd often wondered how he felt about being centuries older than his wife's current age on earth. "Your key will work only when you're both together." *The last thing I need is Josh showing up here when Jennifer marries another man, or if she decides to kick him out after he's told her about Sarnia. Who knows what kind of foul mood he'll be in then?*

"We don't know what to say," Jennifer spoke up, breaking their stunned silence.

"Jennifer is right, Gisabella; your gift to us is over the top!"

"I think it's time I head home," Gisabella yawned, knowing the two were anxious to begin their celebration alone. "Make sure you get some rest tonight, Jennifer, because tomorrow I will be teaching you psychometry."

"Sounds like fun," Jennifer muttered as her stomach gave a nervous twinge.

"Oh, Gisabella *will* have fun," Josh grinned.

"Ignore him. I always do," Gisabella countered, before hugging each of them.

"Let's go to bed," Josh said, doing his best to hide the heavy burden on his shoulders as he took Jennifer's hand and led them in the direction of their bedroom.

~Sorry Talos, but the bedroom is one place you're not allowed. If you're hungry, I left a steak on the kitchen counter for you. See you in the morning,~ Josh messaged as he closed the bedroom door. Talos licked his chops and went in search of his dinner before curling up in front of the fire, full and content.

CHAPTER THIRTY-FIVE

"Good morning, baby," Josh said silkily.

"Good morning, my sexy man." Her love for him was written all over her face.

"Let's go downstairs and make sure Talos hasn't destroyed our home." Josh tried his best to sound upbeat as he led the way out of the bedroom and fell over the large panther curled up right outside the door.

"Talos!" Jennifer greeted, dropping to his level to wrap her arms around the massive panther. "You must be starved. Don't worry, Josh is a great cook and he's going to make us both a big breakfast."

Great! That overgrown cat's already wiggled his way into my wife's heart.

Twenty minutes later, Josh joined Jennifer at the table with two plates while Talos chomped on a variety of frozen meat.

"You'd better hurry or you'll be late. Trust me, you don't want to keep Gisabella waiting for your psychometry lesson," Josh warned.

"Like the last time? Honestly, Josh—that was all your fault. Weren't *you* the one who said 'Gisabella won't mind?'" Jennifer blushed, remembering the time they'd been an hour late.

"Hey! You were the one wearing only a towel."

"Psychometry? Isn't that 'reading' objects?" Jennifer said, quickly changing the subject so as not to have a reoccurrence of tardiness.

"Precisely!" Josh cheered.

Twenty-five minutes later they arrived at Gisabella's house. "Good luck, baby," Josh said, bidding her goodbye as he deposited Jennifer on Gisabella's doorstep.

"Thank you." Jennifer did her best to disguise her nerves. "I have a feeling I'm going to need all the help I can get."

"Jennifer, you're very gifted and possess many natural abilities, so I'm positive you're going to do great. Besides, you'd be hard-pressed to find a better instructor than your grandma."

"You're right on time." Gisabella opened the door wide and invited her granddaughter inside. After giving Jennifer a hug, Gisabella turned her attention to Josh. "We'll be done in four hours."

"So that's when I'll return." Josh's velvety voice did little to disguise the firm undertones telling both women he was serious.

"I'm capable of finding my way home," Jennifer balked, trying to keep some of her independence while there in the other realm. Once back on earth, there'd be no escaping her elite protector's scrutiny.

The look in Jennifer's eyes didn't stop Josh from insisting. "Of course you can, but I'd like to speak to Gisabella afterwards, so we might as well walk home together. Take good care of my wife, old woman—you'd better be kind in your teaching methods," Josh went on, glaring a warning at his longtime friend. He still remembered his psychometry lessons with Gisabella, and the objects she'd placed into his hands: a vial of poison, a dead man's penis, a live cobra, and even the head of Medusa. They haunted him to that very day.

"What are you talking about, Josh? I made your lessons interesting and fun! Thanks to my methods, you were the most proficient out of all of my students."

"That's because all the others ran away from you screaming their heads off!"

"At least they didn't squeal like a little girl!"

"The only squealing that day was yours, when I threw Medusa's head..." Josh's voice trailed off when he caught sight of Jennifer's wide-eyed look of fright. "Now look what you've done, Gisabella," he said, nodding towards his wife.

"*I've* done? You were the one who ran your mouth!" Gisabella turned around with a sweet, grandmotherly smile. "Jennifer, please don't listen to him; I'd never treat you so unkindly. Josh was well-equipped to handle everything I threw his way." When Jennifer's look hadn't softened, she added, "Besides, you haven't seen any snake bite scars on Josh, and he certainly doesn't appear any worse for wear."

"So help me, Grandmamma, if you try to place any horrible items in my hands, I'll set my husband loose on you."

"Not to worry, dear. I promise I have nothing scary in store for you." Gisabella turned towards her previous student. "Now if you'll excuse us, Jennifer and I have a lot of work to do and you've caused enough trouble already." She shooed Josh out of the house, then returned to her student. "The reason I wanted to be the one to teach you psychometry is because I believe you have a natural ability that, when properly developed, will be a powerful tool."

Her grandma spoke in hushed tones as if concerned someone may overhear her, and Jennifer found her behavior odd. No one else was in the house, and Gisabella's entire domain was surrounded by so much protection it was the safest place in all the universes. Her grandma's paranoia was so intriguing that Jennifer leaned forward with interest.

"Psychometry is when a person such as yourself can read the energy of an object. All objects hold clues as to who wore, used, or owned the item, in turn helping you piece together enough clues to know every detail about anyone who's come in contact with the object. In addition, objects often hold leftover energy, so you may feel happiness, sadness, fear, pain, or a plethora of other feelings. It will serve you well to become proficient in psychometry, and will help you determine who you can trust and who is out to get you.

"The first thing you must *always* do is to put protection in place, so you don't inadvertently take on any negative energy vibrations as your own. In extreme cases, energies from items have been known to change people's personalities. For example, a protector came to me when his visionary became bedridden and was hospitalized, unable to walk. After searching the girl's memories, we discovered her dying grandmother had gifted her a necklace she'd worn daily. Because the girl was picking up the energy from the necklace, she ended up with the same symptoms and illness as her grandma. Once it was removed and cleansed of all negative energy, the girl was fine and able to wear the gift."

Gisabella instructed Jennifer to surround herself with protective white light, and to imagine gloves on her hands. "You must do these steps each time you work in psychometry. Being gifted, you may find yourself picking up on the energies around you automatically, so you have to surround yourself with white light protection daily. To start off, it's easier to concentrate on the item's energy with your eyes closed." Gisabella waited until Jennifer was ready for her first object.

Jennifer held out a shaky hand, nervous she might disappoint her powerful grandma who, like Josh, seemed to have high expectations. *Please let me get some information.* When a small object was placed in her hand, she was relieved that many words and feelings flowed into her mind with ease. "Fireplace—I feel like I'm sitting in front of a brick fireplace with a warm fire burning in the hearth." Tears began to prick her eyes and she felt engulfed in overwhelming sadness. "A man is standing behind me holding a sparkling pendant in front of my eyes, before clasping it around my neck. The pendant is a gift, but I get the impression the occasion was filled with sadness." Sorrow consumed her, and her heart filled with grief. The moment Gisabella removed the item from her hand, all emotional ties to the necklace dissipated.

"Excellent," Gisabella applauded. "During my final lifetime on earth, my husband gave it to me before he unexpectedly died." Gisabella left out that he'd been her *preordained life-path husband,* whom she'd been forced into marrying even though her heart had belonged to Merlin. In time she'd grown to care a great deal about the man, as she hoped Jennifer would regarding her own future life-path husband. Jennifer's love for Josh was so strong Gisabella feared she may need to employ extra encouragement in addition to her destiny and the spell she'd put over Jennifer years earlier. "I could tell by the tears in your eyes and the ache in your heart that you took on the energy. The reason you had those feelings is because your protection wasn't strong enough. If it were, you'd have been nothing more than an observer with no emotional ties to the piece."

Gisabella placed the next item in Jennifer's hand and carefully watched her student's expression turn to worry—a sign that Jennifer wasn't trusting the information she was receiving.

"I think this is a dog's toy ball," Jennifer said, waiting for another "job well done."

"Tell me about the very first impression you received when I placed the item in your hand."

"The first thing I saw was fire flying through the air towards me—similar to how I'd equate a flaming cannonball. Then a vision of a snowstorm came into my head, and the snow piled up rapidly while it clung to my hair and eyelashes." Jennifer felt foolish saying the odd, nonsensical descriptions aloud.

"Now that you've said both, which one resonates with you more? Don't think about it—just say the first thing that comes to mind."

"Oddly enough, the flaming cannonball," Jennifer said, even though she was still confused over two conflicting revelations.

"That's accurate! The object you're holding was used during ancient times by soldiers. They'd light the cannonballs on fire and catapult them at their enemies. This particular one was used during a war between territories on earth that I was presiding over. I created a snowstorm to stop the possibility of a deadly fire and to deter the aggressive enemy that threatened the usually peaceful kingdom. Within a few minutes, the wet snow covered the battlefield and extinguished the flames. Both sides sought shelter, putting an end to the conflict." Gisabella inwardly shuddered and blocked her memories so Jennifer wouldn't find out that Josh had been the real hero that day. She could still see him in all his otherworldly glory, flinging boulder-sized balls of ice that immediately cleared the entire battlefield long before the first of her snowflakes had landed. "This is a perfect demonstration that you must always trust your first impression, even if it doesn't make sense.

"We'll do one more before we break for lunch. This piece is unique, so take your time and describe all the information you receive." Gisabella carefully placed the ancient dagger that had separated the two lovers many centuries ago into Jennifer's hands. *I pray Merlin's plan works.*

Jennifer's mind was flooded with photos, words, and emotions before she found herself transported back in time. She saw herself as a young woman dressed in a long, periwinkle dress and sitting with her hands on her lap. Suddenly, her stomach clenched and bile rose in her throat at the unexpected sight of the man in the arena. She couldn't take her eyes off his well-built, masculine splendor, and the way his skin glistened under the bright sun. He wore little more than a loincloth, but the fighter's features were strong, determined, and intense.

The man's wavy brown hair was darkened from exertion and each time he swung his sword, fighting off the other man's attack, beads of sweat followed suit. With each downed opponent, Jennifer's elation grew and her nerves calmed. When the last of the opponents in the arena had been toppled, she wanted to stand and cheer for the superior, unbeaten male. Surely she was looking at Hercules himself! Who else could've rid the entire arena of all the other fighters in record time? The sound of the crowd was deafening—standing, cheering, and throwing flowers out of the stands and into the...*Colosseum?*

Jennifer found she could breathe again now that the man was safe. She was no longer an observer, but had converged with her medieval self to become one as her heart and soul filled with love for the unbeaten man standing alone in the arena. For the first time, Jennifer noticed a foul-looking man seated to her left who evoked a deep hatred inside her. She also suddenly knew that *he'd* been the reason why the beautiful man —her lover—had been forced to fight.

Her attention once again focused on the fighter, who raised his sword in salute to the wicked king seated next to the foul man beside her. The fighter's green eyes stayed fixed on Jennifer, and as if in slow motion, she watched him crumple to his knees as a large man plunged a dagger into his back. Her lover fell face down in the dirt, causing disapproving jeers and mayhem as Jennifer watched him draw his last breath.

"*Demetri!*" Jennifer shouted, bursting into tears at the same time. "How could I have done this to you? I loved you," she screamed, sobbing violently. "I didn't know—forgive me, my love; I didn't know. God forgive me...our poor baby," Jennifer wailed.

"Jennifer! Jennifer, snap out of it," Gisabella shouted as she grabbed the knife out of Jennifer's hand, trying to break the link between Jennifer and the past. Gisabella put her shock from Jennifer's revelation aside, and worked to bring her back to the present. She'd never thought Jennifer would become part of the scene or remember so much detail. "Jennifer, it's me, your grandma." Gisabella grasped Jennifer's shoulders, forcing the girl back to the present. Jennifer hesitantly opened her eyes and collapsed into Gisabella's arms, crying, while the high priestess softly stroked her hair.

Astraea had been pregnant?! Why were there no signs of another soul? What am I going to do now?! Gisabella knew that a love like Joshua and Jennifer's had no boundaries, and there was nothing that would be able to pull the two apart; not Jennifer's destiny, life-path, or any spell. Even Gisabella's own magic might not be enough to make Jennifer forget Josh and marry another man. Gisabella's heart froze. Since she was the one responsible for bringing the two lovers together and for marrying them, *she'd* be the one held accountable if Jennifer refused to go along with her destiny. Worse yet, if Jennifer failed to comply with her life-path marriage, they'd all be banished and their souls destroyed. *Jennifer will never accept another man as her husband! I must talk to Merlin.* The thought was unpleasant, to say the least. *Merlin's going to throw a fit!*

Looking down at the dagger, it became clear that Merlin was right and it was up to Gisabella to set the wheels in motion so that when the time came, Jennifer would lead Josh to the weapon that'd been used to murder him in the Colosseum. The same knife that Astraea had used to take her own life had apparently ended another innocent life that day.

What a poetic ending; the man who'd orchestrated Josh's murder in a former life would die and be disintegrated by the man he'd sentenced to death long ago. Gisabella would see to it that Josh and Jennifer had their revenge.

To abate Jennifer's painful memories, Gisabella first used magic to erase them as well as the vision of her lover's murder. She then added a subliminal message to Jennifer's psyche to guarantee that when the time came, Jennifer would lead Josh to the dagger. She only hoped that her magic was strong enough to block all memories of the dagger and her implanted instructions from Josh, until it was time for Jennifer to lead him to the only weapon that could save the universe. Merlin's warning came to mind: "*The timing must be precise. If Josh finds the dagger or knows of its existence too soon, he'll falter and all hope will be lost.*"

"What happened?" Jennifer lifted her eyes to gaze at Gisabella. She felt completely drained, but couldn't remember anything that had transpired.

"Nothing really—you said a couple of things about this ring before you dozed off." Gisabella held up an emerald ring to further support her lie. "When you're new to psychometry, it can be quite tiring. Not to worry; your endurance will improve with time."

"I'm sorry," Jennifer murmured sleepily.

"You did wonderful, my dear. Why don't you relax while I go and make you a cup of tea?" Gisabella went into the kitchen to sort out her thoughts. Now she had living proof of why Josh had changed their wedding vows—on a subconscious level, he must've remembered his past life's connection to Jennifer. Listening to Jennifer's heart-wrenching tale and seeing her present reaction proved once and for all that the couple's connection on earth had ended far too soon. *No wonder Josh agreed to become a protector in exchange for another lifetime with Astraea-slash-Jennifer!*

"Here you go, Jennifer." Gisabella handed her a cup of a rare tonic created by Merlin. "Go ahead and drink up—it'll help to cleanse any left-over negative or emotional energy you may still be carrying." She watched to make sure Jennifer finished all the potent tea, ensuring Jennifer's memory of the dagger, her past lifetime as Astraea, and their unknown baby was all forgotten.

"Jennifer, why don't you lie down for a while until Josh comes to collect you?" Gisabella suggested when Jennifer's eyes drooped.

"Okay…" Jennifer mumbled.

Twenty minutes later, Gisabella answered the door. "I'm afraid your wife became tired." She pointed to the sleeping figure lying underneath a cashmere blanket on the couch. "Why don't you join me in the kitchen and let Jennifer sleep a little while longer?" She bustled off in the direction of the kitchen with Josh following.

"How did Jennifer's lesson go?" Josh asked.

"She did quite well. Even though I suspected she was born this lifetime with a natural ability in psychometry, I was surprised by how accurate Jennifer was. She was even able to retrieve information from ancient items!" Gisabella blocked all thoughts of the dagger and his previous lifetime with Jennifer from Josh.

"That's wonderful," Josh said proudly. "I should take her home now so we can celebrate privately." He imagined tossing Jennifer over his shoulder to carry her up to their bedroom.

"No wonder Jennifer calls you a scoundrel!" Gisabella chuckled at Josh's lack of discretion, doing her best to act like nothing unusual had happened. "All kidding aside, my granddaughter is one lucky woman!" A soft hue of peach colored her cheeks and warmed her face.

"Thank you. I'll take that as a compliment." His face split into a wide, Cheshire cat-like grin. "Now if you'll excuse me, I need to collect my sleeping beauty. I think it's about time to wake her up, and I'm counting on her being as hungry as I am."

"Sounds like you're putting off telling Jennifer about Sarnia. You should just get it over with—unless you're afraid your wife will kick you to the curb?!" Gisabella heckled.

"Thanks for ruining the moment!"

"My pleasure, Josh," Gisabella said with a wicked grin, enjoying Josh's discomfort. *Poor guy—doesn't he know that Jennifer loves him too much to ever leave?*

As soon as Josh left with Jennifer's sleeping figure in his arms, Gisabella summoned Merlin, who immediately rushed to her side.

"Gisabella, my love," Merlin greeted, taking hold of Gisabella's hands. "Is everything all right?"

"Oh dear, I didn't mean to worry you—everything's fine." She stretched the truth and glanced away from Merlin's beseeching eyes.

"Gisabella, you can't fool me—I know you too well. Tell me what's going on."

"I did as you instructed and everything's all set. Jennifer will lead Josh to the dagger when the time comes." Gisabella swallowed before imparting the reason she summoned him to her side. "When Jennifer was reading the dagger, she went so deeply into the vision that she became her former self."

"That sometimes happens with deeply disturbing items," Merlin reminded.

"Yes, but Jennifer received information that she could've only learned after she'd gone to heaven. Merlin—Astraea had been pregnant with Demetri's child."

"What? How did you miss such an important thing?" Merlin dropped Gisabella's hands.

"The baby must've been newly conceived—possibly only a few hours earlier."

"Where's this child's soul now?"

"I have no idea," Gisabella confessed, wringing her hands.

"The first thing we must do is locate their baby's soul. We can't leave any former soul conceived by Jennifer and Josh unguarded," Merlin warned.

"At least it's the only child either of them have ever conceived in any of their lifetimes…" Gisabella murmured.

Merlin's eyebrows quirked, brightening his foul expression as his next words tumbled out in excitement. "On the other hand, if Josh and Jennifer were to conceive a child reincarnated from their previous baby's soul, it would become the strongest, most gifted being in existence. If we were to make this possible, our family would remain in charge forever!"

"What you're saying is we *must* find their baby's soul? That was almost two thousand years ago!" Gisabella said, her voice rising.

"Then I suggest you get busy," Merlin suggested with a smirk.

"Don't you mean *we*?"

"Fine, I'll help. But it'll cost you." Merlin softened his tone and demeanor while letting his cloak fall to the ground.

"What do you have in mind?" Gisabella asked softly, looking up at her former lover with hope blossoming in her heart.

"I'm sorry for what I said earlier, by the way…of course you couldn't have known about the baby. The important thing is that we found out in time to use this to our advantage," Merlin soothed as he sauntered towards her.

"Thank you for saying that," Gisabella said, her pulse rising.

"The only thing that matters to me now is you, my love." Merlin wrapped Gisabella in his embrace, pulling her tightly against him. "God, how I missed you," he moaned, running his hand through her golden hair. "I'm never letting you go again! So help me woman, if your plan is to leave me after I make love to you, than do it now, because I can't survive losing you again."

Gisabella was rendered speechless as Merlin uttered the words she'd waited centuries to hear.

"Damn it Gisabella, say something!" Merlin poised his mouth an inch from hers, waiting for a sign.

"I love you too much to ever leave you," she whispered.

"Good!" Merlin lowered his mouth to Gisabella's and kissed her the way he used to, before she'd broken his heart by leaving him for her predestined husband. As Gisabella began matching his need, Merlin poured his entire heart into kissing her, bringing to life the once-dormant embers of their love that soon morphed into flames of ardent passion.

CHAPTER THIRTY-SIX

Josh easily carried Jennifer home from Gisabella's house and up to their bedroom, but to his dismay, she hadn't woken up. Once he settled Jennifer in bed, Josh pulled the comforter over her sleeping figure and sat down on the edge.

"You're so beautiful, Jennifer. I don't know what I ever did to deserve you, or how you love me enough to make our impossible marriage work so well. You know I'd do anything to make you happy and to keep you safe—don't you? You are my everything," Josh said softly, looking for a sign Jennifer was awakening. "I have something I need to tell you. I don't know why I kept it from you; probably because I knew it didn't mean anything to me. But I need to be completely honest, so I'm sharing it with you now."

Josh inhaled, hoping to calm his rising apprehension. "I once heard if you have something bad to say, blurting it out is the easiest way, so here it goes: When I left you to get ready for our marriage ceremony, there was a girl waiting for me in my apartment…in my bed. Sarnia means *nothing* to me, and even though she claims we once had an affair, I have no memory of her and I together. Through the years Sarnia has made a few passes at me, but I've always shut her down." *I wish I knew how Jennifer is going to react when she hears this for real.*

"Sleep now, my love. I promise I'll tell you everything as soon as you wake up," Josh vowed, kissing Jennifer's forehead before heading towards the door.

"Talos, stay here with Jennifer and message me when she awakens," Josh instructed the big cat, breaking his strict "cats do *not* enter the bedroom" rule.

~Yes sir,~ Talos purred, eyeing Josh as he walked out of the room. Once Josh shut the door, Talos leapt onto the bed and curled up beside Jennifer.

During the next four hours Josh checked on Jennifer several times, but she hadn't stirred. *What the hell happened at Gisabella's?* Josh gently lifted each of Jennifer's eyelids, discovering that her pupils were dilated and her pulse seemed abnormally slow. *Jennifer's been drugged!* He didn't need to use his crystal ball or psychic skills to know who'd drugged his wife, and anger swelled deep in Josh's chest as all sense of protocol or temper control left him.

~Stay here Talos, and guard Jennifer. Let me know immediately if she opens her eyes,~ Josh ordered before running out.

~Gisabella—you better get your ass over here *now*!~ Josh blasted while pacing to and fro in the family room.

"How dare you use that tone with me?" Gisabella warned, appearing suddenly behind him.

Josh whipped around and confronted his boss. "What did you give Jennifer?! She's been sleeping since I carried her home!"

"Honestly, Josh; *this* is the reason for your shouting?" Gisabella pooh-poohed, rolling her eyes.

"Drugging my wife gives me the right to shout! Why'd you do it? Are you trying to erase her memory like you did mine?"

"Why would I do such a thing? I just gave her a cup of chamomile tea to calm her senses. Even *you* can't find fault with that."

Josh swiped his fingers through his hair while he contemplated his next move. "You're right; I can't be mad at you for *that* particular item. Too bad there's so many other things you've done to Jennifer and I," Josh said in a voice laced with darkness.

"Seriously? You have a list?" Gisabella toyed.

"There's a list all right—a long one that includes so many underhanded things that if Jennifer were to find out even one, she'd despise you."

"Really? What about all the things *you've* done to the poor girl?" Gisabella flung back, trying to gain the upper hand.

"What're you talking about, old woman? I've done nothing wrong."

Gisabella noticed the flicker of doubt on Josh's face as he spoke, and she grinned in victory. *Gotcha!* "Have you told Jennifer about Sarnia yet? I think she deserves to know you had a naked woman in bed on the night of your wedding!"

Josh stifled a groan, aware he was at Gisabella's mercy. His only defense was to go on the offensive, leaving Gisabella with no doubt that she'd better hold her tongue. "You're one to talk in regards to withholding the truth, Gisabella. I'd like to see you explain your reasoning for hiding how Jennifer almost got herself killed! Or what about the fact you've locked her into marrying another man as part of her destiny? What spell do you plan on using on my wife to get her to agree to such a farce?" Josh shouted, his voice booming around the room.

"I won't need to do anything; Jennifer's future lies in her destiny, and nothing will be able to stop her from falling in love with him—not even you." Gisabella's words wavered at the end, but she managed to say them without faltering.

Suddenly a sparkling object flew past Josh's face, grazing his cheek on the way. "Ow! What the hell was that?" he yelped, rubbing the spot and finding a trace of blood on his fingertips. He bent down to retrieve it, and spotted a second shiny item lying a few inches away. He grabbed them and rose to his full height, his heart clenching at the sight of both rings cradled in his palm. *No!*

"How could you?!" Jennifer cried from where she stood in the doorway.

Josh met Jennifer's icy glare and took a hesitant step towards her. "Jennifer..."

"*NO!*" Jennifer shouted, stopping Josh in his tracks. Her eyes, once full of love, held nothing but contempt for him now. "Don't you *dare* come near me!"

"It's not what you think," Josh said, the rings digging into the flesh of his palm as he clenched them tighter.

"Another woman in your bed—*naked*?" Jennifer sobbed. "How could you lie about such a thing?! You promised never to lie to me again, and now I find out that all you've ever *done* is lie to me! I've been so stupid." Jennifer pivoted then, turning her attention to Gisabella.

"And *you*—you're just as bad, if not worse, than he is! What kind of person are you? You call yourself Josh's friend and my grandmother, and have the nerve to pass yourself off as some almighty know-it-all high priestess! All this time I've felt inferior, and was so afraid I'd fail you. You made me feel like I was never going to be good enough to follow in your footsteps, but you know what? I am better than you—*I* have a heart! Anyone who's able manipulate people into doing whatever they want doesn't deserve my respect." Jennifer squared her shoulders, tears continuing to trail down her cheeks. "Did you really think I'd be tricked into marrying another man in eight years? There isn't a drug strong enough to make me forget my vows—plus, I wouldn't even *need* it considering my husband's a lying cheater!"

"Jennifer, please calm down. Let's talk about this rationally," Gisabella said, keeping her tone measured.

"Not on your life! What makes you think I want to listen to any more of your lies? Get this through your head, Grandma—from now on, you're *nothing* to me! I'm done with listening to you and all your stupid high priestess lessons. Find yourself another pawn; oh wait, I forgot—you have Josh! He seems to go along with whatever scheme you come up with, including marrying me for eight years before passing me off to someone else so he can run off with Sarnia!" A sob managed to escape Jennifer before she quickly reeled in her emotions. "Well, not anymore. I quit!"

"Baby, please let me explain—"

"Josh, in case you're too daft to understand what I'm saying, Sarnia is *welcome* to you! I want a divorce!" Jennifer tugged at the chain that held the locket with Josh's heart, but it wouldn't break. *I'll cut it off at home!*

"You can never remove my heart or love from around your neck. No matter what you believe, they'll always be yours. I beg you, Jennifer, please don't throw our love away," Josh implored, praying she'd choose to stay with him.

"Don't. You're one too many lies too late," Jennifer replied, a lump forming in her throat. ~Prepare to transport,~ she messaged Talos, who raced down the stairs immediately. As soon as the panther was leaning against her, Jennifer initiated the instructions she'd read in the high priestess manual, hoping to reappear in her bedroom down on earth.

"*Wait!*" Josh ran forward, helpless to do anything but watch as Jennifer faded away.

"Did you teach Jennifer how to transport?" Gisabella accused, spinning on him.

Josh grasped at his hair, haunted by all the possible risks transporting presented without proper training. "Don't look at me! This is all your fault, Gisabella! If you hadn't twisted my words or pushed Jennifer so hard, she would've never read the high priestess manual or tried to transport without one of us; she would've never *left me*. You'd better pray Jennifer isn't floating around somewhere in space, or that she hasn't converged with Talos into one being!"

"What are you waiting for?! Go get her!" Gisabella croaked, trying to hold back the rare emotional tide that was threatening to drown her.

"Goodbye, Gisabella." Josh's words were as frozen as his darkened eyes. "Don't bother sending anyone after us, or trying to press any charges against Jennifer for illegally transporting; if you do, I'll see to it everything you've ever done comes back to haunt you."

"I'm sorry, Josh; I wish I could take back the things I said. I didn't mean for this to happen." Gisabella's eyes filled with unshed tears.

"As novel as your apology may be, it's falling on deaf ears. If you want to do something useful, pray that Jennifer makes it home—and while you're at it, that she takes me back." Josh glanced down at the rings still sitting in his palm. "I need all the prayers in the universe if I hope to have any chance with her. Let's face it; Jennifer was always too good for me!" Josh slipped Jennifer's rings onto his pinky and transported down to earth, hoping with every fiber that he'd find his wife in one piece and not scattered all over the universe.

"Where are we?" Jennifer asked, wide-eyed and scared.

~I have no idea,~ Talos said.

"I've got a feeling we're not on earth or in Gisabella's domain anymore," Jennifer said shakily. Scanning the small clearing where they were standing, she noticed it was covered in a carpet of thick moss, but found no sign of life, houses, or any other kinds of structures she'd expect to see on her planet. A glance upward proved how right she was. "There are *three* moons!"

~Yes, I can see that,~ Talos agreed, receiving a scowl in return.

Just outside the dimly lit clearing, Jennifer could barely make out some enormous trees covered in cobwebs of hanging moss nearby. A shiver of fear ran through her. *What if I'm in an alternate universe and lost forevermore?!* With no way to backtrack the course she'd taken other than clicking her shoes like Dorothy, her only hope of going home rested in her soon-to-be-ex-husband. *Who am I kidding; now that Josh has been found out, he's surely by Sarnia's side, or worse—holding her in his arms and professing how grateful he is to be rid of me.*

"Oh Talos, what have I done?" Jennifer sunk to the ground and pulled Talos closer for warmth.

~Don't worry, my lady—someone's bound to find us…*eventually*,~ Talos said, licking his chops hungrily.

"'Eventually?!'" Jennifer groaned, burying her face in the panther's dense fur coat but finding little comfort in his low, throaty growls.

~Jennifer! Are you here?!~ Josh called out across the universe, running into his and Jennifer's bedroom on earth. ~Please answer me, baby. I know you're not talking to me, but I need to know you're safe.~ Josh scanned the house for Jennifer's energy, but felt no sign of her. Without knowing the coordinates Jennifer had used to transport home, there was no way of telling whether she was on earth or floating around somewhere, lost in space.

~Talos, can you hear me? Are you still with Jennifer? If so, let me see her through your eyes,~ Josh messaged, to no reply. ~Jennifer, can you hear me?~

Josh tried messaging over and over to no avail, nor could he get a reading on her location with his crystal orb. *If only I could figure out which dimension Jennifer landed in!*

"Where are you, Jennifer?" Josh cried out in anguish, falling to his knees. *Please God, help me find my wife safe and sound.*" Then, Josh did something he hadn't in over a thousand years: he prayed for a *miracle.*

You've reached the end of book one in the Destined To Be Lovers saga.

CONNECT WITH SUZANNE NEMEC

Thank you for reading book one of my *Destined To Be Lovers saga.* If you enjoyed it, please take time to leave a review on Amazon, Kindle, Goodreads, or one of your other favorite online retailers.

I'm currently working on book two and like most readers, I want to know what happens next with Josh and Jennifer too!

For more information on Josh and Jennifer, plus updates on future books, please stop by my website; www.suzannenemec.net.

While you're there, don't forget to sign up to receive my newsletter.

Facebook pages:
Author page: @CrossingAllBoundaries
Reader page: @Destinedtobelovers

Instagram: Suzannenemec
Pinterest: Suzannenemecauthor
Twitter: Suzannenemec

LEARN MORE

If you would like to learn more about astrology, psychometry, gemstone properties, mediumship, and other metaphysical studies, visit Sandy Anastasi at: www.sandyanastasi.com.

53993967R00214

Made in the USA
Columbia, SC
23 March 2019